# The Minors

*A Novel*

Christopher Ludovici

Published by Unsolicited Press



Cover Design: U.P. In House Team



ISBN-13: 978-1-947021-00-6

To my son for the deadline.

To my cats for the company.

To my wife for literally everything else.

# CONTENTS

# PART ONE: MARCH

## SUNDAY HANDS

Nick wasn't going to like Steve Heller.

The moment he pulled up in front of Heller's big stupid house and saw the Prius with the Obama '08 sticker, it was like *here we go* and when Heller opened his door, Nick got a look at the hundred dollar jeans, crisp University of Chicago sweatshirt, and styled *fucking* hair.

What kind of a dickhead put product in his hair on a *Sunday morning*?

"Nick, right?"

Nick nodded.

"I'm Steve, good to meet you. Abbie said great things." He smiled, stuck his hand out; his grip was firm, shake was solid, but his hand was clean and smooth.

Heller led Nick around the side of the house to the back and up onto the deck. The yard was nice, clean, well kept; no way was he taking care of it by himself. Whoever it was though, did good work.

A cold breeze blew through Nick's hair and down his neck; he shivered and absently massaged his shoulder. It'd been so warm lately that he wasn't even wearing a jacket that morning, and now he was freezing his ass off. He wanted to smoke but could tell by looking that Heller wouldn't like it.

"I've been meaning to get this deck fixed up forever," said Heller. "Put a table back here, maybe a grill." He ran his hand over the wood railing. "But first, we had to fix the roof and do some work inside. That took *years.* Then there were cars and clothes for the kids and school." He turned around and looked at Nick. "You know how it goes, right?"

Nick did not know how that went. Nick lived in a twin with three other people. What backyard there was could barely hold them all standing, so the idea of a deck in any condition was out of the question. The reality was that Heller probably paid around half a million dollars for his perfect turn-of-the-century brick and stone house with its big yard at the end of the perfect tree lined street in the perfect neighborhood and then tens of thousands more getting it just the way he wanted it. The whole *idea* of doing that was to separate himself from everyone else. To live in some fantasy with all the other rich liberals who wanted to help the poor and downtrodden, but didn't want to live anywhere near them. Nick dealt with them his whole life. "Sure," Nick said. "I know how it goes."

Heller knocked on the railing. "But hey," he said, and looked at Nick, smiling widely. "That's why you're here, right? Time to get it done."

Nick wished that just once, he could walk into a house without getting a long story about the history of the place and the people in it. He wished that, just once, he could be given a job and left alone.

"Sounds good."

"Yeah, it is. Or it's gonna be. After you fix up the deck, I'm getting that table and grill, maybe get some tiki torches going, sort of a Mediterranean thing, you know?"

There he went again. "Sure."

"After that? After the deck?" He winked at Nick; the guy actually *winked*. "Don't tell my wife if she asks. I mean, obviously she wouldn't just ask, but if you two were like talking or something and it came up, don't mention I said anything because I want it to be a surprise, but… I'm putting in a pool."

He was animated now, walking around the porch and gesturing as he spoke. He was tall, probably six feet, slim, in pretty good shape. Nick figured he went to the gym a few times a week, his job probably had a gym in the building. House this nice, the guy probably spent a lot of time at the office to afford it. And he moved confidently, gracefully; he had been an athlete when he was younger, through high school at least, maybe even into college.

"My daughter loves to swim," Heller was saying. "My parents' place had a pool; she'd swim for hours during the summer. As soon as it got even a little warm she'd start, 'Daddy, is the pool open yet? Daddy, when are Gran and Grandpa opening the pool?'" His voice trailed off, and he stared absently at the grass where his pool would someday be, then a moment later his eyes focused back on Nick. "Sorry about that, got lost in a wave of nostalgia for a second."

"Hey," Nick said, "it happens to everyone." Which was total bullshit; the past was the past and only idiots spent time getting all dreamy about it.

"And the older you get, the *worse* it gets," said Heller. "They moved down to Florida a few years ago, my parents did, retired down there. It broke her heart. The place they got down there has a pool too. But we only get to see them a few times a year. You ever go to Florida?"

"Couple times," Nick said. "A long time ago."

"Disney World?"

"No, it was something else. Like kind of a school trip thing." Nick said, bracing himself for further questions.

"Oh, okay." He didn't care why Nick had been to Florida. "We try and get down a couple times a year. Philly to Tampa's only a three-hour flight and my folks love seeing the kids. The kids love it too. Sam, that's my daughter, she's the older one, she's great about it. When I was a kid, I *hated* going on trips with my family, all I just wanted to go back home and hang out with my friends. But Sam doesn't mind, or at least that's what she says. It's a miracle. And *Oscar*, he just likes running around in the sun and heat in January. And the swimming *never* gets old. Everybody, I mean *everybody*, has a pool down there. Did you notice that?"

"Not really."

"Oh man, they're everywhere. Big houses, little houses. I guess it's just too hot, people can't do without them."

Guys like Heller, rich entitled guys, University of Chicago sweatshirt guys, guys like him never worked for anything, not really. They had rich parents and went to private schools and good colleges and then business school or medical school or law school or whatever and they were set. Everything was in place for them from the moment they were born. These were the kinds of people who put pools into their homes. Sure, they *studied*, and they *practiced*, and they *played.* But work? Honest to god *work?* Shit. Guys like Heller wouldn't even know what that was.

"Anyway," Heller said, waving a hand at the backyard, "that's all happening later. Today, we're tackling this deck." He looked at Nick. "What do you think? What's it gonna take?"

Nick knew what it would take the moment he stepped on the deck, but it was good to hesitate. Listen to their stories, look around, act like he was working out what was obvious from the start. So he walked around the deck with his hands on his hips, looking serious. He crouched down, bit his lower lip, and looked over the backyard.

The thing about guys like Heller was, they weren't necessarily bad guys, they were just... *ignorant.* They thought because they had money and an education that they understood how things worked; as far as Nick was concerned, all that equaled precisely the opposite. Those kinds of guys were so sure they were right about everything that they never stopped to listen to anyone else. They never learned anything. Nick's old hitting coach had a name for guys like that: he called them rubes. A rube always knew what he was doing at the plate, never studied the opposing pitcher, never took any advice on his swing; he'd been naturally great his whole life without ever really having to try, and the idea that he had equals (or superiors) was ridiculous. Rubes were always easy outs, easy to fool because they were always sure they knew what pitch was coming and no matter how many times they were wrong, they kept swinging away.

But that didn't mean Nick could take advantage of Heller. Nick's line of work operated on reputation. He did good work for someone and they recommended him to someone else who recommended him to someone else. Business was going well for Nick the last couple of months and he didn't need to fuck it up by over-charging some guy too dumb to realize.

Nick stood up.

"Well," he said, "some of these boards are rotten, and I'd probably replace the banister if I were you. Probably a good idea to put new steps in too. Then you're gonna want to have the whole thing waterproofed. Figure, day, day and a half."

"Okay," said Heller. "So, how much?"

Nick shrugged. "Depends. Let's say somewhere between eight hundred and a thousand. Depending on how long the whole thing ends up taking."

"Sounds good," Heller said. "Can you start tomorrow?"

Never done a day's work in his life.

"Tomorrow works."

"Perfect. I won't be here, of course, I'll be at the office. But Liz, that's my wife, Liz, she'll be here all day, so she can let you in and out of the house and get you anything you need."

"All right," Nick said. "I guess I'll see her tomorrow then." He turned away and started to trot down the steps to the backyard.

"Hold on a second," Heller called out, "I meant to ask, your name's Nick *Rogers*, right?"

Nick's shoulders tensed up; he didn't turn around. "That's right."

"It's so familiar to me. Do I know you from somewhere?"

"You probably just heard it around the neighborhood. I've done a lot of work around here."

"No." Nick could hear the deck creak as Heller walked toward him. Reluctantly, he turned around. "It wasn't that. In fact, when Abbie was talking about you, your name rang a bell. It's actually why I got your number off her instead of going with one of the other guys we've used in the past, well, that and she said you did great work. But, I really feel like I know you somehow. We never met before or anything? Are you like a junior? Could I maybe know your father?"

Nick laughed. "I seriously doubt it, Mr. Heller. I think I just have one of those names."

Heller frowned. “It’ll come to me. Anyway, see you tomorrow.”

“See you tomorrow.” Nick turned back around and headed to the front toward his truck.

Total rube.

# CIGARETTES

Sam was thinking about cigarettes. Specifically, she thought about why people started smoking and whether *she* should.

Ever since she was little, people warned her about the dangers of smoking. How it was super addictive and terrible and smelled and the people who did it were suckers and she should never even think about it because smoking was the single worst thing a person could ever do and, *she got it already.*

But…

She still wanted to try it.

Despite what she was told growing up, there was less than no peer pressure to smoke. The kids who smoked, smoked; the ones who didn't, didn't. She was sure someone offered her a cigarette at some time, but only as a courtesy. She said no thanks and that was the end of it.

She didn't think of herself as particularly susceptible to advertising, didn't have strong clothing brand loyalties or irrational devotion to one type of soda or cell phone or anything like that. If her desire to possibly smoke was all in the marketing, how had it succeeded where other products had not?

No, the brutal honest truth of it was, smoking was cool. Or, it was to Sam at least. She loved the way it looked, the cigarette dangling from guys' mouths in the old movies her grandmom watched on AMC; the way they cupped their hands over a lighter. She loved the way smoke looked when they exhaled through their noses.

More than anything, she loved when people in movies (in real life too, she supposed, though she had never seen it anywhere but the movies) pulled the cigarette out of the pack with their lips. It was just about the sexiest thing she ever saw.

Sam wanted to be cool like that. She needed to be cool like that. What was the word when people needed something in their mouths? Fixation. That's what they called it, oral fixation. It was one of the stages Freud discovered – she'd read about it in psychology – all these different stages of growing up and how sometimes people got stuck on one and kept doing it forever. There were a whole bunch of them, but the only ones she could remember were oral and anal. Every time their teacher, Mrs. Standish, mentioned those stages someone in the class would snort and everyone would laugh. Mrs. Standish always glared when that happened, but she must have known it would make them laugh. Why keep saying words like oral and anal to a high school classroom anyway?

Is that why she wanted to smoke? Did she have an oral fixation? Would it be bad if she did? It was better than an anal one, right?

She and her friend Becky laughed about it after class. They said that girls with oral fixations would need to go down on guys all the time to get a fix. They teased each other any time one of them would drink anything out of a straw or had a lollipop. But underneath it, she worried. She used to wonder how it would feel to do that to a boy; sometimes the idea didn't seem so horrible. Did that mean something?

Mrs. Standish talked about penis envy too, the idea that women wanted to have penises or always wanted to have sex with them or something like that. If she did have an oral fixation, would smoking cigarettes cure it or make it worse? Back when they took that psych class, neither she nor Becky had any real experience with guys, so it was all pretend - it was safe. That summer though, Sam started dating Martin Reed.

She knew Martin practically his whole life, and he was good and sweet and kind, maybe a little *too* kind. He asked her out, but other than that, he was shy to the point of total passivity. Martin's sister went to Bryn Mawr and she drilled into his head the importance of being respectful to women, and that was *great*, but he wouldn't even *try* to kiss Sam. He stole glances at her when they were on the couch watching TV, and there would be these awkward pauses in their conversation where she could tell he was trying to find the courage to make a move, but he always chickened out. It went on like that for almost a month before Sam got fed up and just kissed him already. After that he kissed her, but when she could tell he wanted things to go farther, he would freeze up again.

She was the one to put his hands under her shirt, and later, the one to unzip his pants and take it out (assuring him "*yes, Martin, I'm sure it's okay*") and put her head down and do it. She didn't particularly like it; not that she had much time to form an opinion, which was good because it kind of smelled, and he didn't give her any warning before he finished, and that was gross, but other than that it was okay. She also didn't dislike it. She liked that it made Martin feel good and she liked the idea of turning him on. She was turned on by the idea of doing it. After four months of safe nervous Martin, Sam decided that a little danger in a guy might suit her better. Maybe she preferred someone a little edgier, a little more confident, a little taller. Sam was tall for her age - at five-foot-seven, she had towered over most of her male classmates for years. It would be nice, she thought, to look up into someone's eyes for a change. Not that she regretted dating Martin, she just outgrew him. But he was the right kind of boy to have as a first boyfriend.

Becky wasn't as lucky.

Becky started dating Tyler, a senior from a neighboring school. They worked together at a summer camp in New Jersey. Sam, flush from her burgeoning romance with Martin, and excited by the idea that they would both have their first real boyfriends at the same time, encouraged Becky's relationship. She should have kept her stupid mouth shut.

Things seemed to be going well. Then, all of a sudden, everything stopped. At first Becky acted like she was fine; she made like the breakup was mutual and that she didn't really like Tyler anyway. That lasted about two days. Then she broke down crying and told Sam everything. Sobbing, she said she really liked him, *really*, and how they had sex on their fourth date (she wanted to tell Sam, but things went bad so quickly after that, she never got the chance); he said they would go to a movie that weekend and then he didn't call. She texted him and left him voicemail messages and tried talking to him on Facebook until he called her a stalker and de-friended her. She felt stupid and used and ashamed.

Ashamed. Over that fucking douche bag.

Sam wanted to go after him with a baseball bat, or at least destroy his car. Becky Schultz was her oldest and dearest friend and that asshole made her feel like dirt. It was unfair - unfair that things went so well with her and Martin, and so badly for Becky. Guilt seeped into her brain and made its way down her spine, until it settled in her stomach. Rationally, she knew she had no control over Tyler, couldn't make him be nice to Becky, and hadn't made him act like such a dirt ball in the first place. But, she had encouraged the relationship and filled Becky's head with unrealistic expectations. Did that all lead Becky to let that asshole use her and throw her away? Sam would be goddamned if she was going to stand by and let that slide.

She found Tyler's address online and was halfway down her driveway with a Louisville Slugger before her dad ran out to ask what exactly she was doing. Shaking with rage, Sam raved. She told him how Tyler used Becky and threw her away, how bad Becky felt, and how Tyler should pay. Tears ran down her face as she confessed to her father how she had unwittingly helped him by encouraging Becky to take him seriously.

Her dad was very understanding and upset for Becky. But he also told her that, as much of a shit as this Tyler was, she couldn't wreck his car with a bat. Sam knew that, knew the whole time. She didn't actually have a plan beyond charging angrily out of the house and was more than a little relieved when her dad stopped her. But it felt good to pretend to take control of things and seek out justice for her friend, if only as a way of coping with her own guilt.

That was the thing about life: you could never be sure what you were getting when you looked into somebody's face; could never be sure where something small might lead. A boy might seem nice, and then turn out to be a jerk. A curiosity about cigarettes might lead to some kind of sexual deviance.

It sounded goofy, sure, but everything starts somewhere.

One time this boy in her class, Andrew Miller, told a story about an Italian opera singer (he couldn't remember her name) who loved being in orgies. Supposedly, she was really into giving head (*giving head,* he said, the phrase made her skin crawl) during these orgies. And, supposedly, she went to a doctor, who told her she was damaging to her throat from the constant blow-jobs. If she kept at it, she would ruin her singing voice. According to Andrew, the singer chose the orgies over singing. Andrew said this woman was so addicted to the rush of sex that she gave up everything else. It sounded like bullshit to Sam, and she said so, but he insisted it was true. His older brother heard the story from a professor in one of his classes at college, some lecture about addictive behaviors. Sam googled it, tried to uncover the identity of the tragic blow-job obsessed, nymphomaniac opera singer, but she never found anything.

Of course, that didn't mean it didn't happen. Anything was possible. And *if* that opera chick really existed, then it was possible that her massive, life-altering obsession first appeared as something small. Like, maybe, a cigarette. Somewhere, sometime, this person did something that led to something else, which led to something else, which ended with her giving up her career in order to follow her obsession. And at the time of that first cigarette, it probably didn't seem like a big deal. It was just one. One. Little. Smoke.

She read once that personality was pretty much fully formed by the time someone was five years old. She couldn't remember *anything* that happened to her before she was five, but that was when all the really important stuff went down. That meant, in a way, she had no control over the person she was. Teachers and guidance counselors and therapists all talked to her about the importance of adolescence because it formed her identity. But if that book was to be believed, her core identity was formed years before, and without much input on her part. All that was left were the details.

So sometimes, when faced with a decision, she froze. Was her desire to smoke the next logical step in some long chain of desires that was set in motion when she was just a baby? Or was it some desperate, pointless attempt on her part to rebel from whatever programming was driving her these last sixteen years? How could she ever know?

Put another way, how could Samantha Elizabeth Heller ever, really, understand why she did anything? And if she couldn't understand *why* she was doing something, how could she go ahead and do it? How could anyone ever expect anybody to-

"*Sam!*" Her mother's voice sliced through her train of thought. Suddenly she was back in the passenger seat of her mom's car, the radio tuned to NPR and her little brother in the backseat humming tunelessly.

"What's up?"

"*What's up*? I've been talking to you for five minutes! Did you hear anything I said?"

"I'm sorry. I was a million miles away. What did you want to say?"

"Well, there really isn't time anymore. We're almost to Becky's."

"Can you, I don't know, give me the gist of it?"

"The *gist*?"

"Yeah, it means the-"

"I know what it *means.*" Her mom wasn't irritated; not really, she just got impatient with Sam sometimes.

Okay, maybe she was a little irritated.

They pulled up in front of Becky's house. Sam unbuckled and leaned over to kiss her mom on the cheek. "I'll be home by dinner. Becky's going to drive me home."

"You're sure she's not going to get distracted by you or anything. She's only had her license a week."

Sam held the door open and was half out of the car. "Mom, I gotta *go.*" She closed the door. "Love you."

"Love you too, sweetie."

Sam tapped the back window. “See you tonight, Oscar!” she called to her six-year-old brother.

“Love you!” he called out, and waved furiously.

“Love you too!” But the car was already pulling away.

She turned and started up the driveway to Becky's house.

# GERTIE

"Why are you being such a jerk about this?"

"Because it's stupid, Dana. You're being stupid."

The conversation was so bad that even going for a run didn't help.

Usually when Nick ran, he slipped into a zone and forgot all his problems. Usually he listened to his music and focused on his breathing and the steady rhythm of his feet hitting the pavement, and pretty soon his mind blanked and he was at peace. He would run three, four, five, sometimes six miles depending on how he felt and how tired Gert looked, though it always seemed like she could go a little farther. Huskies were strong, having been bred to pull sleds; it was why Nick had bought her. He wanted an athlete, like him. He loved running with her more than just about anything, when it was just the two of them - no work, no stress, no stupid girls getting worked up over nothing.

These girls. He was always clear with them. Always. He would tell them, right at the beginning, that he didn't want any kind of serious relationship, or girlfriend, or anything like that. He said he liked them and then, when they were hooking up, he reminded them that it was cool and everything, but that it didn't mean anything. *He said it every time*. And they always said they felt the same way. So why did so many of them go and fuck up a perfectly good thing?

It would be different if he lied, told them some story, strung them along, just to get into their pants. He played on teams with more than a few guys like that. They were assholes. Nick didn't believe in games, and he rarely made the first move. Nine times out of ten it was the girl who jumped *him*, and then, after everything, after his reminding them and their assurances, they always went crazy, treated him like shit, until *he* ended up the asshole.

Sometimes he wondered why he even bothered.

Dana was fun once. They hung out, drank, sometimes they made out, other times they didn't. Things were easy, things were good. Then, as usual, it soured. She started texting him all the time, asking him to shows and bars, or whatever. If he went, she got mad at him for saying the wrong thing, or not being nice enough to one of her stupid friends. If he didn't go, she pouted. Why would he want to hang out with her friends? Most of them were idiots. It wasn't his fault they were idiots. He liked *her*, not her friends. But to Dana, it was a slap in the face.

Nick stopped and waited for Gertie to do her business in front of a tree. She sniffed around its base, then she squatted, peed, stared up at him with blue eyes and wagged her tail happily, her signal that she was ready to start again.

Why would Dana want him for a boyfriend anyway? She was just a kid, barely twenty; he would be twenty-nine soon. When he was her age, he wasn't looking for a girlfriend, and the girls weren't serious either. Back then, girls didn't have expectations; if things didn't work out they didn't lose their shit and make giant scenes; they figured maybe the next one would work out better. Girls back then understood how to just hang out. Seriously, whatever happened to hanging out and seeing what happened?

And now she was pulling this shit.

When Dana first told him she was late, he was cool about it. He went through it before with other girls. He said to wait a couple days and not panic and see what happened. He told her thinking about it too much sometimes caused it to not come. She said she knew that, and she was a little bitchy about it too. And he thought: *why the fuck are you stressing about it then*? But he let it go, he knew better than to take her seriously; he reiterated that they should be cool until a little more time passed. She said okay, and that was that.

Then, a week later, it still hadn't happened, and she was getting really nervous. To be honest, he was nervous too. No way was he ready to have a kid, and especially not with a girl as annoying and clingy as Dana. But again, for her, he was calm. He asked her what she wanted to do— did she want to see a doctor? She said no, because she was still on her mom's insurance and she didn't want to answer any questions. They decided to pick up a test from the drug store. The test was negative. Dana was so relieved, she cried. Nick also felt pretty good. Maybe he should take the whole thing as a sign and stop hanging out with this girl. That should have been the end of it, right?

Wrong.

Dana's period still didn't come a week later. She started getting worked up again. She took the other two tests in the box. They were both negative. But that wasn't good enough anymore. *Now* she wanted to get tested by a professional. And she wanted Nick to take her.

But Nick didn't want to take her anymore. He was tired. He was tired of the drama, tired of the bullshit, tired of the phone calls and text messages and neediness. He was tired of *Dana.* And he told her too, when she asked him to take her. Not at first, of course, first he tried to be nice.

"I can't," he said. "I'm working tomorrow. I need to work all day."

"Please," she said, "it won't take long. We can go early in the morning. The clinic opens at six. I called and checked." There was panic edging into her voice. It pissed him off.

If she just stopped freaking out and looked at the tests, if she just listened to him in the first place, she'd see that this was all in her head. But now, it was his job to get her down off this high ledge she climbed, his job to take time out of his life and put out this imaginary fire.

He could easily have taken her. He didn't have to be at the Heller home at any particular time, but he was standing up for a principle. This girl thought she could get him to do whatever she wanted, whenever she wanted. He had to draw the line. "You should have gone last week."

"I'm sorry, okay? I should have. But, now I need your help. I'll buy you breakfast as a thank you."

Nick sighed. This was getting pathetic. "Why can't you get someone else to drive you?"

“Because,” she pleaded, “I don't want anyone else to know, in case...you know...”

“*It's nothing*,” Nick insisted.

“I know. I know it’s nothing. I’m just... I need to be sure, you know?”

“I already am sure.”

“Okay but...I need to be sure too. And if you can just do this for me, we won’t talk about it again, okay? I promise.”

Nick almost laughed. “How can I believe that?”

“What? Because I’m telling you. I’m promising.”

“You're promising now. You'll say anything *now*. All you care about is tomorrow. I have to think about after tomorrow.”

“I don't understand what you-”

“When something else happens, and you get all crazy again, and you come to me to bail you out. We’ve talked about this Dana; I’m not your boyfriend.”

“I didn't say that you were.”

“Well then, you should stop expecting me to drop everything every time you can’t get a crazy idea out of your head.”

“Why are you being such a jerk about this?”

“Because it’s stupid, Dana. You’re being stupid.”

He knew he shouldn’t have said it the moment it came out of his mouth.

There was silence on the other end of the phone. He didn’t know if he should speak. He went too far, lost his temper. He *liked* Dana, had no desire to hurt her. He just wanted her to relax, not stress so much.

“You're right.” Her voice sounded small, defeated. “I am being stupid. I'll just go and take care of this myself.”

“No, Dana, look…”

She cut him off. “Sorry to bother you.”

And then she hung up.

The run didn't help.

Nick gave up. He sat on the curb, rested his elbows on his knees and went over his options.

He could let things be. Not call Dana back. Not call her ever again. He hadn't done anything wrong, hadn't misled her. What he said was true, even if he said it badly. That must count for something. All he wanted to do was calm her down and she pushed him until he lost his cool. How could he be held accountable for being pushed until he cracked? How was that fair?

But fair or not, that was what was going to happen.

If he just let things lie, he would be the asshole. It didn't matter what he *meant* or *why* he said what he said. All that would matter was that he said it, and never fixed it. Dana would tell someone. She would drink too much one night and tell one of her stupid friends, and the two of them would talk about it and blow it out of proportion all over again. And the next day, the friend would tell someone, and soon enough it would get around that Nick was a big asshole who fucked girls and was mean to them and it wouldn't matter what really happened or how he was manipulated and harassed. All that would matter is what he said.

On the other hand, if he called her back, apologized and patched things up, wouldn't he be endorsing her behavior? Wouldn't that invite more craziness into his life? Or for some other poor bastard down the road? Dana was wrong. She wasn't pregnant, everything was fine and she was overreacting. It was her overreacting that kept her period away. These were all *facts.* He didn't know if she did all this because she was lonely and needed attention, or if there was something genuinely wrong with her. He did know if he gave in to her childish behavior, it would only be to make himself feel better and would, ultimately, be worse for Dana.

He couldn't win.

Gertie put her muzzle in Nick's lap and he absently scratched her head. She closed her eyes and grunted happily.

He pressed his face against hers. “You are the best girl in the world,” he said. “The whole world. C’mon.” He thumped Gertie's side and stood up. They started back home.

Forty minutes later, still wet from his shower and wrapped in a towel, Nick sat on his bed and stared at his phone. Finally, he dialed her number.

It rang.

And rang.

Until her voicemail clicked on.

Nick cursed quietly. Dana always had her phone. Always. She just wasn’t picking up because she was pissed. He was generally against leaving messages; the whole notion of talking to nothing made him nervous and he always felt like he said the wrong thing. In this case, he had to get over it.

“Hey, Dana. Look... about what I said earlier. I mean, I was just trying to calm you down, you know? I wanted to... anyway, if you still need me to take you to the, to that place tomorrow, I can. It’s not a big deal. I mean, I have to work, but I can just get there a little later if you need me to. It’s not that big a deal. So, yeah. Uh, get back to me.”

He hung up.

And then he fell back on his bed and cursed himself for being such a fucking idiot.

# GOLDWELL

"It itches."

"Sam, we're burning the color from your hair. Literally. Of course it itches."

Sam rubbed her neck just below the plastic bag that held her itchy, burning hair and looked up at her best friend. They were in Becky's bathroom. Becky leaned against the wall, thumbing through an *Us Weekly*, while Sam sat on the edge of the tub, wrapped in a towel and kicking at the remnants of her freshly cut hair.

"And it's gonna look okay when we're done?"

Becky rolled her eyes. "Jesus, would you man up? I've done this like, a thousand times. It's not brain surgery."

"I know, but I've never done anything like this before, you know?"

"That's why it'll be so *great*." Becky crouched down and put her hands on Sam's knees. "If you're gonna make a change, it may as well be a big one. So, the long hair is gone, and now we dye it. You're gonna look awesome. *Trust* me. Remember when we pierced our ears? You were nervous then, but what happened?"

"My mom freaked because I didn't ask her permission. Then, she threatened to ground me for a month."

"Yeah, okay, but did you actually get grounded?"

"No, only because Dad talked her down."

"You're missing the point. The point is, everything settled down and you looked great and you've pierced your ears, what, like four times since then?"

Sam tugged on her earlobe, "Five."

Becky smiled, "See? It'll be just like that. Except, your mom won't get so mad this time. You were eleven. Five whole years ago, that's the same as a million. You really think she's gonna get so worked up over a little hair cut?"

"Probably."

"Then why'd you do it?"

Sam didn't know. It would have been easy to check with her mom beforehand, but she hadn't. And now it was too late to do anything about it. She picked up the box of hair dye and examined it. She chose the color purely because she liked the name. "Goldwell," she said.

Becky was staring at herself in the mirror. "What about it?" she asked over her shoulder.

"Nothing. I just like saying the name. Goldwell." She looked down at the box and, after a minute, said, "Hey, do you ever think about, like, what makes us, us?"

"Um, not really. What do you mean 'what makes us, us'?"

"I dunno. Like, our hair's always growing, right? And we keep cutting it off, and dyeing it and whatever. We're always gaining or losing weight, and growing and stuff like that. And, you know how they say we shed our skin every seven years?"

"Sure, everyone knows that."

"So our body is always changing. I'm not the same... thing that I was when I was born. Physically, I mean. I'm not the same. I'm not even the same as I was when we pierced our ears. You said it yourself."

"Yeah, but you're still *you*."

"But what does that mean? Look, who's my favorite band?"

"Gaslight Anthem."

"But they weren't five years ago. Five years ago, Maroon 5 was my favorite band. Now I can't stand them."

"*So*?" Exasperation crept into Becky's voice.

Sam knew it drove Becky nuts when she talked about these things, but sometimes she just couldn't help it. "So, if my body's different, and my mind's different, then what's the same? How am I the same person that I was five years ago?"

"Christ Sam, I don't know, because you just are. I mean, fine, some things are different, yeah, but there're lots that are the same. We're still best friends, yeah? And you still hate mushrooms, and your favorite book is still *Harry Potter and the Prisoner of Azkaban*."

"But what if we weren't still friends? And I decided I liked mushrooms after all? If all that changed, would that mean I wouldn't be me anymore?"

Becky stared at her. "I think I was wrong. I think the bleach has soaked through your hair and is burning your brain. How did you start thinking about this?"

Sam held up the box. "I was looking at the box, and I was thinking about how long it'd been since I cut my hair. Then I thought about that bible story about Samson and Delilah, and about how he kept all his strength in his hair. And then I started thinking 'What if I kept all my strength somewhere on my body like that?' and then I started wondering if I actually *did* keep it somewhere, and where it was. Because that place where I keep all my strength and my sadness and happiness and love and all that, that's *me*, and it must be *somewhere*, and I was just wondering where that was."

Becky laughed. "You got all that from a hair dye box?"

"I guess." Sam shrugged.

Becky laughed again. "Jesus."

Sam looked down. "Forget it. It's stupid."

"Stupid? It's not stupid. I just have *no idea* what the answers are, that's all. Isn't that what, like, philosophers and artists and religious people have been trying to figure out forever?"

"Maybe."

"Well, it's a lot to think about. And it's a little out of my league, at least tonight it is. Why don't we just concentrate on not fucking up your hair for now, okay Samson?"

Sam smiled. "Yeah, okay."

"Good, because that, I know we can figure out."

# RESPECT: PART ONE

"Hey, hey, hey, *hey*!" Tom knocked Nick's hand away from the skillet. "What are you doing?"

Nick shook his hand. "Dude, He said, "I'm not *seven*"

Tom's son Robbie sat on the kitchen floor behind his dad. Thinking Nick was waving at him, he smiled and waved back with one of his blocks.

"Don't act like you're seven then. Don't pick. It'll be done when it's done."

"But I'm hungry." Nick looked at Robbie and scrunched up his face. Robbie tried to copy him, but mostly just blew spit bubbles.

Tom frowned at Nick. "What are you, an animal? You can't wait five minutes and eat off a plate?"

"Five minutes?"

"Five minutes."

Nick crossed the kitchen and opened the back door; he paused halfway out, and pointed at Tom. "Five minutes," he said. Then he whistled for Gertie. She raced through the kitchen and out the back door; he followed, closing the door behind him. Outside, Nick took a seat in the beat-up lawn chair next to the door, lit a smoke, and watched Gertie happily sniff around the small backyard.

Tom got bitchy when he cooked. He'd been that way since they were kids. Nick would go over to Tom's house and find Tom in the kitchen with his mom, cutting up one thing, sautéing another, water boiling, things happening. Tom would order Nick out of the kitchen and Nick would head outside to throw a ball against the wall, or play video games in the den— anything, so long as he was out of the way. After high school, Tom enrolled at the culinary school (which, frankly, Nick didn't even know was a *thing*). Now, he worked as a chef at a retirement home.

It amused Nick how seriously Tom took food. To Nick, food was fuel, something to keep him going from stop to stop. A burger was as good as steak. But for Tom it was something more; for Tom, food was practically holy. It was his way of gathering together loved ones and letting them know how much they meant to him. There was nothing more serious to Tom than a properly prepared meal. And for Nick, the fun was in tweaking his old friend while he prepared that meal.

Val's clunky old Honda pulled onto the driveway. The car stereo was loud enough that Nick recognized the song even if he couldn't remember the name, it wasone of those 80's New Wave one hit wonders from an English band where all the guys looked like extras from The Crow. Or, he guessed because *The Crow* came out in the nineties, everyone in that movie looked like the guys from one of these bands. Anyway. Two years younger than Nick, Val was actually Nick's aunt, but more like a sister than anything else. Growing up, Val and Tom were his two best friends, and no one was surprised when the two of them eventually started dating. They got married and bought a house in town; they let Nick move into the spare bedroom when he lost his place.

The metal gate squeaked and Val, in her Doc Martens, cut across the small patch of grass. She sank next to him and he wordlessly handed her a cigarette. She was ready with a lighter. She inhaled, held the smoke in her lungs for a few seconds, then exhaled through her nose and rested her head against the aluminum siding of her house.

"Rough day?"

Val shrugged. "Not especially, just long. I'm beat."

She took another drag.

"Lots of pissed off people, no support from management. I have to take care of everything myself or nothing gets done. The usual. How about you?"

"Nothing special."

"Did you see about that job?"

Nick nodded.

"You gonna do it?"

Nick nodded again.

They sat there quietly. Nick knew what Val really wanted to talk about, but he wasn't going to give her the satisfaction. Gertie trotted to the back door and batted at the screen. Nick reached up and opened the door for her.

"Did you talk to Dana?"

And there it was.

"Nick?"

Shit. "Yeah?"

"Did you hear me?"

"Yeah." His voice was low, a whisper.

"*Yeah* what? Yeah *I heard you*? Or yeah, *I talked to Dana*?"

"Yeah to both of them."

"So what happened?"

"Nothing really."

"Everything's okay then?"

"As okay as it's gonna be."

"What does that mean?"

"It *means* I don't want to talk about it."

"That means you did something."

"I didn't *do* anything." He felt his heart speed up, his neck get hot.

"Then tell me what happened."

"Val, you're not my mom, all right?" This sometimes worked as a last defense. It sometimes pushed her off, at least for a while.

Not tonight though. "*Tell me.*"

So he told her. He told her everything: Dana acting crazy, he wasn't her boyfriend, Dana being stupid. By the time he finished, there were daggers in Val's eyes.

"Jesus Nick, you're such a fucking idiot."

Nick rolled his eyes. "Whatever." This was exactly why he didn't want to tell her. He knew she would take Dana's side; she *always* took the girl's side. Every time, no matter what. He always resisted telling her about the girls in his life, and she always pushed him (why did he cave?), and then she always got mad at him. She never looked at things from his perspective. It was like she wanted to get mad at him or something. None of it was any of her business anyway. "No, seriously, fuck you. This isn't a 'whatever' situation. You fucked up big this time."

He hated when she got like this, when she acted superior to him. "How? How is any of this my fault? She took the test. It came back negative. I offered to take her to a doctor a week ago. I'm not her boyfriend."

"No, but you acted like it."

"That's such bullshit. When did I ever 'act'" - he put up air quotes - "like I was her boyfriend?"

"How about when you put your *dick* in her, fuckwad? How about then?"

Nick stared ahead angrily - Val got so crude when she was angry. Cruder than usual. It was annoying.

"Yeah, no comeback for that, is there?"

She missed the point, but then, people usually did. Dana was her own person, capable of making her own decisions about her own body. If she wanted to have sex with him, it was her choice. That didn't make him anything to her. If he could have sex with her and not think of her as his girlfriend, then she should be able to do the same. Anything else was just delusional. But nobody cared about that. All Val cared about was the poor girl's *feelings*. How the girl treated Nick, and how Nick treated the girl never mattered against how the girl *felt* about it all. So that's what she focused on. Reality wasn't something that girls worried about when they got mad.

"Let me ask you something Val, why is it always my fault? Did I drug Dana? Did I rape her? Were you even there? Because I seem to remember her kissing me. And I remember her telling me that everything would be okay. How come I'm the asshole for believing her?"

Val looked at him then, and her eyes weren't angry anymore, they were something he couldn't put his finger on. They almost looked hurt. "Nick..." she said, and then her voice trailed off.

"What?"

She looked away. "Nothing."

"No, what were you going to say?"

"Nothing, it's not important."

"That's not fair - you can't push me into talking and then say nothing. You tell me what you were going to say."

She took a deep breath. "I was going to say... that you're right."

"You were?" He hadn't expected that.

"Yes. Not about the way you treated Dana. You were right when you said I wasn't your mom. I'm not. This is none of my business. Just, do whatever you want, I don't care."

"You don't?" In all the times they argued, Val never backed down before. It made Nick nervous.

Val shrugged and said nothing; she kept her eyes on the ground.

He felt his resolve melt. As much as she annoyed him and mothered him and bossed him around, he couldn't stand to upset her. More than anyone else in the world, he needed her to be okay with him. Suddenly, nothing mattered more than getting her to believe in him again.

"Look, I'm gonna fix this, okay?"

"Sure you will."

"I *will*," he insisted.

"I don't see how."

"I'll think of something, okay?"

"What do you mean 'okay'? It doesn't matter what I think."

"I know, I know. It's just..." He wanted to ask her to never look at him that way again. He wanted to say *don't give up on me, please*. But instead he said, "It's just if you think whatever I come up with is good, I know Dana will too."

Val looked at him again. "You better hope so. Come on." She put out the remainder of her cigarette on the concrete ground and stood up. "Let's go eat."

Relief flooded through Nick's body. He put out his smoke too. "All right."

Val stretched out her arms and yawned. "What'd Tom make tonight?"

Nick got to his feet, feeling positively giddy. "Something with chicken; it smelled good."

"You didn't try any?"

"He slapped my hand before I got a chance."

"Oh Nick," Val said opening the door, "when are you gonna learn?"

# RESPECT: PART TWO

She was angry. *Of course she was angry.* They were sitting at the dining room table, Sam's parents at the two heads, with Sam and Oscar on opposite sides. "You should have talked to us." Sam's mom wasn't taking the new hair well. "Your beautiful hair," she said. "What about senior portraits? Did you think about that?"

"Mom, that's like, six months away!"

"Six months isn't as long as you think. We're either going to have to dye your hair again, or cut it again. I'm not sending pictures to Gran, and everyone, of you with half brown, half red hair."

"It's white too," Oscar reminded them.

She and Becky had stripped her hair so that the red would really pop, but also because Sam thought the white roots looked cool.

"Thanks, Oscar," Sam said quietly.

"That's right, Oscar," her mom said, "brown, red, and a stripe of white in between. You'll look like...I don't know what, but we're not doing it."

"So we'll cut it again mom; it's just hair."

"It's the earrings all over again," she muttered.

Sam looked down at her plate. What else could she do? "I didn't think it would be a big deal."

"And it wouldn't have been, if you had talked to us about it first." Sam's mom was big on protocol. Rules were rules. If Sam had a problem with one of the rules she could bring it up, and if she had a good reason, sometimes (though not often), the rule changed. But until the rule changed, it was to be obeyed. That's why they were all at the big dining room table for dinner, instead of the smaller, more comfortable one in the kitchen.

Sam's mom never tired of telling them about her family's Sunday dinner policy when she was growing up. Sam's grandfather didn't ask much from his family. Monday through Saturday they could eat however they wanted, people could watch TV, be out on dates or with friends, or other people could be over or whatever; but Sunday night was family dinner night. Everybody had to be home, there couldn't be any guests, and dinner was served at the dining room table at six-thirty sharp. That was the rule. When Sam's mother grew up, got married, and started a family of her own, she carried the tradition with her. So when Sam walked in the door at six-thirty-five and sat down at the table with her new, short, red hair, her mom went a little ballistic.

"I didn't know it was something we *had* to talk about." While this was technically true, it was nothing more than that. Sam knew very well what her mom was going to do when she walked into the room with her new hair.

"Well, that's why we talk about it, so you can figure it out."

"Anyway, it's done now," Sam's dad cut in, "and there's nothing we can do about it, right?"

Sam suppressed a smile; her dad understood and was coming to her rescue, again.

"Hon." He turned to Sam's mom. "It sounds to me like Sam knows she screwed up by not checking with you, and she won't forget or do it again. Right?" He looked at Sam and raised his eyebrows.

"I won't, I promise mom, really."

"Aside from that, I'm not sure there's anything else to say," her dad said.

Her mom sighed. "I just liked your hair when it was brown," she finally said.

"Is that what this is about? Color? Do you want me to dye her hair brown?" Sam's dad put his hands flat on the table, palms down. "Because if that's what it takes to fix this, I'll do it."

"Daddy!" Sam covered her head with her hands and giggled. He was turning it all into a game, one of his specialties.

"Yeah, let's color Sammy's hair!" Oscar threw his hands in the air with excitement at the idea.

"What do you say, hon? Oscar's in on it too! We could go to the store and get the dye right now!"

"Right now!" echoed Oscar.

"Come on now, this is serious," Sam's mom said, trying to get the conversation back on track.

"Oh, I'm serious," insisted her dad. "I'm as serious as a heart attack! We're dyeing her hair tonight! And if brown doesn't do it for you, we'll try other colors too! Black! Blonde! Purple!"

"No Daddy, not purple! I don't even know if they have purple dye at the store!" They did, and she knew it, but that wasn't the point. Sam was playing now, as much to Oscar as her dad. Pushing his imagination.

"Purple hair, purple hair, purple hair!" Oscar shouted

"Then we'll have to improvise! Oscar," her dad almost bellowed, "get your crayons! I'll start boiling the water!"

"Yeah yeah yeah yeah!" Wild-eyed, Oscar jumped out of his chair and sped across the room, only to be scooped up by their mom, who laughed in spite of herself. "No, no," she said, "no crayon dye jobs today."

"But I wanna give Sammy purple hair!" Oscar looked like he was about to cry.

"Why don't you draw me with purple hair instead? How does that sound?" Her dad had been there for her with her mom; she covered him when Oscar started to get out of hand. They were a team.

"Okay." He was still disappointed, but it wasn't as bad as it could have been. Their mom put him down and he started back towards his room again.

“Hold on,” his mom said, “finish dinner first. *Then,* draw Sam.”

Oscar sat back down. After a moment of eating, he seemed to have forgotten about Sam and her purple hair entirely.

“So I finally got a guy to fix up the deck,” Sam’s dad said. “It’s not gonna be cheap, but Abbie Reisman said he did great work on her kitchen back in February.” Sam watched him, not listening to a word he was saying.

She had the best dad in the whole world.

## MONDAY TOOL

Back in the day, he used music to psyche himself up.

It started in the ninth grade when he was in the weight room and his coach put an old mixtape into the shitty boom box. It was mostly awful stuff from the 80's, like *Van Halen* and *Eye of the Tiger*, stuff coach used back in *his* day to get pumped. It was cheesy but it kind of worked. To this day, his heart started beating faster whenever he heard *Right Now.*

The other guys on the team laughed at the tape behind coach's back. They made their own tapes. Nick was never really into music, but he liked listening to it when he worked out, so he asked some of the guys to make him tapes too. That's where he first heard *Nirvana, Alice in Chains, Soundgarden, Oasis,* and all the other bands he would end up listening to for the next fifteen years. The music helped him center his thoughts and focus his emotions. It helped him get ready for the pain of pushing himself where his body didn't necessarily want him to go.

And that's where he was at seven thirty in the morning—sitting in his truck, down the street from Dana's house, waiting for her mom to leave for work. Somewhere he didn't want to be.

It wasn't that he didn't like her mom, he liked her fine. And it wasn't that she didn't like him. If anything, it was kind of the opposite. There wasn't anything that he could put his finger on; more of a vibe. Like the way she looked at him. She had this way of staring at Nick that made him uncomfortable. She had big, greedy eyes that looked like they wanted to swallow him whole. It freaked him out, made him want to run as far away from her as possible. Sometimes Dana looked at him with the same eyes.

He couldn't deal with two sets of greedy eyes today.

And so, feeling like an idiot, he waited for Dana's mom to leave for work and listened to *Tool* to psyche himself up for the conversation he really didn't want to have.

Fucking Val.

She had her own family; she had a husband and a kid and a job and everything. Why did she have to waste her time worrying about his life? He had things under control. Mostly. And it wasn't like she knew Dana. Val had met her, how many times? Three, four at the most? And only for a couple of minutes at a time. That wasn't any real time. They weren't friends. If they were friends, then Val's overreaction about Dana would totally make sense.

Why couldn't she just leave him alone to take care of things his own way?

He was just about to say fuck it, give up and go home, when Dana's mom finally walked out of the front door, got in her car, and drove off.

He gave it a few more minutes. Let the song finish and his thoughts settle as much as they could. *Just go do this*, he told himself. *Just go make things right with her and you can tell Val that everything's fine and she won't look at you like that again*. He could take a couple more days or weeks with Dana if it made Val happy.

The song ended and he killed the engine.

He took a deep breath, got out of the car, and walked up the driveway. He rang the doorbell twice before she opened the door. When she did, she stared up at him with tired red eyes. She was wearing a loose t-shirt and a pair of faded pink pajama bottoms with little bears on them. Her hair was messy and her skin was raw and splotchy. She hadn't slept much the night before, and had obviously been crying.

Neither of them said anything. Nick realized he had no idea how to begin.

He felt like an asshole. Immediately, he felt his irritation at Dana grow in his belly. Who was this girl to make him feel so bad for something that wasn't even real? How dare she blame him for her delusions. Where did she get the-—

He shut that shit down. Focused. Played the music from the car in his head.

*Calculate what we will or will not tolerate...*

Just like the weight training, push his body where it didn't want to go.

Finally he said, "You weren't picking up when I called."

"What are you doing here?"

"I wanted to talk to you."

"About what?"

"About..." God, he felt dumb. "About yesterday. About what we were talking about on the phone."

"I don't know why, there's nothing else to say."

"I was an asshole yesterday."

She snorted. "Yeah, you were. But it wasn't just yesterday." She wasn't going to give an inch.

"Okay, well, I guess that's what I am, okay?"

She looked at him hard. "What do you mean 'okay'?"

"What?"

"Just what I said, *what do you mean 'okay'?* What is okay?"

Jesus. "Christ Dana, I don't know. I just came over to make sure you were okay. I wanted to see if you still wanted me to take you to the doctor or what."

"Well fine, so you said that. So you can go now."

She was right, he could.

"All right," he said, "if that's what you want. I'll see you around." And then he turned and walked away. He was halfway back to his truck and feeling pretty good about himself when she called out to him.

"Nick!"

Nick closed his eyes and grimaced. Then he opened them and turned around. She jogged toward him, across the gravel driveway in front of her house. Nick saw her bare feet kick up the little stones as she ran and cursed himself under his breath. He was so close to getting out of there. He could have told Val he did all he could and Dana told him to leave anyway. It would have been perfect.

"Wait," she said when she finally caught up to him. "Just, wait. I just want to... Look, I was," she corrected herself, "I *am* really hurt by what you said to me yesterday-"

"And that's why I came, to apologize."

"Yeah, you did, and I appreciate it. But I don't know. I'm gonna need more than that."

He had no idea where any of this was going, and he didn't like it. But he played the music in his head, and thought of Val and pushed through it. "Like what, more how?"

"I don't know. Just, more." She shivered and ran her hands up and down her bare arms. Over Dana's shoulder Nick saw a curtain move in the window of the house next door. Nick imagined people looking out their front windows and seeing a guy in a jacket and sweatshirt standing in front of a tiny barefoot girl in just a t-shirt and thin pajama pants. How did that look?

"Here." He took off his jacket and draped it over her shoulders. "You're gonna get sick if you stand out here much longer."

"Thanks." Her arms emerged from inside the coat and she pulled the collar closed. She looked almost comically small inside his jacket. He had close to a foot and seventy pounds on her. "Can we, talk, later? Like later today?" She smiled at him for the first time. "I got less than no sleep and Alicia's coming to take me to the doctor in half an hour."

He hated Alicia. She was one of the most annoying people Nick had ever met in his life.

"I can take you if you want."

"No, I don't think that would be a good idea. But maybe we can get something to eat after?"

"Well, I mean, I have a job today so I don't really…."

"Oh, yeah, you did say that. Okay. Well, you wanna, like, get dinner?"

Of course he didn't. "If that's what you want to do."

"So, I'll see you tonight?"

He nodded.

"And I can call you, to let you know what happens at the doctor? You'll be around?"

"I'm not going anywhere," he said.

And he wasn't.

Shit.

# MULLET

"Did I ever tell you about when I changed my hair?" Sam's dad glanced over at her for a moment but then focused back on the road.

"Maybe," she said. "But if you did, I don't remember."

"Is that 'I don't remember, so tell me'? Or is it more 'I don't remember because it's so boring that my brain forced me to forget'?"

"Don't be paranoid Daddy and tell me your stupid story."

"Okay, but only because… anyway, I was seventeen and your Grandma Alice and Grandpa Joe decided they were taking the family to visit Grandma Alice's parents, in Seattle. For the whole summer. Normally we'd go out for a couple of weeks in July but Grandma Alice's parents were getting older and she wanted to spend some real quality time with them before they, you know…"

"Died?"

"Exactly. So they decided that we'd spend the whole summer out there, which was fine with me because I had a lot of cousins my age out there and their friends were my friends and I always had fun with them and stuff."

"Lots of cute girls?"

"Exactly again. And it was a good summer too, if you know what I mean."

"Daddy!"

"Hey, I'm just saying. So I was out there and I don't know but I decided to grow out my hair. I didn't go to the barber all summer and by the time we got back home, I had a pretty good, you know, look. My whole life I had the same haircut, I called it the *Dennis the Menace*, with a little cowlick in the back and everything. But now, after the summer, there's this volume that I never had before. I had a whole bangs thing going on; I got, like, scruff growing down my neck; I had hair covering my ears, it was a little curly.

I'm telling you, I got back home and the girls saw me and it was like I was a different person. It was amazing. I thought that hair was going to change everything for me."

"So, what happened?"

"Sam, it was *the worst* day of my life. Two days before school starts, I go to the barber, for the first time in *three months,* just to get a little trim. Just a little one, right? And he massacres my head. He gave me one of those, oh what are they called?" He lifted a hand to the side of his head. "Hockey players have them?"

"Mullet?"

He snapped his fingers, "Yeah, that's it, he gave me a mullet."

"Oh Daddy, that's terrible, I'm sorry. What did you do?"

"What could I do? I went home and shaved my head."

"Did you at least chew out the barber?"

"I couldn't. Gus had been my barber my whole life. He cut my hair along with every other guy I grew up with. I shoulda gone to a hairdresser; it was my own fault really."

"Bad hair cuts are the worst."

"Tell me about it."

"Why didn't you just grow your hair out again?"

Her dad didn't say anything, he just kept driving, but his eyes were slightly unfocused, lost in thought; he did that sometimes.

"Daddy?"

He snapped back, "Sorry, what's up?"

She laughed, "Your hair, if you liked the way it looked long, why didn't you just grow it out again?"

He shrugged. "I guess I was embarrassed to try. I didn't want people to make fun of me. It would have to go through that awkward phase where it's not long yet, but it's not short; I didn't want to deal with it? When you're a guy it can be really hard to change the way you look without getting crucified by other guys.

Girls can do it whenever they want and nobody cares; it's expected. But guys, guys'll rip you up."

Sam shook her head; she loved her dad, but sometimes he could be really dense. "I'm sorry Daddy but that's just crazy talk. Girls are always worried about how they look. And they are horrible to each other about that stuff. I mean, haven't you ever looked at the cover of a fashion magazine?"

"Well sure," her dad said, "but I thought that was more about weight and stuff, and about how attractive they were to men. I always thought girls were nice and supportive to each other, like girl power or something."

"Yeah, well, they're not. Girls want to be attractive to boys, but they're just as worried about how they look to other girls. Maybe more, because at least guys are honest. Girls are super nice to each other's face, but terrible behind their backs. It's kind of the opposite of boys that way. Boys pick on each other, but don't really care, and girls say nice things, but then stab you in the back."

"They do?"

"All the time. It makes you paranoid because you never know if someone actually thinks you look good or if they're only saying it and are gonna make fun of you when you walk away. It's the worst."

"It sounds like it."

Sometimes Sam couldn't tell when her dad was being honest and when he was stringing her along. Being a dad and letting her go on and on about something that was perfectly obvious.

"Daddy, are you being, like, for real right now?"

"Completely. I really thought that girls' body image issues came from men having really high standards. You know, *Playboy* and Gloria Steinem and stuff." His face scrunched up, he actually looked a little irritated.

"All right, it's just that you live with two women, and you've had girlfriends before mom. I figured you would have noticed."

Her dad shrugged helplessly. “I don’t know what to tell you sweetie, I guess I’m just spectacularly unobservant.”

“You know how when we’re watching TV with mom, she always comments on the outfits that everybody’s wearing?”

“Sure, but those are TV people, they aren’t real.”

“What about when she talks about Aunt Sydney and Aunt Carol? She’s always nice when she sees them, but when we’re back in the car… “

“I guess I thought that was sister stuff.”

“No Daddy, it’s all girl stuff.”

Sam pressed her forehead against the passenger window and concentrated on the cool glass against her skin. There was a moment before her dad spoke again.

“*I* cared when other guys picked on me.”

“Well Daddy, I guess you’re just a big girl then.”

“I guess. Hey, listen, as long as we’re talking about all this - your mom and your hair and stuff - you need to talk to her about last night, make things right.”

She sighed, “C’mon…”

“No really, it’s important. You know how these sorts of things matter to her.”

“I thought you were on my side about this.”

“I’m not on anybody’s side, that’s not what this is about. You need to respect your mom.”

“Well, what am I supposed to do? It’s not like I can change my hair back.”

“You’re supposed to talk to her, and you’re supposed to be nice and be respectful.”

“She yelled at you, didn’t she? Last night? After dinner?”

“*Sam*.”

There was no more arguing, she could tell. Her mom got to him. He fixed things and her mom went and messed it up again. Sam crossed her arms.

"All right."

"C'mon, it's not a big deal."

"Whatever, I said I'd do it."

"Don't be like this."

"Can we stop talking about this please?" She turned her head back to the window, and pressed her head against the glass again and didn't say anything for the rest of the ride home.

Sam's mom wasn't home when they got there. She'd gone to pick up Oscar from daycare and would pick up dinner on her way home.

But someone was there.

She saw him through the kitchen window; she went in to get a snack before dinner and, while opening a fruit roll-up, the sound of a drill just outside spun her around in surprise. There was a boy on her back deck. He was crouched down, running his finger around a spot on the deck; an electric drill lay at his feet. He leaned in close to the spot and gently blew. He wiped at it one more time, and then stood up and stretched.

He was tall, thin, but powerful looking, broad shouldered, in a beaten old leather jacket over a grey sweat shirt. Dirty jeans hung loosely from a tool belt, and his work boots were untied. His face was smudgy and unshaven and he had shaggy brown hair that fell into his eyes.

He was maybe the most beautiful boy Sam had ever seen.

She stared through the kitchen window as the boy reached into his back pocket and pulled out a crumpled pack of cigarettes. There was some kind of marking on the side of his hand, a tattoo, like one of those tribal symbols people got. He squeezed the packet and lifted it to his mouth where he, *oh god - he lifted the pack up to his mouth and pulled a cigarette out of the pack with his lips.* All the blood rushed from Sam's head and raced to her pelvis.

Her dad walked into the kitchen and put his hand on her shoulder.

"Mom will be home in ten. She's bringing Chinese. How's that sound?"

Sam snapped back to reality, tore her eyes off the boy on the deck. "What? Chinese? Sure, sounds fine."

"Glad to hear it. Listen, Sam, about your mom…"

He was walking around on the deck, the cigarette in his mouth. Was he done for the day? Staying longer? Who was this boy? "I said it's okay."

"Because I don't want you to think that she…"

She looked at her dad. "Daddy? Really, I'll talk to mom; it's fine. *It's fine.*" She changed the subject. "Who's that outside?"

"Him? He's the guy I hired to fix up the deck. I've been saying for years that I was going to… Oh! That's right!" He pointed at her. "I figured it out!"

"You what?" She had no idea what he was talking about.

"Him." He pointed out the window. "I figured out where I - this is really cool - follow me." He started into the dining room toward the back door.

Sam didn't move. "Daddy, what are you doing?"

"I want to introduce you to him. It's cool, you're gonna think it's really cool, I promise."

"I don't want to meet anybody."

He came back into the kitchen, put his arm around her and lightly pulled her toward the deck. "C'mon, trust me." Reluctantly, Sam followed her dad into the dining room, where he slid the back door open and stepped outside.

The boy had his back to them; he put his cigarette out in a bowl sitting on the banister. He looked over his shoulder at Sam's dad and turned around. "Mr. Heller, I just finished up for the day.

Your wife said I should use this bowl for my cigarettes. I hope that's okay."

"Oh yeah sure, that's fine. I wanted to introduce you to someone." He looked over his shoulder at Sam, still standing in the dining room. "Sam? Sam, come here, meet Nick."

Feeling as self-conscious as ever, Sam went out onto the porch to her dad. He put his hand on her shoulder.

"Nick, this is my daughter, Sam. Remember, I told you about her yesterday?"

Sam felt her ears and the back of her neck burn; this was maybe the most embarrassing moment of her life.

"Sure, nice to meet you." The boy named Nick put his hand out to shake.

She took his hand.

"Good. Thanks."

She managed to meet his eyes for a second; then she had to look away.

"And Sam, this is Nick Rogers. Do you know who that is?" He didn't wait for her to answer. "Nick played second base at East Baxter High School about, what? Ten years ago?"

"That's about right," Nick mumbled.

"I knew I recognized you from somewhere, so I googled you at work today. I followed you some time back when you played around here." He turned back to Sam. "Sam, in his senior year Nick hit .625 with twenty-eight home runs!"

"Twenty-seven," Nick said.

"He was amazing. I used to read about him all the time in the paper; you're probably too young to remember, but Nick here was a really big deal."

Sam heard the sound of her mom's car in the driveway. "Mom's here - I'm gonna go see if she needs any help bringing in food or anything."

"That's a good idea sweetie, you do that," he turned his attention back to Nick. "You know I played in school too, all the way through college..."

Sam fled back into the house and toward the front door as fast as she could without actually running.

She had never been so glad to see her mom in her life.

# BIRTHDAY CARDS

Not even ten o'clock and Dana was already asleep. It made sense, given the last few days. Anxiety kept her up for most of the previous night. When the doctor told her the news, she was so relieved, an enormous weight was lifted off her shoulders. Then the adrenaline kicked in and she was bouncing off the walls for the rest of the day. Nick picked her up that evening, and it was like she was a new person. He tried to connect the sad pathetic girl from earlier that day with the bright, shining one that ran across the yard and practically jumped into his arms before he got five steps from his truck.

Nick lay on his side and stared at the wall. The lights were off, and the curtains were drawn; it was just him and his thoughts. Dana was snuggled up behind him, her arm under his, wrapped around him, her breasts pushing into him in time with her breathing. Her face was pressed so hard against him that her eyelashes tickled his neck as her eyes darted behind her lids. He wished he could sleep, fall into her easy rhythm and drift off himself, but it was too early, and his mind wouldn't cooperate.

He was going to have to stay the night.

He felt so shitty after that conversation with Heller and she was so happy, it was impossible not to be affected by it.

Fucking Heller, why couldn't he leave well enough alone? What was it about some people? They always have to remind everyone how much better they've got it than everyone else. Guy has a good job, a huge house and a beautiful family, but he has to rub it in Nick's nose that he missed his chance at the same.

The wife, Liz, she was so nice when he asked her for something to use for his cigarettes. Sometimes, people got annoyed at him for even asking. He would ask and they'd make this face like he shouldn't be smoking on their property at all. Outside. It was ridiculous. But Liz smiled and said sure, and got him the bowl and that was it. Later, she came outside and asked if he wanted anything to eat or drink. They talked for a few minutes. She was a nice woman. Some people acted like Nick was a thief they'd allowed into their home; they would disappear, but he could feel them watching, making sure he wasn't taking anything or messing anything up too bad. Liz treated him like just another guy she knew; she treated him like an equal.

*You were so great! Why aren't you playing now? What happened? He used to be a big deal.* Thanks a lot, asshole. Right in front of his daughter too. Clown.

He only saw the daughter for that second, but she looked embarrassed enough by her dad's comments that he could tell she was nice. Cute too. Tall and thin like her mom. Hadn't Heller said something about her liking to swim or something? She could probably run track. It would be good for her. She had that long-legged, baby deer thing going. Awkwardness which, properly channeled by a good coach, could turn into grace. And it wasn't just in her body either. She had these big eyes - eyes were important - that darted around nervously; there was a lot going on in there. She just needed a little confidence and she'd be able to take over the world.

The mom had it. One day, the daughter would too.

They were too good for that guy.

He had to move.

Carefully, Nick rolled out of Dana's grip and off the bed. He felt around the floor for his clothes, grabbed his smokes from his jeans, and pulled on his boxers.

Dana groaned sleepily. "Everything okay?"

"Fine, just my leg started to cramp a little, gonna walk it off."

Her eyes were still closed. "Don't have to stay in here, can go watch TV, something."

He could hear it on downstairs, some cop show, or maybe doctors, but her mom was down there and she would try to talk to him. He had no desire to spend an hour sitting next to Dana's mom on the couch making small talk. He was trapped. "I'm okay, just gonna smoke."

"'Kay, g'night." She rolled over and instantly snored lightly.

His eyes adjusted enough to the dark, and he lit his cigarette, lazily wandering around Dana's small room. Next to the bed was a bookshelf filled with books that, other than *Harry Potter*, he never heard of, and a handful of CDs by bands with faggy names that played that emo shit or Euro dance trash that she sometimes played for him.

Across from the bookshelf, on the opposite wall, stood a little desk and vanity, with pictures of Dana and her friends stuck into the mirror frame. Nick sat in the little chair and flipped through the environmental science textbook on the desk; Dana took classes at the community college. Education maybe, or early childhood development? Whatever it was, it had something to do with taking care of kids. And she worked at a local daycare center too. Or she had. Or something.

He leaned in to look at the pictures on the mirror, using his lighter so that he didn't have to turn on a lamp. He had been in her room before of course, but he never really looked at it. Over the years he'd been in so many different girls' rooms that he barely took the time to register the details anymore. There were half a dozen pictures; Dana was in all of them. In the oldest one she looked to be around five - she was dressed like a cowgirl, standing in front of an Old West themed backdrop; she wore jeans, a red flannel shirt, and cowboy boots. In one hand she held a lasso and in the other, a cowboy hat, which she raised to the camera in salute. Her smile was wide and she was missing a tooth.

The other pictures traced her as she aged and, other than the fact that they were of Dana, could have been the exact same pictures that Val or his other aunts or any girl he knew kept on their mirrors: Dana and her friends at birthday parties or the beach; little girls pretending to vamp in their swimsuits. There was a black and white strip from a photo booth of her and a girl Nick recognized but whose name he couldn't remember, making funny faces. She looked about fourteen or fifteen in that one. The most recent one was from her high school graduation: Dana, in her cap and gown, holding her diploma, her mom on one side of her, and two older people, probably her grandparents, on the other. He wondered who took the picture.

He opened a few of the desk drawers and poked around. One drawer had jewelry, another make-up. He thought about Dana sitting at this desk, getting all made up to go out on a date with some guy, making herself look good. He remembered Val, back when she was dating, would spend *forever* getting ready. Doing her hair, or putting on makeup or trying outfits. Did the guy ever really notice? Nick hadn't dressed up for a girl since he was in high school, and even then he never took more than a couple of minutes.

The other drawers were just as predictable. One had journals. Nick paged through a couple of them, they were filled with what looked like diary entries - they were dated, written in different color ink, stuff like that. A few pages had what looked like scribbled poetry, something about dolls and fire. He put them back, and moved on.

In the last drawer was an old pink shoebox. He lifted it out, put it on his lap and opened it. Inside were dozens of old photos, cards, movie stubs and saved notes. Nick grabbed a handful of stuff from the middle of the box and spread it across the desktop.

Mostly there were birthday cards. They weren't in any order, an eleventh birthday card from an aunt was under a seventeenth card from her mom and on top of a ninth from a friend. Some of the cards were dog-eared from being opened and closed a thousand times. Some looked almost brand new. One card toward the bottom of the pile had a six-year-old check for fifteen dollars with *love you, Nana* on the memo. A few had tape around the edges like maybe they decorated a wall once. He noticed that none of the cards were from her dad. Not even one. Nick shook his head and started going through the box more deliberately.

He didn't find a single card.

Why was he surprised? He knew the guy was an asshole.

Still.

Once, a few years ago, a girl Nick was dating actually *did* get pregnant. She asked Nick if he had any opinions about it, and he told her it was her call, he would back her play. What was he supposed to say? She thought about it for a while, and decided to take care of it. He went with her to the clinic and drove her home and did all the things a guy was supposed to do. It wasn't the best time in his life, but he got through it, and that was that. Nick never doubted her decision. Kids were great, but they were a lot of work. He spent enough time around parents to pick that up.

But if she decided to go through with the pregnancy, he would have been in the kid's life. That was for damn sure. Nick always liked kids, got along with them. He didn't know what kind of dad he was cut out to be, but that didn't mean he wouldn't try. He was a fuck-up, but a fuck-up's still better than nothing. A fuck-up's still there. Nick's dad wasn't around for close to fifteen years, and it wasn't like spent time together when he was: never lived with him, never stayed over at his place, never did much of anything. He was just a guy. Once, when he was real young, he asked his mom why his dad didn't come and see him. She just laughed and he never asked again.

It made him crazy; these guys who just went through life making messes and letting other people clean them up.

Dana's dad was pretty much the same. It was one reason they connected. Her dad stayed with Dana's mom until his construction business became successful; then he split and married some other woman. He bought a big house on the other side of town and started a new family. Dana had half-brothers and half-sisters that she never saw, or when she did, they barely acknowledged her. Her dad treated *those* kids right. They dressed in nice clothes and drove nice cars and he gave them money for school and whatever, but Dana and her mom didn't even exist to him. Her mom gave up on him a long time ago, she never asked him for anything, but Dana never stopped looking for that connection.

She talked to him once, on the phone, when she was out with Nick. They were in the neighborhood and she wanted to introduce Nick to her dad. Nick didn't want to go, but the hope in her voice when she got him on the line, and then the sadness when he shot her down, made Nick want to drive over there, kick down the door and knock that fucker on his ass.

Nick scooped the cards back into the shoebox; put it all back in the drawer. Then, he walked over to the bed and carefully got back under the covers. Still asleep, Dana rolled toward him. He opened his arm and she slid her head onto his chest; he wrapped his arm around her and stroked her hair until he finally drifted off to sleep.

# THE GIVING TREE

"Heads up."

Sam looked up from her desk in time to see her mother toss something small to her from the doorway. She snatched it out of the air, a package of Reese's Peanut Butter Cups. She looked at her mother, confused.

Her mother shrugged at the unasked question. "I picked up Oscar's ear medicine at CVS. Thought I'd get you something to eat."

"That was nice." Sam opened the wrapper and took out a cup.

"Can I come in?"

"Of course."

Sam's mom walked into the room and sat on the edge of the bed.

"Want one?" Sam said through the chocolate. She held out the second cup.

"What kind of gift would that be, if I took half?"

"Mom, c'mon."

"Well, okay." She took the candy from Sam's outstretched hand, "Thanks."

"Didn't put up much of a fight, did you?"

"I'm as human as the next woman." She put the whole cup in her mouth and sat chewing. Then, after she swallowed, she said, "Going to bed soon?"

Sam glanced at her clock. It was just after ten. "Probably."

"When did you stop having a bedtime? Do you remember?"

"Not really, not since six or seventh grade, maybe."

"It's funny that something so routine like that could just… slip away and we wouldn't notice."

"I sometimes miss bedtime stories."

"If you like, I can go get *The Giving Tree* from Oscar's room and read it to you."

"I think I'll be okay, thanks. I sometimes miss third grade too, but that doesn't mean I'm gonna go sign up for classes."

Her mom leaned back on her elbows. "That's good, I always hated that damn book."

"You what?"

"Oh yeah, it's the worst."

"I loved that story!"

"I know; I was the one who had to read the thing to you a thousand times."

"I don't believe it." Sam's life was flashing before her eyes.

"And now, somehow, Oscar's latched onto it too."

"Because I read it to him!"

Sam's mom glared at her from across the room. "I should have known."

"How can you hate *The Giving Tree*?"

Sam's mom lay down across the base of Sam's bed and pled her case to the ceiling. "Because it doesn't make any sense. The tree loves the boy, right? And so it gives and gives and gives until it's all gone and then the boy, who never says thank you or anything by the way, comes and sits on it at the end? That's it? That's the whole story? What's that supposed to be about?"

"It's about love," said Sam. "It's about unconditional love and giving all of yourself that you can."

Sam's mom sat up and rolled her eyes. "That's a great message for kids—give up everything you've got until you're nothing but a stump."

"I think it's beautiful," Sam said. "Maybe you're just too cynical to see it now. Too beat down by life."

"Could be," Sam's mom said, "but I'd rather be a cynical tree than a romantic stump."

Sam laughed. "Maybe," she said, "there's a way to find a middle ground."

"Let's hope so, right?" She smiled. "Listen, about the thing with your hair…"

Sam groaned, "Aw Mom, we were doing so well." And they had been too. Dinner passed without incident and after, when her mom disappeared into Oscar's room to put him to bed, Sam thought maybe, this one time, her mom was going to let something slide. Who was she kidding?

Her mom put a hand up. "Just, hear me out, okay?"

Sam sat back in her chair and crossed her arms, then, feeling self-conscious, uncrossed them and let them fall loosely to her sides. That didn't feel right either. She settled on putting her hands in her pockets.

Looking back, the candy was a dead giveaway.

"Okay, so, I wanted to say, I'm sorry."

What?

"Your hair is your hair, and you are certainly allowed to do whatever you want to it."

Sam was speechless.

"At least, you know, within reason."

This was unprecedented.

"I mean, I'd rather you didn't shave your head while you're still living with us, or, like, shave any obscene words into the back of your head or anything like that."

Was this what being in shock felt like? Was Sam in shock?

"It's just… hard, to let go of certain things, you know? It's like bedtime stories: before you know it, you're not even reading them anymore. And when you notice you're not reading them anymore, you panic because, like, what else are you missing? It's a cliché, I know, and everyone told me it would happen, but I didn't believe them, and you know what?"

She looked Sam in the eye.

"They were right," she said. "*They were all right.* You're never really ready for your kids to grow up."

Sam's mom got up off the bed, walked over to where Sam was sitting and hugged her. She let go, but stayed crouched down so they were at eye level.

"But the fact is, you are growing up. Last night I forgot, and I'm sorry about that. It probably won't be the last time I forget either. And I'm sorry ahead of time for when I forget next."

She kissed Sam on the top of the head, and walked to the hall. At the door, she turned around and said, "I really like what you did with your hair by the way." Then she said, "Don't stay up too late." She turned, and walked into the hall, closing the door behind her.

Still reeling, Sam reached up and felt her scalp.

Her mom liked her hair.

# TUESDAY

"What are you doing?"

Nick looked up at the boy staring at him through the screen door. "I'm fixing your deck," he said.

"Why?"

"Because your dad hired me to."

"Are you painting it?"

"Sort of."

"But it doesn't change color where you were painting."

"That's because this paint isn't for color, it's so when it rains the wood doesn't warp."

The boy frowned. "What's warp mean?"

"Warp means, like…okay, when wood gets wet, the water gets into it, and makes it bigger. Then, it changes shape. That's called warping. And because all the wood out here is so close together, when it gets bigger, all the pieces push together and break. Pretty bad, right?"

The boy nodded vigorously.

"So what this paint does is, it keeps the water out of the wood and keeps it from warping and breaking. Get it?"

The boy nodded again. "Mom says I can't come outside until you're done. She says I'll mess up your work."

"You can come out if you want. Just stay off this side of the deck." He gestured around himself. "But if you want to go to the yard or sit on the steps or something, that's cool."

The boy slid the door open and stepped carefully across the deck and down the steps. Then, when he was on the grass, he broke into a run towards a big round plastic turtle. He opened the turtle's shell and pulled out some toys. Nick watched Oscar until he selected the toys he wanted, then, Nick returned to his work.

A few minutes later the boy wandered back.

"Do you have a saw?"

The boy was patiently staring up at Nick from the lawn; he shifted his weight from one foot to the other and gently knocked some sort of plastic toy against his thigh.

"A saw?"

The boy nodded.

"Uh, not at the moment. Why?"

"Have you ever used one?"

"Sure."

"Have you ever cut down a tree?"

"A few times."

"Were they big?"

"Not really. They were just in people's yards and they didn't want them anymore."

"Oscar!" The girl from the day before, Sam, stood in the door now. "Stop pestering him." Sam looked down at Nick and smiled, embarrassed. "Sorry about him," she said.

"It's okay, I don't mind." He didn't. Kids were easy, and fun, and never wanted anything from you other than a few minutes of your attention. Oscar was already trotting back into the yard.

Sam stepped outside. "Everyone says that at first. But then, after twenty minutes of random questions, they see the light. Is it okay if I come out here?"

Nick nodded. "Just stay on that side."

"I'm not interrupting?"

Nick stood up, stretched. "I needed to take a break anyway."

"My name's Sam," she said.

"I remember," he said. "Short for Samantha."

"That's right."

"Someone told me once that they took a poll of what men's favorite names were for women, and Samantha came in first. Ever since then I always remember when I meet a Samantha."

She brushed her hair behind her ear, looked down at the ground. "I've never heard that before."

"Ask your folks who picked your name. Bet you ten bucks it was your dad." He pulled a cigarette out and lit it.

"Can I ask you a question?"

He shrugged. "Go nuts."

"When did you start smoking?"

"A few years ago."

"But, like, after high school?"

He laughed. "Yeah, after high school."

"So, you knew it was bad for you when you started?"

"Sure."

"So, I guess I just don't understand why somebody would start doing something that they knew was bad for them."

She turned away after she said that, and watched Oscar running around in the yard. Nick was halfway finished with his smoke before she said anything again. She brushed her hair out of her face again, her eyes still on her little brother. "Can I ask you another question?"

He laughed again, he liked this girl— the boy too: this family was fun. "Tell you what, you can ask me anything you want on one condition."

She turned toward him, "What's the condition?"

"Stop asking if you can ask me a question and just ask me, okay?"

She smiled shyly, and looked down at the deck "Okay. So, my question is," she looked right at him then, "if I asked you to bum me a smoke, what would you say?"

# NICK

When she saw Oscar out there talking to him, it made her jealous. It was so easy for him to just go up to someone and start talking, like it was the most natural thing in the world. Some of it was his age of course; six-year-olds didn't think about how they looked to other people, but a lot of it was just Oscar. "Oscar has to say something to everyone," her mom always said. Sam was always a quieter kid, more of the slow burn type. Oscar could bounce from emotion to emotion; even when she was his age, Sam was more measured. At least that's what her parents told her; it wasn't like she could remember any of it.

But any irritation she felt toward her brother turned to gratitude when she realized that Oscar could be her 'in' with Nick. She couldn't just go up to him and talk, but she *could* go out and talk to Oscar, get him to leave Nick alone and then talk to Nick about it.

Nick cocked his head like a dog. "What would I say? Didn't you just ask me how someone could smoke if it's bad for you?"

When he said that thing about her name her knees went all wobbly, and when he did the thing with the cigarette she just about fell over. That was when she got the idea to ask him. Sam didn't know if she actually had the guts to ask him until the words came out of her mouth. Her stomach was in knots and her head was spinning, but she said it, she asked him. There was no going back now. "And weren't you just saying something about picking your poison?"

"So, you smoke then?"

She shrugged. "I've smoked."

He squinted at her, and smiled, "You've never had a cigarette in your life."

He totally busted her; how could he tell just by looking at her? Was it so obvious? Sam felt her face flush and her neck burn. All her confidence vanished. She looked away from him, pushed her hair out of her face.

"You just changed your hair, didn't you?"

She looked back at him; how could he possibly know that?

"You keep touching your hair," he explained, "pushing it out of you face like you're not used to it being there. I grew up with a lot of girls; I can tell when they're getting used to a new haircut."

"I pulled it back all the time," she said. "Can't really do that anymore."

"It looks good," he said. "There was a show on when I was in high school, . Your hair looks like the girl's hair on that show."

"What show?"

"I don't remember what it was called. My aunts all loved it; their friends loved it. I think you pretty much had to love it if you were a teenage girl when it was on."

"Wait, your aunts were teenagers when you were in high school?"

"Yeah. Oh. Right. No, my aunts - see my mom was the oldest kid, and I'm actually pretty much the same age as a bunch of her sisters, so we all went to school together. They're really more like sisters than aunts."

That was different. "Huh. My aunts are all in their forties and fifties."

"Anyway, they all loved that show. All the girls in my school did. It was a whole thing."

"But you don't remember what it was called?"

"Sorry. It was kind of a stupid name, I think."

"Do you remember anyone who was in it?"

"Not the names of the actors or anything. But the one girl, the main one, the one with the hair, she was in a movie a few years ago. Val, that's one of my aunts, she dragged me to see it because the girl from the show was in it."

"What movie?"

He smiled apologetically. "I don't remember that either. Sorry. It had a stupid name too though, some kind of fairy thing. It was like one of those *Lord of the Rings* movies, only stupid. Robert DeNiro was in it, and Michelle Pfeiffer."

"*Stardust*?"

He pointed at her. "Yeah, that might be it, or something like that. The girl from the show was like a magic super fairy or something? And, I don't remember, maybe there were blimps. It wasn't a good movie; it was just kind of stupid and weird."

"Yeah, that's *Stardust*."

"Did you see it?"

Sam saw *Stardust*, and liked it; she actually owned it, and knew which character he was talking about. "Yeah."

"Well, the one girl in that, that's who was in the show."

"Interesting." She could look up the actress who played Yvaine and see what TV shows she had starred in.

"Can I ask *you* a question?"

She smiled. "Sure."

"Why did you want to know when I started smoking?"

She took a small step back. "Well, I was just curious. I mean, yesterday, my daddy—- my dad—was saying how, I guess, you used to play baseball or something?"

He paused for a moment, and she regretted bringing it up. Maybe he didn't like to talk about that. "For a while yeah, when I was younger."

No, he seemed okay with it. Better to push ahead than to back off, maybe that would embarrass him more. Besides, he was the one to bring the smoking back up. "Did you smoke when you played?"

"God no. Are you kidding? I had to run like seven miles a day, every day. Besides, my coach would have killed me."

"So, why did you start?"

"I guess maybe I was celebrating the fact that I didn't have to worry as much about that sort of stuff anymore."

They stood there silently for a minute. He was lost in whatever he was thinking about; Sam studied her feet.

"I should get back to work." He put the cigarette out in a bowl on the railing and turned away; then, he looked back over his shoulder at her. "Any more questions though, before I do?"

Why not? It wasn't like she was ever going to see him again anyway.

"Do you have a favorite name? For a girl, I mean."

He laughed when she said that, a sort of barking laugh that deteriorated into a cough. He liked the question, she could tell. He pulled his sweatshirt over his head; he was wearing an old wife beater underneath, the ropey muscles on his arms and back shone with sweat. The tattoo on his left hand ran up his arm to his neck. Sam almost gasped.

"You know," he said, "I don't think anybody's ever asked me that before."

# PART TWO

# CHICAGO

Sam sat on her bed and tried to hold it together.

It still didn't feel real.

Her head was spinning; she wanted to scream. And cry. And break everything in her room till her hands were bloody. At the same time, she wanted to just strip down and get into bed, to lie perfectly still and concentrate on the feeling of the clean, cool sheets against her bare skin. She was going to rip in two.

She picked up her phone, dialed Becky; she needed to tell her what happened. Maybe the two of them could figure it out together. But she hung up after the first ring; she didn't know how she would say it. Part of her felt like maybe there was still a way out of this, some kind of deal or something; maybe she could get her dad to change his mind.

"I have some news," he said during Sunday dinner. "It's pretty important and, I think, pretty exciting."

Sam put down her fork and looked at her dad; he was sitting at the head of the table, waiting, milking the moment. She looked across the table at her mom for some kind of clue as to what he was about to say. But if her mom knew, and Sam was sure that she did, she wasn't giving anything away. Summer was coming; probably it was about their family vacation. Maybe they were going somewhere exciting, like Europe. Maybe they were going to Egypt—that would be exciting. Sam had always wanted to see the pyramids with her own eyes. Or maybe they were going somewhere on the other side of the world, like Fiji or something. That would be pretty cool.

"So," he said after a suitable pause, "the first part of my exciting news is that I got a promotion."

"That's great, Daddy," she said. "Congratulations!"

"Thanks sweetie, but there's more. With this promotion come some changes. For one thing, I'll be making more money, so, Sam, when you get your license, we can afford to get you a car, a new one."

Sam almost jumped out of her seat with excitement. "Really?"

Her dad smiled at her. "Really."

Learning to drive was kind of an ordeal. It started out bad (like really bad), and then settled into more of an irritant than anything else. When Becky got her license, Sam pretty much tabled the whole learning-to-drive thing for the time being, but the idea that she could have a car of her own, and a new one, was exhilarating.

"There's more though," her dad continued. "This promotion means I'll have more work and responsibilities. So, I won't be around as much as I was; I hope that's okay."

Sam looked at her mom; she was still sitting silently, looking at Sam's dad. They must have talked about this already; she wasn't showing any signs of surprise or anything, she must have known all this was coming. That made sense, but she wasn't saying anything either, wasn't adding anything or responding to anything. And no one said anything to Oscar; he half listened, but also played with one of his toy cars, driving it back and forth across the table. That made sense too; it wasn't like there was anything he wanted in particular, wasn't anything that their dad's promotion was going to change for him. Her dad's attention seemed to be focused pretty squarely on her; this was a conversation between the two of them.

"Okay Daddy, if you need to work more, you need to work more. I'm a big girl, and you should take opportunities when they come. Don't worry about me."

"I'm glad to hear you say that, but there's still more."

Her dad took another moment, he rubbed his chin and jaw and over the top of his head. He was gearing up for something and it made her nervous. What was she missing?

"Shoot."

"The thing is, this promotion, it's not just a promotion, it's a transfer too."

"I don't understand," she said.

"A transfer, I've been transferred. To Chicago. I'm moving – *we're* moving – to Chicago. The family is."

"What?"

"They need me to, and I have to go," he was stumbling over his words, couldn't look her in the eye. "I start next week; I'm leaving this weekend. I know this is all sudden, but there's a trial I need to prepare for."

"*What*?"

"You guys are all staying for now. Until you two finish the school year, and while your mom gets the house fixed up and ready to sell."

"You guys are selling the house? Wait-"

"The firm helped me find an apartment for the interim. Once you guys get out there, we can all look for a house together."

Sam was stunned. She looked to her mother to make sense of what she was hearing.

"I know it's sudden, sweetie, it's sudden for all of us," her mother said. "But this is a really big opportunity for your dad and it's a lot more money, not just for things like cars, but for college too."

"But our house, our friends, our life…"

"There's life in Chicago too," her dad said. "There are friends, your mom and I know a lot of people from when we went to school out there. And it's just a year for you; you're leaving after that, anyway."

"*Just a year?*"

"I know it seems like a long time now, but it'll rush by, sweetie, I promise. You can still email and Skype and text and Facebook with your friends here."

"And how about this." Her mother jumped in. "How about we fly Becky out a few times, to visit? We can do that, right?" She looked at Sam's dad.

"Sure, we can," he said, "absolutely."

Sam slumped back in her chair, defeated; she didn't know what to say.

Her dad turned his attention to Oscar. "What do you think buddy?" he said in an upbeat, excited voice. "You ready to have an adventure?"

Sam saw what her dad was trying to do. It was the game. He was taking a serious situation and trying to defuse it by winding Oscar up. But this time, the person he was really trying to defuse was her. A chill ran through Sam's body.

But it took more than one person to play the game. Oscar could often be in his own little world, and for good reason; very little actually affected him. But when he was paying attention he was often very adept at reading the room. And he could sense that whatever was going on wasn't just an adventure. It was big and scary. He looked from his dad to his mom and then to Sam, reading the tension on the three of them. His eyes grew big with alarm. Then he shook his head and looked away.

He didn't want to play.

In her room, Sam sat on the edge of her bed with her head in her hands and pulled herself together.

The reality was, she was fucked. She searched her mind for any reason that they should stay other than for her, and found nothing. Sam's parents met in Chicago, got married in Chicago, and lived in Chicago a few years after that. They'd moved back to Baxter because Sam's dad grew up there, his parents still lived there and he'd been offered a job there. But Sam's grandparents moved down to Florida a year ago, and her dad didn't have any other relatives living close by. All her mom's people lived in the middle of the country so that wasn't any help either.

Her parents had friends, but not any close ones. None worth staying for. And her mother never really liked the area; she thought the east coast was too cluttered; she'd always said she preferred the Midwest. And it wasn't like Oscar had a life to disrupt either; he didn't know where he was half the time anyway. Most of his life was spent being dragged somewhere that someone else in his family needed to be. He had friends, sure, but they were all six-year-olds. They just liked to run around together. He could find those anywhere.

As far as Sam could tell, the only one who was really losing here was her.

But, as selfish as it might be, she still had to try and derail this train.

She knew what her dad *said,* knew that he had taken the job and was *going* to leave. But he hadn't left yet. If she explained to him how important it was to her to spend her senior year at home with her friends, maybe she could find a way to get him to stay for just a little longer.

She was halfway down the stairs when she heard them.

Their voices were low, but edgy. Sam heard her parents argue before and she often chose to respect their privacy, out of respect, but also because she had no wish to be caught eavesdropping. But at that moment, there was nothing more important than the possibility that she might learn something that would help her cause. She tip-toed down the steps until their voices were clear.

"It was a disaster, *disaster,*" her mother was saying. "Sam's miserable, Oscar's scared, the house needs all this work done if we're going to get anything for it, and you're dumping all of it on my lap."

"I can't help it that they need me when they need me," her dad replied. "This trial is part of the job. For the next three months, it is the job. I can't just show up whenever I'm ready. Things don't work like that and you know it."

"This is just so you, Steve. You make these big, bold, plans, and leave everyone else with the dirty work."

"Look, I did what I thought was right. An opportunity came up, and I took it. I'm sorry I didn't have time to talk it over with you, really. But I'm doing this for *us*. You were the one who said things had to change."

"Oh no, don't you dare make out like this is about me. This is all about you. It's what you always do when there's a challenge—you cut and you run."

"Excuse me," her dad was almost shouting now. "*Excuse me,* but I am doing my best here. You said that something wasn't working, and you said that something needed to change. You needed a gesture from me; you said you needed to see that I was committed, yeah?"

"I did," her mother said.

"Well," her dad said, "here it is; here's my gesture. You're always going on about how much you hate it here, how you miss being closer to home. And maybe I did overreact. Maybe if you and I could have a civil conversation; maybe if I didn't end up sleeping in the guest room half the time, we tried to talk about things, we could have come up with a better solution together. But we couldn't, so here we are."

Sam couldn't listen anymore. Trembling, she made her way back up the stairs, down the hall and into her room. Then, she threw herself onto her bed, buried her face in a pillow and screamed as loud as she could for as long as she could.

Her mother.

Her fucking mother.

She should have known.

Sam woke up suddenly, sore and disoriented. She hadn't slept well. She hadn't bothered to get ready for bed or put on pajamas, brush her teeth or get under the covers. Her face was red and splotchy from crying; there was a gross taste in her mouth, and a little puddle of drool on her pillow.

Then the night before rushed back to her and her heart broke again. Her first thought was to say fuck it and stay home from school, but that would mean spending the day alone with her mother. That was the last thing she wanted to do. Besides, she had to see Becky, to tell her the news.

So she got up and got ready for the day. She had no desire to interact with either of her parents so she stayed in her room until she saw Becky's car coming down the street from her bedroom window. Then, she raced down the stairs, out the door, and into the car before anyone could say anything to her.

"Okay, you're pumped," Becky said as she backed the car out of the driveway. "Big test today or something?"

Sam shook her head, "Nope, no tests today, nothing like that. Hey, let's get some breakfast, you wanna get some breakfast? C'mon, we'll go to Denny's."

"You want to get breakfast? What about class?"

Sam shook her head again, "Nah, fuck that, I want an omelet."

Becky glanced over at Sam. "Sam, are you okay? You don't just ditch school, that's not what you do."

Sam slid her hand along the leather interior of the passenger car door. Becky was so excited when she called Sam to say she passed the driving exam. It was one of the best days of their lives, Becky's freedom meant Sam's freedom too. Six months ago, when Becky's mom got a new car, her parents said she could have the old Explorer at the end of the school year if she kept her grades up and didn't get into any trouble. When she got her license, her parents caved and gave it to her early. How many trips would she and Becky have taken in this car? How many times would she have sat in this very seat going off to some movie or party or just to the store and back? And now, how many trips did she have left?

"It is today," she said.

She told Becky halfway through breakfast. It spilled out of her in a long, uninterrupted stream: the transfer, the move, and her dad leaving at the end of the week. She told Becky about overhearing her parents' argument, how her mom let her dad take the fall for everything when she was the one who demanded the change. By the time she finished, Becky looked so crushed that

Sam thought maybe it was a mistake to tell her. But what else could she do? It wasn't like she could just disappear one day without explanation. And besides, things never felt real until she told Becky.

"What are you gonna do?" There were tears in Becky's eyes.

Sam stabbed at her food, "Nothing. Go to Chicago."

"But you can't just *go*, there has to be something…"

"I'm open, what do you have in mind?"

Now Becky was actually crying. "Oh my god, *Sam*," she said, "I can't believe you're leaving."

"I know."

"We've never gone to school apart."

"I know." She could feel her throat tightening up.

"I'm gonna miss you so much."

"I'm gonna miss you too."

"What if," Becky said, "what if you come live with us for senior year?"

"Becks…"

"No really," Becky was smiling and crying at the same time. "My parents totally love you; you're like their other daughter. They say it all the time. You could move into the spare bedroom and, like, we could get your dad to send checks for food and stuff…"

"What, like child support?"

Becky sniffed, wiped her nose with her wrist then cleaned it with a napkin. "Something like that, yeah."

"C'mon Becks, be serious. Even if we could, somehow, talk your parents into letting me stay with them for a whole year, there's no way my folks would go for it."

"Well," Becky said, "what about for the rest of the summer then? Think they'd go for that?"

Sam felt a thrill shoot up her spine, maybe she *could* do that. But it was short lived, "No, no way. We have to move and then there's our family vacation and Mom's gonna want us to get used to the neighborhood and whatever before school starts. There's no way."

"I know," said Becky miserably, "I knew it when I said it—we have vacations and stuff too. I'm going to Camp Carrion to be a counselor in August; there's no way my parents would let me out of that, not with college applications coming up. But, like, I still had to at least say it, you know? See how it sounded or something."

"Oh Becks," Sam said. "What am I going to do without you?"

Becky tried to laugh but it came out more of a choke. "That's what I'm worried about. Who's gonna talk you into doing all the stuff you aren't supposed to do in Chicago?"

"Who's gonna try and get me to drink?"

"You'd never do it though."

"I did!"

"Oh yeah, like *a* beer. Ooh. Dangerous."

"Whatever, I've totally drank with you. Who's gonna talk me into going to parties after curfew?"

"Actually, you wouldn't ever do that one either."

"Who'll shoplift perfume and candy from CVS with me?"

"Well, we haven't done that one in like, five years, but at least it happened."

"Who'll dye my hair?"

Becky said, "You'll always have your mom to dye your hair."

They both laughed at that.

"God, this sucks," said Becky. "One year, one fucking year, before graduation and your dad takes a transfer."

"Well, we have my mom to thank for that," Sam said. "She basically forced him to move, and then made out like he was the bad guy."

"Yeah," Becky shook her head, "that's really fucked up. Why's she so mad at your dad anyway?"

"I don't know. Because she's a bitch?"

"There's gotta be a *reason* though, right?"

"You know what? I really don't care. I don't care what the reason is, because whatever my dad did to her, which probably wasn't anything anyway, she punished *me* for it. Dad gets a promotion, Mom gets to leave Baxter, and I get screwed, and you get screwed. Nothing happens to Oscar and I'm the only one who gets hurt. Fuck her."

"At least," Becky said, "at least she said I could come and visit, right?"

Sam didn't say anything. She was boiling again.

"And they said I could come more than once, right? So, that's cool. I can come out this summer and visit. And I bet my parents would fly me out a couple times too. I bet I can get out there at least four times. Maybe we can do a couple of them over the school year. Like, maybe Thanksgiving or Christmas or something. That might be cool."

"Yeah, it might be, if we can do it. If your parents let you leave for a holiday."

"They'll do it. When Barry lived at home, they let him get away with all sorts of shit like that. And they love you, I can talk them into letting me go, that's not even going to be a problem."

Sam shrugged. "If you say so."

"Trust me. Look, here's what we have to do. I know you, Sam, you're thinking about this the wrong way. You're all doom and gloom and big stuff when we should be thinking practically. What we have to do is break this into, like, quadrants. We always said we're going to the same college anyway, so all we really have to worry about is the time until then. College starts in September of next year, yeah? So that's about sixteen months away. What day is it today?"

"Monday."

"Okay, obviously it's Monday, Sam; I meant what's the date?"

Sam looked at her phone. "May fifth."

"And when's school over? June Fifteenth?"

"Something like that."

"So that's over a month right there, almost a month and a half, guaranteed. Let's say, just to pick a date, that you guys leave for Chicago on the first of July. Because no way your mom's going to make you pack the same time you're studying for finals."

"We don't know that Becks. What if the house sells right away?"

Becky rolled her eyes. "See, you're already doing it, stop being glass is half empty. The point is, we're down from sixteen months apart to fourteen, just like that, see?"

Sam did see. Despite her better judgment, she started to cheer up a little. Things were bad, sure, but Becky could focus on the positive in ways Sam rarely could. It was maybe Sam's favorite thing about her.

They spent the rest of the meal making plans for when and how Becky would come to Chicago and possible times for Sam to come back and visit Baxter. After breakfast, neither of them felt like going to school so they decided to catch a movie instead. After the movie, Becky drove them to the woods on the edge of the Baxter College campus; the two of them made their way through the woods to the clearing, where they used to play when they were younger.

When they were kids, the clearing always felt magical, like something out of a fairytale. The woods on Baxter's campus were the closest they got to an actual forest and they pretended to be lost princesses or orphans or whatever they felt like being on that particular day. In their imaginary adventures, the clearing always represented safety from whatever dangers lurked in the forest. As they got older they would come to the clearing for other reasons; the clearing was a place away from parents and school—there was no homework in the clearing, no grades, no groundings, no responsibilities. Sam went there a couple times with Martin Reed to make out under the stars. She was sure that Becky did the same with boys of her own.

Sam lay in the grass and closed her eyes. She let the sun warm her, and felt the grass tickle her skin. She tried not to think about anything.

Sam didn't tell anyone about Chicago. She knew she would have to eventually, but she didn't want to deal with the drama. Her other friends would want to talk about it and ask questions and it would be too much. She made Becky promise not to tell either. For now, Sam's move would stay between the two of them.

Her dad left the following Sunday. A car came to take him to the airport early in the evening. Sam's mother offered to drive him, but her dad said it would be better if he just got a cab. He packed a few bags with clothes, some books, his laptop. Essentials. The bags sat by the front door all that day, waiting to be taken to Chicago. Sam tried to avoid looking at them, but they were always there, in her peripheral vision as she was going up or down the stairs, or standing in the kitchen making something to eat. Those clean black bags just sitting there.

When the car finally arrived, and the driver picked up the bags, Sam actually flinched. Suddenly it was all real, and it was happening now. The first objects had been moved out of the only house Sam could ever remember living in. It was just a matter of time before the rest of the house would be packed up piece by piece and carried away, taken somewhere she had never been, but she'd be expected to think of as home.

Sam stood in the front room silently and watched through the window as the driver carried the bags down to where the car was parked at the end of the driveway. She didn't want to watch, but she had to; she was afraid if she tried to move she would fall over, afraid if she tried to speak she would start to cry. That she would regress from the young woman that she understood she was, to the desperate little girl she felt inside, who just wanted everything to stay the way it was forever.

But it couldn't, and it didn't. All the bags but one were in the car, the only one left was her dad's laptop bag, the one he carried with him pretty much everywhere. It was strung over his shoulder as he walked down the stairs patting his pockets and mumbling to himself, presumably making sure he had everything he needed for the flight and beyond. Her mother came down behind him, looking tense but focused. It was her *let's just all get through this together* face. She caught Sam's eye and gave her a thin smile. A bolt of rage shot through Sam's gut. There wasn't going to be any solidarity between her mother and her, they weren't teammates working together for a common goal or any of that nonsense. This was on her mother, *it was her fault*, and Sam sure as hell wasn't going to fall in and play the good little soldier.

Her dad called for Oscar to turn off the TV and come say goodbye. When he trotted in, her dad scooped him up into a big hug; he said to be good, that he was the man of the house until they were all together again and that he relied on Oscar to rise to the challenge. Oscar nodded and told their dad he loved him. He kissed Oscar on the top of the head and put him down; then he kissed her mother and said he'd call her from Chicago.

Then he turned to Sam.

She didn't trust herself to even look him in the eye.

Her dad hugged her close and kissed her on the cheek. "It's gonna be okay, kiddo," he said. "Promise."

Sam squeezed her eyes shut and started to shake. He hadn't called her that in years.

"I gotta go, but I'll talk to you tonight when I call mom, and I'll see you in a couple of weeks, okay?"

Sam nodded. She was amazed she could manage that. She heard Oscar sniffle behind her.

"Love you," he said. Then he let her go.

Eyes still closed, Sam listened to her dad walk across the room and out the front door. She heard it shut behind him and Oscar started to full on bawl. She opened her eyes. The last bag was gone, and so was her dad.

"Well," her mother said after soothing Oscar down to a low whimper, "I'm not really in the mood to make anything tonight. What do you guys say we get a pizza?"

"Can we get pepperoni?" Oscar wiped his eyes. He was down, but there wasn't much that pizza couldn't cure.

"I don't see why not. Sam, is pepperoni okay with you?"

Sam looked at her mother. Then, she turned and walked up the stairs to her room and shut the door.

Fuck Sunday dinner.

# THE RULES OF THE GAME

"Oh my God, Alicia, I can see your whole butt!" Dana laughed so hard she started to hiccup.

Alicia looked over her shoulder, flashed a devilish grin and pulled her jeans up. "Let's see you do better in these jeans," she said. "Not like you could pull them off." She leered at her stupid date and smacked her ass. Dana cackled.

*You could wear jeans that don't stop a fucking half inch above your ass crack*, Nick thought, *that would take care of it*. But there wasn't a modest bone in Alicia's body. Nick knew because if there were, he would have been able to see it through her skin tight jeans and baby-doll T-shirt. Date rape walking. Nick never understood how nice girls like Dana, girls with at least some self-respect, could hang out with loud obnoxious girls like Alicia. She was hot, there wasn't any doubt about that, but she knew it, and she played it up too much. Girls like Alicia *needed* you to think she was hot because it was all she had.

This was hell. He was in hell. Hanging out with a bunch of kids at a goddamn disco bowling alley at ten o'clock on a Tuesday night. How much longer did he have to be there? He watched Dana pick up her ball and heave it toward the pins; tried not to flinch as the ball crashed down on the polished lane. It quickly veered to the right and bounced off the bumper in the gutter about a third of the way down the lane; that slowed it down a little; bouncing off the bumper on the other side slowed it down even more. When her ball finally knocked down four pins, Dana spun around and raised her fists in triumph. Alicia clapped and hooted.Her stupid date gave Dana a high five; Nick fought the urge to bury his face in his hands.

Dana looked at him but he had no idea what to say. She managed to knock down fewer than half the pins while using *both* of the bumpers. Was he supposed to be happy for her? He managed a smile and gave her the thumbs up.

"What? How you like me now?" she said, getting up in his face.

"Pretty impressive."

"I pick up the spare here and I'll be closing in on you pretty soon."

Nick glanced up at the score on the monitor, one-forty-two to fifty-four with three frames to go. No. No, she wouldn't. "Your ball's back," he nodded towards the dispenser.

She kissed his nose. "Thanks." Then she grabbed her ball and skipped back to the lane.

He knew she was only kidding, that she knew she had no hope of catching him, that she was just having fun, who cared about the score?

But using bumpers was cheating. It just was. Maybe it wasn't if you were six and still learning, (though Nick hadn't), but after that? Nick never saw the point in playing a game if you didn't follow the rules. He knew what Dana would say if he told her that though, she'd say lighten up, have fun. But taking games seriously was what made them fun. It was fun to be good at them, to see how you got better, to measure yourself against yourself and against other people. That was the beauty of it.

But Dana wouldn't understand that.

For her, a good time was hanging out with Nick (even though he was fucking miserable) and Alicia and Alicia's stupid date (who, by the way, had said, like, ten words to Nick all night; total dickhead) and all three of them could stare at Alicia's ass, whether they wanted to or not, while playing a rigged game. That was Dana's idea of fun.

Alicia's stupid date rolled an eight, then picked up the spare. He wasn't terrible. But he was still a dick.

Nick got a strike on his turn, which pumped him up a little. A strike was a strike, bumpers or no.

Back in the day, the team would bowl on the road. Those games got pretty serious. Like, money serious. Minor leaguers don't make a ton of money, but what money there was flew around. Guys bet on sets of games, whole games, individual frames, individual rolls within frames. They bet on the games being played in other lanes, who the waitress would serve first, who would have to go to the bathroom first.

And they bet on girls. They bet on girls *a lot*. Not that it was hard to hook up with local girls; if anything, it was too easy. Most towns they played in were pretty dead; the games were the only real attraction, so anyone who played was as good as it got. Everyone wanted to say they got to see the next Ken Griffey when he was still coming up.

But that made hooking up *too* easy. It took away the challenge that Nick and his teammates strove for. His celebrity (modest, but still) made it impossible for him to lose. It distorted any accomplishments.

Like bumper lanes.

So the guys found ways to make it interesting. Who got the most numbers from the hottest girls; how far he got on the premises, or in a car right outside the premises. Whatever. It wasn't about the girls; it was about beating the other guys. It was about winning.

Now, *that* was fun.

The game ended two frames or ten thousand years later, depending on how you looked at it, and Nick said he had to go.

"C'mon," Dana said, "one more game, then we can go home…"

Her hands were flat on his chest and drifted down to his stomach. He gently took her by the wrists and stepped back.

"You know I can't. I'm working in the morning. Alicia." He gave her a little wave; he turned to her stupid date who stuck out his fist for a bump. Nick felt his back tense up in irritation as he bumped fists with the jack ass. Then he kissed Dana and left.

She caught up with him as he was getting into his truck.

"Why are you leaving?"

"I told you, I gotta be up tomorrow."

"That's not it," she said. "You've slept over tons of times when you had to work the next day. You're mad about something."

"I'm not."

"You are."

*"I'm fine."*

"You hate my friends. That's what this is."

"Dana..."

"No. You do, don't bother to deny it."

"What do you want me to say?"

"I want you to tell me the truth."

Dana didn't want the truth. It wasn't like this was their first conversation about her friends. She knew he didn't like Alicia, he'd said so, several times. But for some reason, it never got through to her, she never accepted it.

He sighed.

"Why can't you try just once ?" she pleaded. "Alicia's my *best friend*, and you don't even try to like her."

"What are you talking about?" It was hard not to lose his temper. "I've tried. I've tried *a lot*."

"No you haven't, not really. You decided you didn't like her the first time you met her and it's never changed."

"How can you say I never tried? How do you know I didn't try? Maybe I don't like her because she's annoying, and no matter how many times I hang out with her, that's not gonna change."

"She's my best friend," Dana said, as if he missed it the first thousand times. "It's important to me that you two spend time together."

"Then talk to her about it. She can't possibly like me."

"Because she knows you don't like her!"

"Well, that's not my fault! It's not my fault she's loud and, and, fucking obnoxious; she dresses like a -"

"What?" Dana cut him off. "Like a slut? Are you saying she's slutty?"

"Dana, you saw what she was wearing, I could make out the label on her thong *through her jeans!* I mean, who's she trying to impress? You? Me? It can't be that chucklehead in there; he'd probably stick his dick in a light socket."

"Jesus Nick, you just met Dave, and you barely said two words to him. He's totally a nice guy!"

"He's an asshole. He's another suburban kid who thinks he's black. Did you see how he went for a pound when I left? I hate that wigger shit."

Dana looked horrified.

"What?" he said. "Anything else you want or can I go?"

"Just, just go," she said, "I'll talk to you tomorrow." She turned around and walked to the entrance of the bowling alley.

"Can't wait," Nick mumbled to her back and got in his truck. He took a deep breath, rubbed his head, and tried to get his cool back. She started conversations he didn't want to have, pushed them to places he didn't want to go, and got upset at him when they went bad. Why couldn't she, just once, let him go when he said he had to go?

And they did talk the next day; she texted him while he was working and he called her back on his lunch break. And it wasn't any better, and he wasn't surprised. He was trying with Dana, he really was, but she wasn't making things easy.

He'd resolved to give the two of them an honest shot; to be more present and aware and all the other things that Val always told him to do. He made the effort even though it always felt so forced and phony. The whole time, that doubting voice in the back of his head remained, saying *this is wrong; this isn't going to work out*. But he ignored it, pushed past it. He treated it with the same contempt that he treated the doubt that crept in when he played ball. Back then, doubt was the enemy; it was the thing trying to destroy him, keep him from his destiny. The problem was he could never convince himself Dana was his destiny. He was so sure about baseball, it came so easy, felt so right, that when doubt did manage to get hold of him it was easy to banish.

Life with Dana was the opposite. Nothing came easy, nothing felt right; it was almost all doubt.

If he did what she wanted (go out with her and her friends), he was wrong; if he did what he *needed* (go home and get some sleep before work the next morning), he was wrong.

To recap, for the cheap seats: He tried to do the right thing, he went out, had a bad time, pissed Dana off, got into a fight, and slept badly.

And did he get any credit for going out at all? For making that all important effort that Val stressed? Of course he didn't.

So why had he gone out in the first place?

It wasn't like he was a jerk to anyone; he was perfectly nice to Alicia and what's-his-name. He didn't even say he disliked Alicia. Dana was mad at him for the answer she gave to her own question. It was crazy.

So why was he still trying?

What was the endgame? Here he was, months later, right back where he started. He was stuck with an unhappy girl that he never really wanted in the first place, but was still somehow responsible for.

And, appropriately he supposed, he was back working on the same house as he had been all those months ago.

It was like the universe was giving him a sign or something

***

"Sounds like a head case to me," Liz said, and took a sip of lemonade.

He sat on the deck taking a smoke break, and she came to ask him if he was thirsty. He hadn't even heard her walk up behind him and was a little startled when she spoke. She said it looked like he was lost in thought, asked him if he wanted to talk about it.

And he did.

It was weird; there wasn't any reason to tell this random woman his girl problems, and it wasn't like unburdening himself to some stranger, or anyone really, was Nick's thing. In fact, he saw the need to confide in other people, to stress them with irrelevant shit, as kind of weak.

But, for some reason – maybe he was at the end of his rope; maybe he needed that outside perspective after all; maybe he just liked her face or something – when she asked, he told.

And she listened.

*And she was on his side.*

"I knew a lot of girls like that when I was in college." She put the cup down. "Still do. They're not happy unless everything's perfect like they imagined. Let me guess, dad's not in the picture?"

"That's right," Nick said.

"It's a daddy thing. She's just mad at you because he's not around. She makes her own little family in her head, expects you to play this part."

"Totally," Nick said.

"But you're not her dad, you're just a guy she's hanging out with."

Nick really liked this lady.

"So what now?"

"Honestly?" She looked at him. "I'd dump her. I know it sounds cruel, but you're not the guy she wants you to be; you never will be. The sooner she figures that out the better."

Nick nodded. She was right, and he knew it, knew it all along really. It was just what the voice always told him. It wasn't right. He wasn't right for her.

She said, "That must sound cold hearted, huh?"

Nick wanted to laugh. "Not really," he said.

"No, it is. I'm supposed to be all sisterhood and you shouldn't take advantage, but I can't. I hate those types of girls, you know? They're professional victims; they deliberately go after guys who aren't looking for commitment, then expect pity when the guy doesn't want to be her boyfriend."

"Totally."

Liz shook her head. "It's not fair. She's not being fair to you. That girl needs to start taking responsibility for her own actions, stop blaming you for everything. Look, maybe you haven't been the *best* boyfriend in the world, but who is? You do your best, and if she isn't happy with you, she can show you the door. This constant sulking though, it's pathetic."

Now, Nick did laugh. "She's not *that* bad."

Liz laughed too. "I'm sure she's not. I got off on a bit of a rant there. Sorry. That had more to do with me than anything with you or…"

"Dana."

"It had nothing to do with you or with Dana. That's just my stuff."

She took another sip of her lemonade.

"Can I ask you a question," Nick said, "change the subject?" "

"Shoot."

"You're selling your house right?"

She nodded.

"Well, not to be telling you your husband's business or anything, but when I was here a few months ago, he was telling me all about these big plans he had for the backyard and stuff. But when you called me about re-tiling the kitchen, did you say you were moving?"

"To Chicago."

"It's, I mean, that's kind of a quick turnaround, isn't it? He was just going on about putting in a pool and stuff, now you're going to Chicago."

Liz sighed, put her head down.

"Shit," Nick said, "I think he might have said that was a secret. Did you not know that?"

She shook her head.

"Sorry," Nick said. "It's not my business, I just remember these things. You never know when people are gonna want more work, you know? You gotta pay attention."

"No, it's okay. It's not that. I mean, it is, but." She took a moment. "Steve's brilliant, but he's kind of like a big dumb dog sometimes."

Nick had no idea what that was supposed to mean.

"You know the kind of dog I'm talking about? He's chasing after a ball you threw, but then he sees a squirrel out the window and he runs over to bark at the squirrel and bangs into a table and the lamp falls over and breaks? You know that kind of dog?"

She looked at him.

"I'm not making any sense, am I?"

Nick smiled, laughed. "Not really."

"I guess I have no idea what Steve's doing. But I know he's breaking a lot of stuff doing it, and I have to clean it all up."

"Do you want a cigarette?" He held the pack out to her.

"What? No. No. I don't smoke, or, I gave it up years ago when I was pregnant with Sam."

"Okay," Nick put the pack down. "You were just looking at the pack, is all. I thought maybe you wanted one."

They sat on the steps silently for a minute; Nick was sort of amazed. This was, by far, the longest conversation he'd ever had with a customer.

“You know what?” Liz pulled a cigarette out of the pack and lit it with the lighter tucked in the cellophane wrapping. “Seventeen years, never gave in once to temptation,” she said; then she gave him a side glance. “Can you keep this a secret?”

“I told you about that pool.”

She didn’t bat an eye. “The hell with it,” she said. “I’ll take my chances.” She closed her eyes and took a long drag.

Three hours later, Nick was finishing up in the kitchen for the night when she came in looking harried.

“This is way out of left field,” she said, “and I hate to ask, but can you do me a huge favor?”

“I guess it depends on what it is.”

“Sam, you met her last time you were here, I think? She’s with her friend Becky, and Becky was driving her home, and I guess they had some kind of car trouble and now they’re at a garage and they need someone to pick them up, and I would but I have a meeting that I absolutely can’t re-schedule and Becky can’t seem to get either of her parents and -”

“You need me to go pick them up?”

“It would just be such a huge help,” she said.

“Yeah, I can do that.”

“Oh, thank you, that’s such a load off, you have no idea.”

“Really,” he said. “It’s no problem.”

If Sam was surprised to see Nick pull up in his truck and open the passenger door for her and her friend, she didn’t show it. Most likely, her mom told her he was coming, but still, Nick was struck by how natural the whole thing felt. How easy.

Growing up, he was pretty much responsible for getting himself to and from where he needed to be. There were just so many kids, and his grandparents could only do so much. A lot of times he could get a ride from his Uncle Dennis. Dennis had a pick-up. Nick and his friends would pile into the bed of the truck and Dennis would tear through town, blaring the stereo so everyone in the back could hear, turning too fast and screeching to stops at red lights, generally putting all their lives in danger.

He'd spent some of the best times of his life in the back of that truck.

And now, here he was, all these years later, returning the favor. He was helping out, getting the girls where they needed to go. In a pick-up, too. He just opened the door and Sam slid in next to him, the friend following. She shut the door, and they were off.

It was like a sign, reminding him that life didn't have to be as much work as it was with Dana. A lot of the time, things were difficult because they weren't right. If something was meant to be, it would happen. Sam needed a lift, and he was there to give it to her.

They rode in pleasant silence; Nick drove with one arm resting on the open window, warmed by the setting sun. No one asked him a million questions about anything that popped into their head or went on and on about their day. When they got to the friend's house, she thanked him and got out. He took Sam home, watched her until she made it inside, then he leaned back in his seat, lit a smoke, and closed his eyes.

He felt better than he had in a long time. Helping Liz out, picking the girls up, felt *good.*

It could always be like that. No chatting, no pressure, no expectations. He did what was asked of him, and he was appreciated for it.

The way things should be.

# SIGNS

Sam had a secret.

She carried it around with her at school and it gave her a warm feeling in the pit of her stomach. It colored her vision and filtered out voices she didn't want to hear. Sometimes, when she was sitting in class, everything else would suddenly fade away and it would just be Sam and her secret. Sam's secret gave her power, made her feel strong, dangerous, even sexy.

Once, a year ago, Becky took Sam to the Victoria's Secret in the mall to get some lingerie. Becky tried to talk her into getting something trashy like a thong or g-string (not that Sam could ever figure out the difference between the two), but Sam settled on a pair of sheer lacey hip huggers. Most of the time, they sat in the back of Sam's underwear drawer, neatly folded, and out of view. She didn't buy them because she wanted anyone to see them. She bought them when she and Martin were dating, and Becky told her she needed that kind of underwear now. But, she never actually wore them for him. In fact, she probably would have been mortified if he found out she had them. The few times Sam ever wore them, she even washed them herself in the sink so that her mother never saw them. But, the knowledge that she had such an item of clothing was powerful.

Every once in a while, Sam slipped them on, and the moment she did she felt different. The smooth fabric against her skin was a constant reminder that yes, they were there, and yes, she was wearing them. It was like she was a superhero or something, with her costume on underneath her street clothes. Sam was her secret identity; underneath she was, well, she was still Sam, but an older, more adult, sexier Sam.

Walking down the halls she felt like she had a little more shimmy in her step, a little more swagger. She was more confident, more alive. She held boys' gazes a moment longer than usual, and liked to believe they noticed. During class, she daydreamed about pulling a random hot boy, Scott Temple for example, into the stairwell and jumping him. They wouldn't talk; she would just kiss him. At first, he would be confused, shocked even, that quiet, sweet, Sam Heller would be so bold. But that would quickly become a turn on and he would really get into it.

His hands would start up on her shoulders in a defensive position, like he was going to push her away. But they would quickly move to hold her; first, they would slide around her and rub her back and neck. Then, slowly, they would make their way down her back to her jeans. His hand would slip under her jeans and feel the fabric of her underwear and he would pull back for a second and look at her; she would look back at him with a wicked smile. Then he would smile back and…

That was it, really.

She had other fantasies of course—ones that went farther, that were dirtier, more explicit. But that was her favorite, because it felt more attainable.

The fantasy wasn't about sex really; it was about the power to take control of a boy and bend him to her will, and it was about that moment when he recognized there was more to her than he ever imagined.

Sam felt that way more and more these days.

Nobody, other than Becky, knew that she was leaving at the end of the year, and she made Becky promise not to tell anyone else. At first, it was because Sam didn't want to think about it, didn't want it to be real yet. And she didn't want the drama that came with people hearing. Didn't want to have the same conversation over and over again, didn't want to keep crying. But she did, too; she wanted that rush of emotion and intimacy. There was this part of her that was afraid not enough people would be upset. She wondered who would actually care. She knew some of her friends would, but for others, she wasn't so sure. She didn't want to tell the world she was leaving forever and have the world be all like, *Cool, have fun in Chicago*. Shrug and walk away. She wanted her leaving to mean something, and the longer she waited to tell people, the longer she could hold onto the idea that Baxter High School would never be the same without her.

That was where it started.

In her imagination, boys who secretly crushed on her called her because it was their last chance to do so. And the thing was, fantasizing aside, that was essentially true. Sam's tomorrows were winding down, at least as far as Baxter was concerned. It was really happening. Little by little, the truth of her leaving was sinking in, and while that knowledge brought all the pain and sadness she expected, it brought something else too, something she never really considered. It brought freedom.

Sam's whole life was a war between her rational mind and her wilder impulses; a struggle between her desires to act out versus her more sober understanding that those actions had consequences. As much as she might want to pull Scott Temple into the stairwell, she knew that, when it was over, Scott would walk away from her, straight to his friends, to tell them the crazy thing that just happened. Some people, like, say, Becky, lived their lives ignoring that other practical voice. It led to heartbreak and pain, sure, but it also led to exhilaration.

Sam was haunted by the voice.

It was overwhelming. Every decision in her life was analyzed from a thousand different directions, considered from every conceivable angle. Is this okay? Is this the right move? How will this look to me down the line? How will it look to other people? And when she did take a risk and try something new, like the recent hair controversy, her mother usually ended up coming down on her like a ton of bricks. God, imagine if she actually did something that mattered. It'd be the end of the world. No wonder she was so self-conscious.

You would think that kind of pressure would quiet the wild side down; that it would make it go away. You would be wrong. It almost seemed like the more reasonable Sam behaved, the louder the voice got. The voice yelled and screamed and roared. It said *forget about tomorrow, forget about tomorrow, forget about tomorrow.* Then the voice repeated the words her parents used to tell her when she was young, *it's never tomorrow,* they would tell her, *it's always today.* It was like, why spend time worrying about something that would never come? And the answer was because, somehow, no matter what her parents or the voice said, it was tomorrow too. Somehow, it was always today and tomorrow at the same time.

Until now.

Now, there truly was no tomorrow to worry about.

Now, today was all that was left.

Now was her chance to put aside the rational side, and maybe let the wild child come out and play.

Now, who cared what her mother thought about how she behaved? She was selfish enough to force her dad to take a new job, move the whole family halfway across the country without even stopping to *ask* any of them how they felt about it. How she felt about it. Sam took her mother's feelings into every decision she made, into every step no matter how small.

And this was how her mother repaid her.

Fine.

You don't give a damn about me?

I don't give a damn about *you.*

Period.

Anyway.

The point was, now Sam could try being a little more dangerous. Yeah, okay, there was addiction and pregnancy to consider. But, plenty of people drank once in a while without becoming an alcoholic, and certainly, people aren't impregnated every time they have sex. People *lived*, were teenagers, and they made it through okay.

This was her chance.

Nick was back.

She ran into the house after school, just to drop off her bag and pick up her phone charger while Becky waited outside in the car, and saw him on his knees by the sink. She froze, astonished. He looked up at her and smiled.

"Hey," he said, "Sam, right?"

Sam nodded. She felt dizzy.

"You ever ask your folks who picked that name?"

"Oh, yeah I did." She recovered enough to not only answer the question, but make it sound casual too. Nice.

"And?"

And? And what? She was looking at his arms and completely forgot what they were talking about. She considered running out of the room and hiding in her room until he left.

Then she remembered. "It's my aunt's name, my *mother's* sister."

"You didn't know you were named after your aunt?"

She was so nervous during that conversation she was lucky she remembered her name at all, let alone where it came from. "Don't change the subject, the point is, you were wrong."

He shrugged. "Not necessarily, now you have to find out who named you aunt. If it was your grandpop, then I'm still right, just off by a generation."

Sam laughed, in relief that she got through the conversation without saying anything stupid or fainting, but also, new project!

Outside, Becky honked the horn; Sam jumped ten feet in the air.

"He's back," Sam said to Becky when they were halfway between their houses.

"Who's back?"

"Nick."

"Nick?"

"Nick, the boy, the *guy* Dad hired a couple of months ago to work on the deck?"

Becky pulled over to the side of the street and killed the engine, "Wait a minute, is that the super cute boy you were obsessing about? The tall one, with, like, the tattoo on in his hand?"

"Okay, first of all, I wasn't obsessing over him, I just mentioned him a couple of times. And second, the tattoo wasn't just on his hand, it was his whole arm."

"I stand corrected. Clearly, you weren't obsessing at all. But, that's who we're talking about? That's who's in your house right now?"

Sam nodded.

"Awesome." Becky started the car back up and made a wide U-turn.

Sam didn't like where this was going, "What are you doing?"

"I want to see him."

"What? No! Becky!"

"C'mon," she said. "You tell me this guy— your walking wet dream—who you've been talking about for two months and were never going to see again has somehow, miraculously, re-appeared in your kitchen, and you think I'm not gonna go check him out?"

"Becks, c'mon, let's just go to your place."

"This is a sign, like, from God or something. This guy was meant to marry you, and I'm gonna see him."

Sam felt panic edge into her voice. "Becks, please, all right? Just don't do this, okay?"

"The hell I won't."

"Look." They were almost back to Sam's house; her mind raced. If Becky saw Nick then she would say something or do something and Sam would never be able to speak to him again, she just knew it. "If we go in now, just to look at him, it'll be weird and obvious. You'll see him when you drop me off tonight."

"He'll be gone by then."

"Then, you can see him tomorrow!"

Becky looked over at her, "He'll be there tomorrow too?"

"Yes."

"I have your word? I can see this mystery man of yours tomorrow?"

*"Yes!"* Sam was practically in tears she was so nervous. She had no idea if Nick was going to be back or not, but she couldn't walk back into the house. Not now.

Becky drew the moment out. "Weeell," she said, enjoying watching her best friend suffer, watching her squirm. "Okay." She did another U-turn back towards her house. "But, I better get to see this boy."

Sam sighed; she felt a thousand pounds lighter. "You will," she said. "I promise."

And she did.

Becky's car broke down later that night on the way back from *Barnes and Noble*. They were at a stop light and when the light turned green, Becky stepped on the gas but nothing happened. It just sat there. The engine was running, but it wouldn't go. People behind them honked and she rolled down the window and waved people by. They stayed through two light cycles before a guy actually got out of his car and helped them push the car off the road and into the Wawa parking lot.

It took twenty-five minutes for the tow truck to pick them up; when it did, they rode with the driver back to his garage.

Becky called and texted both her parents to see if they could get a ride home but neither of them responded, which wasn't a surprise; they were terrible with phones. Sam's mother got mad at her if she didn't call to check in, like, every fifteen minutes, but Becky could disappear for a week before her parents would notice she was gone, they could silence their phones to watch *Breaking Bad* and forget to turn the sound back on for days. So Sam called her mother, who sounded pissed, and told her she couldn't come because she had some important meeting to go to, but then she said she'd take care of it and hung up before Sam could protest.

Five minutes later, her mother called back to say *Nick* was coming to pick them up. Sam was mortified. She told her mother she could just call one of her other friends or a cab or walk, *anything else*, but her mother said Nick already left. He would be there in ten minutes.

Becky's eyes glowed with excitement when Sam told her.

"It's a sign," she kept saying, "It's a sign, it's a sign, it's a sign!"

***

"Oh my God. Mom. Are you kidding me right now? Are you kidding? How could Becky's car breaking down possibly be my fault?" Sam's mother was home less than five minutes before she started figuring out a way to make Sam feel guilty about what happened.

"I'm not saying it's your fault. I'm saying you need to be more self-sufficient. I can't always drop everything when something comes up. With your dad in Chicago, I have to take care of you and your brother, get the house fixed up to sell, *and* get us packed up to move. I have so much to do, and so little time. Nick was willing to pick you two up, but I doubt we'll always be so lucky."

"Excuse me? Did I *ask* him to come get us? No. You did. You asked him before you even checked to see if I could get anyone else!"

Her mother laughed, but it was tired sounding, hollow. "C'mon Sam, I'm not saying-"

"Whatever." Sam spun on her heels and just walked away.

Sam sat on the edge of her bed fuming. The arrogance of her mother, the gall, to use the move, a move that she herself forced, as some kind of weapon against Sam, it was enraging. Then – then! – to make it out as if calling Nick was Sam's idea, like she asked for it. Like it was something she wanted. Sam would have rather walked home than been in that car with him.

That car ride was twenty of the longest minutes of her life. She was miserable; she barely said a word the whole time. Even Becky, who was so excited to get to see him, and who Sam was afraid would talk his ear off, was intimidated ("he's really hot," Becky said the next morning, *"really"*). Sam wished Becky would say something, anything, just to break the silence.

And the thing of it was, when she talked to him earlier in the day, in the kitchen, it had been nice. It made her happy afterwards.

And now, it was gone.

Now, if he came back, she didn't know if she could ever talk to him again.

And her mother thought that was what she wanted.

It was like her mother was actively working against her. Every time Sam felt she got a handle on things, her mother would step in and shake them up again until Sam lost her grip. Sam accepted that they were moving, accepted that everything she knew and loved was being ripped away from her for no real reason. And she tried to make the most of the time she had left in her home, and with her friends. And her mother was undermining that too.

For no reason.

Here was this boy, the beautiful boy, dropped into her life by God or chance or whoever, and, for some insane reason, he seemed to like her. Okay, probably not *like* like her, but still, he remembered her, and seemed to not mind talking to her. *And he was in her house*. How awesome was that? And then her mother just sends him out, like an errand boy, like a chauffeur, to pick her up, at a *garage*. That was so her mother. She didn't think of people as *people,* they were just pieces on a board, to be moved and used as she saw fit.

Sam thought that maybe, and she'd never admit this to Becky, but maybe Nick being in her house really was a sign. A sign of… something, she didn't know what. A sign maybe that she should listen to that voice telling her to use her remaining time in Baxter to cut loose a little. To push things, see what happened. Maybe… maybe, Nick picking her up was a sign too, a sign that one of the things that needed pushing was her mother. Maybe that power that she was feeling at school needed to be exercised at home too. Maybe she needed to put her foot down.

Her mother was taking so much away from her.

She wasn't going to take this away too.

The next day Sam walked straight home after school. The walk gave her time to gather her nerves and figure out what she was going to say in case he really was still there. She saw his truck parked in front of the house when she turned the corner to her street. Her stomach clenched and a shiver ran up her spine. She thought about calling Becky, going to her house and waiting for him to leave, or at least letting her come over. That way, she would have moral support. Like a wing man. But no, she had to do this herself.

Sam took a breath, tucked her hair behind her ear, and went in the house.

# PERMIT

"Hey."

Nick looked up at Sam; she stood in the kitchen doorway, hands on the straps of her backpack, one foot flat on the ground the other behind her and on the tip of her toes, like she hadn't fully committed to coming into the room.

"How's your friend's car?" He stood up. How tall was she? Five seven, eight? Even without the shock of red hair, she'd be easy to spot in a crowd.

"Huh? Oh, fine I think." She shrugged. "I mean, they said it'd be a couple days to fix. But, it's *getting* fixed, so…y'know, that's good." She walked into the kitchen, dropped her bag on a chair.

"It just means you'll be doing the driving for a while."

"Me? I don't have my license." She opened the fridge, took out a can of soda. "Do you want anything to drink?"

"Sure, I'll take a Coke. You don't have a license yet? How old are you?"

"Seventeen next month." She handed him a can, then opened her own.

"Did they raise the age requirement or something?"

"No, it's still sixteen."

"So what's the hold up?"

She shrugged again. "Just haven't gotten around to it I guess."

Nick was stunned. "Haven't gotten around to it? *Haven't gotten around to it?* What's more important than getting your license? I started driving when I was fifteen, got my permit on my sixteenth birthday, and my license two weeks later."

She laughed. "What can I say; I'm just not as focused as you."

"Guess not," he said.

"You know one of the things I've been doing instead of learning to drive? I've been watching *My So Called Life*."

It took a second for him to place it. "Oh, the show! The one with the girl with the red hair I was telling you about, right?"

"Angela."

"Yeah, Angela. You found that show?"

"It wasn't hard, you said that it starred the fairy girl from *Stardust*; I just looked up Claire Danes, and she was the only in one show."

"Okay, but then you actually watched the show?"

She shrugged again. This girl shrugged a lot. "It was streaming on Netflix."

"Wow," he said. "I'm impressed. Does it hold up?"

"It's pretty good," she said. "I mean, the clothes and music are pretty cheesy in places, but Claire Danes is really good. And the two boys are good too, Jordan and Krakow."

"Krakow, right," he said. "He was the one with the big Jew-fro?"

Sam took a sip from her soda. "It's pretty hilarious."

"It's on Netflix? We have that. Maybe I should check it out, watch it with Val, relive the old days."

"Val? Is that one of your aunts who's your age?"

"Actually," he said, "she's a year younger. But close enough." He was kind of amazed. "You remember that?"

She smiled, brushed her hair behind her ear. "I have a good memory."

He shook his head. "Well," he said. "I'm impressed."

Sam smiled. He liked this girl, liked her family, liked the house. He was thinking about it the night before after dropping Sam off. So many clients Nick dealt with were rude, dismissive, entitled assholes. Actually, most of the people Nick met in *life* were like that. It was such a relief to spend time with people who were just nice. People who listened when he talked, didn't twist his words around or think he was trying to juke them out of money.

The Hellers though, they treated him nicely. They treated him with respect. And it started with the mom, with Liz. The dad, well, okay the dad was kind of a dick, but he was gone anyway, in Chicago, so Nick didn't worry about him. But Liz was all right. She was nice to him from day one, offering him the ashtray for his butts instead treating him like a criminal for daring to light a cigarette.

And it turned out Sam was cool too. He remembered having a good feeling about her when he was working on the deck, but the fact that she remembered so much of what they talked about and found and watched *My So Called Life*? That just confirmed it.

Hell, Nick even liked the little kid, what's-his-name, Oscar. They were only in each other's company for a few minutes, but in that time the kid walked up and talked to Nick like they were old friends. A lot of the little kids Nick met were so shy they couldn't say three words to him. But Oscar didn't seem to be afraid of anything.

*This is what a family should be like*, Nick thought. *How a home should feel.*

"So," Sam said, "my mom hired you to fix our kitchen too?"

"Among other things."

"Like what other things?"

"Like lots of things. Before a house goes on the market, it's gotta be in tip-top shape so it can sell for as much money as possible. Your mom wants me to do work in the kitchen, bathroom, some painting."

"You can do all that?"

"I can do all sorts of things." He wiggled his eyebrows. "I can even drive."

"Shut *up*!" She punched him in the shoulder.

"I'm sorry; I can't get over it - what sixteen-year-old doesn't learn to drive right away?"

"Whatever, it's hard to get your license these days. Maybe when you were my age you could just go and get it, but now you have to, like, log all this time driving first. You have to have fifty hours with an adult. They have to sign forms and everything."

"Okay so, that sounds like a pain in the ass, but doable."

"Yeah, well, my dad works all the time, and, now he's in Chicago and none of my friends are old enough to teach me."

"What about your mom?"

Sam laughed. "No. Just, no."

"What? Why not your mom?"

"Because she gets super tense whenever I try and drive with her, and that makes *me* tense, which makes her more tense. It's a whole tense thing. The last time she took me driving, I almost drove into a ditch. So, I'm not doing that."

"Yeah, maybe that's not such a good idea. What about other relatives? My uncle taught me how to drive. Got any uncles around here?"

She shook her head.

"Well," he said. "I'm all out of ideas."

She took a step toward him. "Hey," she said. "Why don't you teach me?"

"You want me to teach you?"

"Well, you were just saying I need to learn, right? And I need someone to teach me. You're here. You're around. You think it's a big deal, so teach me."

He laughed, he couldn't help it. "Teach you? You just punched me!"

She smiled wickedly. "Imagine what I'll do if you don't?"

The thing of it was, he couldn't really think of a reason *not* to do it. It might be fun, and it felt right, like picking her up the night before. Besides, he liked her, and it wasn't like he was doing anything else. Why not help out?

"If I say yes," he said, "and I mean *if*, do I have to do all fifty hours, or can we just try it out and see what happens?"

Her smile widened. “We can totally just try it.”

“Okay,” he said, “here’s what you do— you check with your mom to make sure it’s okay with her, and if she gives the okay, we’ll go out after I finish up here for the day. We’ll see what happens, but no promises, okay?”

She jumped in the air, clapped her hands, squealed. “Thank you,” she said, “thankyou thankyouthankyouthankyou.” She threw her arms around him, hugged him tightly. Then, she sped out of the kitchen.

Nick smiled, shook his head.

Kids.

# THE WOODS

"Shut up!"

"Swear to God."

"And you actually said, 'Imagine what I'll do if you don't'? Those were, like, your exact words?"

"Pretty much."

"Samantha Heller," Becky said, "you little slut!"

Sam called her the minute she was in her room, flush with victory. She closed the door, put on some music, loud, so there wasn't a chance of being overheard, and dialed her best friend. Her heart pounded, her head spun, and she felt more alive than ever.

It was perfect, beyond perfect, it was some kind of beyond perfect thing that there wasn't a word for yet. He talked about her not driving, and then they talked about *My So Called Life*, and she thought about it and she remembered how in the show Jordan taught Angela how to drive, and she was like, *I should've asked him to take me driving, how cool would that've been*? But it was too late, the moment passed.

But then, through some miracle, he brought it up again. It was… whatever that beyond perfect word was. Time slowed down and she knew what she was going to say, it was like everything was in slow motion and she had the time to shape everything she said for maximum coolness.

"Becks, I was *amazing*."

"Yeah, you were!" Becky sounded almost as happy as Sam felt. "You're some kind of super chick or something." Sam laughed, she loved Becky so much. Who was going to cheer for her like this in Chicago?

"It got better. At the end, after he said he'd take me? I totally hugged him."

"Stop it."

"I did."

"You're killing me, you're killing me. When did you get this cool?"

"I dunno Becks, I was just outside my house, you know? And his truck was there, and I was thinking about how I'm leaving and it was like, what do I have to lose? What's the worst thing that could happen? So, I'm like, talking to myself, right? Psyching myself up? And I'm telling myself, *look, just go in and say hi, or whatever, and see what he does.* I mean, it's my house, isn't it? I have a right to be there."

"Yeah," Becky said, "totally."

"So I go in, and I say hey, and he just, starts talking to me. He asks about your car."

"He did? What'd you say?"

"I said it was getting fixed."

"Did he say anything else about me?"

"Becks..."

"Sorry, I'm just, I don't know, excited for you. I know I said you should talk to him, but I never thought you'd actually do it."

"What can I say? I guess I'm a new woman."

"Or something. Hey, I gotta run, but call me after you get back, okay? I wanna hear everything."

And her mother's face when Sam told her. Her mother's face. That alone would have made everything worth it. Sam waited until the last moment to tell her; she didn't know if or how her mother would try and stop her from going, but she didn't want to give her much opportunity.

She stayed in her room until five, did homework, poked around online, killed time. Then she took a quick shower and put on a pair of cute shorts that she thought made her legs look good, and a blue and white striped t-shirt. "Mom," she said. "Nick was going to take me out driving when he finished. Can we use Dad's car, or should we just use Nick's?" They were all in the kitchen; Nick was packing up his stuff.

"What?"

"Dad's car," Sam pressed. "Can I use it or should we use Nick's? Cause I think it would be better to learn on Dad's. I'll probably actually drive it sometime so it'd be good to learn. And Nick has a truck, so it might not be a good idea to use that. Better to get used to a car first, right?"

"Wait," her mother said, "hold on, back up. Nick's teaching you how to drive?"

"Well, you know, not really. I know the basics from Dad, but he's gonna drive around with me so I can get the hours on the road to take my test. I mean, *somebody* has to. And didn't you guys tell me I was getting a car?"

"Yeah, but-"

"And weren't you just saying the other day," she interrupted, "that you were really busy and didn't have much time to get things done?"

"Well, I did."

"Well," Sam said, "Nick's old enough to take me, and I have to do it, so..."

Her mother looked at Nick; she didn't seem totally convinced. "And you're okay with this?"

Nick washed his hands in the kitchen sink. "It's okay with me if it's okay with you," he said over his shoulder.

"Well," she said, "I hadn't really, I mean, I wish you all gave me a little more *time* to..." She trailed off.

And that was it. Sam had her, there was nothing her mother could say at that moment to stop her from going, and she wasn't going to just say no without a reason. If it had been her dad, then she might have, probably would have, but in front of someone not in the family, another adult especially, her mother wouldn't just shut her down.

"Sure," her mother finally said, "I mean, if you're both okay with it."

"Thanks Mom," Sam said, and turned to Nick, "I'll be outside by the car." At the front door, she took one last glance over her shoulder at her mother. She stood in the same spot in the kitchen, looking at Sam. She looked confused; not unhappy, not mad, but a little nervous, maybe. Sam turned back towards the front door, towards the car, and the rest of her day with Nick. She smiled.

Suck it, Mom.

The first time Sam drove a car was almost a year ago, the first Saturday after her sixteenth birthday. She was so eager to learn and her dad promised to take her out as soon as she got her permit. Her birthday was on a Thursday, and she rode her bike to the DMV to get her permit that very morning, missing the first two periods of class in the process. She was two months older than Becky, and the two of them planned all the places they would go once Sam got her license, which she would do the second she was able. They would go to the movies, and to the mall, and to restaurants and everywhere they always went, but it would be different because *it would be under their control.* No working out schedules for pick-ups and drop-offs. No calling home to check to see if those schedules could be changed if something caught their eye. Once Sam got her license, it would be just the two of them.

So she pedaled to the DMV and took the test for her permit and it was a breeze. All she had to do was take a test on a computer, answer a bunch of questions about how far away from a fire hydrant she was supposed to park and who goes first at a four way stop sign. Sam had other, older, non-Becky friends who'd gotten their permits and they'd told her what to expect. The whole thing was easy-peasy, less than half an hour and she was out of there.

Her dad was in the middle of a case at work and by the time he got home that night the sun was going down and it was too late to take her out. Friday was the same story, but he promised to take her out first thing Saturday morning. Sam couldn't sleep that night, it felt like Christmas Eve. She tossed and turned in bed that night, trying to relax but unable to keep the images of herself in the driver's seat, her music pumping through the speakers, out of her head. Maybe she and Becky would go to the beach, just the two of them on a day trip. They needed to be able to use a car for the day, but if she could drop her dad off, and he was willing to take the train home, maybe she could use his. Or she could go down to Savannah, Georgia for a weekend. One of her favorite movies was *Midnight in the Garden of Good And Evil.* She rented the movie one night knowing nothing about it, just that the title was neat, and she fell in love. When she saw that it was based on a book, she bought the book and it was even better than the movie. The city in the story was so wild and strange and unique, she knew she had to go someday and see it for herself. Now that she was going to be driving, maybe it was finally time to go. Or she could go to Boston. Or Manhattan, or that one bridge in Maryland that was a couple miles long. She always wanted to drive that. No wonder she couldn't sleep.

Her eyes popped open before seven that Saturday morning, it was the first time that happened voluntarily in years. Oscar was awake of course; he sat by himself in the living room, cartoons on the TV, a bowl of cereal next to him. Her mother was there too, dozing on the couch, a book resting on her chest. Sam smiled; she remembered when she was too young to just be awake and alone in the house; soon, she'd be able to be alone wherever she wanted. Her dad though, was still asleep. Sam knew better than to wake him up. Like Sam, he valued his weekends, especially when things were busy at work. Some days he would be gone before Sam woke up in the morning and didn't get home much before she was going to bed. As much as she wanted to get on the road, she wasn't about to keep him from getting his sleep. Instead, she made herself a bagel and sat with Oscar watching his cartoons until her dad woke up a few hours later.

He milked it of course, took his time having his breakfast and getting ready to go. He took forever to get dressed, pretended he couldn't find his keys; he went up to her mother and said, "Hey, didn't you get into a long conversation with your sister the other day that you wanted to tell me about?"

"Oh that's right," her mother said. "She was telling me about how she's gotten into knitting. And I asked her how you go about that, and she said all you have to do is -- you know what? There's a lot of terminology involved, and I wrote it down, let me go get my notebook."

"Brilliant," Sam said rolling her eyes, no stranger to her parents' routines. "Hilarious, c'mon Daddy, let's *go*." She grabbed him by the arm and dragged him out to the car.

Her dad backed the car out of the driveway and into the street. Then, he got out and walked around the car, and got back in on the passenger's side. Sam sat in the driver's seat for the first time. She adjusted the seat and mirrors, buckled her seatbelt and started the engine. She felt her heartbeat in her ears. Finally, when she was ready, and when her dad was ready, for the first time, she actually stepped on the gas.

And everything changed.

Her dad told her that driving was easy, that all a person needed to do was keep her foot on the gas and her hands on the wheel and the car would do the rest. Her friends who drove told her basically the same thing. So Sam was shocked by how, the first time she stepped on that pedal, panic swept across her body. It wasn't that she was misled; the physical act of driving was as easy as everyone said. What Sam was unprepared for was how her perception of speed suddenly drastically shifted. How going twenty miles an hour, a speed that seemed like a snail's pace from the passenger's seat, now felt life-threatening when she sat three feet to the left.

Sam heard once that the average person could run a maximum of eleven miles an hour, and then not for very long. Oh sure, some people could run way faster than that, but they were like Olympic athletes, genetic freaks of nature, and it was for about ten seconds at a time. Most people, regular folks, didn't top ten miles an hour in their whole life.

And here was Sam, all of a sudden going double that.

It was alarming.

Here she was, in charge of God knew how many thousands of pounds of steel, travelling at speeds faster than her body was designed to travel, and she was responsible for making decisions about where that steel was supposed to go? And on top of that there were thousands, millions, of other piles of steel hurtling around, even faster than she was, that might run into her at any second. Okay, there weren't any other piles of steel in her immediate vicinity, but still, they were *around*, they could be, eventually *would* be. And besides, there were other obstacles; there were trees and stop signs and curbs. If she hit any of those she could still get hurt. Hell, if she broke too fast she could slam into the steering wheel or something. *What kind of horrible machine was this where she could hurt herself by stopping too much?* And, oh my God, what if she hit a person? What if there was someone on the sidewalk and she wasn't paying attention or something and she just clipped them a little? Fifteen miles an hour, was that a killing speed? Was it a maiming speed? Should she feel better knowing that she was probably only going to maim someone instead of kill them?

What gave her the right to cripple someone just because she wanted to go to the mall?

She crept down her street on that first day, refusing to go over ten miles an hour. Her dad tried not to get frustrated but he was clearly confused. Why was the girl who was so eager to learn to drive as recently as that morning suddenly so terrified? Sam tried to explain it, how the physical reality of driving so thoroughly annihilated any fantasy expectations, and how the depth of her disappointment made it worse. She craved her license for so long, and now that it was in her grasp, the discovery that it wasn't as easy as she imagined, the responsibility that came with the freedom, she didn't know if she could handle that.

It was devastating.

Her dad tried to cheer her up. He told her she was thinking too much. He said she should be proud of herself for taking driving seriously, that most kids her age would just rush out without considering the consequences of their actions. He told her it was okay, that it got easier, got better. It helped, a little.

Things did get better, and she got better, but it was never quite the same. Or rather, it was never the way she wanted it to be originally. The freedom she craved wasn't going to be found in driving. She went out a few more times with her dad, and gained more confidence, but then his workload got heavier again and he couldn't take her out. So her mother took over. And that was a disaster. Her mother was good at many things, but teaching Sam to drive wasn't one of them; her tension from the passenger seat radiated, her instructions to Sam came out clipped and abrupt, more like commands than guidance. Whenever her mother said anything, the muscles in Sam's back clenched up and she felt bad, like she did something wrong. Those trips were so stressful that she lost all the nerve she managed to build up, along with any enthusiasm. The idea of spending fifty hours in a car with her mother just to get a license seemed like more trouble than it was worth. Before the summer was over, Becky got her license and Sam pretty much abandoned any notions of driving herself.

Walking out of her house with Nick, she was surprised that Nick took the keys from her. She assumed that she would just start driving, like she did with her dad.

"Nope," Nick said. "For all I know you'll drive straight into a tree or something. We're gonna go somewhere with a lot of open space, go over basics like speeding up and braking, making turns, stuff like that. If you've got those down, *then* you can take it out on the road."

"C'mon," she said, "I've driven before, I just need the hours."

"Hey, you want me to teach you?"

Sam nodded.

"Then we're doing it my way. First, you're showing me you know the basics, got it?"

Sam felt a wave of pleasure run through her body; she got in the passenger seat.

Sitting next to Nick as he drove her dad's car, she wondered if maybe she was getting that feeling of freedom back. Maybe learning, not with her mother or with her dad, but with Nick, listening to him, learning from him, someone new, someone interesting, someone more her age, maybe that was the key. As Nick drove, she felt that old excitement return to her bones, but it was different now too, better. She knew there were responsibilities that came with the license, and she was ready.

She tried to absorb every aspect of the moment, the sight of the houses and trees rushing by, the feel of the leather seat against her legs. The breeze from her open window through her hair, the sound of the music playing on the car stereo, some classic rock song she knew but couldn't name, and the smell of the boy sitting next to her, the sweaty but not smelly odor of a body that worked all day. She wanted to roll the windows up and live in that smell, to keep it forever.

Nick pulled into the empty parking lot of the high school and came to a stop.

Nick directed Sam to speed up and slow down, make turns, and come to a full stop. She backed up and pulled into a few of the parking spaces. Sam felt better and more confident in her driving. She had to admit she was a little worried that the self-doubt of the early days was going to come back. But it didn't. Neither did the tension she felt when she was with her mother. If Nick was worried about being in a car she was driving, he wasn't showing it. He seemed cool, calm, and collected. Of course, they were in an empty parking lot. Still, he was so relaxed, Sam had no doubt he would stay that way when they went out on the open road.

She would be, too.

After about fifteen minutes of Sam making lazy circles around the parking lot and demonstrating various simple maneuvers, Nick told her to stop and turn off the engine. He got out of the car, walked around to the front and leaned against the hood. Sam grabbed her bag from the back seat and got out. Nick took his cigarettes from his pocket, held the pack up to his mouth and pulled a smoke out with his lips, just like the first time. Sam reached into her bag, grabbed the pack she had in there all week, and tried to get her lighter to spark. It wouldn't. Nick looked at her quizzically.

"Since when do you smoke?"

Sam shrugged, "For a while now. Can I get a light? This is broken or empty or something."

Nick laughed, "It's your life, I guess." He tossed her his lighter.

"Thanks," she said, and lit her cigarette.

It was, in fact, the fifth cigarette she ever smoked, from the first pack she ever bought, purchased a week ago from the Wawa up the street from her school. The one with the creepy older guy who worked there in the afternoons and who stared at all the girls and didn't card.. She always thought smoking would be difficult, that she'd hate the first few and cough a whole bunch and generally look like an idiot. But it wasn't that way at all. The first time she actually smoked was alone, in the woods, the day after she bought the pack. She went for a walk by herself after dinner; her dad wanted to talk about Chicago, see how she was dealing with everything, but Sam still didn't want to talk about it, or anything really, with either of her parents.

So she grabbed her MP3 player and her bag (with the cigarettes tucked safely inside a zipped-up pocket) and went for a walk. She needed to find somewhere secure, somewhere private. She didn't want her parents or anyone who knew her parents to see her, obviously, but she also wasn't keen to be seen by anyone her age either. If she ended up coughing or puking or anything like that, she wanted to do it alone. She decided to walk through the woods at Baxter; it gave her the privacy she wanted and she'd been there the day before with Becky, so it was fresh in her mind.

She didn't cough, or puke, or any of that. She pretty much liked it right away. She opened the pack, taking care to stuff the plastic from the wrapper into her bag. She always loved the idea of smoking, but hated seeing loose wrapping and spent butts on the ground, like it somehow wasn't littering or something. She put the cigarette in her mouth and it felt right. She liked the weight of it, the feel of the paper against her lips and the taste of the tobacco. When she inhaled for the first time, it was weird no doubt, but a good weird, not a sick weird. She felt… something, some kind of rush of something she couldn't put her finger on, but it was exciting and calming at the same time. She exhaled, worried that maybe people got sick from their first cigarette because they didn't know how long to hold the smoke in their lungs. And, again, it was fine, good.

She finished the cigarette, ground it out in the dirt, but wrapped it up in the plastic from the wrapper and found a garbage can to throw it out on her way home.

She felt another wave of panic just before she went back inside her house. What if her parents somehow knew she smoked? What if she was sloppy and someone saw her in the woods? Or throwing out the butt, or even buying the pack the day before? What if they were waiting by the door right now to bust her? She lifted the collar of her shirt and sniffed it; did it smell like smoke? She couldn't be sure.

Her best bet, she figured, was to run upstairs right away, take a shower, brush her teeth and change all her clothes. If her parents somehow caught her before that, she was dead; there was nothing she could do. But they didn't, and she wasn't. She went in the house and up the stairs as quickly as she could without drawing attention to herself, showered, brushed, and changed. Then, because she needed to know if they were able to tell, she went into the living room to watch the baseball game with her family. Her parents were on the couch, her dad on one end nursing a beer, her mother on the other end, a book in her lap, with her feet resting on Sam's dad. He called out encouragement to the television and absently massaged her mother's feet with his free hand. Oscar sat on his knees on the floor in his own little world, pushing his toy cars around.

Sam took a seat on the floor in front, resting her back on the couch; her father ruffled Sam's hair. She reached up, took her father's hand in hers and gave it a reassuring squeeze. He squeezed back, then pulled away. Sam sat wordlessly and watched the rest of the inning, feeling connected to her family and at the same time, infinitely apart from them. The memory of that cigarette in the woods glowed warmly in her stomach. When the inning ended, she stood up, kissed the top of her dad's head, and went upstairs to her room.

"So," Nick said, stretching, "this is the car you're going to be driving when you get your license?"

"I don't know," Sam said. "This is my dad's car. Or, it was. I don't know how it's getting to Chicago, or why he didn't take it with him. I think he must have a car there now. So maybe we're selling this one before we leave? I mean, he likes new cars, and he's had this one for a couple of years now. That's usually how long his cars last before he trades them in or whatever. Why, does it matter?"

"It matters some, mostly just what kind of transmission you have. You know, stick or automatic."

Sam shrugged, "Probably it'll just be automatic. That's what my parents drive; it's easier, right?"

Nick nodded, "Yeah, it's easier to learn, but it's not always easier to drive. The thing about a stick shift is you have more control over the car. If you're driving an automatic, it shifts for you, and that makes it harder to regulate speeds, see what I mean?"

"Not really."

"Okay, the gear your car is in determines how fast it can go. When it's in first gear it can't go much higher than fifteen miles an hour. To go higher, the engine has to shift to second. You know how when you're speeding up it sounds like the engine is straining for a second, working harder, and then it settles?"

Sam nodded.

"That's the sound of the engine shifting gears. In an automatic, it does it on its own, but if you have a manual, you shift it yourself with the stick, right?"

"I guess."

"Okay, so, let's say it's snowing and there's ice on the road. You're going to be driving really carefully so you don't skid or whatever. If you're driving an automatic, it's harder to keep the car under a certain speed, say twenty miles an hour, because the engine decides for itself what gear to be in. It thinks you want to go thirty, it shifts for you. But if you're driving a stick shift, you can keep it in second, and the car won't go over thirty. It just won't. It can't. So it's easier to keep control, get it?"

Sam said, "I never thought about that."

Nick flicked his cigarette away; Sam was only halfway through hers. "No reason you should have," he said. "Things like that, someone has to explain them. That's how it is."

"Maybe I should learn stick then."

"Maybe you should. Winters in Chicago are supposed to be pretty nasty, yeah? It could get icy. The other good thing about stick is, it's cheaper, so you can get a nicer car if you can handle a manual transmission."

"I guess you know stick, huh?"

"Sure."

"Was it hard to learn?"

"It sucked. But I was glad in the end. My uncle Dennis taught me to drive, and if you think driving with me is boring, you should have seen what I had to go through."

"What could possibly be more boring than driving in an empty parking lot?"

"He took me to a little incline, and made me sit in the driver's seat and stay in one place with the engine on."

Sam laughed, "What?"

"Getting a car to start moving is the hardest part with a stick shift. You know how in movies and TV and stuff, when someone's learning to drive, the car's always all jerky? That's them trying to get into first gear. You gotta take your foot off the clutch and press the gas at pretty much the same time, but if you give it too much gas, the car lurches forward real fast. Too little and it stalls out and you have to start the engine again. After first gear, it's easier because the car's already moving forward, so you can shift from first to second then third and on and on without a problem. First gear's the bitch of the bunch. So Dennis, he wanted me to get the hang of that before anything else.

"He takes me to this incline, where if there weren't any brakes the car would slowly drift backward, and he has me sit there for close to an hour, in first gear, just applying enough gas to keep it from going backward, but not enough to go forward. He said it would teach me how to ease the car into first gear, and not freak out if I had to start driving while on a hill, likeif I was at a red light or something. We did it every time, until he was sure I'd be able to do it on my own."

Sam scratched her hip absently, "Did it work?"

"Pretty much. I was great when I was with Dennis. But the day I got my license I took his car to go pick up this girl. I went to her parents' house, picked her up. I'm totally cool. Then, first red light we hit, when it turns green I panic, stall the car out. I start it again, stall it again, over and over. The people behind us start honking, that just made it worse. We sat through three cycles before I could get it going."

"Oh my God." Sam wasn't sure if she was supposed to laugh or not. "That's so embarrassing."

"Yeah, it was pretty bad, but after that I was fine. I didn't get anywhere with the girl though, maybe if I'd gotten through that first light."

A sort of excited/nervous spasm shot through Sam's stomach. She didn't know how to respond, or if she was even supposed to.

Nick clapped his hands together. "All right," he said authoritatively, "I think that's enough of my life story for one day. It's also enough of this driving around a parking lot shit. You're ready to go out on the road. Feel up to it?"

"Absolutely."

"Then let's do it."

Nick rolled his eyes when Sam jogged over to a garbage can to toss out her cigarette butt. She got into the driver's seat, started the engine and drove across the parking lot, trying her best not to jam her foot on the gas and hurry the hell up. After what seemed like an eternity, she was at the exit.

She put on her blinker, looked both ways and when Nick gave the okay, made her way into traffic.

*The Minors*

# CATCH

“Ready? Here it comes.”

Nick tossed the ball underhand to Oscar. It arced lazily through the air, bounced off Oscar’s outstretched glove, and fell to the grass at his feet. He picked it up, reared back and heaved. The ball sailed over Nick’s head and landed ten or so feet behind him. He trotted over to where it lay, and tossed it back again.

Nick hadn’t played catch with anyone in a long time, let alone someone as young as Oscar. Back when he played, the team sometimes went to the local schools and worked with the kids. And when he was in high school, kids used to come by all the time, though most of the older ones were too in awe of him to say anything. Everyone was certain he was the next Griffey; some asked for autographs, stuff like that. But the real little kids, the ones who were too young to know any better, asked him if he wanted to play in their games.

And sometimes he would. It was actually something he liked doing, teaching kids, working with them, watching their skills improve. It came more naturally to him than for a lot of the other guys. Growing up, the only time Nick really felt like he belonged was on a field. It seemed wrong to not at least try and give that feeling of peace to some other kid. The excitement on their faces when he agreed to be on their team, or play catch, or help them with their swing, or whatever, just seeing that excitement was about the best Nick felt outside of actually playing.

“I like to play catch with my dad,” Oscar said as the ball bounced off his open glove, “but he’s in Chicago.” He picked up the ball and threw it back to Nick.

Nick managed to catch the ball this time, “So I heard,” said Nick as he tossed it back.

Bounce; pick up, “Did you play catch with your dad when you were little?” Throw.

Catch. “Nah.” Toss.

Bounce; pick up, "Why not?" Throw.

Catch. "He wasn't around." Toss.

"Oh." Bounce; pick up. "Are your parents divorced?" Throw.

Catch. "My parents were never married." Toss. "It's like the same thing."

Bounce; pick up. "Danny Eisenson's parents are divorced; he sees his dad on the weekends." Oscar launched the ball back at Nick. "Did you see your dad on the weekends?"

"Lift your glove a little higher when I throw you the ball. Hold it face up, with your palm facing up. Use your other hand to trap it in there. Always use two hands when you catch." Nick tossed the ball back to Oscar.

"You're not using two hands."

"When you get to be as old as me you can use one hand. But until then, two hands."

He threw the ball back to Oscar who, using two hands, managed to get the ball into his glove before it bounced out and onto the ground. "That's better," Nick said, "let's try it again." He threw the ball again; again it bounced out of Oscar's glove before he could trap it with his right hand. But he was getting closer.

Oscar threw the ball again. He said, "My dad says you used be a baseball player before."

"That's true."

"My dad said you were real good."

"That's nice of your dad to say."

"Were you?"

"For a while."

"Why did you stop?"

"I got hurt."

"One time I saw a guy run into a wall trying to catch a ball. He hit his face and was all bloody and stuff. Did you do that?"

"No."

"What happened?"

"I hurt my shoulder," Nick said. "It wasn't during a game. It was an accident, I was doing something that I shouldn't have been doing and I hurt it."

"What were you doing?"

"Something I shouldn't have been doing."

Oscar kept pushing, "What was it?"

"It doesn't really matter. I just couldn't play baseball for a long time afterward."

"Does your shoulder still hurt?"

"Sometimes. Not really, though. No."

"Then why didn't you go back to playing after?"

"I tried," Nick said, "but I was too old by then. I missed my chance."

"Oh," Oscar was quiet for a little while. After they threw the ball back and forth another four or five times, he asked, "Did that make you sad?"

"That I was too old to go back?"

"Uh huh."

"Yeah."

"Oh," Oscar said. "I'm sorry you hurt your shoulder."

"Thanks," said Nick, "I am too." It was weird; he didn't ever mention this to anyone , and now here he was standing in someone else's backyard talking to a six-year-old, telling him things he didn't normally want to talk about. Things he usually kept to himself unless he was furious or falling down drunk.

"It's okay to be sad about things like that," Oscar said.

"I guess that's good," said Nick.

"Mom says when you're used to things being one way, and then it changes, even if it's a change you're okay with, you usually still get sad."

"That's probably true."

"I'm sad about moving," said Oscar. "Mom said it's because moving is a big change. She says it's okay to be sad, but I'm still sad."

"Right," Nick said, "I guess that doesn't really change anything then."

"I like our house; I like my room and my school and my friends. Mom says I'll like Chicago. But what if I don't? Did you have your own room when you were little?"

"No, I had to share."

"I don't want to share a room with Sammy," Oscar said. "Did you know that we were the first people to live in our house, ever?"

"I didn't."

"It was new when we got here. No one ever had my room before, but now, someone else will. That makes me sad too. I don't want anyone else to have my room. It's *mine*."

Oscar threw the ball to Nick with what felt like a little more force. Nick figured that Oscar wouldn't have cared one way or the other about moving. Over the years, Nick spent more than his fair share of time around people preparing to move. They hired him, like the Hellers did, to fix up the house, get it ready to sell. He had tons of experience around stressed out people packing up their junk to move somewhere else. Nick heard somewhere once that moving was one of the top five stressful things a person could do, and that sure seemed to be the case, because the people in those houses inevitably ended up snapping at one another over some little thing.

It was amusing to see people lose it like that with one another. Nick grew up and then played ball without space of his own, so he never put much stock in where he lived. He crashed on too many couches and threw his stuff into too many duffle bags to ever develop much attachment to places or things. It was all basically the same. What always mattered to him was the team. Nick figured Oscar would be more like that, just throw stuff in a box and he'd be good. Or, not.

Sam being angry made sense; she was leaving behind a life, and didn't get much say in the matter. At least that's what she kept saying. Over and over. Liz said something about how difficult it was for Sam to acclimate to the news. How she was acting out more, pushing. Liz said she was worried about it. If Oscar was unhappy too, that could only make things harder.

Nick said, "Maybe you'll like your new room too."

"But is it going to be new like my room? Or was it someone else's first?"

Nick didn't know what to say to that, so he didn't say anything.

"Are you going to paint my room? Mom said you're painting some of the rooms. Are you painting mine?"

"I don't think anyone's said anything about your room, but maybe."

"Well," Oscar said, "*I* want you to paint it. And paint it orange, I hate orange. That way, it's not my room anymore and no else will ever have my room."

"I'll talk to your mom about it," Nick said. "See what she has to say."

Then, as if on cue, the porch door opened and Sam stormed out, followed by Liz.

"*I'll get to it,*" Sam was saying. "How many times do I have to tell you?"

"You don't have to tell me at all," said Liz. "Just do it and I'll stop reminding you."

"Whatever, I said I'd do it, I'll do it. Can we please just drop it?" She focused on Nick and Oscar in the yard, "Hey, you guys are playing catch? Can I play too?" She bounced down the porch steps and across the grass to where they were standing.

“Sure,” Nick said. “Why don’t you take over? I could use the break.” He handed the ball to Sam, walked over to the porch steps where Liz sat and took a seat next to her.

As soon as Sam’s back was turned, Liz looked at Nick and put her finger to her temple, pantomimed shooting herself in the head, complete with eye roll and slow motion recoil. It was actually pretty good.

Nick smiled, *what are you gonna do*?

Liz held up a finger, *Here’s an idea*. She pointed at Sam and raised her thumb again, and repeated the shooting motion. She looked back at Nick, eyebrow raised, *how does that sound?*

Nick shook her off.

Liz shrugged, “Worth a shot. Seriously though,” she said, with actual words, “it’s really great how you spend time with the kids; I know they love having you around.”

“Oh, hey, no sweat,” Nick said. “They’re good kids. Despite, you know, everything.”

Liz leaned back on her elbows, stretched her legs out. They weren’t bad, long and strong. *Definitely* used to run, maybe still did. “It may be no sweat for you,” she said, “but it helps me out a lot. It’s not easy keeping track of two kids on your own.” Her hair was back in a ponytail; she reached back, pulled out the band, and let it fall over her shoulders. “I don’t know how single parents do it. It’s been three weeks since Steve left, and I feel like I’m going to explode.”

“She giving you trouble?”

“That? That was nothing.” Liz sighed. “It’s fine I guess, or maybe it’s not, I don’t know anymore. They’re going to Chicago next week to spend Memorial Day weekend with Steve. I want her to pack a bag of stuff that she can leave there. Sort of like a little start to the move, you know? That little scene was because I asked her if she’d thought about what she was going to pack. She decided to be a pill about it. I took the bait. It was stupid.”

"I don't know. You want her to start taking stuff to Chicago, so she should start taking stuff. It has to happen eventually. Nothing stupid about that."

"Well, trust me, it was," Liz said. "I have to pick my spots with her these days. Sam and I, the last couple of years, have been…difficult. Everybody said it would be, you know, all that typical mother-daughter stuff? You figure, as a mom, that you know it's coming and you'll just ride it out, but when it happens, you can't help but take it personally. It's like, I can't do anything right anymore, and she's so *angry* at me all the time. And I know, I know, that's how it goes, but sometimes? I think she really hates me."

"She doesn't hate you," Nick said. "Look, I didn't have actual sisters growing up, but I had aunts close to my age, and they were like sisters, and they fought with their mom all the time. They grew out of it. So will Sam."

"Maybe," said Liz. "A month ago, I probably would have agreed with you. Now, with everything that's happening, I just don't want to lose her, you know? Me and my mom were at each other's throats all the time when I was a kid. We probably still would be except I moved a thousand miles away. I wanted it to be different for me and Sam. I wanted us to be, not *friends*, but something better than I had with my mom."

"Okay," Nick said, "but you still have to do your job. You still have to get her where she needs to be, and you can't beat yourself up every time she gets huffy."

"No, you're right, you're right. It just makes things worse, but I can't seem to stop doing it." She lowered her voice, "I could really use another one of those cigarettes right about now."

"So have one," said Nick.

"Don't tempt me. I have enough headaches as it is. Steve's the one that can to talk to her, not me. When Steve was here it would sometimes make me so mad how it seemed like it was just the two of them no matter who else was in the room. I mean, yeah, I admit I was jealous, but it was more than that. He had a habit of undercutting me. He could connect with Sam so quickly, so easily, it made me look even worse. It drove me nuts." She laughed. "But I'm telling you, now that he's gone? I'd take their little world and her in a good mood over all this conflict."

"Don't you have, like, friends with teenage daughters you can talk to? Someone who can give you advice or something?"

Liz spat out another bitter little laugh, "It's probably really pathetic to say this? But, no, not really. I *had* friends, growing up and when we were in Chicago. But by the time we moved here, we'd decided I was going to be a stay at home mom. I was thinking about going back to work when Sam made it to high school, but then Oscar came along, and it all started over.

"Anyway, I just never really got the chance to meet anyone around here. I did a couple of mommies groups when the kids were young, but I never clicked with anyone, and I'm friends with some of Steve's work friends and their wives but I don't know, they're not real friends. Not the kind you can talk to. Most of the friends I have left are still in Chicago or back home. We talk, but not more than a couple times a year, and they're all working moms, if they have kids at all. When I talk to them about Sam I always feel like some refugee from another age."

"Maybe," said Nick, "but you care about your kid and want to have a good relationship with her. I mean, I was raised by my grandmother mostly, and she's definitely from another age. She taught me, all of us, to believe that kids should respect their elders. I look around and see kids talking back, being disrespectful," he shook his head. "I don't like it. Maybe if those kids had moms like you, who cared about them, they wouldn't turn into little punks."

Liz laughed at that, a good laugh, with none of the bitterness from before; she put her hand on his shoulder. "Punks, huh? Listen to us," she said, "old before our time. Let's talk about something else instead. How're things going with that girl?"

"Who, Dana? Status quo, I guess. I haven't talked to her in a couple days."

Out in the yard, Oscar's throw went wild to the right and bounced over to where Nick and Liz sat. Nick picked it up and tossed it to Sam, who caught it, and threw it back to Oscar. Nick watched her throw.

"Sam used to be a dancer, didn't she?"

"She took classes for a little while when she was younger. How did you know that?"

"She steps forward onto the toe when she throws, see?" Nick pointed, "And when she releases she keeps her knee locked. It stays perfectly straight and she pivoted on her hip instead. Like a ballet dancer."

Liz whistled, "I'm impressed," she said. "That's a pretty sharp observation."

"It's easy if you know what to look for."

"Did you ever think about coaching? Like as a job."

"You mean high school or something? I did for a minute, but you need to have a degree for that."

"So go to college."

Now it was Nick's turn to laugh. "Sure, you got sixty thousand spare dollars lying around?"

"All right," she said, "what about Little League, then? You're good with kids and obviously know a lot about the game. You should use that somehow."

Nick smiled at her, "What are you, my guidance counselor now?"

She squinted, put a hand up over her eyes and looked at him. "Something like that. I told you I used to have a job. I taught eleventh grade English for three years before I gave it up. I guess that eye for potential never quite goes away."

"Well, teach," he said, "I think that's all a conversation for another time. I should probably get going."

"Fair enough," she said, punching him lightly on the shoulder, "to be continued."

# HOW SOON IS NOW?

Fifty hours is a long time. Like, a little more than two whole days long. Sam drove with her dad for six and her mom for three, which left forty-one hours until she could get her license. Realistically she wasn't going to spend all forty-one of those hours with Nick, but she was going to take whatever she could get. They drove every evening that week and into the next. When Nick finished working on the house, Sam always stood at the front door, keys in hand, ready to go.

Those hours were some of the happiest of her life.

During class her mind drifted ahead to that afternoon, seeing him, what she would say to him, what he might say back, how she could find out everything about him without, you know, *looking* like she was trying to find out everything about him.

It wasn't like anything happened; she drove around the neighborhood and he sat next to her, occasionally making suggestions or telling her where to go. On the Monday of the second week he turned the radio to a hard rock station. Sam originally asked if she could listen to music, but Nick said he needed to make sure it wouldn't distract her. By the third mopey grunge song she wished he was still making up his mind. Sam gave him grief about having to listen to old people music and he told her as long as he was teaching and she was learning, they would listen to what he wanted, and besides she probably listened to, like, Lady Gaga or Ke$ha or the *Glee* albums or some other gay shit like that.

It annoyed Sam that he assumed she was just a teenage girl who worshipped at the altar of Gaga (not that she didn't, she loved Lady Gaga. Lady Gaga was epic, but that wasn't the point.); as it happened, her music tastes were very eclectic. She went online, read reviews, stuff like that. Becky's older brother texted her links to websites of bands he saw or read about, and she and Becky checked them out, and a lot of the time they were good; Sam learned about a lot of bands that way. She said that tomorrow she was bringing her MP3 player and they were listening to *her* music, then he'd see how gay her music was.

Besides, she told him, he shouldn't be using *gay* as some sort of insult.

And anyway, what about the music he liked? What about all that dour, angry 90's stuff? She saw videos for some of those songs, and those guys all had like, long hair, nail polish and sometimes they wore skirts and whatever? Why weren't there any girls in those videos? What were they so depressed about anyway? So maybe Nick shouldn't be the one pointing fingers at people's music.

Nick nodded, said fair enough, as far as he was concerned she could play whatever she wanted, provided it didn't distract her. That night Sam made sure her MP3 player was completely charged and filled with her favorite bands that she also thought Nick might like. She wasn't going to play any one album, she figured she'd just hit shuffle and see what came up. And just to be safe, she took off her Lady Gaga and Ke$ha.

C'mon though, *Glee*? Who did he think she was?

But he was right about one thing; playing her music did distract her. The first day driving around with it she kept worrying about what Nick would say. When he didn't say anything, she worried about why he *wasn't* saying anything. Did he not like it? She wanted to skip around, find her favorite songs, but she knew she couldn't. She travelled in plenty of cars where people drove with one hand on the wheel, and the other fiddling with their radio or phone, but she supposed they didn't do it while they were learning.

Her MP3 player played Modest Mouse. It played Gaslight Anthem, MIA, Neutral Milk Hotel, and Eminem. No reaction to any of it.

Eventually she couldn't take it anymore and asked, okay maybe accosted him, about why he didn't like her music. He was surprised, said he didn't know what she was talking about. She reminded him about the conversation from the previous day; he laughed and said he completely forgot about it. He said he was never much of a music guy, but from what he could hear, her music was fine with him and she could play it if it made her happy. It just couldn't interfere with her concentration.

After a week and a half of driving she had it pretty much down, but she only had six hours logged. That, along with the time she put in with her parents, still meant she needed thirty-five more hours before she could take her test.

"Listen," Nick said that Friday before he took off, "I have to run a bunch of errands tomorrow, head over to Home Depot, get some new shoes at the mall, shit like that. I'm gonna be driving around most of the day. If you *want*, you can chauffer me around and get some more time in."

"Sure," said Sam, "sounds good." She could reschedule her plans with Becky.

That night she tried not to freak out. *It's not like this is a date,* she told herself. *Yeah, okay, if this were a boy from school and he asked you to spend the day with him, you might think it was a date. But this isn't a boy from school and it's not a date.* She repeated it to herself over and over, and, as much as she believed it, as much as she knew it was the truth, there was the other voice, the one telling her *yeah, but...*

Nick picked her up a little after eleven the next morning. His eyes were bloodshot, his hair was scraggly, a cigarette was hanging from his lips and he was wearing what looked like the same clothes from the day before; Sam woke up hours ago and changed clothes three times.

"Morning sleepy head," she said. "Did you just wake up or something?"

Nick tipped his Mountain Dew toward her in greeting, "Breakfast of champions," he said. He tossed her a Dunkin' Donuts bag, "I got an egg sandwich, thought you might want a donut or something. Take one," he said, "the rest are mine."

"Thanks," she said, and pulled out the glazed.

"I'm gonna run inside, use your bathroom real quick, cool?"

Sam shrugged. "Knock yourself out," she said. She took a seat on the curb and munched on her donut while she waited for Nick. When he came back out a few minutes later he looked much better; he'd splashed some water on his face and through his hair. His eyes were still bloodshot, but his skin had a little more color.

"Ready?" he said.

She held her keys, jingled them, "Where to?"

Nick got into the passenger seat of her dad's car and rubbed his eyes with his palms. He yawned. "Home Depot first. Then we'll hit the mall, sound good?"

"You're the boss," Sam said, and started the engine. She took her MP3 player out of her bag and was plugging it into the stereo when Nick put his hand on hers (!) and gently pushed it away.

"Let's hold off on the music for a little, okay?" He smiled, "I guess I partied a little too hard last night; I'm still working it off."

"Like I said, you're the boss." She put her MP3 player back in her bag and pulled out of the driveway.

He looked at her. "You have no idea what I'm talking about, do you?"

"Sure I do."

"No you don't, you've never been hungover a day in your life."

"Oh my God," she laughingly insisted, "I totally have."

"Sam, Sam, Sam," Nick tilted his seat back and closed his eyes. "What are we going to do with you?"

He bought a bunch of stuff at Home Depot. Nick tried to explain what it all was, since a lot of it was going to be used in her house, but it all looked like cans of goop to her. The only thing she could identify for certain was the orange paint.

Home Depot always both fascinated and made her nervous at the same time. It was just so *big*, and it was filled with whole aisles of stuff like doorknobs. The idea that there was a place you could go that had hundreds of doorknobs delighted her. She never thought about doorknobs, never considered them as aesthetic objects or art or anything; to her, they were just the things that let you open doors. But a place like Home Depot reminded her that every doorknob was somebody's choice. Some person's job was to design and build different looking doorknobs. Every day they went to work and came up with a doorknob no one had ever seen before.

Was there anyone out there with a real passion for designing doorknobs; someone for whom designing doorknobs was a life-long dream? How much did a person make designing doorknobs? Could you make a lot of money from it? Was there anyone who got rich from it? When that person had children, would people say the child came from "doorknob money?"

And then, someone else picked that doorknob out, from hundreds or who knows, maybe thousands, of different designs. Did a designer ever notice his doorknob on someone's front door? Did he feel proud? Did he ever tell the person whose door it was that he designed their doorknob? Sam decided she wanted to meet the person who designed the doorknob on her front door. That'd be pretty neat.

Lots of Home Depot's rows had that effect on Sam. Filled with things she saw every day but never considered. The variety made her head spin. Doorknobs, and mail boxes, and light fixtures, and on/off switches, and door hinges, and locks and on and on into infinity.

And that was what made her nervous.

Sometimes, when Sam was out at places like that, she got overwhelmed by all the detail, all the variety that existed in even the most insignificant things. With so many subtle choices, how did anyone ever know they were getting the exact right one?

She had the same problem at grocery stores. She hated going food shopping because there were always so many versions of the same basic things that she never felt confident in any of her choices and inevitably ended up frustrated with herself for not being able to pick out cereal. Her mother didn't make it any easier, standing behind Sam, sighing impatiently, "C'mon Sam, just pick one, they're all the same." But they *weren't* all the same, that was the problem. If they were all the same, then there wouldn't be so many choices and she could grab any box. But Sam's mother could never see that.

She never saw anything. All she did was make things more difficult than they had to be.

They were standing in the parking lot, catching a smoke before going to the mall when Sam's phone rang. She glanced at the caller ID and hit ignore.

She must have looked irritated or something because Nick asked her who called.

"No one, just my mom."

"Why didn't you pick up?" he said.

"I don't want to talk to her right now. She's just gonna ask where I am and when I'm going to be home and blah blah blah."

"It's not like she's gonna stop calling though."

"How bout I send her a text?" Sam took her phone out of her pocket, wrote *busy, talk later,* and hit send. She looked at Nick, "Good enough?"

Nick shook his head, "You shouldn't be so hard on her; she's doing her best."

Sam took a drag, "That's her thing, *doing the best she can*," she shook her head. "What does that even mean? How am I supposed to know what the best she can is? I'm just supposed to trust her?"

"Well yeah, pretty much."

Sam rolled her eyes, "Whatever. She always gets people to feel sorry for her; me, dad, you, then she can get us to do whatever she wants."

"Hey," Nick said, "at least she cares about what you're doing."

"She cares about controlling us, getting her way."

"Still, she's around, she cares about you. That's better than nothing; it's more than I can say about *my* mom anyway." Nick flicked his butt away and got into the car.

Sam stamped out her cigarette and walked to the trash can to throw it away, all the while turning this new nugget of information about Nick over and over in her head. In the time they spent together he so rarely volunteered anything about himself, even small details. And for him to trust her with something like this; this was no small detail. She decided not to follow up, to play it cool. Nick told her something personal, something that must be painful; if he wanted to talk more about it he could, but she wasn't going to push the matter. It was enough that he said anything at all.

Next on the agenda was the mall so Nick could get some new running shoes, which worked out really well for Sam, who wanted to get some new shoes herself.

For such a casual dresser, Nick took his sneakers very seriously. After going to three different stores, and looking at dozens of shoes, Nick settled on a pair of black and white Nike free runners. Sam picked a pair of lo-top Chuck Taylors. Nick grunted disapproval at her choice and warned her that Converse wore out quickly and didn't give any arch support. But Sam didn't care about arch support; she liked her news shoes, liked the way her feet and ankles looked in them. She especially liked the red and white checkered coloring of the cloth; it reminded her of picnic tables on warm spring days.

Walking out of the store, they bumped into Amelia Grudin, a girl from Sam's grade. They weren't friends exactly, but they were friendly. Amelia was the kind of girl Sam hung out with a couple of times because she was a friend of a friend. Amelia was with another girl, Sara Stevens, who Sam knew even less, and thought was kind of a bitch. Not like a total bitch, just always getting the leads in the school plays and musicals, and kind of stuck up about it.

That didn't mean she was incapable of being nice though. Amelia and Sara kept stealing glances at Nick while they talked, and Sam introduced him as her "friend." Nick said hey to the girls and then Sam said Nick was teaching her how to drive. Nick said how it was the only time she listened to him, and that he tried to stop her from getting ripped off on a pair of shoes but she ignored him. Sam checked him with her shoulder, and said knowing about driving and knowing about shoes were two different things entirely. She looked to Amelia and Sara for support. They just kind of stood there for a second; they looked unsure of what they were supposed to say. So Sam said goodbye, slid her arm around Nick's, and led him toward the exit.

She *loved* her new shoes.

The mall was around the corner from Nick's house, so they stopped to drop off his stuff. Nick lived in a house that was like two houses connected in the middle. Each side was a separate home, but they had identical front doors, windows and porches.

Sam followed Nick inside as he carried the stuff from Home Depot. His phone started buzzing; Nick looked down at the caller ID and grimaced. "I gotta take this," he said, "just stay here a minute, okay?" Then, without waiting for an answer, he disappeared from the kitchen to the back of the house, leaving her alone.

Sam leaned against the kitchen counter and brushed her hair behind her ears; it always made her nervous to be in someone's house for the first time. She was never quite sure how to act. Her mother always stressed the importance of being polite, and Sam had trouble even taking a seat in a house she'd never been in without first being invited to. And to be alone in a room was torture. She didn't want to give off an impression like she was snooping around or acting like she owned the place.

She knew these feelings were irrational and silly. Knew that, for instance, Nick wouldn't get mad if he came back into the kitchen to find her sitting at the table; but that sort of rational thinking never actually held up when she found herself in the moment. Part of the miracle of Nick was that he was in her house and her car, everything was on her turf. She could be herself around him because she was always so sure of her physical surroundings. At no point was anyone ever going to barge into her kitchen and ask her what she was doing there.

As if on cue, the back door opened, and a woman walked into the kitchen carrying two grocery bags. She threw Sam a curious glance, put the bags on the counter.

"And you would be…?" she said.

"My name's, uh," Sam stood straight up, anxiety flooding her, "my name's Sam." She pointed toward the doorway Nick had disappeared through, "I'm just waiting for Nick."

The woman snapped her fingers and pointed at Sam, a sort of smirk on her face. "Of course you are," she said.

Whoever this woman was, she didn't seem too happy to find Sam in her kitchen. Sam tried to explain herself, "Nick's working on my house, like, contracting work? And he's teaching me how to drive."

The woman was putting groceries away, not looking at Sam. "I'll bet he is," she said.

How had she pissed this woman off so quickly? Maybe she was already in a bad mood, or mad at Nick about something else, or maybe mad at Nick for bringing Sam over? Oh God, was this Nick's girlfriend? Nick hadn't mentioned a girlfriend, but maybe this was her and she was super-jealous and suspicious or something.

"Are you, um, his girlfriend?"

The woman laughed a short loud bark. "No," she said. "God. No. I'm his aunt. I live with him; or, more like he lives with me. My name's Val."

Sam was relieved. "Right! The one he watched *Stardust* with!"

Val turned her attention back on Sam, "Sorry?"

Somehow, Sam messed up again. "*Stardust*, the... Claire Danes was in it. He told me you liked her cause of *My So-Called Life*, and you guys went to see it?"

Val frowned and nodded, "Right, *My So-Called Life*, sure, why not? Use whatever's handy I suppose." She chuckled and shook her head again. Then, she plugged her MP3 player portable speakers by the fridge. She fiddled with it a minute; then a song came on that Sam recognized.

Sam was very confused. No matter what she said to Val, it was wrong. She stood there silently, miserable. Where was Nick? She wanted to get out of there. At least there was music she knew and could concentrate on. Without thinking about it, she sang quietly along: *I am the son/ and the heir/ Of a shyness that is criminally vulgar/ I am the son and heir/ Of nothing in particular.*

This time Val looked at her with open hostility. She said, "What, did Nick tell you I was a big Smiths fan too?"

"What? I don't know what you mean."

"The song," Val said. "You were singing it."

"Yeah," Sam said, "I love this song. I used to listen to it all the time."

"Are you fucking with me?"

"Why would I..." She couldn't bring herself to actually use the word *fuck*; God she was such a baby, "do that?"

"This is one of Nick's weird jokes, right? If it is, I'm gonna put him through a wall."

How could this possibly be a joke? What was even funny about it? "I don't... I don't understand..."

"Like you told Nick you liked the Smiths, and he told you to tell me if we ever met so I wouldn't give him shit or something?"

"I just like the song, I don't know who does it. I wasn't *told* to do anything." Sam was trying not to cry now; she really felt like she might lose it.

"Wait, you don't know who The Smiths are? How do you know the song then? How did you" - she did an exaggerated impression of Sam's voice - "'listen to it all the time?'"

"*The Wedding Singer,*" Sam said. "It's on the soundtrack."

"Figures," Val sneered, turning back to her cabinets, "fucking soundtrack."

So now there was a problem with *how* she knew the song? Did that make her some kind of a poseur? She never *said* she was anything! Sam couldn't hold it back anymore, her throat started to close, tears welled up in her eyes.

Val turned back and saw Sam's face. "Hey, whoa, Jesus, don't cry," she said, "I'm not… I was just being a bitch, okay? I'm sorry, it's just, it's been a week, you know? And when I came in and you were in here and I didn't know who you were… but that's, that's not an excuse. I really am sorry. Yelling at a kid for no reason, *Jesus,* what am I? Look, let's just, let's start over, okay?"

Sam wasn't sure she wanted to start over with this girl; she was mean. Still she was in her house. "Okay," she said.

"Hi," Val said and walked across the kitchen to Sam, hand outstretched, "I'm Val."

Sam took her hand, shook it, "Sam."

"Hi Sam," said Val. "You're a friend of Nick's, right?"

Sam sniffed, nodded.

"Well, any friend of Nick's," Val said. "Sit down."

Sam sat down on a wooden chair next to the table.

"Did you want something to eat or something?"

Sam shook her head.

"You sure? I got cookies…"

"That's okay."

"C'mon, I was just awful to you for no reason; the least I can do is feed you some junk food."

Sam fought back a smile. "Okay," she said. So maybe this girl wasn't all bad.

Val pulled a bag of Oreos from a cabinet. "So that's the only Smiths you know?" All Val's anger was gone now; she spread a handful of cookies across a plate and poured a glass of milk into a plastic cup.

"I guess, I mean, maybe not. Maybe I've heard other stuff and just not known it was them, you know?"

"You've never heard *Please Please Please*, or *Pretty Girls Make Graves*, or *There is a Light That Never Goes Out*? You've never heard any of those?" Val put the plate of cookies and cup of milk on the table in front of Sam

Sam picked up an Oreo, took a bite. She shook her head, "Should I have?"

"YES!" Val shouted and threw her hands in the air. "They're totally amazing songs! And The Smiths are the best band in the world! Like, ever!"

"Okay," Sam laughed now, "I believe you. Where should I start?"

"Where should you start? With all of them, every album, there's no-" she cut herself off - "you know what, I'll make you a CD, okay? I'll make you a CD and I'll give it to Nick and he can give it to you and you can listen to it, okay? How's that sound? Do kids still do that? Listen to CDs?"

"Not really," said Sam. "But you can make it if you want to. I'd like that."

"You'd like what?" Nick walked back into the room.

"Val's making me a Smiths mix," Sam said.

Nick rolled his eyes, "Awesome, another little dark fairy in the world."

"Nick doesn't like anything that isn't crotch-rock or grunge," Val said. "If it's not Guns N' Roses or Nirvana or something like that, it's off his radar."

"Oh my God, you're right," Sam said laughing, "I was playing music when we were driving, and he kept making these faces the whole time."

Val laughed too.

"Yeah, okay," Nick said, "not everyone likes English guys singing about comas or whatever."

"Whatever's right," Val said. "Where've you been, anyway? It's rude to leave someone standing in a strange house, what the fuck is wrong with you?"

"It was just for a minute. Dana's been calling all day. I just needed to see what she wanted."

"Who's Dana?" Sam asked.

Val mouthed the word *girlfriend.* Sam's heart sank a little.

"She's not my girlfriend," Nick said. "I mean, yes, okay, technically she sort of is. But…" he trailed off.

"But nothing," Val said, "she's your girlfriend. End of story."

"I don't want to get into this with you right now," Nick said. He turned to Sam, "You ready to go?"

Val said, "Are you gonna apologize for making her stand here while you were talking to your girlfriend first?"

Nick glared at his aunt, "What are you, my mom?"

"It's okay," said Sam, "I didn't mind."

"Anyway," Nick said, "if that's everything," he looked back at Val who smiled at him innocently. "Sam, are you ready to go?"

"Sure."

"All right then, let's get out of here."

"Bye Val," said Sam. "It was nice to meet you."

"It was nice to meet you too Sam," she said. "I'll get that CD to you soon."

Sam followed Nick outside to the car. So, on the one hand, she made friends with Nick's scary sister/aunt. That was good. On the other hand, turned out he had a girlfriend. That was disappointing. But, it didn't sound like he was too keen on her either.

That was something.

# LITTLE GIRLS

"I don't like how much time you're spending there." Dinner was done, they were walking back to Nick's truck, and she finally started talking about whatever it was that pissed her off this time. Whatever it was that caused the angry bitchy Dana to show up, as opposed to the sullen, pouty Dana he usually got when she was unhappy.

"What?" Nick tried not to laugh in Dana's face, but she made it hard. This was why she was so touchy all night? Why she barely ate anything at dinner and was so quiet? It was because of his job? Unreal.

"You heard me," she said. "Every time I call you're with those people. I don't like it."

Nick rubbed his eyes with his thumb and forefinger. "Dana, I work for 'those people.' It's how I make money to do things like take you to dinner."

"It's how you make money? By, just hanging out with those people? You're being paid to take that girl driving every night?"

He told himself that couldn't be it, that he misheard her. "You have to be kidding Dana; tell me you're kidding, and you're not mad because I'm teaching someone how to drive."

"I'm mad," she said, "because when I call you, on a *Saturday*, that *girl* is at your house. And then, when we're out at dinner the next night, you go on and on about how your aunt, who I'm barely allowed to spend any time with, and is like your *best friend*, is making her a mix? How am I supposed to feel about that?"

Christ. This was jealousy. She was jealous of a sixteen-year-old girl. "So there's something wrong with me trying to be nice to someone now, with Val being nice to someone? That's wrong too? I have no control over who Val likes and doesn't like, or who she talks to, in her own home. I didn't know she was gonna come home, Dana; I just had to stop by and drop off some stuff. We would have been in and out of there if *you* hadn't called and needed to talk. If you're gonna get mad at someone for that, get mad at yourself."

"Well, why were you out there with that girl in the first place?"

Well, that had no effect; he responds reasonably, she changes the subject. Classic Dana. "You never told me teaching someone how to drive a car was one of the things I wasn't allowed to do."

Dana laughed, because she got to do that; Nick had to stifle his laughter because he had to be the adult. He bobbed and weaved like a goddamn butterfly in the breeze while she could say whatever she wanted, because she was the irrational one, the childish one. And God forbid the adult ever got to call the child out on her bullshit. "It's not about that and you know it," she said.

"No Dana, I only know what you tell me. You just told me it was about my teaching Sam to drive, so that's what I'm gonna respond to. The next thing you tell me it's about, I'll respond to that."

"That's right," she said, wild-eyed, "I'm a crazy irrational bitch who's gonna freak out about whatever she wants to freak out about."

"I just said I can only respond to what you tell me is bothering you." It was true.

"Well now I want to talk about that girl. She's what's bothering me."

"Would you stop calling her 'that girl'? God, Dana, you make it sound like, like…" he trailed off.

"Yeah, I do." Dana said. "Because that's what it looks like."

"Jesus Dana, she's a *child*, okay? A child." It was all such a charade. He couldn't just say *you're being ridiculous. Think about it—if your jealous thoughts were correct, about my making a move on a child, I could go to jail.* If he said anything like that, though, it would give the idea some kind of credence, like he's already considered it or something.

"She's sixteen Nick."

No shit. “Yeah, sixteen, a child. Under the law and everything, one who’s stressed because she’s fighting with her mom and her dad’s gone and I’m just helping out. So whatever you’re worried about, just put it out of your head.”

She practically growled. “And I’m sure the law’s the only thing keeping you away from her.”

“*Dana!*” He was trying so hard not to lose it; if she were a guy he would have put her through the fucking wall for saying something like that, but, a girl was allowed to go off on these paranoid flights of fancy. He leaned his elbows against the hood of his truck, held his head in his hands. Tried to keep it together. Why was she trying so hard to make him into the bad guy? “Jesus, watch yourself. That’s really over the line.”

“So, you’re telling me, if this girl was two years older, you wouldn’t at least be thinking about it?”

“Dana, I’m not kidding, I’m not going down this road with you. No way. No how.”

“Just answer me one thing, Nick, can you do that for me? Just tell me this, what does she look like?”

“What?”

“Did I stutter? What. Does. She. Look. Like?”

“Like, I don’t know, like a girl.”

“Is she cute?”

“What? Dana she’s a little girl.”

“*Is she cute?*”

“I don’t believe we’re having this conversation.”

“Let me tell you something - if a girl asks a guy if another girl’s cute, and he refuses to answer? That means she is.”

Nick threw his hands up in frustration.

Dana did the same, mocking him. “That’s it?” She said, her eyes welling up, “Don’t know what to say to that? Here, this is all you have to say, tell me she’s not cute. That’s all. Say she’s, like, two hundred pounds, or has a big birthmark on her face or a big nose or something. Can you do that?"

Nick ran his hands through his hair, "Dana," he said, "My not answering your question is not proof that she's cute. I'm not answering because what she looks like has nothing to do with anything. You shouldn't care what she looks like because I don't, because, and I'm only going to say this one more time, *she's a child.*"

"So she's cute."

Nick wanted to scream.

"I knew it," Dana said, as the tears started down her cheeks, "no one ever goes out of their way to help ugly girls."

He wanted to feel bad that she was upset and angry enough to actually cry. But he couldn't, because no matter how mad she was, it was all in her head, and there was nothing he could do about any of it. But she was taking it out on him, and that made him angry. "Dana," Nick said, "whenever you come down off whatever crazy mountain you've decided to climb tonight, you're gonna feel so stupid about all this."

"Probably," she said, "probably I will. But even if I do, and I manage to convince myself that I was being stupid? *I'll still have been right.*"

She turned and walked away from him. He didn't follow.

What was going on?

First Val got on him about Sam, and now Dana. Seduce a sixteen-year-old girl? How could they think he was capable of something like that? Val was nicer about it, sort of, or at least she didn't try to make him feel like as much of a dirt bag. He tried to put it behind him, to look at Val's little lecture as misguided but basically good-hearted. She was just trying to make sure that Sam wasn't going to get hurt, he could respect that. But now Dana came at him with the same shit, but way nastier.

"Cute kid," Val said when Nick returned from dropping Sam off the day before.

"Yeah, she's all right."

"You're not into her right?"

"Val, don't be stupid."

"Cause you know she's into you, right?"

"What did I just say about being stupid?"

"I'm just telling you what's what."

"How could you possibly know anything after talking to her for just two minutes?"

Val rolled her eyes, "I didn't have to talk to her at all to see it. Just don't do anything you're gonna regret later. I mean, I know that's kind of your specialty, but just this once."

"Hey," Nick said, "I'm not the one making her mixes."

"Like I said, she's a cute kid. So don't fuck anything up." And that said, she turned and left the room.

So Nick had no real desire to go home and see Val, but he didn't have anywhere else to go. The original plan was spending the night at Dana's, but that obviously wasn't happening. He could go to a bar if he wanted, just have one drink andsee what games were on. But he wasn't fooling anyone. The mood he was in, there was no way he was just having one drink; he'd lose the whole night in there. There wasn't much worse than working hung over. So maybe he'd take tomorrow off; would that be so bad? He was supposed to start on the Hellers' downstairs bathroom, replacing some of the pipes in the sink, but he could put it off until Tuesday.

But no, that wouldn't be fair to Liz. He might not have much to be proud of these days, but when he said he was going to do something, he did it. His reputation as a contractor was sterling; he wasn't going to do anything to damage that. Once you start slacking, it was hard to stop.

And he was supposed to take Sam driving too.

A surge of guilt washed over him, followed immediately by anger. Why was he feeling guilty about something that he knew was perfectly innocent? Why did he let Dana and Val get to him? And why were they so eager to demonize him anyway? He was only trying to help out where he was needed, just like he did at home. What was wrong with that?

His anger bounced back and forth between Val and Dana. On the one hand, Val's accusations hurt because she should know him better. She seemed to be saying he couldn't see what was going on right in front of him, which was pretty insulting. It was possible that maybe Sam had some sort of harmless crush on him, sure, but that was all it was, harmless. It was possible to think someone was cute or nice or whatever without wanting it to go anywhere. And he had no intention of taking advantage, if she even had a crush on him. He'd been around plenty of girls who had crushes on him where nothing happened. On the other hand, Val was looking out for his best interests. Even if she was suggesting what she was suggesting, it came from a place of love and concern. And she wanted to make sure Sam didn't get hurt. In a way, he and Val were on the same page; they wanted what was best for Sam.

Dana though, she didn't want what was best for Sam. She didn't want what was best for Nick either, or for anybody who wasn't herself. She saw Sam as competition, which was twisted and sick. Dana didn't care that Sam was just a kid, didn't care that she needed to be helped out and looked after the way all kids do. She didn't want Sam to get in the way of her spending time with Nick, and if she did, then she was Dana's enemy.

Maybe she really didn't want him to have any kind of life outside of her. Maybe she didn't want him to feel good about himself. Dana was unhappy, that was just the truth, and she liked it that way. She loved the drama that came with misery. And she made Nick's life miserable because it was the only way she knew to be close to him. His happiness with anyone else was a threat to her.

The more Nick thought about it, the more sense it made. He felt so good after spending time with the Hellers. He liked helping them. He said as much to Dana, and she was weird about it.

Whereas, if she came to him and said she found something that made her feel good about herself, he would be happy for her. That was a normal reaction. But Dana was concerned, upset almost. It seemed odd to him, but he figured she was upset about something else. Only, the weirdness never stopped. Every time he talked about the Hellers, she became quiet and squirmy. He could ignore it until tonight, when he finally pushed her to tell him what was wrong and everything blew up.

As childish and selfish as Dana could be, he never would have thought she was capable of this. To actually be angry at Nick just because he was feeling good about himself, and to channel that anger into rage and jealousy at an innocent girl. It was terrible. And, ironically, it confirmed exactly why he liked spending time with Liz and her family so much. It underlined why he was starting to prefer spending time with the Hellers over just about anywhere else.

They didn't play games like Dana did, or make cruel accusations like Val. They accepted him and liked him as he was. Liz liked him because he showed up on time, did his job, and was nice to her kids. Sam liked him because he treated her with respect and took her driving. Oscar liked him because, well, it seemed like Oscar liked everyone, but that was okay too. The point was, he did what he was supposed to, and they were grateful. He could talk to them, be himself, and they didn't judge him. Unlike Dana and Val, who read into everything he said and did in order to tease out the darkest possible interpretation. The Hellers treated him more like family than his actual family did.

There was nothing he could do about Val. She was the way she was and nothing could ever change that. And she was the closest thing he had to a sister and he loved her. But Dana, something needed to change there.

Maybe Liz was right.

She said Dana was a head case, setting Nick up to fail by asking him to be something else. Liz said Dana didn't have a father so she dated Nick because he was older than her and she could punish him in ways that she couldn't punish her dad. She said Dana was passive aggressive and put him in positions where she knew he would act badly so that she could feel sorry for herself. It made a lot of sense. Nick thought how nice it was to have someone who listened to him and didn't immediately think he was the bad guy.

Nick's phone buzzed to life on the passenger seat. It was Dana. Nick debated not picking it up, but she knew he had his phone with him, and would keep calling, getting angrier and angrier until he did. Better to get the conversation over with. Just try to pacify her, calm her down, maybe spend the night over there after all. Things would be better in the morning.

"Why don't you break up with me?"

Okay, no beating around the bush. Not even a hello. Fine, if that was how it was going to be, that was how it was going to be. "I don't know Dana, you seem to have all the answers today, why don't you tell me?"

"See, I've been thinking about it, and I really don't know. I mean, do you even like me at all?"

"Of course I do, don't be ridiculous."

"I don't think you do. People don't treat people they like the way you treat me."

There was no right answer to that. "Dana, I like you."

"Really," she spat, "what do you like about me?"

"Look, I like you, okay? You're asking me right now, in the middle of a fight, what I like about you and I'm not going to be able to think of much. No one can do that, it's why we're fighting. I mean, do you like me right now?"

"No," she said, "I don't. I really, really don't."

"Well there you go. It's hard to remember why you like someone when you're mad at them."

"But that's the thing. I don't think I like you much when I'm not mad at you either. I used to like you a lot, before I got to know you. I used to think you were interesting and sad and beautiful. But now, now I don't know anymore. But I do know that you definitely don't like me."

"Dana, if I didn't like you, why would I still be with you?"

"I don't know, because I let you be mean to me and still let you have sex with me?"

"Wow. Okay." He let that sink in. Let it roll around in his head for a minute. "So, if you think that's what I think about you, and you clearly don't think much of me, I think the question isn't why am I still with you. It's why are you with me?"

"Because," her voice cracked, she was starting to cry, "I fell in love with you before I realized what an asshole you were, and now I can't break up with you."

She'd never said that before. "Dana-"

She cut him off. "I know you're an asshole, and I know you don't like me, that you probably never did, and I don't like you anymore. I know all that, but I can't seem to stop loving you."

He was speechless. It had been a long time since someone told him they loved him.

"So I keep doing this, letting you hurt me and getting mad and forgiving you and letting you fuck me, because I love you and I need you."

He was really out of his depth.

"So, I'm asking you, please, just break up with me; because I don't have the strength to break up with you."

"Look-"

"No, Nick, no 'look', just tell me it's over and walk away. I can't take it anymore; I can't keep feeling this way. It's killing me Nick, it's killing me."

Suddenly, Nick was angry. No. More than angry, he was furious. She had the nerve, to say that to him. To drop that bomb, and then tell him it was killing her? She could be that melodramatic, that selfish, that cruel? Did she have the slightest idea what hearing her say that would do to him? Did she even care? Of course not, because all Dana cared about was herself, and her stupid fucking psycho-drama. She wanted to break up with him, but she still wanted to be the victim.

Enough. He wasn't going to be her bad guy any more.

"You know what Dana? No. If this relationship is so bad for you, and hurts you so much, then you can end it. I'm not gonna be your bagman."

"Please, I don't want-"

He cut her off. If he wasn't allowed to talk when she was giving her little soliloquy, then she couldn't talk during his. "I'm tired of your bullshit, Dana. If you want this to be over, you're gonna have to pull the trigger yourself. I'm not your dad."

"I never said-"

"I'm not your dad Dana," God that felt good to say, "I'm not your dad, and you're a big girl who can make her own decisions. You figure out what you want to do. Then you can call me." He snapped the phone shut and tossed it on the seat beside him. Then he had a better idea, he grabbed his phone, and *turned it off.* He wasn't going to turn it on until the morning. Maybe he'd even wait until the afternoon. See how she likes that.

He drove home feeling really good; he was finally standing up to her. That night he slept well, and when he woke up the next morning the good feeling remained. It stayed with him all through the day. He told Liz about the night before and how Dana tried to manipulate him into breaking up with her and how he stood his ground. Liz said it sounded like it was a hard night, but also like he made the right decision. She said Dana needed to learn to take responsibility for her own feelings and stop blaming him for everything.

Nick didn't turn his phone on until after he took Sam driving. She was going to see her dad in Chicago that weekend, and couldn't stop talking about it. How stressed she was about the whole thing, how she was glad to get to see her dad and to get away from her mom (they got into another fight—Sam missed curfew a few times, but only by, like, ten minutes, and her mom was pissed about it. She was gonna be seventeen in *three weeks*, when was her mom gonna stop micro-managing her whole life?), but how she didn't want to move to Chicago and how that made the whole thing so awkward. Nick sat there the whole time, listening, letting her vent. See Dana? He wasn't such an asshole; he cared about other people, listened to their problems. People liked him, and he liked other people. It wasn't that complicated.

Loving him was killing her. What a bitch.

When he finally turned on his phone there were four messages from Dana, each one more desperate than the last. By the last one she was in tears, saying he was right about everything, apologizing for everything she said, begging for his forgiveness. She'd do anything he wanted, *be* anything he wanted. Just please, call her back.

Nick smiled.

Now they were getting somewhere.

# ANTS

Sam shook the last ice cube from the little plastic cup into her mouth, then crushed the cup and put it in the pocket of the seat in front of her. She pressed her forehead against the window and looked down at the ground crawling by far below her.

Everything looked so small from up in a plane. It was one of those trite observations that drove Sam nuts whenever she flew anywhere because she couldn't help thinking it with profound amazement. Because it was true. Everything really did look so small. Sam got the window seat whenever she could and, when the plane finally lifted off, kept her eyes glued to the tarmac, watching the earth fall farther and farther away. She picked a point on the ground and focused on it for as long as she could. Then, she switched to roads – watched how the cars on a big wide interstate slowly looked less and less real, and more like abstractions of cars, like toy cars. And then she wouldn't be able to see any cars all. Just road. It was the same with houses. First, she was able to see all the houses, then just the big ones, lots of them with pools (Sam always wanted a pool); then, only big clusters of buildings.

She knew life went on down there of course, that she was speeding over it from such a great height that it became indistinguishable from itself.

Oscar slept in the seat next to her, his legs sprawled across the front of his chair, his arms at his sides and his head hanging limply. A small string of spit hung from his open mouth.

Sam admired her brother's ability to fall asleep at the drop of a hat. He slept in cars, on buses, trains, and when he was young, the baby seat on the back of a bicycle. Conditions had to be close to perfect for her to drift off. It was one of the few traits she shared with her mother. And a hard airplane seat that wouldn't recline no matter how hard she pushed the button, was far from a perfect condition. She wasn't tired, anyway; it wasn't even five o'clock.

She opened *White Noise,* the book she bought specifically for the flight home, but fifty pages in and it still wasn't interesting. She picked it because she read somewhere that it was considered to be one of the best books of the last fifty years. So far she couldn't see why. It was just pages and pages of lists of things that a guy saw at a grocery store. Sam closed the book, put in her headphones, started *The Queen is Dead*, and returned to the window.

Her dad explained to her once, that one of the ways the brain developed had to do with a person's ability to recognize the independent existence of other people separate from the individual person's perception of them. He talked about how, like, when there's a little baby, and someone plays peek-a-boo and the baby gets all excited and amazed, it was because the baby really thought the person popped out of existence for that second. They were just *gone*. If you saw someone pop in and out of existence you'd probably be pretty amazed too, right? No wonder it was so hard to disobey her parents; they were sorcerers for the first couple years of her life.

Anyway.

Her dad said that was one of the first ways people understand reality: what they see is, and what they don't see isn't. The next step, he said, had to do with understanding other things in relation to the person. So, if a baby or toddler is in a tall building or plane, and they see all the little people running around like ants, they think that's how small the people are. The kid just thinks they're little people running around down there.

The next step is when the little kid thinks that the little people are big people who got little because the little kid went far away from them. This one was a little more advanced because it started to introduce the idea of spatial relations. That kid thinks that the act of walking towards a person actually makes them larger. Or coming down on an airplane makes the city grow. Everything is relative to the person, who is the only constant in the universe.

The last step is the realization that, no, it's the perception of the individual that makes it seem like the other person or building or whatever is getting bigger or smaller. The last step is when you realize that the distance you have from something affects how you perceive it. All that growth happens in the first couple of years when you're learning to walk and talk and stuff, which made sense to Sam, because the more you actually get to interact with the world, the more of an understanding you get of how it actually works.

Her dad told her all that years ago, and she wasn't sure if she remembered it exactly right, but the important part, at least to her, was that she always remembered. The importance was that things rarely change. What changes is how you see something based on your distance from it.

Sam sat in her seat on the plane, headed back home to Baxter. She pushed her head against the glass trying to watch the people she couldn't see, but who she knew were there, and thought about the weekend she had just spent with her dad in Chicago.

She had mixed feelings about the visit. In the weeks since she learned of the move, and since her dad left, she tried to make peace with the idea, tried to minimize the loss she felt, and looked for any possible upsides. She thought about getting the car, a sense of freedom. She thought about how, if they weren't moving, she wouldn't have gotten to know Nick or Val, wouldn't be close to getting her license. She repeated to herself that it was just a year, then she could decide where to live for the rest of her life. She could go back to Baxter if she wanted to, go to the college or just live there and commute to another area school. But no matter how many ways she looked at it, she couldn't get the math to add up. The loss she felt from leaving always dwarfed the benefits she managed to find. She just didn't want to move to Chicago.

But her dad was already there. Her poor, lonely daddy. Cut off from his family and friends, all by himself in a big lonely city. He was being punished, all because her mother got it in her head, for whatever stupid reason, that a new life, a new beginning, was needed.

Sam missed her dad so much. She talked to him every day, unless he was too busy with work. But on those days he at least texted her to apologize and tell her how much he missed her and was looking forward to her visit. He worked extra hard so he could spend Memorial Day weekend with her and Oscar.

Sam wanted her dad to be happy, wanted to have a good trip for his sake. And at least she would get away from her mother. Every time she talked to her dad and heard his sad tone, or saw his tired eyes and the bare walls behind him over Skype, she got a little angrier at her mother for putting them all in this situation.

And the madder she got, the harder it was to simply live with her mother. Everything she said and did drove Sam nuts. So Sam started fighting back; started standing up for herself. If, in her mother's judgment, it was in her family's best interest to be ripped apart and her husband to be buried in work halfway across the country, then maybe her judgment was not very good at all. Maybe her mother wasn't so worthy of her respect.

The bottom line was, Sam didn't like being angry. She didn't like holding grudges. She *wanted* to enjoy Chicago despite all the reasons against it. She knew kids who held onto pain and anger like it was their best friend. They dressed in black and were sullen and hostile, behaving exactly the way she imagined angry teenagers would behave. It was frankly embarrassing how many kids wallowed in misery, thinking it made them special, when in fact that behavior made them indistinguishable from one another. She never wanted to be one of those kids.

Their dad met them at the airport just past the security check point. They saw him standing there, at the end of a long hallway, his neck craning as he tried to spot them through the crowd.

"Dad!" Oscar shouted, tugging on Sam's shirt and pointing, "It's Dad!" Then he broke into a run.

Sam's instinct was to run too, but she didn't. She wanted to stretch the moment out, savor it. She watched her dad as his face lit up when he saw Oscar and then scooped him up in a big bear hug. Oscar, now in his father's arm, said something to him and pointed to her. Her dad followed Oscar's gesture, and at last saw Sam. Their eyes met, and he smiled.

But it wasn't the same smile that he gave Oscar. His smile for Oscar was big and bright, the kind given to a child. Sam's smile was different. It was calmer, as if a great tension lifted just by seeing her with his own eyes again. Sam smiled the exact same way right back at him. She was with her dad again. Finally. Her dad wrapped his free arm around Sam and she buried her face in his shoulder.

"Hi Daddy," she said and began to cry. "Missed you."

"Missed you too, kid. I missed both of you so much. But now you're here, and we have the whole weekend ahead of us. What do you guys want to do first?"

"I don't know," Sam let go of her dad and wiped her eyes and nose. "Oh," she said, "I got your shirt wet."

"That's okay," he said. "I've got more. How about you Oscar, what do you want to do?"

Oscar thought it over and said, "I'm hungry."

"Of course you are. Let's eat! How does pizza sound?"

"Pizza!" cried Oscar.

"That sounds like a yes to me," their dad said. "Sam, how does it sound to you?"

Sam felt herself beam; it was just like it used to be, like it was supposed to be. "It sounds great."

"Great! And not just any old pizza either, we're going to have special pizza."

"Special pizza? Special how?" Oscar asked, his eyes wide with curiosity.

"Special Chicago style deep dish pizza. It's like… super pizza. You're going to love it, promise."

"Whoa," said Oscar, his mind blown.

"Now," their dad said, "do we need to pick up any luggage or anything before we head out?"

Sam shook her head, "It was all carry on."

"Travel light, I love it." Then he paused, "But didn't Mom want you to pack a bag of stuff to leave here?"

"She did, but I never got around to it."

"Bet she didn't like that."

Sam shrugged, "What can I say, I got places to be, things to do."

"My baby's in demand." He put his arm around her and the three of them started toward the exit. "How could it be any other way?"

They took the shuttle to their dad's car, a brand new black Audi with GPS and a phone dock and all sorts of other cool stuff, which was okay. But, in the back seat there was a little cooler, and in the cooler was a cherry Dr. Pepper just for her. *That* was impressive. Sam sat in the passenger seat, twisted off the top of the soda, and took a long satisfying drink.

"So," her dad said after they'd been driving for a few minutes and Oscar had passed out in the back seat, "Did you bring your permit with you?"

"Uh-huh."

"Maybe we could go out tomorrow for a little if you want."

"Maybe," she said, "I haven't really done much city driving though."

"Then this is a perfect opportunity to learn," he said. "Your mom says you're getting a lot of practice at home. How's it coming? Still worried about fifteen miles an hour collisions?"

She grinned. "Not so much these days," she said. "I should have my fifty hours soon."

"Given any thought to what kind of car you might want to get?"

"Not too much. The only thing I was thinking was maybe I'd get something with a stick shift."

"Really," her dad said. "That's news. What made you think you might want that?"

"I dunno," Sam said as gazed out the window, "I like the idea of having more control, especially in bad weather."

Her dad nodded, "Good thinking. Are you learning on a stick now though?"

"No, I'm using your old car."

"You'd have to find someone to teach you I guess."

"You don't know how to drive stick?"

He shook his head, "Never learned. Your mom either."

"I wouldn't use her even if I could; she'd freak the first time I stalled out, and I'd have a panic attack and never drive again."

Her dad chuckled, "You're probably right," he said, "but if it's what you want we'll figure out a way to make it happen. How hard can it be?"

The house her dad bought, the house that was going to be her house in a matter of months, was in Hyde Park, just off Lake Michigan. Her dad graduated law school nearby at The University of Chicago. Driving around the area her dad pointed out the various landmarks both personal ("your mom and I used to eat there all the time, really excellent sweet and sour chicken.") and historical ("That's the house Obama lived in when he taught here.")

He pointed out all the beautiful old brick mansions that sat on tree lined streets. He told her about the history of the place, how it was the place for old money back in the early twentieth century. Then, he said, it went through some hard times in the seventies and eighties, but things settled down thanks, in no small part, to its private police force. In fact, Hyde Park had the second largest private police force in the world, after the Vatican.

Her dad talked about the presence of the University in the area, how long it had been there and how it actually owned a lot of the land in Hyde Park. He talked about it being one of the top law schools in the country (like Sam didn't already know that. Every year when U.S. News released its law school rankings her dad rushed out to pick it up, and if it wasn't in the top five, he was inconsolable for weeks.) He said the public school system wasn't that great but he was sure he could get Sam and Oscar into the area Lab schools, private schools that were connected to U of Chicago.

Sam wasn't sure about that last bit. She'd gone to public school her whole life and this whole transition was going to be tough enough without dealing with stuck up rich kids.

Finally, they pulled up to the house. Sam was impressed. First of all, it was big, not that her house back home was small, but this house was Big. Like three stories big, built from massive grey stones and burgundy siding, with great big windows and a big chimney running up the side. Just, Big. It was flanked by tall trees and there was even a modest yard surrounded by a fence, which her dad described as *wrought iron*. Sam looked at the house and had to admit, it looked exciting.

Inside was a different story. It might have been funny how modestly her dad was living in such a large house if it weren't so sad. Sam walked through empty room after empty room, no furniture, no pictures on the walls, no bookshelves or books or lamps or rugs or anything. Dust sparkled in beams of light that poured in through the curtainless windows, and the sound of her footsteps bounced off the hardwood floors. There were a few items in the kitchen, paper plates, a bowl, plastic silverware, milk and beer in the fridge, peanut butter, bread, and cereal. The garbage can overflowed with Chinese takeout containers and pizza boxes.

Two rooms had air mattresses for them to sleep on, while their dad had a futon set up in the master bedroom. The bathroom next to her room was spotless, folded towels rested on the counter next to the sink, and an unopened package of toilet paper sat on top of the towels. Every room was just waiting for their stuff to be shipped over from Baxter to fill it up and make it their home.

But it wouldn't be.

This was not her house, and no matter how they dressed it up, it never would be. They could re-create her room down to the cracks in the paint and the dust bunnies in corner, but it still wouldn't be her room. It would never be more than a hollow reproduction. What made her house, *her house,* wasn't the stuff inside it; it was the experiences she had there. The life she lived. You can't just move that. And to suggest otherwise would be... disrespectful. Sam's home meant too much to her for her to disrespect it like that. She'd live in this house for a year, because she had to. But it would never be her home.

The only place in the house that looked even remotely inhabited was the living room. There was a black leather couch and matching easy chair. A coffee table sat in front of the couch that already had a couple of coffee ring stains. Against the wall opposite the couch, a giant TV hung from the wall and below it was an intricate looking sound system, wirelessly connected to sleek speakers around the room. Or at least that was what her dad said. He went on for a while about the setup of the room, about the TV, how it was 3D and it could surf the internet and stream Netflix and a bunch of other stuff he hadn't figured out yet. He also got a 3D Blu-Ray player, some 3D movies, and a bunch of glasses. It was all some sort of package. Sam didn't understand most of it, and what she did understand, she didn't really care about. She went to a couple of 3D movies and thought the effect was pointless and sort of annoying. Plus, she hated the glasses.

But her dad wanted to use the glasses to watch one of the movies he bought and he wanted to do so with them. It was why he bought the system in the first place. He said, that the guy at the store said, that most of the really good 3D movies were family films, animated stuff, so he got a bunch of those. He envisioned many nights of the whole family sitting around the couch enjoying the 3D together.

They ordered pizza to be delivered from Giordano's, choosing a "famous" deep dish pizza and fries and mozzarella sticks and breaded mushrooms and sodas and cheese cake for dessert. It was enough food to last the entire weekend. Her dad said when he was in law school, he and their mom got pizza from Giordano's all the time. He said it was the best. Sam thought it was okay, too much sauce, and way too heavy. After one piece, she couldn't eat any more. Her dad kept asking if she wanted to try anything else and

Sam kept begging off, which was a shame because she loved breaded mushrooms. Oscar was like some sort of bottomless pit; he ate his piece of pizza and most of the fries and drank two glasses of root beer and still had room for cheese cake. Only the mushrooms went untouched. Oscar hated mushrooms; their dad didn't really care for them either, he'd pretty much gotten them just for Sam.

The 3D was pretty much a bust too. They decided on *Despicable Me*, a movie Oscar already adored. But fifteen minutes into the movie, Sam's glasses started acting up; they kept switching on and off for no reason. It was annoying, but not a huge deal – she could just read or something while Oscar and their dad finished the movie. But her dad wouldn't hear of it. He bought the 3D TV so they could all enjoy movies *as a family*. How could they enjoy it if all the glasses didn't work? He paused the movie and fiddled with the glasses, put them on the charger, maybe the batteries needed to be charged; but no, it was all charged up. He even unscrewed the glasses to get to the batteries. Sometimes with these sorts of things, he said, you just needed to take the batteries out and put them back in. Sometimes, that was all it took. Not this time; the glasses still switched off.

Oscar was cranky, his glasses worked fine, and he wanted to watch his movie. Sam said it was okay, *really*, she didn't care. She could watch the movie with the glasses off. She didn't care if the picture was a little blurry; they could figure it out later. But her dad couldn't let it go. He just bought the damn things, and they were breaking already? Unacceptable. He called tech support. They were going to get this straightened out here and now.

Oscar was near tears, but her dad kept the movie paused. Finally, Sam suggested they restart the movie? That way Oscar could still watch his movie without anyone else falling behind in the plot that they all knew by heart. Sam restarted the movie while her dad left the room, presumably so he could let the tech guy know what he thought of their product without being overheard by children.

What was going on with him? Why was he being this way? He was tense. He wasn't just going with the flow like he usually did. He was forcing things, like her mother; it was making everything worse.

Five minutes later, her dad was back, smiling. The problem, he said, wasn't with the batteries, it was with the light. If it was too bright in the room, then the glasses automatically turned off. Sam was sitting too close to the window; the light coming in caused interference. All she had to do was sit somewhere else and it would be fine. Tomorrow they would go out and get some blinds to hang so it wouldn't happen again.

Sam couldn't enjoy the movie even if her glasses worked. The whole thing was too much trouble, too much work, for something she didn't really like to begin with.

It all just felt wrong.

Later that night, Sam lay on the air mattress in the empty what-was-soon-to-be-her-room, and tried unsuccessfully to fall asleep. The emptiness of the house pierced her senses and spread into her brain. She couldn't stop seeing the bare walls, hearing the echoes in the hallways, smelling the musty odors of the undisturbed rooms. She heard activity outside the windows; there was a soft rustle of wind through the trees, the rumble of cars making their way down the street, and the soft sound of conversation between people somewhere close by.

Sam felt like crying.

Everywhere around her, just a few feet away, life was happening, but it was outside, just out of her reach. She was stuck in this sterile room in this empty house. She thought about her room back in Baxter, her warm safe room where she slept most every night of her entire life, filled with her bed and desk and all her clothes and books and music and pictures and everything that was her, and it all felt so far away. She thought about Becky; was she awake? Was she out with friends? Was she drinking in the woods, or at the benches in the square outside Baxter Pizza? Was she sitting up with her family in the living room watching TV? Or maybe she was asleep by now, in her own bed, her head resting on her favorite blue and white striped pillow she'd had since she was seven, with her ceiling fan cooling down the room.

Becky's was the first friend's house where Sam ever slept over. They were in the second grade, and it was such a big deal talking their parents into it. They stayed up until ten (again, *huge* deal) watching scary movies, and when it was time to go to sleep they crawled into Becky's bed together and drifted off, talking about all the things they were going to do the next morning. She woke up a little before midnight in a dead panic. Her parents were only a couple of miles away, but it felt like they were on the other side of the world. Suddenly, her need to see them, to have her mom kiss her on the forehead and her dad bring her a glass of water overwhelmed her. All of a sudden, things were moving much, much too fast and she needed to be in her own bed in her own room like she never needed anything before. Sam leapt from the bed and flew out of the room, her heart pounding and tears streaming down her cheeks. Becky's parents were in the living room watching TV. Sobbing, Sam confessed that she made a horrible mistake thinking she was old enough to stay away from home and she had, had, *had,* to go home *right now,* please.

Becky's parents talked her down. They said they understood, but why not sit up with them for a few minutes, try and calm down, and if after fifteen minutes she still wanted to, Becky's dad would drive her home. Sniffling, Sam agreed, sure that fifteen minutes later she would still insist on that ride home. She took a seat on the couch between Becky's parents and tried to figure out what was going on in their show. Something about a clumsy French cop whose boss hated him and a girl who might have killed someone. Only, the clumsy cop didn't think so and his butler kept attacking him and… the next thing she knew she was back in Becky's room and it was morning.

After that first night, Sam and Becky slept over at each other's houses dozens of times without incident. As they got older, they did it less and less, and when Becky got her license they pretty much stopped all together. The whole "sleeping over" thing seemed kind of silly when you could come and go as you please without needing someone else for transportation. They would hang out until Becky or Sam got too tired and then Becky would go home or take Sam home or whatever.

Now Sam would probably never sleep in that room again.

Sam wasn't sure, but she thought her brand new out-of-the-box air mattress might have a leak somewhere. It was hard to tell, but it seemed like the mattress wasn't as firm after an hour. She felt like maybe she was slowly sinking into the center of the thing. She rolled off the mattress, found the switch for the air pump and turned it on. The noise of the mattress was horrible, and she couldn't tell if it was firming up or not. She turned it off after a minute, and got back into bed, miserable.

Finally, when Sam couldn't take the naked white walls, ambient noise outside, and (possibly?) deflating air mattress anymore she got up and went to the living room, pillow in one hand, sheet in the other. She hoped to find her dad there, watching TV maybe, or working on his laptop, but he wasn't. But at least there was furniture. Sam put *Avatar* in the blu-ray player, not because she had any desire to see it again, but it was long and she hoped to fall asleep before it ended. She drifted off just as Jake was picking out his flying lizard thing.

She woke up the next morning with a crick in her neck and a cheese Danish on a paper plate waiting for her on the coffee table. Her dad and Oscar had been up for over an hour and already went to the bakery around the corner and picked up a box of pastries. Oscar was sitting on the floor, his back leaning against the table, watching cartoons and happily munching on a croissant. Her dad sat beside her in the recliner and sipped from a cup of coffee.

"Well," her dad said, "she lives. That's a relief."

"Morning," croaked Sam.

"Good morning, sweetie. How'd you sleep?"

"Not great. I had to come out here and watch TV until I finally drifted off."

"I'm sorry," her dad said. "First nights in a new place can be rough. It'll get easier though, I promise."

Sam didn't say anything, but she smiled and nodded at him sleepily. She picked her Danish off the table and took a bite. She watched Oscar's show without paying attention as she chewed.

"We've got a big day ahead of us," her dad said. "Lots to do. We're going to the pier and the museum, and the park. It's gonna be great."

"Oh Daddy," Sam said. "Can we just take it easy today? My neck's sore from sleeping on the couch and I could really use a nice low-key day. Can't we do all that stuff tomorrow?"

Her dad waved a dismissive hand at her. "You're saying that because you just woke up. All you need to do is get going, and you'll be good. Besides, I already told Oscar all about the museum and he's excited for the dinosaur exhibit, right buddy?"

Oscar nodded vigorously without taking his eyes from the TV.

"See?" Her dad winked at her, and smiled reassuringly. "We're gonna go see Sue the T-Rex; she's twelve feet tall and forty feet long. It's the best, most complete Tyrannosaurus skeleton in the whole world. We gotta go check that out, right? You can rest up tomorrow. C'mon, just get up, you'll feel like a million bucks in no time."

Sam rubbed her eyes with her palms. "Sure daddy," she said, "whatever, it's your trip." She rolled off the couch before her dad could respond, went to her room, grabbed a change of clothes and got in the shower. She wondered, as the water rinsed the bad night's sleep out of her, when her cool easy going dad had been replaced by this new model who put on a show about being relaxed, but had apparently micro-managed every second of their weekend.

And what was with using Oscar on her like that? *Oh, Oscar'll be super disappointed if he doesn't get to see his dinosaur exhibit.* How weak was that?

Weak and, as it turned out, ironic, because on their way to the Field Museum their dad got a call and said he had to make a quick stop at work. Meet up with another lawyer working on his case. The day, which wasn't going particularly well, wasn't getting any better. The pier totally sucked, nothing like walking around when you were sore already to make a bad mood worse. And it wasn't helping, Sam thought, that if she'd been able to go when she was ready, she might have actually enjoyed it. Her dad noticed she was unhappy of course, and tried to cheer her up. But if he really cared about her feelings, he wouldn't make her go out when she didn't want to. He was being such a hypocrite. And that was how she felt *before* he said he had to go to work. So, if she didn't want to do something, she had to suck it up and go with the plan, but if work needed something everything changed?

Good to know.

Their dad worked in a tall modern building downtown. He had a spot in the parking garage with his name on it. He pointed it out to Oscar, trying to impress him, but it didn't really work. Oscar didn't appreciate being jerked around when it came to dinosaurs. If it was possible, Sam was even less impressed than her little brother. She grunted responses to any questions and hung back a few steps as they walked through the lobby of his building. In the elevator, he apologized again.

"I'm really sorry about this, guys," he said, "we've got this case coming up, and I've been really swamped. I wanted to free up this weekend so it could be just the three of us, but I have to take care of this one thing, then we can get to the museum."

Oscar stared angrily ahead. He wanted to see his T-rex.

He looked at Sam. "I know," he said, reading her thoughts, "and I'm sorry."

"Hey," she said, "priorities, right?"

Her dad looked miserable. Good, she thought. Why should she be the only one?

The elevator doors opened to a really plush floor that seemed pretty full of people for a Saturday. A woman's head popped out of an office and focused in on them.

"Steve, hey," she said, "sorry to call you in on your big weekend, but I just need five minutes." She came out of the office and walked toward them. She was young, on the small side, with short brown hair, and stylishly dressed in a red, wide-collared blouse, and pre-worn jeans. Pre-worn clothes bugged Sam and so did the people who wore them; they projected an intimacy that wasn't authentic.

"It's all right, Nat, these things happen. Kids, this is Natalie, one of our associates at the firm. Nat, these are my kids. Oscar," he ruffled Oscar's hair, "and Sam."

"I know who they are," she said smiling at them. "You kids should hear how much your dad talks about you," said Natalie. "And the pictures, so many pictures. I feel like I already know you."

Oscar shook Natalie's outstretched hand dutifully.

"I really like your hair, Sam," Natalie said as she gripped Sam's hand. "Did you dye it yourself?" Natalie was smiling warmly at her. It was creepy.

"Pretty much."

"Nat, can you hang out here for a minute with these guys? I'm gonna talk to Bolano," their dad said. Then he looked at Sam and Oscar. "I'm really sorry, guys. I just need five minutes to explain something to one of my bosses," he said. "Our trial strategy. But Nat's here, and she'll get you anything you want, if you get thirsty or hungry or anything. Right, Nat?"

Natalie nodded enthusiastically. "Sure thing," she said. "We'll be fine, won't we?" She looked at them and smiled.

Sam wanted to say no, we won't be fine. She had less than no desire to make conversation with some overly friendly girl trying to score points with her dad. She wanted say to her dad, *just leave us here, alone, and take your little friend with you.* But her manners kicked in and she kept her mouth shut. Her dad spun around and hurried down the hallway and disappeared into an office.

"So," Natalie said to the two of them, "are you guys enjoying your trip to Chicago?"

"We're going to the museum to see Sue the dinosaur," said Oscar.

"Sue the dinosaur!" said Natalie in that fake high-pitched voice that people used to talk to kids and which drove Sam nuts. "That sounds exciting!

"We were supposed to go after the lake, but we had to come here instead."

Natalie frowned sympathetically. "That sounds frustrating," she said, "but I'm sure it'll only be a few minutes; then I'm sure you'll have a great time at the museum." She looked up at Sam. "What about you Sam? Are you having a good time in our city? I know your dad was really excited for you to come."

Sam scratched her shoulder, this woman's chipmunky enthusiasm made her itch. "It's okay, I guess," she said.

Natalie put her hands on her hips and scowled (did this woman have an off switch anywhere?) "Only *okay*? It's the third biggest city in the country! There's so much to see and do. How can it only be okay?"

"I don't know," said Sam, "it just is. Maybe we're not doing the right things." She didn't try very hard to keep the irritation out of her voice; Natalie's face twitched and she turned her attention back to Oscar.

"What else do you want to do besides see dinosaurs?"

"Natalie?" Sam jumped in before Oscar could respond. "Where's the bathroom?"

Natalie smiled brightly and pointed, "Just down the hall and to the left. I can take you if you want."

Sam smiled back sarcastically. "No worries. I'm sure I'll be able to find it on my own, thanks."

She didn't have to go to the bathroom; she just needed to get away before she heard another second of Natalie's fake talking. She just had to get away for a second and gather her thoughts. She thought about taking the elevator down to the lobby, going outside and catching a smoke, but it was too risky. What if her dad came out before she got back and Natalie went to get her and she wasn't in the bathroom? Or what if one of her father's co-workers saw her down there with a cigarette in her mouth and told him later? She didn't know who any of them were or what they looked like, so it wasn't like she could look out for anyone. No, it'd be better to play it safe and kill time in the bathroom for as long as she could.

Now she was hiding in bathrooms.

Awesome.

Sam pulled out her cell and dialed Becky, but her voicemail picked up right away. Probably her battery ran out and she hadn't noticed yet.

"Hey Becks," she said after the beep. "I'm just killing time in a bathroom, avoiding the most annoying woman in the world and waiting for my dad to finish talking to one his bosses so we can get back to the most annoying trip in the world. I swear to God though, if he pushes me to one more *stupid* touristy…" She paused, re-considered. "Okay, it's not that bad. It's actually, it's fine. I'm just annoyed because I didn't sleep good last night and we've been running around all day and… I'm just being stupid. So call me back later and we'll talk and I'll tell you how stupid I'm being and you can tell me I'm an idiot. Love you." She killed the call.

Sam wet her hands in the sink, ran them through her hair and looked at herself in the mirror.

Saying it out loud made her realize how she sounded, so irritated and so angry and over what? What was wrong with her today? Why was she being such a pill about everything? She could see how hard everyone at her dad's office worked, understood how much he must have busted his butt to get this weekend free. Why was she so intent on having a bad time? She was being really childish and she didn't like it.

This weekend was important. It was important to her dad, and to Oscar and her mother and it was important to her. She needed to nut up and stop being such a baby. This move was happening; she was going to be living in Chicago before the summer was over.

She needed to accept it and start finding things to like about it, because being a baby was only going to make things worse. She didn't like sleeping in an empty house for a weekend? How many nights had her dad slept there? And when he did it, he was completely alone.

And she felt like crying again.

But this time it wasn't because she was feeling sorry for herself like the night before. This time it was frustration at herself and pity for her dad. He worked so hard, all by himself, and she had the nerve to come here and give him grief because everything wasn't perfect from the get go. She was so spoiled. Spoiled and entitled. And she didn't like Natalie. Why? Because of the pants she wore? Because Natalie tried to be nice to her, make her feel welcome in a place she didn't want to be? Sam looked at herself in the mirror.

"You're being a real bitch you know," she said to the reflection.

Well, not anymore.

Her dad was back; she saw him as she came around the corner, talking and smiling with Natalie, his hand on Oscar's shoulder, holding him close.

"Hey," she said brightly as she skipped up to them.

"Hey yourself," her dad seemed a little taken aback by her improved mood, unsure how to proceed. "Ready to go?"

"If you're done here, sure."

Natalie looked down at Oscar, "So, you're going to get to see those dinosaurs huh?"

Oscar nodded, smiled.

Natalie looked back up at Sam and her dad, "Then what's on the agenda?"

Sam's dad looked at her, "After that," he said, "I don't know. Whatever Sam wants to do, I think. She's been a pretty good sport about running around, doing what we want to do; tonight, we'll do what she wants."

"Oh Daddy, it doesn't matter to me. We can do whatever you guys want."

But her dad wouldn't hear of it. "We'll figure something out. Maybe we'll get some stuff for their rooms. That could be fun, right? New stuff for the new house?"

"Sure Daddy, that sounds great."

"There's a little store a few blocks from here," Natalie said. "I pass it all the time. They've got like, weird little knick knacks and foot stools and lunch boxes and stuff like that. Maybe you guys would like it."

"Great idea Nat, thanks, that sounds perfect. You should see Sam's room in Baxter, it's so well decorated."

The old Sam, the one from just a few moments ago, would have been irritated at her dad's overly enthusiastic selling of her room. The old Sam would have found it embarrassing. The new Sam, however, rolled with it. "That's nice of him to say," the new Sam said. "But it's just a room."

"She's being modest," her dad said, "She put a lot of work into that room. I remember, a couple of years ago, Sam and her friend spent all weekend cutting pictures out of magazines. Where did that pile of magazines come from anyway?"

"I think mom got them from one of her doctor friends. They'd just been piling up in her waiting room."

"Huh," her dad said, "I don't think I knew that. Anyway, she and Becky spent all Saturday ripping out pictures, cutting out faces and images, and then on Sunday, they hung them up in Sam's room. It was really… creative."

Again, old Sam: getting more and more embarrassed at her dad's sharing of details about her private life with a stranger and using words like *creative* to do it. New Sam: cheerfully appreciative, and modest. She said, "Most of those pictures aren't even up anymore."

"You know," said Natalie, "that reminds me. Back in law school, my aunt got me a bunch of magazine subscriptions: Rolling Stone, Spin, Entertainment Weekly, that sort of stuff. I didn't have time to read actual books, so I figured I'd read magazines, which I also didn't read. But I didn't want to throw them out, so I started throwing them in this old suitcase thinking I'd read them later. For years. And I still have them. If you want, you could have them, cut out the pictures."

"Wow, Nat, that's really generous, thank you," said Sam's dad.

"Yeah, but I don't want to take all your collection," said Sam.

"Oh, don't worry," Natalie said. "I'm only carrying them around out of habit. Believe me, it'd be a relief to get rid of them."

"How about that?" her dad whistled. "Lucky thing we stopped by."

The old Sam was straining to let loose. *No, I don't want to hang up pictures from your magazines. Please, stop talking to me and leave me alone, I don't like you.* But the new Sam stayed in control, "Thank you," she said, "that's really nice of you."

After all, where was the harm? She brings in the magazines one day to work; Sam's dad plops them in her room and forgets all about it. By the time she was back in Chicago it wouldn't even be a memory.

The rest of the day was much easier. After the office, they went to the museum, then ate dinner in town at some fancy restaurant, and went home. Once Sam curbed the nasty, things went smoother. Occasionally the bad Sam whispered to good Sam about this or that, looking for the worst, most offensive interpretation of some small moment. But she ignored her. Sam was a passenger, seeing the sights and making notes of what was interesting enough to revisit when she returned. The other voice was a stowaway, trying to ruin an otherwise pleasant trip. That voice was nothing but trouble.

It was a little passed eight that night. Sam, her dad, and Oscar were watching *Coraline*, when the doorbell rang.

Her dad paused the movie, jumped up, “I’ll get it,” he said.

Oscar looked at Sam, curious. Sam put her hands up in the air: *I don’t know what’s going on either*.

A second later her dad reappeared with Natalie; she was pulling a suitcase on wheels behind her. “Look who it is!” he said.

“I didn’t have anything to do after work,” Natalie said, “and I figured, why not? I’ll take Sam her magazines now, before I forget.”

Inside the old Sam screamed at new Sam for not listening to her. But what could she do now? “Wow, that’s really nice, thanks.”

“It really is,” her dad said, and trailed off. Sam was terrified he was going to ask her to stay.

“Well,” Natalie said after a thousand years, “I should probably get going.”

“Hey, thanks again for stopping by though, dropping these off,” Sam’s dad said. “It was really thoughtful of you.”

“It was,” Sam said, “thanks.” Sam stuck her hands in her back pockets, gently rocked back and forth on her heels. She didn’t know how to act. This woman had just come and given her dozens or even a hundred magazines. How do you respond to that? Do you hug the person? Shake hands?

“Well I hope you get more use out of them than I did. See you guys around.” Natalie turned around and headed back to the front door. Sam’s dad disappeared with her. After a minute he popped back into view, came back to the couch and sat down.

He put his hand on Sam’s knee. “That was nice of her, wasn’t it?”

Good Sam and bad Sam could agree on one thing: they really didn’t like Natalie. “Super, super, nice,” she said.

Her dad put the movie back on.

Sunday was the low-key day her dad promised it would be. They hung around the house for most of the day, watched TV, fooled around online, did the kinds of things they would have done if they actually lived there. Sam spent some time on her own exploring the neighborhood. She walked around Hyde Park and the University campus, talked to Becky for close to an hour. It was a nice day, not too warm, breezy. When Becky had to go, Sam popped in her ear buds and listened to her MP3 player, taking in the area, letting it soak into her as an actual place, as opposed to the tour her dad gave them two nights earlier. She admitted that it was very pretty; she was used to living in a college town from Baxter, so the whole feel of Hyde Park was comfortably familiar, like a more urban, super-roided up version.

Every fall in Baxter, a new group of nervous college freshman arrived and cautiously made their way around town, getting to know its features and quirks. They usually looked scared, those kids. Sam always wondered what she'd be like her first year away from home. Over time, they all got used to the area, of course, made it their new home. She used to sit in town and watch the college kids and try and figure out what year they were in based on their behavior, their body language, how comfortable they seemed with one another, and even how excited or nervous or bored they sounded.

She looked around. There were kids everywhere, younger kids, older kids, high school looking kids. They all managed to survive living here, they were all basically her age, and they all got along, just like those kids who came to Baxter every year.

Maybe it wouldn't be such a bad place to live; it could be like a test for when she went to college in a year. Like the shallow end of the pool or something—in the water, but safe at the same time. She could try to make new friends, deal with not being in Baxter, and all with her family waiting at home. That could actually be good, in the long run.

It was all a question of identity. Who did she want to be? Did she want to be the girl who, when faced with a situation she didn't like, threw a big fit and made everyone around her miserable? Like her mother? When her mother had a problem, everything stopped until it was fixed. Or did she want to be more like her dad? Someone who rolled with things, worked with them, found the good in everything and focused on that. Her dad didn't want to be living in Chicago any more that she did, but he did what he had to do to make the best of it. She should do the same.

It occurred to Sam that she had no idea where she was; it was somewhere on the U of C campus, but how she got there and how she'd get home eluded her. She called her dad and he asked her to describe her surroundings, what did the buildings look like? When she got to the big churchy building, he told her to stop. He said that was Rockefeller Chapel, he knew where she was. Go wait by the chapel, he'd get Oscar, pick her up and the three of them would get dinner.

They ate at an Italian place near campus, another spot that her dad went to all the time when he was in school. After that, they stopped in a Barnes and Noble so Sam could get a book for her trip home. She liked the cover for *White Noise,* and decided to give it a shot. They went home, made some popcorn, and turned on the TV. Everything was better, everything was moving much easier.

But still, there was the suitcase.

She brought it into her room after Natalie dropped it off, put it a corner, and left it there. On the one hand, she wanted to embrace the positive aspects of things. The woman was nice enough to dig out these old magazines and drag them all the way to her house. And going through the magazines would make her dad happy. He didn't say anything about it, but she knew he wanted to. Her dad was like that, always looking for ways for people to like things or each other, looking for positive connections. It was one of her favorite things about him.

It would be such a small thing really. She could tear out, like, a dozen pictures or something, tape them up. Maybe line a corner of her room with them.

No big deal.

Still.

She couldn't bring herself to do it.

The suitcase sat where she left it in the corner of her room. *Maybe when we come back*, she told herself, *when I've got all my stuff here and I know how it's all going to look and it's actually* my *room as opposed to* a *room that will be mine soon*. Maybe then it won't be so hard. By then, the pictures would be a small part of a larger whole. Maybe then it wouldn't make her feel so bad to even think about going through the suitcase.

Maybe.

After brunch on Monday, they packed up their stuff and went to the airport. Sam told their dad he could just drop them off at the terminal, but he parked in one of the garages and walked them to the security checkpoint where he hugged them both tight.

"I had a really great time with you guys this weekend," he said.

"Me too," said Sam.

"Me too," said Oscar.

"And just think," her Dad said, "next time you guys are here, it's going to be for good."

"That'll be something all right." Sam smiled, tried to look positive. Tried to feel positive.

Her dad said, "Listen Sam, I know this hasn't been easy for you."

"Daddy," she said, "I'm fine."

"No," he said, "it's okay; I know it's been hard. It's been hard on all of us, and I know that you really tried this weekend. I really appreciate it."

Sam shrugged, "It wasn't a big deal. I had fun."

"I'm glad to hear that," he said. "Love you."

"Love you too, Daddy," she said, and hugged him again.

Her dad picked Oscar up, "Are you gonna miss me?"

Oscar smiled and nodded.

"Are you gonna be good for your sister on the trip home?"

Oscar nodded again.

"Are you gonna be good for your mom when you get home?"

A third nod.

Her dad squeezed Oscar, "That's my boy. Remember, you're still the man of the house until we're all together again. I'm counting on you. Love you."

"Love you too," said Oscar.

Her dad put Oscar down, then he stood and watched as Sam and Oscar made their way through the security line, put their luggage on the x-ray conveyor, and went through the metal detector. Then, right before they turned to walk down the terminal, Sam looked one more time to see that, yes, he was still standing in the same spot. She waved to him one last time and he waved back; then she took Oscar's hand and turned the corner toward their gate.

Sam pushed her head against the window on the plane, felt the cool surface of the Plexiglas against her forehead and thought about her dad standing alone at that checkpoint. She thought about him watching her and Oscar until they disappeared, then going back to his car by himself, and driving back to that big empty house.

She knew he had wanted for them to have a good time on the trip and like Chicago so badly that it made her ache inside. Her dad wasn't uncomfortable and lonely, he was cool and fun. He didn't push things; he just let them happen and worked with what he got. That was the person who'd raised her, the person she loved so much. She didn't like how out of synch he'd been, how hard he'd tried. How much he *needed* for things to go according to plan. Even after things settled down, she could feel his anxiety hovering in the background just out of reach. Like he always wanted to ask her: *Is this all right now? Am I doing good now?* There was something desperate about the whole thing, something pathetic.

She hated herself for how she felt;for how she could think such terrible things about the person she maybe loved most in the world. But she couldn't manage to eradicate the feeling; it was just, *there*. Why couldn't she just take her dad's excitement and nervousness as sweet and leave it there? Wouldn't it be worse if he didn't care?

Exactly when did she get so judgmental?

Chicago.

It messed everything up. It took her wonderful, perfect relationship with her dad and made it awkward. It took (she was sure) a perfectly nice person in Natalie, and made her seem creepy and clingy. It took her, Sam, a nice girl, a good daughter and sister, the kind of girl who didn't make snap judgments, and turned her into a bitch. The kind of person she hated; the kind she'd sworn to herself she'd never be. One day in Chicago and she was ready to commit murder, over what? Going to the park? Someone daring to offer her free magazines?

It was crazy.

Sam chewed that last ice cube from her drink and looked down at the ground crawling along deceptively slow, far below her. Life was happening to thousands and millions of people right in front of her and she couldn't even see it. Amazing. Soon enough, she'd be back on the ground with them, but things wouldn't be like they'd been, she knew that now. Things were different. She was different. It was like somehow, that thing that she thought as a kid was true after all.

She went up, and everything got all small, and when she came down, nothing was the same size as it'd been before.

# MOTHERS

Usually Sam talked a blue streak while she drove, about school, about her friends, about Oscar or her dad, or whatever went through her mind at that moment, and there was always something.

He didn't really listen to her, not closely anyway. He kept up with what she said for a while, but then, he started to lose the thread (he couldn't keep track of who said what and what this or that might mean to someone), and his thoughts always drifted off on their own.

It was a good thing the two of them had going. Sam got her time on the road, and she got to go on and on about whatever she wanted for an hour, and Nick got to do his good deed for the day, and he kind of liked her little monologues. It was like white noise; he could relax, focus on nothing in particular. Sam's talking was the line in the center of the road endlessly running toward them, ceaselessly, peacefully, comforting. She was a careful enough driver that he didn't have to watch every move she made anymore; all he did was get in the car, pick a destination for her and then sit back and not worry.

And he did listen sometimes. Unlike a lot of girls (unlike a lot of people), Nick knew Sam seemed self-aware enough to understand that her need to talk and other people's capacities to listen weren't always in synch, and she accepted it. So, if there was something she actually wanted to say to him, a conversation she wanted to have, she let him know and he started paying attention.

Mostly though, Sam just seemed happy to talk.

Today was different; today Sam got in the car with a quiet *Hey* and didn't say anything else. She drove in relative silence for the next ten minutes, only opening her mouth to respond to whatever questions or commands Nick gave, and those responses where short and clipped.

"Okay, what's going on?" He said when he couldn't take the crushing silence for a minute more.

She kept her eyes on the road, playing innocent, "What? Nothing. I'm just driving."

"Exactly, just driving. You've said like five words this whole time. Usually I can't get you to shut up."

"I don't know, I guess I'm just feeling quiet today."

"Sam, don't bullshit me, okay? I know when someone's feeling quiet and when something's up. If you don't want to talk about it that's fine, but don't pretend there's nothing up when something clearly *is*. That's insulting."

"All right," she said, "I don't want to talk about it."

"Okay," Nick said, "fair enough."

They drove in silence for another minute; then Sam said, "You grew up here, right?"

"Sure did."

"Did you ever think you were going to leave? Like for good?"

"I was planning on it."

"Oh right," Sam said, "'cause of the baseball?"

"Yeah," he said, "'cause of the baseball."

"Then I guess you were looking forward to it, huh?"

"I guess I was."

"Didn't you like it here though? Didn't you have friends and stuff you didn't want to leave behind?"

"Sure," he said, "I liked it here okay, and I had friends."

"I just, I always planned on leaving, you know? Like when I went off to college or whatever, I was gonna go to California or Portland or somewhere on the other side of the country and have a big adventure. But… me and Oscar were in Chicago over the weekend, you know? And we saw our new house and the neighborhood, and it was *nice*, I'm not saying it wasn't, but it wasn't, like, home."

"Obviously," Nick said. "It won't be home until you've lived there."

Sam said, "Right? That's what I was trying to say to Mom, but she was mad at me because I wasn't like all of a sudden super-psyched about going or something. She doesn't care about Baxter so I shouldn't care either."

***

"She said what?" They were in the kitchen; Liz was making dinner; Oscar was playing in the other room and Sam was upstairs. "That's absurd. I asked her if she was excited about moving now that she'd been to Chicago and seen the house, and she jumped down my throat. And of course, I care about Baxter; I'm just trying to be upbeat about the move. Whatever I say is wrong; if I talk about the move, I'm pushing too hard, if I don't, I'm pretending everything's okay and not facing reality."

***

"Whatever," Sam said in the car the next day. "She's mad because I'm not as on board with her big move. She's happy so everyone has to be happy or it ruins the whole thing for her. But she has no idea how hard this is for me, has no idea what I'm leaving behind. All she cares about is *family*," she sneered. "But it's not family like a typical family, it's family like a unit in the army or something. Mom has this idea of family that's really strict -- it's only what she wants, and if you don't want the same thing, it's your problem."

***

"I know how hard this is for her," Liz said. "All she's done for a month is tell me how hard this is for her. Like I never moved before. Like I never went anywhere new when I was her age, or had to start over. And where did she get this notion that this move is my idea anyway?" She was in the front, weeding; Nick was lending a hand. "I have no idea where it came from. She tells everyone I want to move, that I pushed for it, but *I never did that.* I shouldn't be surprised though. This is what she does, something happens in her life that she doesn't like, she blames me."

***

"Of course, she says it wasn't her idea," Sam said. "Of course, she says I'm blaming her. She sees how unhappy it's making everyone and she can't take it back. Mom's got this thing about rules and how things *should* be so that she can do whatever she wants without worrying about how everyone feels about it. It's not her, it's just the rules. She can't ever be the bad guy."

***

"I'm *always* the bad guy! That's all I've ever been to her! Steve's good, I'm bad. Steve's fun, I'm a kill-joy. Steve's daddy-do-no-wrong, Mom's a selfish cunt. *If she had any idea…*" Liz stopped, closed her eyes, took a deep breath, and took another drag on her cigarette. "Look," she said, "don't, uh, don't tell her any of that, okay? Don't tell her I said that?"

Nick shrugged, "Sure." It was weird being so immersed in family drama, being the go-between, but kind of fun too.

"Thanks," she said. "I'm glad she has you to talk to. Normally, I wouldn't ask you to keep something from her that I said, but Sam and Steve have this great relationship and I don't want our shit to spill over into it. I'm just… it's hard, sometimes, you know? It's like, Steve the dad is different from Steve the husband, and I need to be sure not to punish Steve the dad for Steve the husband's behavior."

Nick shrugged again, "If you say so. Sounds to me, though, like you're making this more complicated than it has to be. It sounds to me like this guy's letting you swing for something you didn't do. It's a pretty shitty thing to do."

"I can see how it might look like that, but it's way more complicated," she said. "I'm hungry; are you hungry?"

"I could eat," Nick said.

"C'mon, I'll make us some lunch."

They got up from the back porch, and went into the kitchen. Liz opened the fridge, "I'm in the mood for something light," she said. "Salad okay with you?"

"Sure," he said, "whatever."

"I think I have some chicken in here," Liz said, sorting through the fridge. "We could break it up and put in the salad if you want some protein or something."

"Really," said Nick, "whatever you're having is good. I'm not picky."

Liz started taking various vegetables out of the fridge. "The thing about Steve is," she said, "he's got that lawyer thing, where he can be so good with people that it inadvertently makes other people look bad. Her whole life, Sam's had this dad who makes everything look so easy, and that's good because it makes her feel safe and loved. But it makes me look awful in comparison."

"Sure," Nick said, "I know what that's like. Some guys are so good they end up showing up everyone else."

Liz pointed the tip of chopping knife at Nick, "Exactly," she said.

"But the thing about those guys," Nick said, "as good as they are, they don't always make the team better. Sometimes they end up pissing everyone else off and poisoning the team. Every coach I ever had said if you're really good, you make everyone else around you better."

Liz sighed, "Yeah, I see what you're getting at, and I wish it were that simple, but what can I do? It's not like I can trade him or cut him and pick up another dad. It doesn't work that way. Besides, he's a *good* dad. He can be a shitty husband, but he's a good dad. I can't get rid of him just because he pisses me off."

She put down the knife, looked at Nick, "I mean, I don't know, maybe it is me, you know? I mean, back when I was teaching? There were some kids—nothing they did was ever their fault. Some other kid was doing something worse, and that kid didn't get in trouble. There was an emergency at home; they had some big project due in another class, it was always something. It was never just that they were being stupid or lazy or whatever; there was always an excuse for why they weren't responsible for their own actions. Maybe I'm that way. Maybe that's what I'm doing with Steve, blaming him because I'm a lousy parent."

"I'm sorry," Nick said, "but that's just ridiculous. I come here and I see you busting your ass every day, doing everything you can for those two kids, and I never hear them say please or thank you or any of that. I mean, I know it's not my place and Sam's a good girl and I like her and everything, but I think you need to set her straight about some of this stuff."

Liz laughed gently. "I remember when I was a kid, my mom did what you're saying— she thought things were, I don't know, unfair? Between her and me and my dad. I guess in a lot of ways I was like Sam, I was really close with my dad and not as much with my mom. So she started to bad-mouth my dad to me, tried to bring him down to her level you know? But it backfired; it just made me more defensive of him and angrier at her."

She was silent for a minute, Nick wondered if he was supposed to say something. But then she said, "Maybe this is, like, karma. Now here I am, standing in her shoes, with the same choices."

"Well I don't know anything about karma," said Nick, "but I don't like seeing someone not get credit for all the work they do. I mean maybe your mom was a good mom, maybe she wasn't, but you are, and you deserve credit for that. Or some slack at least."

"You notice, so there's that, and maybe someday Sam will too."

He should have kept his mouth shut. All that talk about moms and karma and everything, it was like some sort of omen.

The very next day he and Sam were running errands again, this time for a one day roofing job he had across town. After Home Depot, Nick had Sam drive back to his place so they could drop off the supplies before continuing their drive.

Val was there when they walked in; Gert was at her feet watching her chop up meat. She stopped begging long enough to sniff Sam and lick Nick's hands. Robbie sat on the floor playing with his little toy cars. Sam introduced herself to him, sat down on the kitchen floor in order to more closely examine every toy Robbie showed her. He pushed the cars around the linoleum making driving noises. Robbie squeaked with pleasure at the attention he was getting from the new person in the house.

"I was just at Mom and Dad's," Val said.

"Okay," Nick said, "so?"

"So, Barb was there."

Nick almost shouted, "What?"

Robbie looked up, Sam too.

"She wants to talk to you."

Nick sat down, "Yeah, well, we all want a lot of things."

Sam asked, "Who's Barb?"

"Nick," Val said, "you know she's not leaving until she talks to you."

Nick put his head in his hands, "*Fuck!*"

Val said, "C'mon, language." She gestured toward Robbie.

Nick didn't look up, "I know, I just…"

"Who's Barb?" Sam repeated.

Nick clapped his hands on the table. "All right," he said, "if that's what it takes to get her to leave, I'll do it. I'll do it today. Whatever it takes to get that bitch to go back where she came from."

"Seriously?" said Val. "What did I just say?"

"Guys?" Sam said. "Who's Barb?"

"Barb," said Val, "is Nick's mom."

***

"It's good to see you sweetie," his mom said. "You look good."

What else could he do? Val was right, if she wanted to see him, if that was one of the reasons she was back in town, then she wasn't leaving until she did. Nick dropped Sam off at home, got his truck and drove straight over to his grandparents' house; he picked his mom up and the two of them got a table at Bertucci's. They walked in a little after four - an off hour on an off day. Who wanted fancy pizza in the middle of the afternoon on a Thursday? Not too many people as it turned out, what looked like business meetings that ran a little late (judging by the clothes anyway), and a handful of high school kids. He asked the hostess for a quiet table toward the back. She said it wouldn't be a problem, and took them to a booth in the corner farthest from the front door and bathrooms.

They took their seats, and made awkward small talk until the server came and took their order. It wasn't until their drinks arrived that Nick decided to cut to the chase.

He took a sip from his iced tea, "What do you need Mom?"

She looked surprised, a little hurt. Sure she was. "What do I need?"

"What do you need?"

"I don't know, to have lunch with my son I guess. See how his life is."

"Right," he said, "okay. That's how we're doing this. Uh, life is fine. How is your life?"

"Did it ever occur to you," she said, her mouth tight with displeasure, "that this might be the reason I don't come see you very often? This attitude of yours?"

"Gosh mom, I hope so," Nick said. "That was always the idea."

His mom shook her head. "All I wanted," she said, "was to have a nice lunch with my son. Catch up; see what he's up to. I should have known."

They sat silently for a few minutes, his mom sulking and Nick trying not to notice. A feeling started to creep up Nick's neck. He fought it. His mom, and sometimes he wondered why he bothered to think of her that way, had been nothing but trouble for him his whole life. He knew, *he knew*, that this caring act was just that—a bullshit smokescreen to get something out of him, just like it always was. How could he possibly be feeling bad for her right now?

Nick weakly threw his hands up. Unbelievable. But not really. This was going to take as long as she wanted. Just like always. "I'm okay Mom, I'm good."

"Your work's going okay? Still fixing houses?"

Nick nodded.

"Are you seeing anyone?"

"Yeah, sort of, I guess."

His mom smiled, "*Yeah, sort of, you guess?* What's that supposed to mean?"

"It means," Nick said, "that it's complicated and I don't really want to talk about it."

"Fair enough," his mom said, leaning back in her seat. "I've had my share of those types of relationships. What else is going on? Playing any ball?"

"No Mom, not in a long time."

"Ever get out to the batting cages, anything like that?"

"No."

The server came back to the table with their pizza. Nick picked a slice off the platter, started to eat. His mom took her slice and put it on her plate; she took a napkin and laid it on top of the slice, soaking up the excess grease. "Have to watch my weight," she said to him in explanation. "It's a tough world out there for a single girl." When she was satisfied, she took the napkins off and started to eat.

"What about you, Mom?" Nick said when he'd finished his slice. "What are you up to these days?"

"I'm up in Weston," she said, "working reception at a dentist's office. It's okay, the money's you know, so-so, but the people are nice so…" she trailed off.

"You gotta like your co-workers."

"I guess that's why you work alone, huh?" She smiled.

Nick laughed in spite of himself. "I guess," he said.

"It's a nice place, Weston. Ever been there?"

"I drove through it a few times."

"Maybe you can come up, we can spend some time together."

"Maybe," he said.

"We should try and do that," she said. "If I'm even there that much longer. I might have to get a new place. I don't know if it'll be in Weston or if I'm going to have to move, start all over again somewhere else. It's funny, I picked on you a little for saying you were *sort of* in a relationship, but I really shouldn't. I just got out of a relationship, a pretty serious one. It was a *disaster*."

Nick groaned inwardly; he didn't have any desire to hear about another one of his mom's loser boyfriends or the bullshit drama that inevitably came with them.

"I was with this guy, Lyle. We were together for over three years. Lyle was a mechanic; he used to own his own garage, fixing transmissions. He said he lost it because of 'bad investments,'" she put up air quotes, "which I later found out meant *gambling*. He ended up having to sell the place, and stayed on as an employee until they fired him. Lyle says it was because the guy who bought it was an idiot and didn't know how to run the business. He says this new boss couldn't handle having a guy around who knew how to run things so he canned him. Right. So Lyle's broke and loses his place and, of course, ends up moving in with me."

Nick's stomach twisted, his mom laughed bitterly. "My luck, right? Guy was still married the whole time we were together. They were legally separated, him and his wife, but not officially divorced. That way he didn't have to pay any support or something. His wife lived in Jersey with their two kids; he told me he went to see them on the weekends?" She shook her head, "But that wasn't it at all; really he was going to Atlantic City. Of course, I only found this out after I'd spent years giving him money for gas or tolls or just to take those little kids out to dinner while he was down there. And every time something went wrong with the car, it was: *I wouldn't ask, but I'm going to see the kids this weekend.* I swear I must have put I don't know how many thousand dollars into that man before I found out the truth about him."

He could see it clearly now, the destination she was heading to, was headed to the whole time, and he realized that, somehow, he was disappointed. Somehow, despite the mountain of evidence screaming to the contrary, there was a little bit of his mind that allowed itself to believe that she was actually there just to see him. To check in on her son and see how he was getting along. Nick's temples throbbed, anger grew. He knew it, had known it all along. There was no such thing as an innocent visit where she was concerned.

"So I confronted him about it, when I learned the truth—this was three, four months ago. And Lyle, Lyle starts crying and apologizing. He *begs* me to forgive him, goes on about how gambling's an *addiction*, a *disease,* and how he's going to go into treatment if I'll just take him back."

"Mmm," said Nick.

"And you know, like an idiot, I *do*, and things *seem* okay. He's not going to A.C. anymore and he's looking for work during the days. But one day, I'm looking at one of my credit card statements? And there are a bunch of huge charges that I don't recognize at some website that I've never been to. So I check it out of course and it turns out it's one of those online gambling sites. *Turns out* Lyle hasn't been looking for work at all; he's just been going to these sites, on a computer I bought him by the way so that he could have his own space to look for work, and on that computer he's been going to these sites and gambling again. He had a good streak at first I guess, but it went bad like it always does and he ran out of money and had the nerve to use one of my credit cards!"

She took another slice off the platter, blotted up the grease again. Nick sat and waited for her to finish her story, filled in equal parts with rage at his mom and twisted satisfaction as his suspicions were confirmed.

"Well, he gave me the same addict song and dance when I confronted him with the bill, but this time I wasn't having any of it. *This time* I stood my ground, no more excuses." She sighed. "So that's the last I'm gonna see of Lyle. But it's not the last I'm gonna have to think of him. He left me in a pretty big hole. I don't know how I'm going to pay my bills or if I'm going to be able to keep my place." She trailed off, took a long sip from her drink.

"Unbelievable," said Nick.

"I know," she said. "I always manage to find the losers."

"I'm not talking about *Lyle,* Mom. Fuck Lyle. I'm talking about you. So that whole *I want to find out how you're doing* you laid on me a minute ago, was just an act after all. You're here because you need money."

"I didn't say that," she said.

"Come on," he said. "How dumb do you think I am? You come here and tell me this sob story about this guy who stole all your money and how you're broke now and maybe can't keep your place and I'm supposed to think you're not looking for a handout?"

His mom's eyes narrowed. "First of all," she spat, "I didn't ask you, or anyone else in the family, for a thing. Second, so what if I had? Would that have been such a crime? I'm in trouble here, real trouble; I could end up bankrupt over this. Isn't family around to help you when you're in trouble?"

"It shouldn't be the *only* time you see them, Mom. You know, I actually thought for a minute that you might be interested in how my life was going. How should I feel knowing that was all an act to get money out of me?"

"Maybe I'd talk to family more often if they weren't so suspicious of me," his mom said. "Maybe, I'd ask you more about yourself if you didn't twist everything I said to make me look terrible."

This was so typical of her, so fucking typical. She was always the victim, no matter what. "Is anything ever your fault, Mom? Like, ever?"

"So it's my fault that Lyle stole from me? My fault that he took my credit card and maxed it out without my permission?" She crossed her arms. "I guess I just shouldn't try to have a life, shouldn't try and be happy. I deserve to go bankrupt and get kicked out of my house. And why, because you don't think I was a good enough mother to you?"

"You weren't a good enough mother?" He tried to keep his voice down; everything came out as a sort of growl. "*You weren't a mother at all,* Mom. Do you really not get that?"

"So I guess dropping out of high school, having to get my GED instead of a diploma, that doesn't really count. I gave up my youth for you, and you're not even the slightest bit grateful."

It took all his strength not to scream at her, not to knock everything off the table, the drinks, the pizza, everything, and grab her and shake her. "You're talking about five years, Mom." He held up his hand, fingers splayed. "*Five*. Last time I checked childhood was about thirteen years longer than that. You did a little less than a third of a job and then you bugged out. So no, I don't really rate it as much of a sacrifice."

"I left," his mom said, "for your own good. You were better off without me. Do you think I liked being away from you? Working long hours and living in one room apartments?"

Nick rubbed his finger and thumb together for her, *the world's smallest violin*. "Heartbreaking stuff Mom, really."

His mom said, "You act like I just disappeared, went to the other side of the world. There were some years when I wasn't as… good a mom, as I should have been, okay? I admit it. But I was a kid; I didn't know what I was doing. And I came back, didn't I?"

"Yeah Mom, you did. Coincidentally you started giving a damn about me around the same time it looked like I might end up playing ball. When that disappeared, so did you. Again."

His mom didn't say anything; she just sat there, staring at him with cold hard eyes, her second piece of pizza virtually untouched.

"I don't understand," he finally said, "did you think I didn't remember that or something? Did you think I'd forgotten?"

His mom exhaled, shook her head, pursed her lips. "I don't know," she said. "I don't know what I thought. I don't know what I thought or what you felt or how we got here. I don't know why we can't have a simple meal without it turning into an argument about the past. All I know is, things are falling apart for me, and when things are falling apart, you're supposed to be able to go to your family. So that's what I did. Everything in my life's turning to shit and I thought it'd be nice to have a meal with my son. But I don't even get that."

She stared out the window, savoring her own miserable circumstances. Then she said, "I mean, do you have any idea how embarrassing this is for me? To have to come home and admit how badly I screwed up? Do you know how many people, including some of your aunts and uncles, have been waiting for a moment like this, to rub my nose in every little mistake I ever made? To laugh at me and say I told you so?"

Nick's shoulders slumped; he ran his hands through his hair. He was tired all of a sudden, tired of being there, tired of the conversation, tired of her. "How much money do you need?"

"You mean total or to get through the next few months?"

"Just….I don't care; just give me a number. How much?"

She thought about it, or pretended to anyway. After a minute she said, "Two thousand dollars?"

"And if I give it to you, if I give you two thousand dollars, you'll go away and leave me alone?"

She looked at him. "Is that what you want?"

"That's what I want."

"Well," she said, "I mean…I need the money, so… if that's what it takes, I guess I have to."

He swore that he'd never do this. Never play this game with her. Other people could, but not him, this was his mother after all. There had to be a line.

"Okay, let me think about it."

***

Nick took a drag from his smoke, exhaled through his nose. They sat on the back porch steps again, waiting for Sam again. He came over early because he needed to talk to someone about all this, someone who wasn't involved, wouldn't be influenced by personal feelings about his mom. Liz said absolutely, to tell her all about it. Then she poured them both some lemonade and bummed a cigarette off of him.

Nick began: "My mom was only seventeen when I was born, a junior in high school . My father was a senior named Ron Rogers; they weren't even really dating, or they weren't boyfriend-girlfriend anyway. She told him about the baby, about me, and he told her he would stick around, help raise me. But he split the minute he graduated."

"Yikes," Liz said. "Have you ever met him?"

"Couple times," he said. "He'd be in town to see his family or whatever and one of my uncles or aunts would take me by to see him. It was always weird."

"I'm sure it was."

"I mean, I'd be looking at this guy, and I wouldn't feel anything, you know? Like, this wasn't my dad. I didn't have a dad. This was just some guy. Some guy I'd see around sometimes."

"That's pretty fucked up," said Liz.

"I guess," Nick said. "But you want to know the really fucked up part? At least, to me? This guy Ron took off two months before I was born. My mom knew he was gone, like, gone, gone. But she still gave me his name. I'm not Nick *Strakovsky*, I'm Nick *Rogers*.

It's like she was saying to me from day one, *you're not mine, you're his, and I'm just the one stuck with you.*"

Nick took out another cigarette, lit it with the first. A cool breeze blew across the backyard and through his hair; out of the corner of his eye he saw the automatic sprinkler in the neighboring yard click on. It had been a long time since he'd told any of this to anyone.

"Not that she was stuck with me for long. We lived at my grandparents' house until she got her GED; then she took off too, left me with them. I guess she figured they had so many kids of their own they wouldn't notice one more.

"She disappeared for three years. Went to New York or something. There're different versions of where she went and why. I suppose I could figure the truth out if I cared enough. She came back when I was five and lived with us again for a few years. My grandparents only took her back because she said she wanted to be a better mom to me. And for a while she was, she helped me get ready for school in the morning and played with me at night. But pretty soon she was out partying at night again and wouldn't get home until like, three or four in the morning, so she stopped helping me in the mornings. Then, when she got a job as a waitress she was gone in the afternoons too. Pretty soon it was back to the way it was, with my grandparents in charge and she was just another kid in the house."

"God," said Liz.

"It was better that way anyway," he said. "Barbra Strakovsky was never cut out to be a mom. She moved out again when I was in second grade. She didn't disappear this time; she got some place in town with a friend of hers. She said she was going to come get me eventually, when she was sure she could support us both, but it never happened. I saw her every couple of weeks when she came over for dinner; then it was every couple of months. She came by to ask my grandparents or one of my aunts or uncles for a favor, or for money, and she put in some face time with me so she didn't look totally evil I guess. But as soon as she got what she wanted she was out the door again."

"Did anyone ever not give her what she wanted? Not give her the money or whatever it was she needed?"

"Someone would try that every once in a while, but it was always more trouble than it was worth. She was so awful if she didn't get what she wanted; it was always just easier to give it to her so she'd go away."

"Even her parents gave in?"

"They had six other kids to worry about; seven if you counted me, and I wasn't even the youngest. But I always said I wouldn't do it, I wouldn't give her anything. The only time she even pretended to be a good mom was when I was in high school and in the minors. Then I constantly got calls from her, talking about how proud she was of me and how rich and successful I was going to be. How she'd come see me when I played in New York and L.A. and places like that. The houses I'd have, the stuff I'd do. I'd tell her there was a long way to go before anything like that happened, but she wouldn't listen. And when I got hurt, all she could talk about was how she wasn't going to see me in all those cities. All she could think about was what she lost. She stopped coming around again after that."

Liz looked genuinely upset. "I don't understand," she said, "how someone could treat their own child like that. How they could just ignore them. It's your *child*."

"Like I said, it's better that way. If I'd spent more time with her, I just would've ended up getting sucked into more of her bullshit. I'd have ended up taking care of myself most of the time, making my own meals, cleaning up the house. Probably would've gotten my ass kicked by one of her asshole boyfriends a few times, moved out when I was old enough and ended up some piece of shit somewhere. I know guys that happened to. At least I got raised in a good home by people who loved me."

"Yeah, but maybe she would've grown up, you know, rose to the occasion."

Nick said, "Whatever. That's her problem, not mine."

"I don't know it sounds like she's trying to make it your problem. Two thousand dollars is a lot of money. Can you afford that?"

He nodded. "It wouldn't be nothing, but I could do it, yeah."

"And she could go bankrupt if she doesn't get the money?"

"That's what she *says.*"

"Would she just make something as serious as that up?"

"Sure, or exaggerate. I wouldn't put it past her. For all I know there wasn't even a Lyle."

"So, you think she could just be lying about *everything*. Why would she lie like that? Is it," she lowered her voice, "drugs? Does she… do… that?"

Nick shook his head. "She's not into anything like that. I mean, when she was younger I think she got high from time to time. I seem to remember something about that, and she drinks, but who doesn't? No, she's just terrible with money. She buys things she can't afford, leases nice cars, and forgets to pay bills. She digs these holes for herself and then says whatever she has to in order to get out of them. All she wants is the money. She doesn't give a shit how she gets it."

Liz exhaled, leaned back on her elbows. "Wow," she said, "what a bitch."

"That's my mom," said Nick. "When I was a kid, she used to make me so mad I'd start shaking, like actually physically shaking. I'd puff my chest out and be all like *it's fucking bullshit that people give her whatever she wants and she doesn't ever get called on any of her shit* and blah, blah, blah. And now, here I am, all these years later, and I'm gonna do the same thing."

Liz looked at him. "So, why are you going to do it then?"

Nick ground his cigarette out in the bowl they were using as an ashtray. He watched as a bird landed on the tree branch. The bird spread one of its wings, poked around between the feathers with its beak, and flew away.

"Because," he said, "she's my mom."

# DRUNK GIRLS

And just like that, the house sold. Her mother announced it to her and Oscar over dinner the Friday before finals started. She said she had something to tell them about the house. Sam figured it was another lecture about picking up after themselves or not walking on the front lawn or some other equally boring reminder. But it wasn't. Her mother said someone put in a bid, and they accepted it, and they were moving in two weeks.

That was it.

Sam was shocked. It wasn't supposed to happen this quickly. For the last month and a half, all she heard about was how bad the housing market was and how it was possible that the house might not sell for months. Her mother nervously checked the listings and remarked on how some other, nicer, houses were still available after such and such an amount of time, and how far the asking prices had fallen. She couldn't stop worrying about it. If all those other houses hadn't sold yet, what chance did they have? There was talk they might have to move to Chicago before it sold, and it would become this albatross around their necks, gathering dust fifteen hundred miles away.

But while her parents panicked, Sam rejoiced. If the house didn't sell, they didn't have to leave! Yes, okay, sure, she knew they couldn't stay in Baxter forever; it wasn't like her dad was going to be able to transfer back from Chicago (although, it might not be impossible, and how amazing would that be?), but they could stay longer, at least through the summer.

She could have one last summer at home before everything changed. A summer of sitting on the quad of Baxter's campus, reading in the afternoons or swimming at the swim club or getting ice water at the Anthony's. Her nights would be spent at the theaters where she saw *The Harry Potter* movies (oh, it bothered her that she wouldn't be able to see *Deathly Hallows* with Becky when it came out in the fall) and *Pan's Labyrinth*. She would catch fireflies with Oscar in the backyard, go to parties with friends, and spend late nights with Becky doing nothing at all. Maybe her dad could come back for the Fourth of July and they could have the picnic in the gazebo in the park like they did every year for as long as she could remember. Maybe this year she could invite Nick to the picnic; why not? She had friends over for the Fourth picnic before; Becky at least stopped by every year. Nick was her friend, and Oscar liked him, her mother too. He was practically family.

Spending the summer in Baxter meant she could finish her driving requirements with Nick. How many hours did she have left, twenty, twenty-five? That was a full day, guaranteed, she'd be spending with him, just the two of them, in that little car. She could get a full day of his time, jokes, conversation, and errands. A full day of his presence, just his physical presence, a day of seeing him out of the corner of her eye, sitting next to her, not really always paying attention, but *there*, with *her*. She'd get a full day of his voice and his eyes and his smell. All for her.

And, who knows, maybe more.

She was getting along with Val and liked her a lot. She listened to The Smiths mix all the time and made sure Nick told Val. She asked Nick to ask Val to make more mixes, of music like that, from that time. Val was, apparently, happy to do so, because Nick showed up with three more mixes of mostly British new wave bands like Joy Division and Happy Mondays, but also American bands like Pixies and Talking Heads.

Sam devoured the music, read up on the bands she liked the most, and bought a bunch of albums off iTunes. Every time she drove with Nick, she told him to tell Val about some new (for her at least) group she'd fallen in love with thanks to Val's recommendation.

Maybe she and Val could be friends too. Like, outside of her friendship with Nick. Why not, right? Val was younger than Nick, and she seemed to like Sam. Maybe, with time she could get to know Val and they could forge a relationship of their own, and after the inevitable move to Chicago, they could be Facebook friends and Sam could keep talking to her about music and Val could tell her how Nick or Robbie were doing.

Maybe she could babysit Robbie sometime. Sam loved kids; she'd babysat when she was younger. It was the closest thing she'd ever had to, like, a real job. She only met Robbie the one time, and that was a short visit, but she thought he was really cute and he seemed to like her. Val even said something about it, something like *he's usually so shy around strangers*. If Robbie liked her, maybe she could watch him sometime for Val so she could go out with her husband, on a date or something. She could even do it for free. After all, Val and Nick did so much for her; this could be her chance to give back to them.

The summer and all its possibilities spread out before her like an open road. So much she was going to do, so many new exciting things she was going to experience for the first time, and so many beloved traditions she would do one last time before saying goodbye. Someone, fate, God, the housing market, would step in and give her the gift of one final glorious summer in Baxter. It was going to be epic; it would be the best summer of her life. She'd make sure of it.

And then, it was gone.

Just like that.

She felt her summer suddenly ripped away from her. Like whiplash or something; . in her bones, she felt it.

It was all gone now, all of it. No more lazy afternoons under the shade of the big trees on Baxter's campus; no more sitting around Becky's house searching the guide on the TV and trying to figure out what to do; no more friends; no more parties; no more swimming; no more pizza in town; no more anything. The next two weeks would be devoted to finishing school, packing, and leaving.

Sam couldn't believe it.

She stared down at the lasagna on her plate. A minute before, she was so hungry she could have eaten two or three helpings, but now her appetite was completely gone. Lasagna was her favorite food in the entire world; just thinking about it usually made her ravenous. At that moment though, the thought of taking another bite made her nauseous. Her heart sank even further; now, on top of everything else, her favorite food might be tainted—like the time she was in fourth grade and threw up after drinking too much Juicy Juice. She has never able to even think about drinking Juicy Juice since.

She should have known something was up the second she smelled the lasagna. Her mother was trying to butter her up, trying to soften the blow. But instead, she had gotten so excited about the food she hadn't thought about anything else. She was softened up all right. Her guard was as down as down could be, and the news totally blindsided her.

Sam held her head in her hands, squeezed her eyes shut, tried not to lose it. The room was spinning. Somewhere inside her a voice was asking what she was expecting. She knew this was coming, knew the move was happening, and she was making peace with it. It was her fault for dreaming up the elaborate fantasy that was now crashing around her. *You're being ridiculous,* said the voice, *childish and stupid. It's your own fault for allowing yourself to think there was any other outcome. This way that you're feeling right now? This is your fault. Yours.*

"Sam?" There was real concern in her mom's voice, "Sweetie, are you all right?"

"I'm okay Mom"—her voice was breaking; she cleared her throat— "I'm fine."

To her right, she heard Oscar sniffle, start to cry. He was upset because she was upset, gauged his response by how the rest of his family acted. So really, this was her fault too. The voice told her so.

*It's not enough that you hurt yourself,* it said. *You need to upset your poor baby brother too? You're selfish, you're pathetic.*

Sam couldn't take it anymore. She pushed her chair back, ran from the table up to her room, where she could at least break down without worrying about who it hurt.

An hour later, she had a plan.

Quietly, Sam opened her bedroom door and made her way to the bathroom as carefully as possible. She didn't want her mother to call up to her, didn't want to see her or hear her voice until she was composed and prepared. Sam was off guard once tonight, not again.

In the bathroom she scrubbed her face, removed every trace of redness, puffiness, every trace of every tear. She brushed her hair, smoothed out the bed head. She wondered who would dye her hair for her in Chicago and she started to break down again. Two weeks. She braced herself on the sink, pulled herself together, and continued preparing for her conversation with her mother. She finished her hair, splashed a little more water on her face and even brushed her teeth. Because, why not? She looked at herself in the mirror.

She looked cool, calm, and collected.

She looked as mature and responsible as she could remember.

She was as ready as she was going to be.

Her mother was downstairs, in the living room with Oscar. Not surprisingly, Oscar seemed to have recovered from his own crying spell and forgotten it; he was sitting quietly, turning the pages of his *Otis* the tractor books. Their mother sat beside him, talking the story through with him. Sam stood in the entrance to the living room and went over what she was going to say one last time. When she was as calm and as sure of herself as she could be, Sam cleared her throat. Her mother looked up at her with nervous eyes and smiled.

"Sam," she said. "Hey. How're you feeling?"

Sam said, "I'm okay. Sorry about running out like that. I was just, I don't know..." She trailed off, this first step was crucial. Would her mother take the bait?

"No, I understand," her mother said. "You were overwhelmed. It's really big news, and even though we all knew it was coming, it was going to be a shock when it did."

Her mother couldn't have said it better if Sam had given her the lines beforehand. "It was just so, *sudden*; it was like, one minute this was our house, the next it wasn't. It was just too much; I needed time to adjust to the change, I guess." She walked into the living room and took a seat in the chair opposite her mother.

Careful…

"Sweet heart," her mother said, "you were upset. It's okay. You didn't do anything wrong."

"I left the table in the middle of dinner; I upset Oscar."

"It's okay honey, really. It was a lot to take in, and Oscar's fine. You're being too hard on yourself."

"That's nice of you to say," Sam said. "But I know I haven't always been so easy to live with since Daddy left. I've been a pill, and I'm sorry about it."

"We all know how hard this is for you, sweetie," said her mother. "More than any of us, this is a big change for you."

Sam said, "Exactly!" She tried not to get too excited, not get ahead of herself. This was it, this was where she was going to make her case. She needed to play it just right. "Exactly. It's such a big change, and it's so hard to get my head around and it's just been so… hard."

"No one's expecting you to be perfect, Sam," her mother said, smiling. "It's going to be an adjustment."

"That's just it," she said. "It is an adjustment, a huge, *huge* adjustment. And I just don't know if I'm quite ready to make it."

"I understand," her mother said, sympathetically, "but it's one we're going to have to make. We can't stay anymore. Dad's in Chicago, he's got the new job, and the house is sold. Sometimes we have to adjust when we're not ready to yet. Sometimes we adjust because we don't have any other choice."

Here we go. "Well, I get that. I really do. Really. But, and here's the thing, I don't know if I don't have any other choice just yet. And," she started speaking quickly now, "don't say anything, okay? Because I've been giving this a lot of thought and it's gonna sound, I don't know, but I've thought about it, and I think it's worth listening to."

Her mother looked cautious, but not disinterested. It was, all things considered, the best face Sam could hope for. "Okay…" she said.

"Okay," Sam stood up, faced her mother, and took a deep breath. "Here's what I'm thinking. We sell the house, right? And in two weeks, you and Oscar go to Chicago"—this was it, this was really it, her last shot—"and I stay with Becky and her family for another month or maybe the rest of the summer."

"Sam--" her mother said.

"Just, *listen,*" insisted Sam. "Becky suggested it the day I told her, and she's brought it up, like, a *thousand* times since. She even asked her parents once if I could stay for a while, totally on her own; I didn't ask her to and I wasn't even there for them to feel guilty about if the answer was no, and they said it'd be okay. They said it'd be no problem."

Her mother was shaking her head sadly. Desperation crept down Sam's spine.

"It wouldn't have to be for the whole summer; it could just be for a month or two. Or even just a couple of weeks, just to let me say goodbye. Please, Mom. Two weeks. It's just, it's nothing."

"I know sweetheart, I know it feels that way," her mother looked like she might cry herself, "but the answer's no. You have to come with us."

"But, *why?* I don't have to. I can stay with Becky. I *can.* Why can't I just stay here with her a little longer?"

Her mother sighed. "We have to do this all together as a family. It's nice that Becky's parents said that, and maybe, later in the summer, you can come back for a weekend or she can come to Chicago or something, but you have to come with us. This family's been fractured for long enough already with your dad being gone. We need to start being a whole family again."

Sam stood in front of her mother, devastated. That was it. Her last shot. And it failed. It was over. She was going and there wasn't anything she could do about it.

She turned around and calmly went back up to her room.

She sat on the edge of her bed and went over the conversation in her head, looking for where she messed up, the flaw in her logic, and found none.

There was no reason she shouldn't be allowed to stay with Becky for at least a few more weeks. No reason at all. If her mother was to be believed, then she understood how difficult this was for Sam. How painful it was to be ripped from her friends, from her home, from her whole world. She actually said she understood how difficult it was. But she wasn't demonstrating any understanding.

It wasn't as if she was trying to move in with Becky; wasn't like she was asking to finish her senior year in Baxter. She just wanted a few extra weeks. Maybe a month. But it didn't matter how reasonable her request was, her mother wasn't going to cave. Because her mother didn't believe in compromise when it got in the way of what *she* wanted. If she knew how difficult this was for Sam, then she didn't care.

She didn't. Not one bit.

Shaking with rage, Sam pulled on the gingham Chuck Taylors she'd gotten at the mall with Nick, grabbed her phone from her bedside table, and stormed out of her room. Sam needed to get out of the house. Clear her head a little.

"Sam?" her mother called out to her as she raced down the steps. "Can we talk?"

Sam turned where she stood, halfway between the stairs and the front door, and looked at her mother. She was standing in the dining room; plates were stacked on the table behind her. Sam heard the sound of the TV in the living room where Oscar was watching one of his shows. "What?" she said. "What now?"

"I just wanted to talk some more," her mother said, and moved between Sam and the door.

Sam laughed at her mother. "You want to talk some more? About what? What did you want to talk about?"

"Well," her mother said, "I was hoping we could talk more about Chicago."

"Why? Why do you want to talk about it? Is there anything I can say to get you to let me stay?"

Her mother sighed again; Sam was really starting to hate that sound. "Sweetie," she said, "there's just a lot going on right now, and I need you to trust that I-"

And with that, Sam lost it. "Trust you? *Trust you? Fuck* you! You don't care about me, about how I feel! All you care about is yourself and your own stupid plans! I'm never trusting you again!" She pushed past her mother and ran out the front door into the night.

She didn't know whose party it was. Baxter College owned the house and used it during the school year for various events – one of several big, beautiful houses made available to visiting professors or speakers, or to throw fundraisers or parties of their own. When summer rolled around, the houses were empty. If someone knew the right people, a house could be rented for a night. Someone, probably a senior, got ahold of one of the houses on the edge of campus and was throwing a big, end-of-the-year party. As long the drinking didn't get out of hand, and no one got hurt, the town was cool with whatever went on there.

Sam knew about the party before the fight with her mother; Becky was already there and she'd figured on making an appearance, but not staying too long. Parties were something she took in small doses. There were elements of them that were great: she liked being surrounded by people she knew in a different setting; liked seeing people she didn't count as friends but still liked okay; and she liked to dance. There was usually good music. But there was always the whole alcohol thing. People always drank at parties, and people who drank too much and did or said something stupidt got boring quick.

She didn't have a problem with drinking. She usually drank a little, just to loosen up, but didn't like the idea of getting, like, *drunk* in front of her classmates. People who got drunk did dumb things, and those things got out and were remembered and talked about long afterwards. She hated, for instance, that she knew that Sarah Fletcher and Brandon Williams made out at Elliot Tarr's party over winter break even though Brandon was dating Shelly Marks at the time. It wasn't like any of those people were friends with her, or that she was interested in how they spent their time, it was just something that happened and somehow everyone knew. And then Shelly made a big show of how she dumped Brandon and how he was a huge tool and broke her heart and it was all a big soap opera that Sam wasn't interested in watching but that she heard about anyway. It just wasn't worth it, as far as Sam was concerned, to risk that kind of public humiliation, just to have a little fun. She had to live with these people after all.

But that wasn't true anymore, was it?

Becky was in the backyard, drinking a beer and talking to Cameron Rose; they were standing next to a giant oak tree from which a string of lanterns was tied. The lanterns stretched from the tree across the lawn and over the dozen or more kids in the backyard and wrapped around a post next to where Sam stood on the back porch. Music blared from speakers mounted on the side of the house behind her. She made her way down the porch steps and across the yard, giving out hellos and hugs on her way. She caught Becky's eye halfway across the yard; Becky broke into a smile and started toward her. The smile, however, faded as soon she got a good look at Sam's face.

"It's over," Sam yelled over the music. "Mom told us at dinner. The house sold. We're leaving in two weeks."

Becky looked shocked. "What do you mean you're leaving in two weeks?"

She told Becky the whole story. Becky threw her arms around Sam, squeezed. "Jesus," she said. "Sam! What are we going to do?"

Sam looked at her best friend. "Drink," she said. "I'll be right back."

Sam didn't care much for the taste of alcohol. She had beer and wine before and champagne and a lot of different liquors, but it was always the same. So she generally stuck with mixed drinks, rum or jack and coke, whiskey sours, and screwdrivers. Screwdrivers were her favorite. Usually she filled the cup a quarter of the way up (Becky called it *two fingers* when they were feeling sophisticated) of vodka and filled the rest of the cup with orange juice. Nursing a screwdriver or two over the course of an evening typically left her nicely buzzed without pushing her over the edge.

That night though, the edge wasn't something she was worrying about.

She filled the cup a third of the way with vodka (a whole extra finger), poured in the orange juice and drank it all down at once. The cold juice hit her empty stomach with shock, but it was quickly overtaken by the warmth that radiated from even the coldest of alcohols. Sam closed her eyes, grimaced; the orange juice was strong, but couldn't entirely eradicate the vodka's bitter taste. She poured herself another drink; this time the cup was half vodka, half orange juice. She drank that one as quickly as the first, and chased it all with some Coke, just to get that fucking taste out of her mouth.

She found Becky pretty much where she'd left her outside.

"Here's the thing," Sam said over some hip-hop track she didn't recognize. "I feel like shit right now, and I really don't want to. I can feel like shit tomorrow and for the rest of my life, but tonight, I want to have fun, okay? Can we just have fun tonight?"

Becky put on her best, bravest smile. "It's a deal," she said.

So Sam danced. Inside, the music was clearer and the DJ was in there and it was filled with kids and they were all dancing and she joined them. She put her hands over her head and she closed her eyes and she danced. She didn't always know the song; when she did, she sang along. But, either way, she danced. She danced by herself, and she danced with Becky and she danced with other girls she knew and boys and anyone. She danced and she smiled and she laughed and she drank and she danced.

There was a pulse growing inside her; it beat in time with the music. The pulse was warm and satisfying. The pulse was happy. It wasn't her heartbeat, but, like her heartbeat, it coursed through her body, through her skin and blood and bones. It relaxed her muscles and soothed her nerves. She felt the fear and anger fall away as the pulse's steady rhythm took over. The pulse told her that she felt better; maybe it wasn't going to last, maybe she'd wake up in the morning and things would be exactly as they were before and she would be miserable again, but tonight she was going to feel good. For this one last night, she was going to cut loose and finally let herself be herself and see where the night took her. The music was good;it was loud and it was fun, and she could dance. That was all she wanted to do. The singer was saying something about waking up together and the day becoming the night and she felt like he was singing to her, just to her. She looked around at all the people around her, all the faces she knew for so long, and, for at least this one moment, everything was how it should be. She was surrounded by people she grew up with and kept pace with and even if she didn't know all of them, she *knew* them, because she had the same experiences with them, saw the same things, breathed the same air. Fewer than five feet away was Alex Johnson who she once saw fall into a lake during Devin Fox's ninth birthday party. He danced with Mindy DeRicco, who everyone used to say stuffed her bra. Out of the corner of her eye she watched Rob Singleton, who painted his face green every day one summer at camp and would only answer to "Hulk." He shouted something to Allan Wick, the first black person she ever knew. She was overcome with love for all these people she'd watched struggle and work and try so hard to figure out the people they were going to be, and none of it mattered anymore because in this moment they were beautiful; in this moment they were perfect.

Everyone on the dance floor, everyone at the party, everyone she knew and grew up with, they were all one big entity, one big consciousness experiencing life together through a thousand different sets of eyes. She wanted to reach out and hug everyone at the party, everyone at her school, everyone in her town. She wanted to hug them close and whisper *thank you* in their ear. She wanted to thank them for letting her live with them, letting her know them, letting her grow up with them. There was so much that went unspoken for so long, so much she needed to say to them, so that when she was gone they would know that *she* knew how amazing they all were. How wonderful and unique and special and perfect they were. She wanted to tell everyone she knew just how much she appreciated the simple act of making eye contact with her, but she couldn't. So she danced instead. She thought about her mother at home, her dad in that big empty house in Chicago, about her grandparents in Florida, and her other relatives all over the country. She thought about Oscar and Nick and Val and little Robbie and everyone else who wasn't with her in that moment and she realized that, as much as she loved them all, she didn't need them. In that moment, she didn't need any of them. She wished them all the best, yes, even her mother, but they weren't what mattered— they weren't *her.* All she needed, in that moment, was the music and the people around her, the people that she'd shared so much with. She was where she was supposed to be. She needed to lose herself to the seething mass of bodies, to give up her identity and all the hopes and fears and pride and shame to the heaving, sweating, physical reality of the present.

She was hot, her hair was pasted to her forehead and her clothes were sticking to her body. She reached down, grabbed hold of her top and peeled it off, up over her head, leaving only the thin black tank top she wore underneath. It was a shirt she only wore around her house by herself; on any other day, at any other time, she would have been mortified to be exposed like that. But in that moment, she surrendered to the swell, surrendered to the flesh, surrendered to the moment. She took her greasy sweaty top and threw it as far as she could, she didn't care if she ever saw it again.

When she got tired of dancing, she took a break, got another drink, went back outside to catch her breath and get some fresh air. Becky was out there too.

"How many drinks have you had?" Becky asked.

Sam said just the two so far, on her third. Becky looked at her a little funny, said okay, but told her to drink some water too. Sam laughed, and promised she would (Becky was such a good friend); then she saw a group of kids by the side of house smoking and talking. They weren't kids that Sam hung out with; they wore black clothes and were always together and laughing at the stupid things other people said or did. They didn't wear make-up or big boots or put stuff in their hair like goth kids on TV, but they *did* wear black and seemed to always be together. Whatever, who cared, labels like that were dumb anyway. The point was, kids used to laugh at them when they were all younger, but now everyone was kind of intimidated by them. Everyone said they were mean and kept to themselves because they thought they were better than everyone else. There were all kinds of rumors about them, that they all were, like, super-smart and brilliant artists and stuff and could have graduated early and done whatever they wanted if they just cared enough but that they didn't because they were almost *too* smart or something and all they cared about was doing drugs and stuff like that. Sam heard this sort of stuff for years and had been intimidated by the very existence of the scary kids in black. But why?

She was gonna go talk to them.

The scary kids in black stood together at the side of the house, secluded. They saw her coming toward them and shot her a look, sort of confused, like they were wary that someone was in their space. She stopped when she saw the look on their faces, almost turned around, and went back inside; she felt so good she didn't want to ruin it by getting rejected by a bunch of stoners. But the pulse wouldn't hear of it, *give them a chance,* it said. So she did. She walked up to them and pulled out a smoke, asked for a light. They struck a match, held it out for her; she leaned in to the flame and lit her cigarette. They smiled at her, said they didn't know she smoked. She told them they didn't know a lot about her, and maybe if they bothered to find out they could have all been friends. She smiled while she said it though, so they knew she was fucking with them. She asked what they were doing at the party; they said they were invited. She thought that was funny, that they came to a dumb party like this. She laughed. She told them about how she was always intimidated by them because of everything that everyone always said, and they seemed genuinely surprised.

*And it turned out they were all really nice.* They said they didn't think they were better than anybody; they kept to themselves because they thought no one liked *them*. They just figured everyone thought they were big weirdos. Sam said she didn't think they were weirdos. She thought they were brave to be themselves; she said most people weren't that brave. And she didn't not like them; she didn't know anyone who didn't like them. Everyone she knew just thought they were all too busy being super smart and weird and stuff and didn't have time for anyone else. They found that hysterical. They said they didn't know how everyone got the idea they were so smart; they weren't any smarter than anyone else. In fact, most of them were barely passing. Sam said yeah, everyone knew that too, but everyone decided it was because they were like, *too* smart for school and they were failing because it was too easy and beneath them or something. Well they thought that was *hilarious,* and all at once, Sam did too. All the misunderstandings and miscommunications people were always having, all because no one ever actually talked to each other. She was intimidated by these kids for as long as she could remember, and it turned out this whole time they felt the same way about her.

It was so funny.

But it made her sad too, and she said so. People were *so nice,* she said, all they had to do was talk to each other and everyone would see they were all the same. Why couldn't she do this before? Well, they said, we know now, that's something right? She told them they didn't understand, because it was too late. She told them how she was moving in two weeks. No one knows, she said. It was a secret. But it was official now and she didn't care who knew any more. They said they were sad to hear she was leaving because they'd never get to know her. She said she knew, right? It was awful. But hey, they should totally exchange numbers and become Facebook friends and when she came back to visit (because she was absolutely coming back, she was going to make sure of that), they could all hang out because now that she knew how cool and not scary they were, she wanted to finally get to know them.

What if she was as wrong about other people as she'd been about the (it turns out not) scary kids in black? She was leaving so soon and her memories of all the people she knew might not even be of who they were! It might just be some stupid *idea* she had of them that was totally unfair to them. That wasn't fair to anyone.

It was an overwhelming thought.

She needed another drink.

She told the (not) scary kids in black she'd return later and made her way back inside, to the bar.

She noticed, as she walked, that she was feeling a little dizzy. Probably because she stood still for too long after dancing for as long as she had. She'd been sweating when she danced too, with her heart racing. And was she hungry? Her stomach felt something, she wasn't sure if it was hunger, but it was something. She tried to remember when she ate. Was it dinner? No, because she had, like, a bite before her mom said they were leaving and her appetite disappeared. She ate some pretzels earlier in the evening, but not more than a handful. She should probably eat something. There was food inside too. Like chips and cookies and stuff. She thought she remembered seeing pizza in there. If not, maybe she'd just go get some, or order it or something. Yeah, that was a good idea; pizza definitely seemed like a good idea. She had money on her, right? Where was her wallet? She'd find it. Maybe Becky would want to go in with her on a pizza.

Becky wasn't interested in pizza; she looked at the cup in Sam's hand. "How much have you had to drink?"

"I don't know," Sam held her hands a foot apart and laughed. "How much is this?"

Becky laughed too, but not really. "Uh huh, really though, you're hitting it kind of hard, aren't you? Maybe you should take a break for a little." She reached for Sam's cup.

Sam held the cup out of Becky's reach. "Becks, I'm *fine*, you're worrying too much. I do the worrying," she patted her chest, "remember? But we're not worrying tonight. Tonight we're having fun." She tried to pull Becky into a hug, but Becky pushed away.

"Seriously Sam, take some advice from someone who's been there. You need to pace yourself, okay? It's really easy to overdo it if you're not used to it. Have you had any water?"

"Yes."

Becky was unconvinced, "Really?"

"I told you I had." Actually, she wasn't sure when or if she'd had any water; it was getting kind of hard to remember when she'd done what, but it was annoying that Becky didn't believe her. Why did she care so much anyway? Sam could take care of herself.

"Well, drink some more, okay? I'll go get you some right now." She looked Sam in the eye. "Stay right here, okay?"

Sam rolled her eyes, "Whatever."

"I'm serious. Just, I'll be right back." Becky turned around and disappeared into the crowd.

Sam finished off the drink in her hand. She loved Becky and all, but she was starting to be kind of grouchy. All those times she told Sam she needed to relax and not think so much, just have a good time. Now she was finally following Becky's advice and Becky was being all tense about everything, like she was Sam's mother or something. Sam came to the party to get away from her mother.

Scott Temple stood by himself in the far corner of the room; he looked at her. She liked Scott Temple; he was tall. She gave him a big smile and he smiled back; then he raised his cup to her in greeting, waved her over. Scott Temple wanted her to come over to him. Scott Temple. Scott Temple from her underwear fantasy was inviting her over.

She still felt dizzy—if anything, she felt even dizzier—but she centered herself, took a deep breath, and walked over to him as smooth and sexy as she could manage. She wasn't entirely in control though; it was like she was in some kind of dream.

"I just heard a rumor," he said when she was standing in front of him. "Are you moving?"

She nodded; Scott Temple was the cutest boy in her grade, the cutest boy in the whole school. "Good news travels fast I guess."

"I don't think it's good news," he said.

"Me either," she said. He had big shoulders. She liked shoulders.

"Then, why did you say it was *good* news?"

Did she say that? "I don't know," she said. "I guess it sounded good at the time."

He laughed. "That's funny," he said.

He was cute when he laughed. One time during gym, they were all outside and Scott Temple took off his shirt and she almost fainted. "You said it," she said. "I'm a riot." She tipped her cup up to her mouth, but it was already empty. "You can ask anyone." She stared into her empty cup.

"I don't have to ask anyone," he said. "I can see it for myself."

When did she finish her drink? How long had she been holding an empty cup?

"I'm gonna miss it," he said.

"Me too," she said. "Miss what?"

He laughed again. "That's what I'm talking about. You're really something."

"Oh yeah," she nodded her head vigorously, "you missed out on this one buddy, I can tell you that right now."

"Maybe," he said. "Then again, maybe not. Give me your number. I'll text you," he said. "We'll finally get the chance to know each other, even if it is right before you leave."

"Oh sure," she said, "you say that *now*, but when tomorrow comes around where will you be?" She smiled and closed her eyes. She was starting to feel sleepy.

"Hey, do you wanna... nah, never mind." He looked down at his beer.

"What?"

"No," he said, "it was corny."

"*What*?" Who was this boy that he was playing coy with her? She was too tired for his shenanigans.

Then Scott Temple looked at her with his big green eyes. "I was going to ask you if you wanted to, I don't know, go upstairs where it was quieter and talk *now* or something, but it sounded like some cheesy line, and so I decided not to say it."

That was all? "Oh sure," she said. "We can do that."

He smiled, "Really?"

"Yeah, why not?" It wasn't like he wanted to go somewhere far away or something. "It's just over there." She pointed over her shoulder toward the stairs. She saw Becky then; she was holding a water bottle and looking around. She almost called out to her, so she could meet Scott and see what a nice guy he was. Becky always thought he was gross and sleazy but Sam always thought she was wrong about that. Now she could come over and meet him and see that Sam was right all along. Then she remembered that Becky was being a big killjoy and she was mad at her. So she didn't say anything.

"Cool," he said. Scott Temple took her hand (like they were little kids crossing a street!), and led her toward the stairs.

Suddenly, Becky was standing in front of them. She didn't look happy.

"Sam," she said. "Can I talk to you alone for a second?"

"Now?" She was so tired she was practically falling over; she wasn't sure if she would  be able to stand if she let go of Scott Temple's hand.

“Right now.”

“Can it wait? Me and Scott were about to go upstairs.”

“Yeah, I can see that,” she said. “Hey Scott.”

“Hey Becky,” said Scott Temple.

“It’s important, Sam.”

Sam sighed. Becky was great, but sometimes she could be pretty dense. “Okay, one minute.” She let go of Scott Temple’s hand. “I’ll be right back,” she said to him, “right back.”

“I’ll be right here,” he said.

Becky led Sam a few steps away, and turned around so they were out of earshot. “What are you doing?”

“What do you mean?”

“I mean, why are you going upstairs with that creep?”

“Scott’s not a creep. And why shouldn’t I go upstairs?”

“Uh, because you’re drunk? And because that guy’s just gonna try and get in your pants.”

“You don’t know what you’re talking about,” Sam said, angrily; she’d just about had it with Becky. “Scott’s totally a nice guy; you’ve never even given him a chance. And so what if I’m a little drunk? You were always telling me I should try it.”

Becky reached out to her, “Sam-”

“*No!*” Sam pulled away from Becky, “I can take care of myself!”

She went back over to Scott Temple, took his hand. “Sorry about that, Scott,” she said.

“*Sam*,” Becky pleaded as they started up the steps.

“I’ll talk to you later, Becks,” Sam called out over her shoulder. She didn’t even turn around.

Scott Temple found them a room towards the end of a long hallway. It was dark and they could barely hear the loud music playing downstairs and outside. Sam sat on the edge of the bed and tried to get back into her good mood. But it was hard.

"She just made me so mad."

"I know how it is," Scott Temple said. "Friends are great, but sometimes they can get a little weird when something they don't understand is happening."

"Totally," Sam said, and fell back on the bed.

Scott Temple leaned back and rested his head on his hand, his biceps bulged. "But it's okay; she'll be okay."

"I just, I was in such a good mood, you know? And now it's ruined."

"Doesn't have to be," Scott Temple scratched his chin. "You know what might help?"

"What?"

Scott Temple smiled, "Another drink."

"Yes, please," she said, and held her empty cup up in the air. "I'll take another screwdriver. Heavy on the driver." She laughed at her own joke. Scott Temple was right; she *was* funny.

"Got it," he said, and then he was gone.

Sam stayed where she was lying on the bed. She was tired; getting mad at Becky had used up all her energy. It felt like she could fall asleep right there. Why didn't she? It was a nice, soft bed, and that's what they were for. Why couldn't she just go to sleep right there? There was a reason she couldn't, she knew it. She was waiting for someone, who was it again? Scott Temple. Scott Temple was the boy from her fantasy. She liked that fantasy, it made her feel all warm in her tummy just thinking about it. Scott Temple was getting her a drink,. He was so cute. Maybe she'd just rest for a minute, get her strength up.

Sam's eyes shot open at the sound the creaking door.

“Sorry that took so long,” Scott Temple said. “I got caught up in something downstairs.”

How long was he gone? Had she been asleep?

“Here we go,” Scott Temple said, handing her a cup. “A beer for me. A screwdriver for you.”

Hey! Another drink! Sam sat up, “Yay!” she said sleepily, as she took the cup. “These’re my favorites.”

Scott Temple sat on the bed next to Sam, close enough that their hips touched. Sam drank the contents of the cup in one long gulp. Scott Temple took the empty cup out of her hands and put it on the floor; he brushed her hair behind her ear. Then, his hand slid down her face to her chin; he turned her face so that they were looking at each other. She tried looking at him but she was having trouble focusing on anything.

He leaned even closer, their faces were practically touching. “You’re really pretty, you know,” he said.

His hands were rougher than she’d imagined. She could smell the sweat and alcohol on him.

He kissed her on the cheek, pulled back, looked her in the eye, then he kissed her on the cheek again and then down on her neck. His kisses were sloppy and wet. They felt kind of gross. But she liked the way his head was resting on her shoulder. She leaned her head on top of his and closed her eyes. She was so, so tired.

Scott Temple kept kissing her neck; he put his hand on her shoulder and gently pushed her back onto the bed. Sam let herself fall without struggle. Deep inside she felt that something was happening that she should pay attention to, something that was maybe important. But she was exhausted and the mattress was so comfortable and all she really wanted to do was sleep.

He leaned over her, still kissing her neck and shoulders. His hand was under her shirt, massaging her hip. Sam felt heavy and sludgy all over. She tried to move her arms, but they were heavy like lead. Scott Temple’s hand moved across her stomach; his fingertips brushed under her jeans, under the waistband of her underwear. His hand worked up her stomach toward her chest, pushing her shirt up. Sam laughed as his fingers brushed over her belly; she gathered enough energy to weakly push his hand away. He stopped for a second, and she opened her eyes and looked at him. Or rather, at the blur that she thought was him.

She tried to open her mouth, tried to speak, but her jaw wasn't working the way it should. Then she couldn't keep her eyes open anymore and she fell back into the fog.

Dimly, Sam felt Scott Temple lift her tanktop all the way up and kiss her bare chest; her skin was moist and sticky from his saliva. He was lying on top of her now, pinning her leg with his hips. He spread her legs and rubbed the inside of her thigh. His hips pushed up against her leg, grinding. His hand made its way up her thigh. From far, far, away she heard the pop on her jeans unbuttoning and the sound of her zipper going down.

Scott Temple's hand slipped under her pelvis and lifted her up; his other hand started roughly tugging her jeans and underwear down off her hips.

All she wanted was to sleep. She was as tired as she'd ever been, but there was something keeping her from letting go. The part of her that wanted her to pay attention screamed that she really needed to get it together, but everything felt so far away and so unreal. Her body was unresponsive and she couldn't keep any thought in her head. Her jeans were completely off now; she felt the shiver of goose bumps along the inside of her legs. There was another zipper sound.

Suddenly there was a loud crash. Scott Temple cried out, then nothing. He was gone. Sam managed to get her eyes open and focused enough to see him pinned against the wall by a boy in a leather jacket. She couldn't make out who he was, his back was to her. But he was big, big enough to hold Scott Temple up against the wall so high that his feet weren't touching the ground.

The tall boy was yelling at Scott Temple, and Scott Temple looked scared. He tried to respond, but seemed to have trouble on account of the other boy's forearm pushed into his chest. The boy released Scott Temple, and he crumbled to the floor. Then the boy seized Scott Temple by the collar of the shirt and drug him toward the door, threw him out of the room, and slammed the door. Finally, the boy turned around and Sam saw his face. She smiled.

"Nick," she said, "when did you...?" The effort of saying all those words was too great for her, and she finally surrendered to sleep.

## FROM DUSK TILL DAWN

He hadn't actually sat down and watched it in years.

The first time he saw it, he was in high school and it blew his mind. He never cared much about movies; it was just on one morning and he was sitting on the couch cooling off after a long run. He flipped through the channels and stopped on the image of George Clooney glaring and pointing a gun right into the camera and telling everyone to "*be cool.*" Nick always thought Clooney was sort of a pretty boy and a pussy, but he looked badass there, holding that gun, a wicked tattoo running up his neck. Nick figured he'd watch for a while, maybe see where it went. The story started dragging after the shoot-out in the first scene; Clooney and his brother were bank robbers who kidnapped a preacher and his family and it was just going on and on. Nick was about to change the channel when this super-hot Mexican girl started dancing with a snake. So he figured he'd stick with it at least until she was done dancing. But, as she was wrapping up, shit went nuts; the hot girl turned into a giant snake and bit Clooney's brother. Suddenly everyone was turning into vampires and ripping everyone else apart.

It was awesome.

He must have watched it a hundred times after that. It was one of the only movies he ever bought for himself. It was just so gory and funny and strange. And Clooney was fucking amazing in it. Nick loved the way he managed to be both an utterly ruthless badass who killed without a second thought and a nice guy who still loved his brother and be nice to the preacher and his family when they didn't fuck with him. He showed the movie to all his friends and girlfriends, when he was older, teammates. He'd take it on the road and watch it in his hotel room or on the bus. He even got a tattoo that looked like the one on Clooney.

There wasn't a reason he stopped watching it, he just sort of did. There were no new friends to watch with or they'd already seen it or whatever, and he practically had the thing memorized anyway. At some point, he lost his copy, during a move, or maybe he lent it to someone and forgot to get it back. The point was, it was gone and he never replaced it.

But that night when he got home from Dana's and there wasn't anything interesting on TV, no baseball or basketball, just a *Family Guy* he'd already seen a million times, he checked on demand and there it was in the Fear Channel section. What the hell. He settled in on the couch, opened a beer, and hit start.

He was about twenty minutes in—Clooney and his brother were at the motel with the bank clerk—when his phone rang. He didn't even want to look and see who it was. He was in a good mood; Gertie was on the couch with him, her head in his lap and grunting happily as he pet her ears. He was settled into an old favorite movie and halfway into his second beer and the phone could only bring trouble.

But he did look, and when he saw Sam's name on the caller ID his curiosity got the better of him.

"Hello?"

"Is this Nick?" It was a girl he didn't recognize. She sounded nervous, and there was a lot of noise in the background.

"Yeah," said Nick. "Who's this?"

"My name's Becky, I'm a friend of Sam Heller. You drove me home once."

"Okay," said Nick. "Why are you calling me?"

"I think Sam's in trouble."

Nick turned off the TV and grabbed his jacket from off the arm of the couch.

"Where are you?"

He called Liz on his way to the party. She was in a panic. She filled Nick in about the fight, and how Sam ran out of the house afterwards. She called Sam a dozen times to find out where she was, make sure she was safe, but it went straight to voicemail every time. She tried calling Becky, same thing. Hours passed since Sam disappeared and Liz was on the verge of calling the police.

Nick gave Liz the gist of what he knew. He said Becky called him because she was afraid Liz would be mad; he said Sam was at a party and drank too much and he was going to pick her up.

He didn't go into the rest of what Becky told him. No sense in scaring her more over something that might be nothing. Probably was nothing. Better be fucking nothing. And if something *was* happening, better that, if there was something to tell, it had a happy ending. Happy as in something *could* have happened, but Nick would put a motherfucker through a window before it did. Just the thought of some piece of shit taking advantage of that little girl…

Nick turned the music all the way up and leaned on the gas.

A nervous looking girl sat on the porch; she was up and running to his truck before it even came to a stop. He only saw Becky once before, a while ago, and it wasn't like he paid much attention; but she looked familiar, and she was sure as shit acting like she knew him. Her eyes were puffy and her makeup was smeared, she'd obviously been crying. She looked terrified.

"I'm sorry about this but I didn't know what else to do."

"Where is she?"

"She's upstairs, I don't know which room," she said. "Goddamn Scott Temple fucking preppy asshole piece of shit. He came down a little while ago, right before I called you, and talked to a few of his friends. I kept trying to go up but they got in my way, blocked me. They were laughing."

Of course they were. Nick knew guys like that; he grew up with them. Guys who thought they could take whatever they wanted and intimidate anyone that got in their way. "They can fucking try to stop me."

He saw the friends the second he was inside the house. Three dicks with shaved heads in soccer shirts posted at the bottom of the stairs. They were clearly blocking the stairs from anyone they didn't like. The same thing used to happen when he was their age. He hated it even then. The dicks were laughing and drinking; two were sitting on the bottom step, a third stood over them, leaning on the banister. Entitlement radiated from every inch of them; the smug little shits were used to being the biggest, baddest guys in the room.

The dicks saw him coming, Becky right behind, and stopped laughing. The standing one started toward him. Some guys thought that *thinking* they were tough actually *made* them tough. Fucking jokes. All you had to do with guys like that was push a little and they'd fold like a house of cards. Nick shoved the first dick aside, hard, and focused on the two still sitting on the bottom step.

"*Move,*" he said.

They moved.

He went up to a long hallway with a half dozen doors. Nick and Becky went down the hallway checking each door. Two of the rooms were empty, two had other kids in them, one was a bathroom. The last door was locked.

"Stay there," Nick said to Becky. Then he reared back and kicked as hard as he could.

It was dark in the room, but Nick could make out two people on a bed. A guy was leaning over a mostly naked girl lying on her back. The guy was shorn like the dicks downstairs; he was hovering over the girl, fiddling with his pants. He spun around toward the door; Nick got a clear view of Sam's unconscious face and her bright red hair.

He was across the room in a second, pulled the fucker off the bed, and threw him across the room.

"Nothing happened man, I swear!" the kid stammered as Nick advanced. "I'm sorry! Nothing happened, nothing happened, nothing happened nothing happened noth-"

"*Shut up!*" Nick punched the kid in the stomach, lifted him off the ground and slammed him against the door. There was an audible *thock* as the kid's head bounced off the hard wood. Every impulse in his body screamed at him to shred the cocksucker, to break every bone in his body. The fucking little would-be rapist asshole had it coming. It wasn't like he probably hadn't done this a dozen times before with a dozen different girls. It wasn't like he wouldn't try it again.

Something smelled. Nick looked down and saw the growing stain on the front of the kid's pants. It was fucking pathetic, but it cleared Nick's head, reminded him it was just a kid he was dealing with. A fucking degenerate would-be rapist kid, but still just a kid.

Nick put his face up close to the kid's; tears ran down his cheeks. "Listen to me," he said. "You're never trying this little stunt again as long as you live. Do you understand?"

The kid nodded.

"Good. And if you ever, *ever*, talk to Samantha Heller again, if you talk to her friends, if

you *make eye contact* with any of them, I will find you and I will end you."

"I promise," the kid whispered. "I'm sorry, I'm sorry, I'm sorry."

"Get the fuck out of here." Nick eased off, let the kid down off the door; then he punched him one more time, same spot as before. The kid coughed in surprise, doubled over in pain. Nick grabbed the kid's collar and threw him out of the room. Then he turned around and looked at Sam.

She stared at him with cloudy, unfocused eyes; he knew that look. She was tanked, like, gone tanked, and naked form the waste down. Nick focused tightly on her face as another wave of rage came over him. She smiled dreamily.

"Nick," she slurred, her words sliding into one another. "When did you...?" and then her eyes closed and she was asleep.

He stepped into the hall; Becky hadn't budged from her spot. A small crowd was gathered behind her. The cocksucker was gone, but there was a hole in the plaster wall where he'd crashed into it. Whatever, it wasn't his problem. Nick closed the door, waved Becky over.

"We're okay. She's not in the best shape, but nothing really bad happened."

"Are you sure?"

"Yeah, it was close, it was real fucking close, but he didn't… she's okay." He took a breath, gathered his thoughts as best he could, blood pounded in his ears. "Look, she's not, you know. You should probably go in there, get her together. I'll wait out here."

Becky nodded; she slipped past Nick, opened the door, and disappeared into the darkness of the room, closing the door behind her. Nick stood in the hallway and waited. The group of gawkers at the end of the hall stood and wordlessly watched him. All these kids, all these fucking little rich kids were downstairs having the time of their little lives while upstairs a girl came within a fucking baby hair of getting raped. None of them looked out for her when she was getting falling down drunk; none of them seemed to care when she was carried upstairs by a fucking troglodyte who set guards at the steps. Oh, but when a fight breaks out, when someone might get their ass kicked or there was a little drama to witness, you couldn't keep them away.

"The *fuck* are you looking at?" he roared. "Go back to your stupid fucking party, show's over!"

The door opened and Becky stuck her head out. "We're good," she said, "but I don't know how we're getting her out of here."

Inside Sam sat on the edge of the bed, her head hanging limply, eyes closed. Becky managed to get her dressed, but it was pretty obvious she wasn't in any shape to walk anywhere on her own.

"All right," Nick sighed, "let's do this. *Sam!*"

Sam's head shot up and her eyes opened; she fixed him with a glassy stare. "Shup?" she mumbled, "timesit?"

"It's time to go, come on." Nick helped Sam to her feet; put his arm across her back, holding her up. "We're gonna walk out of here, okay?"

Sam snorted, wiped her nose with her free hand and coughed. "Kay," she said, "cool, cool."

"Go make sure the hall's clear," Nick instructed Becky. "Make sure your fucking *friends* aren't out there gawking."

Becky leaned out the door. "All clear," she called.

"Check the stairs; we'll be there in a minute. All right," he said to Sam, "here we go."

Sam shuffled out the door and down the hallway, shoulders slumped, arms hanging at her sides. She moved like a zombie, swaying from side to side with each step. A couple times Nick had to grab her again, steady her so she didn't fall. The whole thing was maddeningly slow, but it wasn't like he'd never walked a drunk somewhere before; hell, he'd taken his turn being the drunk plenty of times. He stopped Sam at the foot of the steps and took stock of her state: she didn't look good: her eyes were hooded, her mouth hung open, and she kept snorting. She was basically asleep on her feet. The stairs would be tricky, and there were certainly more gawkers on the first floor. The thought of those little assholes watching her stumble down the steps and out the door turned his stomach; if he had to give them a show, it sure as shit was going to be as short as possible.

Becky stood at the bottom of the steps. "Open the door," he called to her. Then he scooped Sam up and cradled her in his arms; she buried her face in his neck and fell back asleep. He carried her down the steps, past the large crowd of kids gathered by the steps and out the front door.

"Are you gonna get in trouble?" Becky asked as they all crossed the lawn. "You know, for what you did to Scott in there?"

"Doubt it," said Nick. "To that guy, the only thing worse than getting beat up is talking about it. Besides, what's he gonna say? *I was about to rape an unconscious girl when a guy came in and kicked my ass*? It'll be fine. Get the door."

Becky opened the passenger side door of Nick's truck. Nick slid Sam onto the seat and buckled her.

Becky asked, "Are you taking her home?"

"That's the plan," said Nick. "I'm sure she'll call you tomorrow or something." He walked around to the other side of the truck.

Sam's eyes shot open at the sound of the engine roaring to life. She looked around, confused; then she focused on Nick. She smiled and mashed her hand against the window controls, rolling it down. She snorted and spat out into the night. She turned back to Nick.

"Where're we goin'?"

"I'm taking you home."

Sam violently shook her head. "Oh no," she said. "No, no, no, no, no."

"Oh yes," Nick said, "it's been a long night. Your mom's worried sick about you."

"Not going home," insisted Sam, still shaking her head. "Wanna stay with you."

Nick laughed. "You can't stay with me. You're going home."

"*No,*" Sam said. "Don't wanna go home, never going home again. Wanna stay with *you!*" She turned and spat out of the window again. There was an edge to Sam's voice that made Nick pause. She seemed to be waking up more, seemed more animated. She really didn't want to go home. When he talked to Liz earlier, she was on the edge of panic herself. How would she react to seeing Sam in this condition? Maybe it would be better to keep them separate until things calmed down a little.

He called Liz and filled her in. He said he had Sam and she was safe, but needed to sleep the night off. He said she was resistant about going home and he was bringing her to his place. It was better that way; it would give Liz a chance to get some sleep. If Sam was there, Liz would be up all night making sure she was okay. Nick said he wasn't going to sleep any time soon anyway, so he'd take care of it. Things would be better in the long run.

Liz agreed. She didn't seem too happy about it, but she agreed. She didn't like that Nick was so coy about where Sam had been and what she had been doing either. She made Nick promise to come by in the morning, before Sam came home, and fill her in.

"Okay," Nick said to Sam. "I talked to your mom; you're staying at my place tonight, but you're going home in the morning. Understand?"

Sam smiled at him. "You're the best," she sighed. Then she spat out the window again.

"Sure I am," he said. "Hey, can you stop spitting out the window please?"

"Can't stop," she said.

"Why not?"

"Because I'm a gangster."

Nick burst out laughing, "Because you're a *what?*"

"I just told you," she said. "I'm a gangster." She spat again.

"Fair enough," he said. "You keep on keeping on."

Nick drove Sam across Baxter; it wasn't even midnight yet. He'd been to parties like that. Somebody got a hold of an empty house on campus. Those parties were the best, there was music and drinks and drugs and girls and there were no rules. But the thing about no rules was it meant you had to make up the rules yourself, had to be responsible about being irresponsible. You had to know when a guy wasn't good to drive or a girl was too far gone to make a move on. It was harder on girls; they had to know their own limits, because if they didn't, there was always someone waiting to pounce.

That's what made it special for them, the taking of something not offered.

Baxter was full of guys like that, entitled little shits with rich parents who didn't care what their kids were up to. They always played soccer or lacrosse, drove around town in their fancy SUVs, blaring hip-hop and dressing like they just bought the whole

American Apparel catalogue. Fucking kids thought they could get away with anything.

He looked over at Sam, asleep next to him in the truck. Her legs were curled up beneath her and her head rested against the base of the open passenger side window, her red hair fluttering madly in the breeze.

The porch light was on when they pulled up, but the rest of the house was dark. Nick carried Sam the gangster inside and laid her on the couch on her side. He could hear the TV in Val and Tom's room, the volume low. Nick put a bowl on the floor under Sam's head and an old towel under the bowl. He draped a sheet over her body and tucked a pillow under her head. Then he went to the kitchen, pulled a beer, the cheese, mustard, and roast beef out of the fridge, and made himself a sandwich. Back in the living room he grabbed the remote off the coffee table and took a seat in the easy chair next to the couch. Gertie wandered into the living room, from where she'd been sleeping on Nick's bed, and rested her head in his lap. He looked over at Sam; she was totally out.

He turned the TV on, scratched Gert behind the ears, and restarted his movie from the beginning.

## SOAKING IT UP

Where was she?

She was on a couch in a living room; there was a sheet over her, and her head, which was *pounding*, was resting on a pillow. She could see out a big window that looked onto a street she didn't recognize. She tried pulling herself up, to take a better look around, but it felt like her bones were grinding together and the slightest movement made her stomach lurch and her head swim. Better to lie still for a little while, figure things out from there.

The room looked vaguely familiar; she must have been in it before, but she couldn't remember when or why. She wasn't at a friend's house. The couch felt worn, the cushions a little thin; it didn't *feel* familiar. Sam tried to stay calm. Wherever she was, however she got there, she appeared to be safe. It was morning, she was dressed, mostly anyway (she groaned inwardly at the immerging memory of throwing her shirt away at the party); the bottom line was, she was okay. Sam racked her brain, *who did she know that could have brought her here?*

She retraced her steps from the night before.

As well as she could anyway.

There was the fight with her mother. She went to the party; talked to Becky (did Becky know where she was? She should find her phone, call Becky), drank, danced, drank some more, danced more, and drank more yet again. Then things got really fuzzy.

She definitely remembered being outside after that, going over to the scary kids in black, remembered smoking with them, talking. What did they talk about?

And then she went back inside, right? She couldn't be sure, but she felt like she must have because she had a dim notion of talking to Becky again, and Becky wanting her to slow down, drink some water. And then, something happened.

Because she was mad at Becky.

Why was she mad at Becky?

Was Becky mad at her?

Or she was worried.

She was worried because Sam was doing something, and she didn't want her to do it. But she was going to and…

Wait.

Oh, God.

Did she?

She didn't…

Oh no.

She remembered.

She was talking to Scott Temple. That was what it was.

She was talking to Scott Temple and they were going upstairs, and Becky didn't want her to go because she thought Scott Temple was a jerk and Sam got really mad at her and went upstairs anyway, and then… nothing.

She couldn't remember anything after going upstairs.

Total blank.

What happened after that?

Had she?

Nooo. No way.

She hadn't, like, made out with Scott Temple, had she? Surely she'd remember making out with Scott Temple.

Then again.

She was awful drunk.

God, if it was true, let her please remember making out with Scott Temple.

She had to find out what happened last night and how she got… wherever it was that she was now. Sam looked around again; her phone was in her purse. Or at least, that's where she kept it; it was where it was supposed to be. Find her purse, find her phone, call Becky, figure out what the hell was going on. It was a plan.

But she couldn't see her purse.

After what felt like an hour, and using more effort than it would normally take her to lift up a car, Sam propped herself up on her elbows and got a better view of the room. A table and chairs occupied one corner of the room. The table was clear, as were the chairs, no purse there. A plate and empty beer bottle lay beside the easy chair next to the couch. Sam's stomach lurched again at the sight of the bottle, but she maintained her balance. She wasn't about to lie back down now.

The door was behind the chair. Sam heard music on the other side of it. Life! Maybe whoever was on the other side of the door could give her the answers she needed.

"Hello?" She intended to call out, not to yell, but to raise her voice enough to be heard. But it came out in a croak, barely above a whisper. She coughed, cleared her throat, tried again.

"Hello?"

Same result.

Her throat was swollen and her mouth tasted like the inside of an ashtray. Jesus, they weren't kidding when they said hangovers sucked.

Sam reached up, grabbed the back of the couch and pulled herself into a sitting position. She brought her legs down onto the floor, her ankle bumped into a red bowl that sat next to the couch and sloshed the contents around. Sam leaned in close to see what was in the bowl, but reared back in shock and disgust when the stench hit her.

Yeah, that was vomit.

That was her vomit.

Okay.

That was vile.

Sam sat rigid on the couch, clutching the cushions as tightly as she could. She squeezed her eyes shut and tried not to moan, throw up, pass out, or some combination of the three. It was a fact. She'd never felt so bad in her life.

When the room finally stopped spinning, or slowed down enough for her to move, Sam struggled to her feet. Then with one hand resting on the wall for support, and oh so slowly so that her bones didn't shatter, Sam drug her useless body across the room and through the door to the other side.

"Look Robbie," Val said. "*It's alive!*"

Robbie smiled up at Sam, said a string of nonsense and laughed.

"Val?" Sam said. "What am I doing here?"

"You had a wild night from what I heard." She stirred the contents of a red plastic bowl; its twin sat in the living room filled with puke. Sam's stomach twisted again. She took a seat at the table and held her head in her hands.

"Okay," she said, "but why am I *here?*"

"Nick said you needed someone to pick you up at some party, and you were mad at your mom, so he got roped into doing it. You refused to go back to your place, so he brought your drunk ass here." Val put down the bowl; she took a cup from a cabinet and filled it with lemonade from the fridge. "Drink," she said.

"Uh…" Sam pushed the cup away.

Val pushed it back. "Drink," she said again.

Sam took a reluctant sip. It was the best lemonade in the world. She drank the whole cup.

"It's good, right?" Val said. "You were dehydrated, drinking dries you out. And the puking doesn't help."

"Yeah," said Sam. "Sorry about that."

Val shrugged. "I'm not the one who has to clean it up." She took Sam's cup and re-filled it; put it back down on the table.

"You left most of the contents of your stomach in that. I'm making pancakes. You should try and have one; they'll absorb whatever alcohol's left in you."

Gertie trotted into the room and up to Sam. She pressed her muzzle into Sam's arm, licking until Sam pet her. "Thanks," she said. "I guess I overdid it. I'm kind of new to this drinking thing."

"So Nick tells me." Val took a skillet from the cabinet, put it on the stove, and lit the burner.

"Where is Nick?"

"Nick," Val said, "is at your house trying to settle things up with your mom for you."

"Oh."

"Yeah, oh. You really put her through a ringer. And I gotta tell you, if you were my kid and you ran out on me like that and turned your phone off? You'd still be walking funny when you had kids of your own. I can't imagine what would've happened if any of us tried some shit like that with our folks."

Sam put her head back in her hands.

"I mean you seem like a good kid, and I hear this whole moving thing's been rough on you, but Jesus." She poured some batter from the red bowl onto the skillet. "You're lucky Nick showed up when he did."

"Wait," said Sam, "what do you mean?"

Val turned from the skillet, looked at Sam. "What?"

"What do you mean, *I'm lucky Nick showed up when he did.* Why am I lucky? Did something happen last night?"

"Just, things could have gotten out of hand is all," Val said, turning back to the pancakes. "I knew plenty of girls that had too much to drink one night, next thing you know…" She pointed over her shoulder at Robbie. "Oh yeah," she said, "it happens."

Sam didn't know what to say. She expected this kind of talk from her mother, not from Val. She was so angry last night, so desperate to feel anything else. She wanted to hurt her mother.

Sam wanted to make her, for one night at least, feel out of control, to feel that fear and uncertainty that Sam lived with for the last month. But why? What good did that do? What did it change? She was right back where she was, worse even, because now she was in serious trouble.

The more she thought about it, the more right Val sounded. She imagined her mother calling her phone over and over, going to voicemail and panicking. She thought about her calling Sam's dad, her dad stuck in Chicago unable to calm her down. He'd call repeatedly to see if there was any word yet; each time her mother said no, he'd get a little more frightened, a little more helpless.

She *was* lucky nothing bad happened. She could have been hurt at the party or wandered off into traffic or something. It terrified her how little from the previous night she could actually remember. How could she put herself in that kind of position? And for what? To prove some point? That would have been no consolation if she woke up in the hospital or choked to death on her own vomit somewhere. She felt like she knew someone who knew someone who died like that. Maybe one of Becky's distant relatives or something, some kid went off to college and drank himself to death. And it didn't really matter whether she actually knew someone or not. It happened all the time and it could have happened to her.

She bet whoever it happened to, their family was *wrecked.*

She thought with disgust of the joy and empowerment she felt storming out of the house the night before. She wanted to hurt and scare her mother, she knew she was succeeding, and she was glad.

Regret flooded her. She was a terrible daughter, a terrible person. Tears welled up in her eyes.

"Okay, okay," said Val as she put a plate in front of Sam, "don't make a federal case out of it. You fucked up, it happens."

"But," Sam sniffed, "but all that stuff you said. I scared my mom, I could have been hurt or raped and no one would know."

"Yeah, but you weren't." Val sat down across from Sam, put her hands on the table. "Look, all that stuff I said was true, you fucked up, but you're okay now. Your mom's okay. Everyone's okay. This crying thing you're into right now? That's just the hangover talking, for real. Feel bad, but don't fall apart on me here."

Sam ran her hands through her hair. "But what do I do now?"

"What you do now is go home and apologize until you're blue in the face. Maybe save some of those tears for then. Your mom will either chew your ass out or be so glad you're safe that she lets you slide this one time. If you get punished, you sack it up and take it, because you deserve it. If you slide, be fucking grateful, because she'd be totally in the right about burying you for the rest of your days."

"Okay," said Sam.

Val stood up, made a face, "*Okay.*" she said mockingly, but then she smiled. "I'm gonna go bring some pancakes to my husband," she said. "You sit here and eat, drink some more lemonade, watch Robbie, and try *not* to cry anymore. I'll be right back."

Sam sat silently and picked at her pancake. She ripped a third of it off, and dropped it at her feet for Gertie, who wolfed it down and looked back up at her, ready for more. The pancake tasted fine, but her body fought against it. Val said she would be hungry eventually, but the way Sam felt, she didn't know if she'd ever want to eat again. Why did people drink if this was the result? She thought back to all the books, movies, and TV shows she'd seen where the characters were hungover and still went about their days as if nothing was wrong. She always kind of figured a hangover was nothing more than a headache and a bad taste in the mouth, maybe some nausea. The heels of her feet hurt. No one ever said anything about the heels of their feet.

Across the kitchen, Robbie picked up a brightly colored plastic box, covered with buttons and levers. He carried it to Sam, dumped it in her lap and looked up at her. "Urt," he said.

Sam cocked her head and looked at him, trying to understand, "Urt?"

Robbie nodded. “Urt,” he said again, and mashed the buttons on the box. “Urt,” he said.

“I don’t, I don’t know what that means,” she told him.

“It means he wants you to turn it on,” said Val, walking back into the room. “Hit the big red switch on the top.” She took another plate from the cabinet, and stacked it with pancakes.

“Oh,” Sam said, “okay.”

She flipped the switch and the box came to life, the buttons all lit up and tiny music burst from the speakers. It felt like someone was shaking her aching head as hard as they could. It was the worst thing in the world. Robbie cried out in delight, smiled up at her.

“Robbie honey, go play with your toy in the corner,” Val said. “Aunt Sam isn’t feeling good.”

Robbie took his death-box and started across the room. Val put down a hand to stop him. She dropped to her knees, turned him around. “What do you say to Aunt Sam?” she asked him.

Robbie looked at Sam, or he looked at the space around her. “Tan gu,” he said.

“You’re welcome,” Sam said.

“Very good,” Val said to him, “go play.” She kissed his head, and sat beside Sam. “All my boys,” she said. “I don’t know what they’d do without me.”

“Where’s your husband?” Sam said. “Why isn’t he eating down here with you?”

“Because today is Saturday,” said Val. “And Saturday is homework day. Tom’s taking classes online, he catches up over the weekend.”

“What’s he taking classes in?”

“Business mostly, some accounting too. You know how Tom’s a chef, right?”

Sam nodded.

"His dream's always been to own his own restaurant. To do that though, you need money, to get money you need a loan from a bank. To get a loan, you need an education." She paused, "Well, you don't *need* one," she said, "but it helps a whole lot. Tom went to the culinary school in the city? And he got his degree and everything, but to a bank, that means fuck all. So he's getting another one, this time in business and management."

"That's cool," Sam said.

"I sure hope so," Val said. "I'd hate to think he spent all this time and money for nothing. It's going to take years as it is."

"Oh."

"That's what you gotta do though, you gotta be patient and you gotta be dedicated. Fortunately, Tom's a patient, dedicated guy. The world needs more guys like him, instead of all the fuck-ups, you know?"

Val looked at her, maybe for confirmation of some kind. Sam didn't know too many fuck-ups, so she just laughed.

Then Val said, "And you know who's the biggest fuck up I knowj? I mean the biggest dumb ass *what were you thinking* idiot I've ever seen?"

"Who?"

"Nick," Val said. "My nephew Nick. I know you like him and think he's great and all, and that's wonderful. But believe me, if Nick hadn't told me you were moving anyway, I would have told you to get as far away from him as possible. Everything he touches turns to shit."

Sam just stared at Val, blindsided.

"Don't get me wrong," Val said. "I love the guy and everything, but he's not to be trusted. I've never met a more self-destructive person in my life. Do you know why he didn't make it to the majors?"

"I know he got hurt." She wasn't sure they should be having this conversation.

"Yeah, but do you know *how* he got hurt?"

"I guess not."

"He got hit by a pitch, hard. Those boys down in triple A, they all throw a thousand miles an hour, and they got no control. So, Nick takes one real high on his back, bruises his shoulder, he has to go on the DL for a while. You know what that is?"

Sam nodded.

"Now the doctors tell him he'll be good to play again soon enough, but he has to take it easy for a little while, and do you know what he does? That dumb asshole goes and gets into a bar fight, the bruised shoulder gets dislocated and he's out for the rest of the season. He was never the same player after that; he got released less than a year later. All because he couldn't listen to the doctor's advice."

Val got up and poured herself some lemonade. She refilled Sam's cup and put a little in a sippy-cup for Robbie while she was at it. Sam hoped their conversation was over.

It wasn't.

Val sat back down. "After that he was just different. Or maybe he wasn't, maybe that was the problem, I don't know. But things were definitely different; he alienated all his old friends, didn't get any new ones. He went through girls like tissue paper. I keep hoping one day he'll grow up, but I'm not getting my hopes up anymore..."

She got quiet.

"Guys like Nick," she finally said, "they always think they know best. And they never listen to anybody, not doctors not friends, not *family*, not anyone. They always crash, always. And they burn whoever's near them when they do."

Sam stared down at her empty plate. She didn't know what else to do. Wasn't it bad enough that she was hung over without having to listen to this?

Val went on. "I don't want you to think I'm telling you this to be mean or something," she said. "Nick's like a brother to me, and he's the best friend I've ever had. But at the same time, he has a really bad habit of hurting the people who care about him. That's just a fact. And I would have hated to see it happen to you. Me and Tom? We're his family, we're used to it. We can take it. But you're just a kid—there's no excuse for him to get you caught up in his shit."

Robbie ran over and handed his mom one of his toy cars, breaking her train of thought. He bounced his stomach on Val's chair as she and drove the little car on her thigh, making little *vroom, vroom* sounds. Robbie squealed with delight, ran back to his toys, grabbed another car and brought it back to his mom, who repeated the motion. He did it again, and again, each time bouncing off the chair excitedly. On the fourth trip Robbie picked up the car, ran over to Val, and ran into the chair, then, instead of handing his mom the car, he stood there with a confused look on his face; he opened his mouth, and threw up.

"Oh, little man," cooed Val. "Little man? What happened?"

Confused, Robbie looked at the vomit on the tile, and then up at Val with eyes that seemed to say, *why did you do that to me*?

Sam knew just how he felt.

## MATCHES

Sam threw up the first time around one-thirty, just as the movie was winding up and Nick was drifting off to sleep. She moaned softly and he looked over just in time to see her heave. He had zero desire to catch shit from Val about puke on her couch. He leapt from the chair, over Gertie sleeping at his feet, and directed Sam's head over the bowl just as the first wave hit, holding her hair back. The vomit was thick and soupy; out of the corner of his eye he saw what looked like a mixture of brown sludge streaked with a variety of bright colors. Okay, no M&M's for a while. The bowl was almost full before she stopped, and only a few drops hit the towel beneath it. She never opened her eyes.

So it was a good news/bad news kind of thing. On the one hand, she hadn't woken up to throw up, which was bad if she had anything else in her system, threw up more, and was on her back at the time she did again. There was that. On the other hand, judging by the bowl, it was possible her stomach was empty and she was in the clear.

Possible, but not all that likely, and better safe than sorry.

Nick emptied the bowl in the toilet, grabbed a Mountain Dew from the fridge, sat back in his easy chair and looked for something else to watch.

*SportsCenter* was over and the west coast *Baseball Tonight* was into its first commercial break when she started again. This time the puke was mostly clear with a little bit of orange. The citrus and stomach acid burnt his nostrils. Nick started to gag a little himself. Sam coughed a few times then was still again. That had to be it. He couldn't imagine the girl's stomach could hold anything more.

Gertie trotted over to the bowl from where she'd been sleeping and sniffed at it curiously. She made a face, turned and walked away. Wow. He'd seen Gertie eat cat shit happily—the dried shit of a cat. Even she was turned off by Sam's vomit.

Nick stood up and nudged the bowl toward the couch with his foot. She could clean that one up herself when she woke up in the morning.

He looked down at her face, she looked so peaceful. The only sign that she was ill at all was a little string of vomit that started at her bottom lip and trailed down to the couch cushion. Back in the kitchen, Nick poured some water in a glass and dampened a washcloth. He went back into the living room, went down on one knee and put the cup down beside him. Gently, he wiped Sam's forehead and cheeks. Then he wiped her lips, cleaning the dried vomit that was flaking in the corners of her mouth and catching the spit trail.

"Sam," he said. "*Sam!*"

Her eyes opened and she looked at him like he was a bug flying around her head. "What?"

"Drink this." He handed her the cup.

Sam batted him away. "Don't fucking tell me what to do," she said.

Nick rolled his eyes. "*Drink it.*"

"Okay," she said. "Jesus." She took the cup and drank the water in one long gulp. A good portion of it ran down her chin and neck onto her chest. When she finished, she handed him back the cup and glared at him. "Happy?"

"Very," Nick said.

"Good," Sam said, "maybe now I can get some sleep." She lay back down, closed her eyes and was out like a light again.

Sam was still asleep when Liz called at eight the next morning. She asked him to come over. Nick, who'd finally fallen asleep in the easy chair only a few hours earlier, hauled himself up. He left after explaining to an angry Val why there was a sixteen-year-old girl passed out on her couch.

"Don't get me wrong," she told him, "I'm glad she's safe and everything. But I don't understand why *you* were the one she called."

"Sam didn't call me, her friend Becky did."

"What*ever*. The point is, whoever it was that called you, why was it you who had to swoop in and be the hero? Why didn't this Becky call Sam's mom, or another one of her friends or something?"

"Couldn't tell you, ask her. I was just trying to help out."

"Okay, but why is she *here*?"

Nick felt his temper flare. "I told you, she didn't want to go home last night. What was I supposed to do? Leave her on the street?"

"You could have just taken her home anyway. She is a child, you know. Children do things they don't want to all the time because an adult, that's you by the way, tells them they have to."

"I don't know why I didn't Val; I guess I'm just not very good at this sort of thing, seeing as how I've never fucking done it before. I figured with Sam trashed and Liz on the edge of a panic attack, it was a better idea to let the two of them cool off before they saw each other."

Val narrowed her eyes. "Something's going on here, something weird. This isn't you, you're not acting like *you.* What's the deal with you and these people? Why are you so involved in their lives all of a sudden? I mean helping out, teaching that kid to drive was one thing; it was a little out there but I could see why you'd do it. She's a sweet kid and it was harmless, but now you're rescuing her from parties and huddling up with the mom like you're her dad or something."

"I'm not trying to be her *dad* Val, Jesus-" he stopped himself. "You know what? I don't have time for this right now, okay? I don't have time for one of our regular *what was Nick thinking* conversations. I have to go talk to Liz so I can get the girl *out of your house*. We'll continue this when everything's settled, okay?"

He left without waiting for an answer.

Nick drove and smoked and fumed.

Why did Val have to do that? Why? He was trying to do the right thing here, trying to be the good guy, and somehow it was still wrong. Should he have left Sam at that party to get raped by that fucking douchebag? Said, *sorry, I can't get too involved; my aunt says it's weird*? Should he have taken her home and made things worse with Liz? Said, *here's your daughter, she's pretty fucking hammered and you look pretty edgy yourself—anyway good luck!?*

What if he took Sam home and she'd choked on her vomit because there wasn't anyone there to check on her? What if that had happened? He should have said that to Val. That would have been awesome if he'd thought to say that. Damn it. He would have liked to see her try and turn that into one of his mistakes.

Knowing Val, she would have found a way.

It was just—this was supposed to be the thing he did that was good. He was being helpful. Why couldn't Val see that? She never saw anything decent that he did. Val could like Sam and be nice to her, make her mix CDs or whatever and there wasn't anything sinister about it, but when he was being nice it was weird.

Nothing he did mattered because it was always, always, always wrong.

By the time Nick pulled into the driveway of the Heller's house he was so tired of the whole thing that he was determined to say whatever he needed to say to get Sam home and be done with them. No more driving with Sam, no more talks with Liz or games with Oscar. The whole reason he was doing any of it in the first place was to feel good. But Val ruined that. Better to wash his hands of the whole family.

But the second Liz opened the door and he saw how sad and tired she looked he forgot all of that and just wanted to help again.

"Thanks for coming," she said. She was wearing sweatpants and an old T-shirt. "I set up a play-date for Oscar; figured it'd be better if he were out of the house when Sam gets back. It was hard enough calming him down after she stormed out last night."

"I wouldn't worry about that. She's looking at a monster hangover when she wakes up."

Motherly concern flashed across Liz's face. "Was she really drunk? Like really?"

"She was pretty sauced, yeah."

Liz waved her hands at him to come inside. "Okay," she said, "what happened last night? Gimme the scoop."

"Are you sure you want to hear this?"

"It's why you're here. Better I get it from you and I can process it before I see her. Maybe avoid more drama."

"All right," Nick said, "but I don't know all that much. I was only there for the end, you know."

He told her what he knew, about getting the call from Becky, about the party and about finding Sam with the douchebag. He cleaned that part up a little; PG-13'd it to avoid upsetting her. He did say that Sam seemed out of control and that the douche was taking liberties, but he downplayed the severity of said liberties. If Sam remembered it and wanted to tell her mom, that was her business, not his. He told her about carrying Sam out to the car, about her treading consciousness, about the spitting (Liz laughed at that. "A gangster? Where did that come from?"), and about the puking. Mostly, he said, it seemed like a night that turned out okay, but was better not repeated any time soon.

"Oh Sam," Liz said sadly when he finished, "what am I going to do?" She pulled a pack of cigarettes out of her purse but her lighter was dead. "Shit," she said as she tried again and again to spark it, "nothing's working."

"Here," Nick dug a box of matches from his pocket, tossed them to Liz.

"Thanks," she said. She lit her smoke and tossed the box back.

"I thought you didn't smoke in the house," Nick said.

She looked at him sadly. "Really, at this point, who gives a fuck, right?"

"I guess," Nick said and lit up one of his own. "Can I ask, what's all this about anyway? This fight you two had?"

"What do you think it was about? What is it always about with her anymore? It was about Chicago."

Now it was Liz's turn to talk and Nick's turn to listen. She told him about the house selling, and the move and how sudden it was. She told him about Sam's reaction, how she came to Liz with the plan to stay with Becky, and how she exploded when Liz said no.

"I don't know," she said, "maybe I should give her plan more of a chance, maybe it seemed like I dismissed it out of hand. But I didn't want to get her hopes up about something that just wasn't going to happen."

"It's okay to say no to a kid, you know," Nick said. "In fact, it's kind of important."

"Yeah, but there are better ways to say it." Liz lit another cigarette. "I just, it felt like the conversation was going so well. It felt like we were communicating for the first time in, God, in forever. It felt like we were really seeing eye to eye. I thought maybe we were finally coming out of whatever this is we've been stuck in for so long. I was so unprepared once she got to her point. I thought… I don't know what I thought. Maybe I thought we were so close to really connecting, I just got impatient and jumped the gun." She took a long drag on her smoke and nodded her head as she exhaled. "That was it," she said, "definitely. That was where I fucked up. That was it right there. *Damn it.*"

Nick jumped in; he couldn't listen to it anymore. "Hey you gotta stop this whole *it's all my fault* nonsense, because it's just not true."

"Yeah, but-"

"Yeah but nothing; look, you're too hard on yourself. Period. Sam's a great kid, and I like her a lot, but she's the one who fucked up here, not you. She's the one who ran out of the house and didn't answer her phone and scared you. How is it you're the one feeling bad about it? She's got you so turned around that you're apologizing for her hurting you. Excuse me for saying so but that's ridiculous. There's no excuse for what Sam did, running out on you last night. None. And she's lucky nothing bad happened to her. You're not going to be doing her any favors by convincing yourself otherwise."

"I know," she said. "I know. But I see Steve, and he's just so *good* at talking to her, so good at seeing things from her perspective-"

He cut her off again, he couldn't help it, he was on a roll, walking around the room and gesturing as he spoke. "I'm sorry," he said, "but I have to say this. For weeks I've been hearing from you and Sam about what a great father this guy is. How he's so good at everything. But I can't help thinking that a good father backs up the mother. A good father doesn't just take off and move on a moment's notice and leave all the dirty work to the mom. And maybe, just maybe, if that good father hadn't spent so much time trying to understand Sam's perspective and spent a little more time teaching her to respect yours, none of this would have happened."

She laughed, but he could see her eyes welling up. "What are you, my contractor or my therapist?"

"Neither," he said taking a seat on the couch. "I'm just a guy who doesn't like to see a good person beat herself up over something that isn't her fault."

"I appreciate that," she said. "I really do. Sometimes it gets really easy to believe the worst about yourself when everyone you care about seems to be telling you it's true."

"Well don't," he said, "because it's bullshit."

She sat down next to him on the couch. "Thanks," she said, "thanks for everything. Thanks for the pep talk, thanks for helping with Sam last night, thanks for talking with me all the times you have."

"It was no sweat," he said.

"No, see, now you're doing it," she said. "Now you're the one not believing the best in yourself. It was a big deal you helping out, it made all the difference. I would have been lost without you. Really."

"It was a pleasure," he said standing up. "I'd do it again in a minute."

"I know you would," she said. "It's why you're such a good guy."

She surprised him then—she got to her feet, leaned in, and kissed him softly on the cheek. He turned to look at her, and her face was still there, head cocked slightly, hovering inches away from his own.

He looked at her, she was looking right back.

She wasn't backing away.

And neither was he.

She kissed him again, tentatively, this time on the mouth. Her lips lingered on his for a moment. They were warm and dry.

She pulled back again, looked at him again.

He could feel her breath on his face, smell her shampoo.

She looked at him and he knew what he was supposed to do next. Knew what he *wanted* to do next. On the one hand it all felt so familiar, automatic even. All he had to do was just let go. But he also knew that this time it was different. This wasn't some chick he met at a bar somewhere, or some local girl he got drunk with too late one night. Once he crossed the line it could never be uncrossed. But she was looking at him, and he knew what he wanted, and he could see she wanted it too. And she wasn't going to be standing this close to him forever.

Fuck it.

He wrapped his arm around her waist and put his hand flat against the small of her back. It felt good, felt right. He pulled her body up against his, and he kissed her. Her arms slid up his back and gripped his shoulders; her lips parted and her tongue slid into his mouth.

He pulled off, kept his arms around her, kept his body pressed against hers; he went just far enough to get one last good look at her, to see if she was taking this as seriously as he was. She looked serious enough. “What exactly are we doing here?” he said.

She didn’t say anything; she took his hand and led him up the stairs and into the bedroom.

# DODGING BULLETS

"Oh, little man," cooed Val. "Little man? What happened?"

Robbie looked down at the vomit on the tile and then back up at Val, confused. "Tuck," he said.

"Yeah," she said, "I can see that." She looked at Sam, "I think someone got too excited running back and forth so soon after drinking that lemonade."

"Yeah," Sam said, "the same thing used to happen with my little brother."

Val turned back to Robbie, gave him a big reassuring smile. "Did you hear that? Aunt Sam says this sort of thing happens. Oh well." She pulled Robbie into a gentle hug. "Let's clean it up."

Robbie watched his mom drape a towel over the wet spot on the tile. She glided it around in a small circle with her foot, and when she picked it up, the tile was clean again.

"See?" She knelt down, eye to eye with him, and smiled. "No worries."

Robbie smiled back at her, "Nowrs," he mumbled.

"That's right, no worries."

He laughed, hugged her, and toddled back to his toys.

Robbie's vomit incident seemed to distract Val totally from what she'd been saying. And for that, Sam was supremely grateful. She mumbled something about being tired, put her dishes in the sink, and slipped back into the living room. She flopped down onto the couch. She was miserable, turning over what Val said and trying to piece together the missing portions from the previous night. Whenever Robbie or Val came into the room, she closed her eyes to avoid any more unpleasant conversation.

And by the way, what was that all about? Why was Val being so hard on Nick? What did he do other than be totally helpful to Sam when she needed him? It pissed her off that someone who described herself as Nick's friend could speak so badly about him to someone she hardly knew. Maybe he *had* made trouble in the past, but the Nick that she knew, *her Nick*, was one of the few people she could actually count on these days. Why else would he be over at her house right now, trying to straighten things out with her mother?

He still wasn't back. She didn't know when he left, so she had no idea when to expect him. She thought about calling him, but what if he was in the middle of some intense conversation with her mother and she asked for the phone? Sam wasn't up to talking to her mother yet. She could ask Val when he left, but she couldn't handle another lecture about the perils of drinking or respecting her mother or Nick and his shortcomings; not when she was probably in for more of the same at home.

It was agonizing; she was waiting an indeterminate amount of time to be sentenced for crimes she had little to no memory of actually committing. It felt like she woke up hours ago, but when she looked at the clock, she saw it had been just over ninety minutes. Maybe, Sam thought, she could call Becky and get a ride home from her. Would that be rude though? Would it seem ungrateful somehow, or maybe impatient? Maybe she needed to sit and wait as part of her punishment. She just needed to know what she was supposed to do. Nick might be relieved not having to take her home after everything. There was no way he was happy babysitting a drunk girl on his Friday night, and then having to smooth things out with her mother first thing the next morning. Maybe getting a ride from Becky would spare him some trouble.

She looked at the clock and resolved to give him fifteen minutes to show up, call, or for the universe to give her some kind of sign that she was supposed to sit and wait a little longer. Then again, she could get some answers if she called Becky, fill in some of those blank spots.

Talking to her mother was going to be stressful; there was no getting around that. So the more prepared she was for that, the more in control everything else was, the better it would be for the two of them. Maybe she and Becky could get some breakfast. The pancake felt pretty good going down, maybe get some more of those somewhere, maybe with bananas too. Her stomach growled.

How about that? She *was* getting pretty hungry. Val was right on the money on that one.

Thirteen minutes went by and she was pretty much convinced that calling Becky was her best option—go to breakfast and leave Nick out of anymore drama. Then, she heard his truck pull quickly into the driveway and idle as he walked in the door.

He had a short exchange with Val in the kitchen, then he stepped into the living room and waved for her to get up.

"Let's go," he said.

She collected her stuff and wordlessly followed him to his truck.

Questions raced through her mind at a million miles an hour as they rode back to her house. What did they talk about? What was her mother's mood? Was she mad? How mad? What did Nick say? Did he stand up for her, or did he think she fucked up too? Why did he come get her? How did he know where she was? Had she called him or something? Did he know what happened to her last night?

Whatever happened, Nick wasn't talking, like, at all. He put the truck in reverse as soon as she was inside and her seatbelt was buckled. He didn't say a word, no *hello,* no *how're you holding up*, nothing. He barely even looked at her. It was awful.

Now Nick being quiet wasn't, in itself, that big a deal. He was a quiet guy, and there were lots of times the two of them drove and he said two or three words to her over an hour. But that was different. In those cases, Sam talked and talked as she drove; ran her mouth about whatever it was that occurred to her. It was a way to pass the time, work out whatever it was that happened to be on her mind that day. It was harmless and fun; at least, for her it was. Nick was important as a listener the same way he was important as a driving instructor. He really just had to be there. She knew he wasn't really interested in the things she talked about when she drove, and she didn't mind. Occasionally, she called him on not listening to her, but it was never serious, she was glad he was there at all.

The point was, usually when they drove and Nick was quiet it was because there was nothing for him *to* say. Now, he had a lot of information she could use. And his silence made her itch.

Was she supposed to talk first? Was that how it worked? If so, where was she supposed to start? Should she apologize? Ask him if he was mad at her? Try and find out what happened the night before? Ask him what he and her mother talked about? Try to gauge her mother's mood? See if he knew how much trouble she was in? Nick got along with her mother pretty well, seemed to like her, did they talk about how dead she was when she got home and he wasn't saying anything because he didn't want to be the bearer of bad news? If she chose the wrong topic, maybe it would make things worse. And the ride from Nick's house to hers wasn't all that long; there were so many different ways the conversation could go and every minute they didn't talk meant less information.

The pressure was unbearable.

Why didn't he just *say* something?

Sam sat in her seat and was miserable. He must see how agitated she was, must have some memory of being in a situation similar to hers and being desperate for some kind of break. He was angry at her. That was the only explanation. She said or did something really bad the night before to alienate him, something terrible she couldn't remember.

She hadn't, like, *tried* anything, had she? That would be beyond any horrible thing she could imagine, if she actually made some kind of move on him. But it would explain the sort of weird vibe he was giving off. It couldn't be, though, because there was no way. Just no way. Of course, if you asked her the day before, she would have said there was no way she would ever actually make out with Scott Temple either, and apparently that actually might have happened. Maybe in her drunken state, she tried to go two for two or something.

Maybe that's who Sam Heller was. Maybe you get a couple drinks in her and she'd mount anything handy. Maybe she really was just some trashy slut who needed an excuse. Maybe she was just a stupid selfish horrible girl who was mean to her mother and rude to her friends and ruined everything and didn't deserve a friend like Nick. She didn't deserve anything good.

Mean.

Bitch.

Slut.

Sam's throat started to close up. Tears stung her eyes. But she refused to cry, refused to feel sorry for herself. She was responsible for everything that happened, and she was responsible for any fallout that might come from it. She was the one who ran out of the house the night before, to go to that party, to get stupid, falling-down, black-out drunk. No one made her do any of those things. If she cried, Nick would probably feel sorry for her and forgive her for whatever she did that upset him and she didn't deserve to be forgiven.

Growing up, whenever Sam made a simple mistake, like lose something or break a dish by accident, her mother always said to her *and what have we learned*? It drove her nuts; it came off as patronizing and condescending. It was the kind of thing adults said to kids that seemed to mean one thing and actually meant the opposite. *And what have we learned* sounded like it was about growing up and taking responsibility for something, but actually it was about saying *you're still a kid and you did something stupid and I'm going to rub your nose in it because I'm an adult and I can.* There weren't lessons to be learned from everything; sometimes bad things just happened by accident and there was nothing you could take from it to make sure it didn't happen again.

That was how she felt about it before anyway.

But, sitting in Nick's truck, facing the colossal mess she'd made over the last eighteen hours and trying to figure out the best way to clean it up, she couldn't help thinking it. *And what have we learned*? What did she do, what were the consequences and how could she make sure it didn't happen again?

Maybe she was wrong about *and what have we learned* all along. Maybe it really was about not making excuses but instead resolving to grow and be stronger.

Maybe it was what she had to do right now. Just own up to her mistakes, no excuses, no qualifications—just apologize, and take the consequences. And if those consequences involved alienating Nick and upsetting her mother, she should be less worried about how mad Nick was, and concentrate on doing whatever needed to be done to get him less mad at her. Maybe, if instead of trying to figure out what her mother was going to do to her, she should concentrate on how she was going to make it up to her. How she was going to get her mother's trust back.

Maybe instead of feeling sorry for herself because everyone was mad at her, she could focus on their needs instead of her own.

Maybe that was what she could learn. If Nick needed his space, and what she wanted was for him to be okay, then that was what she would give him. Space. She might want to talk to him and ask him what was wrong and make sure he wasn't upset with her, but that would be for her benefit, not his. Same with her mother—if Sam had to sit on her ass and do nothing for a while in order to prove to her mother that she was sorry for what she did, that was just what she'd do. And it wasn't like last night was an isolated incident either. They'd been butting heads for a while now, and it just got worse since they learned about the move. After all, if Sam were in her mother's position, if she had a consistently bitchy daughter, who ran out of the house, disappeared without giving any sign of where she was going and showed up the next morning, she'd be furious too. She'd probably want to drop kick the kid into the next county or ground her until she left for college.

Of course, if her mother actually did ground her, that would really suck. She only had two weeks to see a lot of people and say good-bye. So hopefully it wouldn't be that. Hopefully she'd get reamed and punished and everything, but maybe she could talk her mother into not grounding her, maybe put that off until they got to Chicago or something. That would be fair too. Because, after all, there's punishing someone and then there's *punishing someone*. Surely the special circumstances would give her some kind of-

No, see, she was doing it again.

Right there, she shifted from looking at things from her mother's perspective right back to her own. It was going to be hard, this whole mature outlook thing, it was really easy to lose it and fall right back into being her old, selfish self. But Sam was determined; she was going to grow up, be the type of person that deserved the love and respect of people like her mother and Nick. No matter how long it took to do it, no matter how hard it was. She was going to do it.

Nick turned his truck onto Sam's street and her heart raced.

This was it. This was her moment of truth, the moment when she faced her own mistakes and bad behavior and took the consequences. What had Val said? *If you get punished, you sack it up and take it, because you deserve it.* That's what she was going to do, she was going to go in there, take whatever her mother dished out and she was not cry or negotiate or complain. Whatever happened, she deserved it. She deserved every last drop of it. She deserved to be yelled at, deserved to have Nick not want to see her any more, deserved to be grounded for the rest of her time in Baxter.

She would show her mother what she learned.

Nick pulled into the driveway, put the truck into neutral. Sam unbuckled her seatbelt and opened the door. "Thanks for the ride," she said. "Sorry about, everything, I guess."

"Don't worry about it," he said, the first thing he'd said to her since the house. "I'll see you around."

"Yeah," she said, "see you."

She stepped down from the truck, closed the door and watched as it backed out of the driveway and drove down the street. She wondered, as she watched it stop at the stop sign at the end of her block, turn and disappear, if it was true. If she really would see him around or if that was their last time together.

But those were concerns for another time.

Sam jumped a little when she walked into the house and the screen door slammed shut behind her. It did that sometimes. She sort of expected her mother to be waiting outside for her, or just inside the door, but she wasn't. Instead, Sam found herself standing in the entry room of her house feeling very much at a loss as to what to do next. Everything felt slightly different than when she'd walked out the night before, everything looked different.

She heard a door open upstairs and footsteps in the hallway, then coming down the stairs, and then her mother emerged.

She looked tired. She wore beat up old jeans and a faded t-shirt; she wasn't wearing any make-up and her hair was wet and unkempt, hanging limply at her shoulders. She had just gotten out of the shower and, suddenly, Sam found it impossibly sad. Involuntarily, she pictured her mother waiting up all night, calling her cell and not getting any response. She pictured her mother, bags under eyes, sick with worry, finally hearing from Nick that Sam was okay, how relieved she must have felt. Her mother wanted to shower all that off herself before she met with Sam. Wanted to wash the previous night away and start fresh.

Her mother stood across the room, staring at Sam. She didn't say anything; she just stood there, hands at her sides, looking nervous. Sam imagined her mother going over what she was going to say as she got ready for Sam to arrive home. How she might have worried about what Sam would think of her, how she might have wanted to look her best for Sam, and so she'd taken a shower and changed her clothes.

Her mother looked impossibly fragile and vulnerable and *human*. And it was all because of Sam. She reduced her beautiful strong proud mother to the beaten down little person standing before her. And, in that moment, all of Sam's resolve to take her punishment like an adult melted away and she just lost it.

"I'm sorry Mom," she said, tears streaming down her face. "I'm so, so, sorry. I'm sorry, I'm sorry, I'm sorry, I'm sorry, I'm sorry."

"Oh, baby," her mother said advancing toward her, "don't cry."

Sam fell to her knees. She cried so hard it was hard to breathe. "I'm just so stupid and so sorry and I never should have run off like that and I'm sorry I worried you and I'm sorry I was so mean like that and I'm sorry, I'm sorry, I'm sorry, I'm sorry."

Sam's mother knelt down and wrapped her up in a hug. "It's okay," she said. "Shhh, now, it's okay."

"It's not okay," Sam insisted. "It's not. I was so mean. And it wasn't just last night. I've been so awful ever since Daddy left. I've been mean and horrible and selfish and I'm so sorry."

"It's okay," her mother said. She was crying now too; Sam felt her tears on her hair. "It's okay. You've been under a lot of stress. This has been really hard for you. I know that."

"You must hate me."

"Sweetie, no. I don't hate you at all."

"Well you should," Sam said. "I would if I were you."

Her mother laughed. "Well, then it's a good thing you're not me, isn't it?" She put her finger under Sam's chin, lifted her face until they were eye to eye. "Listen," she said, "people make mistakes all the time, Sam. It's what we do. But we have to be able to forgive each other. That's the really important thing, that we can forgive each other when we make mistakes."

"Do you, Mom? Do you forgive me?"

"Of course I do, baby. You could never do anything that I couldn't forgive."

Relief flooded Sam's body. She believed her mother. There was something in her face, something in her tone that told Sam she understood and that her words were genuine.

"Thank you Mom," Sam said. "Thank you, thank you, thank you." She buried her face in her mom's shoulder, breathed in the fresh scent of soap and shampoo. She was okay, everything was okay.

"People have to be able to forgive each other, Sam," her mother said again. "We're only human."

That night, for the first time since she was a very little girl, Sam went to bed just after eight. She lay in her soft bed with her head on her favorite pillow with her Snoopy pillow case and nuzzled her feet against her fresh clean sheets. Her bed had never felt so good.

She went over the events of the last day, all the mistakes she made, all the ways she scared the people she cared about and who cared about her. She thought about how vulnerable she must have been the night before, how out of control and helpless. So many bad things could have happened to her; she could be in a hospital right now, or worse. But she wasn't. Nothing bad happened, not really. She didn't get hurt, hadn't hurt anyone else, and she didn't get in trouble either. She was really pretty lucky, dodged some pretty big bullets. She took a reckless leap, one she wasn't anxious to repeat, and survived. Maybe she could survive Chicago too.

And, in a way, maybe it was all for the best. Sure, things were weird with Nick, but he'd get over it. She'd make sure of that. But she felt better about her mother than she had in months, maybe years. Before, she was so hurt and angry that she only saw her mother as just that, a mother, an authority figure who existed only to make Sam's life miserable. Seeing her mother so frail that afternoon reminded her that her mother was a person too, someone doing her best, like everyone else. It had only been a few hours since their reconciliation, but Sam felt closer to her mother, more in synch, than she could ever remember.

And maybe it sounded silly, but those realizations, as shallow and obvious as they were, made her feel so much *better* about everything. Better about herself, her relationship with her mother, and Chicago. She'd felt, over the last month, like she was moving through a fog, like she wasn't really *her* anymore. But the last day had managed to exorcise whatever it was that was haunting her, and she was firmly back in control of herself again.

Finally, everything was okay.

She was safe.

And she wasn't afraid.

*The Minors*

# FAITH

Dana was talking, but he wasn't listening.

He was tired, and his stomach sort of hurt, and he really wanted to be home resting.

After he dropped Sam at her house, Nick went home and took a much needed nap. Then he went for a run with Gertie, showered, and picked up Dana. Nick told her the night before that he'd take her shopping today. His impulse was to cancel of course, to just get some distance between himself and everything that happened before he saw anyone. But, for some reason, he couldn't bring himself to do it. He picked his cell phone up half a dozen times with every intention of calling Dana and begging off and, when he finally called, he chickened out and said he was double checking what time she to be picked up.

What was going on with him?

It wasn't like Dana would be crushed if he rescheduled; he was only taking her to get new pants for her hostess job at the restaurant. And he was tired and needed to think things through. The smart thing was to tell Dana he'd take her some other time and let that be it. But there was a tension in his gut that wouldn't let him cancel.

Was it guilt? Was that what he felt? He felt guilty because he cheated on her? That would make sense; he did something he ought to feel guilty about. But he didn't think that was it. The thing was, he didn't feel like there was much to betray when it came to Dana. They weren't married and they weren't going to get married either. Their relationship had been circling the drain for a long time. And it wasn't like he *planned* to have sex with Liz. It just sort of happened.

He looked at Dana; she faced away from him, holding a pair of pants up against herself and looking in a full length mirror. She was still talking. He nodded noncommittally at whatever she said. She'd be better off without him anyway. He knew that, he'd always known he was wrong for her. Too distant, too cranky, too *old*. And whenever their relationship ended, she'd be unhappy about it for a little while, but she'd get over it quicker than she-

"Nick?"

"Huh?"

Dana laughed. "Do you wanna eat or what?"

"Oh, I don't care. Do you?"

She laughed. "Space cadet? What've I been talking about the last two minutes? Yeah, I'm starving, I wanna eat."

"So let's eat," he said.

They went to the Ruby Tuesdays. Dana talked about some new girl at work she hated. "She might be the dumbest person I've ever met," she said. "Like, it doesn't matter what your last name is, she'll ask if you're related to someone else with the same last name. It could be, like, *Jones*, you could be Nick Jones, and she'd be like *Oh, I worked at blah blah blah with a guy named* Steve *Jones, are you two related*? Swear to God."

"That sounds pretty stupid all right," said Nick.

She bit a mozzarella stick in half. "I know it's not such a big deal. I sound all bitchy and whatever, but it gets *so annoying*, and if that was all she did, if that was it, then it wouldn't be so bad, you know? I could live with that, but it's like, all the time with her. Oh, like the other day? We were getting ready to open the restaurant, right? And Ted asked her to refill some of the ketchup, and yeah, that's usually a bus-boy job, but we were short staffed that day, and she was all like…"

He tried to pay attention, he really did. But the knot in his stomach was still there and it gnawed at him until it consumed his thoughts. He kept returning to that conversation—after everything had happened, when they were lying in bed and her head was on his chest and her hair was spread all over his torso.

Liz turned her head so she could look up at him, "Do you feel bad?"

"What, like, guilty bad?"

"Yeah."

He picked a few strands of hair off his chest, released them, and watched them float back down onto his body. "Should I?"

"I don't know," she said, "maybe. I mean, this is pretty serious what we just did, isn't it?"

Nick shrugged, "I guess that depends on what you mean by serious. It's not like we killed somebody or something."

"Well I guess *that's* a relief." Liz frowned at him. "It's good to know you don't think I'm as bad as a murderer."

"That's not what I'm saying. You're missing the…look, all I mean was… I wouldn't have done it if I didn't want to, okay?"

"People want to do things that are bad all the time."

"Well, this isn't one of those times."

"How do you know?"

"Because… because I just *know*. I know how I feel, that's all. Do you feel bad? Is that what you're trying to say?"

"No, that's not it."

"Then what's the problem?"

"Don't you ever feel bad about *not* feeling bad?"

"Not really. That's not how it works."

"Maybe it should."

"Maybe, but it's not."

She brushed her hair out of her eyes, and stared at him. "Why are you here?"

"You said you wanted me to come over last night."

"No, I mean, why are you *here*?" She waved her hand over the bed.

"Because I like you?"

"Yeah, but that can't just be it."

"Why not?"

"I don't know," she said. "How about because I'm married?"

"Okay, but I'm not."

"So it's okay, because you're not the one doing the cheating? Is that it?" Liz sat up and studied him; she pulled the sheet over her chest.

"That's not what I said."

"Isn't it?"

"No."

"Then what are you saying? Because that's what it sounds like."

"Hey, Liz, hold on a minute."

"You don't know me, you know." She was more worked up. "You don't know about my life, about what I think and feel. I'm not some dumb girl or bored slutty housewife looking to get laid."

"Hey," he took her by the shoulders, looked her in the eye. "*Hey*. Relax, okay? I never said any of that. Don't like, freak out on me here. You made a decision, all right? You did. You decided this was something you wanted to do. I did the same, and here we are. That's all this is. This is only as big a deal as you let it be. You're not the first person to slip up in your marriage. You'll survive."

Panic shone in her eyes—then, it was gone, and Liz was back. She smiled sadly, touched his cheek. "I'm sorry," she said, "you're right. I'm just, I don't know, adjusting or something."

"Yeah, well, that's okay. Just don't put words in my mouth."

"No, yeah, I'm sorry about that. It's just, there's a lot to take in." She bugged her eyes out, laughed. "Woo, right? Wow. Finally, after all these years, here I am. Who would have thought? What's that saying, life's like a maze when you're looking forward, but when you look behind it's a straight line, or something, you know what I mean?"

"Sort of, I guess," Nick said. "Actually, no. Not really. I mean, I understand in theory, but I don't know what it means for you. You aren't saying this was like destiny?"

"No. Well, yeah, in a way. It's complicated. It means…" Liz said, then trailed off. "It means, okay, it means that when I was a kid, my parents had a bad marriage, like really bad. And where we lived, at that time, divorce wasn't something you did. Or it wasn't something my mom did anyway. Small town, religious, she didn't want the shame I guess. So they were miserable, and they hated each other, and me and my brother, you know, we took sides. And, we took our dad's side, because he was fun, and he gave us money for stuff, and we got along with him. Mom was all gloom and doom and misery and dad was sunshine and light and all that shit. Can I get a smoke off you? Mine are still downstairs."

Nick rolled out of bed and grabbed his jeans from the floor; he pulled out the packet of cigarettes and matches and, after lighting one for himself, tossed them to Liz. "Thanks," she said, inhaling hungrily and exhaling with more calm. "So Mom hated Dad, and Dad hated Mom, and we loved Dad, and Mom hated that. So she decided to do something about it and, brilliant strategist that she was, she decided the way to do it was to tell us all about what a shit our dad was." She looked around the room, her eyes lit up when they fell on a coffee mug sitting on her bed side table. She grabbed it and flicked her ash into it.

"Brilliant, right? Instead of becoming a better parent herself, she makes him look worse. Bring him down to her level. Well, it turns out that Dad's been cheating on her for years, which makes sense because I can't imagine the two of them had a very intimate relationship, and she decides to fill us in on as many of the details as she can think of."

"Wait," Nick said, "what do you mean details?"

She gave him a sober look. "*Details*," she said. "The kind you don't want to hear about a parent, especially when you're in the eighth grade."

"Holy shit," said Nick.

"Yeah," Liz said, "holy shit. So, and I think I told you this before, the plan backfired, at least with me. I got so mad at her for telling me all that shit about my dad that our relationship was just broken pretty much forever."

"Good," Nick said. "Fuck her."

"Big time. But the problem is, the plan sort of worked too, because it did change the way I looked at my dad. I mean, I think even then I understood why he'd need to look outside his marriage for some affection, but at the same time, he's still running around on our family, you know? I mean, the guy didn't have the guts to divorce his shrew of a wife but he could bone his secretary in his office every day?"

"Yeah," Nick said, "but..."

Liz put a hand up, stopping him. "No, I know, I know, and that's not the point. I got over the whole thing a long time ago. Or at least, I made peace with it. The *point is*, the whole thing, the cheating, the choosing sides, the anger; it all made me a very loyal person. It made me someone who never wanted to go back to that kind of situation again."

She stubbed out her cigarette in the mug.

"So two, two and a half months ago, right after you finished fixing the deck actually, my car needs some work done, so I take Steve's car for the day. And I find an empty condom wrapper in the back, behind the driver seat."

She took a breath, brushed her hair behind her head. "It must have fallen out of his pocket and he didn't notice it. I had done food shopping and the bag fell over and spilled onto the floor of the car and I was rooting around down there. Anyway, right away I knew. I knew because I had my tubes tied after Oscar and there's no way it's Sam and no one else is ever in the car. It was his. That was the only explanation."

She paused again, took another deep breath. "And it was just like, that mother fucker, you know? That mother *fucker*."

She sniffed, shook her head. "I'm not gonna sit here and say his was any worse than anyone else in some other relationship just because it happened to me. But how many times, *how many fucking times*, did I cry to him about how much my dad's cheating hurt me and my family? And he had the, the, the fucking *balls* to go out, and do it to me? After all that?"

She stopped talking, wiped a tear from her eye.

"You don't have to tell me this if you don't want to."

"No," she said, "it's okay. I haven't really talked to anyone about it." She took another moment to collect herself, then started again. "So, I confronted him about it. And he copped to it right away, which is what he does by the way. Steve's whole thing when he's in trouble is total honesty, total disclosure, that way he can feel like he's still the good guy, you know? 'Cause he's being all mature and forthright. I married a stand-up fucking guy."

She lit another cigarette. "Turns out him and one of the new associates from the office were sleeping together for months. All those late nights, all those" - air quotes - "*working dinners*, the son of a bitch was really sticking his fucking dick into that goddamn whore."

Nick raised his eyebrows at that.

"I should have seen it before," she said, pointing at him with her cigarette. "He was being so nice to everyone:getting to all that fucking work on the house he'd been promising for years, talking about going to Europe for a vacation in the summer. I should have figured something was up right then. Steve's a nice guy, but he was being too nice. He was being guilty nice. But, like a fucking sucker, I didn't think anything. And that wrapper totally blindsided me."

She smashed her cigarette out even though it wasn't half finished. "So he's really sorry and he doesn't know how it happened and that shit. And I'm thinking: *you don't know how it happened? Of course you fucking know how it happened,* I *know how it happened. The little cunt was into you, and you were super nice to her because you have to be liked by everyone and it got in your head–that's what happened.* But that's not what I say. I say, *I don't give a shit how it happened,* which is sort of true, *I just want you to fucking fix this before it permanently destroys our family.*"

She lit a third cigarette. "So, a month ago, we're eating dinner and he goes, *we're all moving to Chicago*, just like that. No discussion, no warning, it's a done deal. And the kids, the kids are going out of their minds, because their whole world is ending and they don't know why and I can't tell them why either..."

"Why?"

"Why, what?"

"Why can't the kids know? Or, at least Sam. She's been thinking you were behind this whole move for the last month."

She cocked her head and looked at him. She smiled. "Were you like, not listening at the beginning of my little monologue?"

"But this is different. This isn't you telling Sam something to hurt her or your husband, this is you correcting a mistaken impression and clearing your name. She had a right to know why all this is happening."

Liz shook her head sadly. "It's not that easy," she said. "If I told Sam what her dad did, it's not like she'd be reasonable and adjust her perspective. It would be catastrophic to her and Steve's relationship, make her last year with us hellish, and who knows how that would affect Oscar."

"Yeah, but if you don't tell her the truth, she's just gonna keep on hating you."

"She'd hate me if I told her too, for showing her something about her dad that she didn't want to see, and it's possible she'd never forgive me. I never forgave *my* mom. She's gonna hate me either way, at least this way she keeps her good relationship with her dad, and we have a shot to patch things up down the line."

"So," Nick said, "what are you going to do?"

"What do you mean?"

"I don't know...what are you going to do about everything I guess?"

She shrugged her shoulders. "I'm gonna go to Chicago, raise my kids, live my life."

"So, you forgave him?"

She shrugged and studied her cigarette. "I don't see what other choice I have."

"You could leave him."

She laughed gently. "I couldn't do that. Couldn't do that to my kids. It would be… I'm just not even going to go there. It's funny, when I was little I used to spend a lot of time thinking about my soul mate. You know, when would I meet him, what would he be like, all that. In my fantasy, my soul mate would come and I would instantly recognize him and he'd sweep me off my feet and everything would be perfect. It was all super romantic. But I got older, and I found my soul mate, or mates, and it wasn't Steve. Turns out, your soul mate isn't a person who you date or marry or anything like that."

If she said God or Jesus was her soul mate, he was going to have to get out of there, fast.

"Your children are your soul mates, like, literally. They're a piece of you. Your body, blood, everything. They are individuals but they're you too. But the thing about soul mates, you think they're going to fix you but you have to fix *them*. Soul mates are a responsibility. And you force yourself to grow up so that you do the best you can for them."

She smiled at him. "See," she said, "that's the thing I don't think you can understand until you have kids of your own. You've been such a big help this last month, and whenever I try and thank you, you say something about how it's *no sweat*."

"Because it's not," Nick said. "It's fun."

"Exactly," she said, "Kids can be fun for a month, anything can be fun for a month when you get to go home at night. It's easy to care when you have no real responsibility. Let's see how much fun it is when you can't leave, when you really disappoint them, when you let them down. Let's see how much fun it is when you've hurt them and you know it and they know it. When they know that something happened that you could have avoided, and you didn't because you were stupid and selfish."

She sighed, "That came out more, hostile, than I meant it to. I'm just pissed. Okay. It's like, Steve fucked up when he did what he did. But I'm not making a bad situation worse by throwing a big public fit and leaving him and disrupting my children's lives just because he was an asshole. That wouldn't help anything. Besides, it's not like I don't love Steve. He's mostly a good husband and a great dad. He just made a mistake. A really, really, *really*, big mistake. One that, if he ever repeats, I will nail his ass to the wall. I may want to do that right now, I may *want* to kick Steve's fucking head in. But when something matters, like really? You do it even if it doesn't feel right or good. That's how you know it's important."

"And keeping your family together is important. I get it."

"It's the most important thing in the world."

"So, why do this with me?"

That stopped her. She sat on the edge of the bed for minute, thinking. Then she got up. "Honestly, I don't have a good answer. I wish I did. I mean, you know, I like you. I know that sounds stupid and like a fourteen-year-old, but I do. You've been so great this last month and I've felt less alone. I'd been feeling alone for a long time. Even when Steve was around, I felt alone, and it felt like you and I connected and I hadn't felt that in so long that…it was just a good feeling and I went with it. And I think that, in the end, this," she gestured to the bed, "what we just did, it's been such a big part of my life for so long now, I guess I needed to try it for myself."

"And now that you've done it? What do you think?"

She chewed on her lip, looked at him with nervous eyes. "And now I don't know," she said fearfully. "I don't know."

"…And it's not like I don't know what it's like to be new somewhere," Dana said. "We all go through it, but, come on, you know? Put in a little effort to get to know the people around you before you go making a joke like that."

"Totally."

"Right? Like, Tasha's half Puerto Rican, and thank God she wasn't there, because if she had been? She would have gone after him and I don't know if we could have held her back because, well, she's kind of a big girl and…"

There was something, something not right. He knew it the moment she said she didn't know how she felt. He was fine until she said that, but there was something in her eyes when she said she didn't know. The knot in his stomach wouldn't let him let it go. Something, something Liz said about responsibility maybe. About letting people down. He couldn't stop thinking about it.

"Why do you like me?"

Dana looked at him, startled. "What?"

"Why do you like me? Why do you like dating me? What do you get out of it?"

"I don't… why are you asking?"

"It's like, people do things for *reasons,* right? Like, there are reasons that you want to be with me. I'm wondering what they are."

"Oh, uh, okay." Dana ran her hand through her hair. "Well," she said, "I mean, you're nice."

"No I'm not. Not really."

"Well, you *can* be nice. And when you are, it's really sweet."

"Okay," he said. "Why else?"

"Um," she looked like she was thinking hard, "I don't… you're cute, and, you take me places?"

"Dana," he said, "this isn't a quiz. There aren't right and wrong answers. I just, we fight, you know? And I haven't always treated you the way that I should, and you're still here, and I want to know why."

"I guess, because I think you're sorry for the way you treated me, and you won't do it again."

"But don't you ever worry I will?"

"Will what?"

"Will treat you badly again. Will hurt you again."

She leaned back, her eyes widening. "What is this? Are you not telling me something?"

"No, that's not, that's not what I'm trying to say." The problem was he really didn't know *what* he wanted to say. "I just what to know why *you* think it."

"Because, I just, I believe that you won't."

"You believe I won't?"

"Yeah."

"And that's it? That's the only reason? You're just trusting that I can be good to you based on some vague belief?"

She frowned at him. "I'm sorry," she said, "I'm just not sure what other reason there *is*."

# GRADUATION

Things settled down after that.

On Monday, the last Monday Sam would ever have classes at Baxter High School, it seemed like everyone heard about the mysterious boy who came and took Sam from the party. Like, carried out, taken. Details beyond that were sketchy; everyone agreed that he appeared shortly after she went upstairs with Scott Temple. Beyond that it was pure conjecture, and anyone who knew anything more wasn't saying. Certainly not Scott, who left the party in a hurry. And, while he looked okay Monday morning, he sure didn't want to talk about getting tossed out of that room Friday night. And some people were saying, though none to his face, that part of the reason he was in such a hurry had a lot to do with a certain stain that may or may not have stretched from his crotch all the way down the inner leg of his jeans.

Nobody said any of this to Sam, or, at least, not directly. What they did was—okay, no one was going to talk to Scott or any of his slimy friends, because what were they gonna say? And no one wanted to talk to Sam, because for all anyone knew, she was traumatized or something. And no one could talk to the mystery boy, for the obvious reason that no one knew who he *was*. So what people did was, they talked to Becky. Every theory or question or possible clue was floated past her for confirmation or denial. Becky wasn't very forthcoming, but she at least was *there*, and had apparently called the guy. That was pretty much all she'd say. The boy was a friend of Sam's that Becky called because she thought Sam had a little too much to drink and needed a ride home. But that didn't stop people from asking, and whenever they did, she told Sam what they asked her and the two of them laughed about it.

Becky told Sam what really happened, of course. Sam called her Saturday after she had her talk with her mom and took a shower. She was nervous about what Becky was going to say, about what happened in that blank spot in her brain where Friday night should have been. Becky set her mind at ease. She said yeah, she called Nick, but that was because she thought Sam overdid it and needed a ride home and she wasn't in shape to drive. She said yeah, Sam went upstairs with Scott Temple, but it wasn't like anything happened; there wasn't time and besides, Sam was pretty trashed at that point, she couldn't even really hold herself up (which was why Nick ended up carrying her to the car), so the idea of her doing anything with him was pretty impossible.

As for Nick and Scott, that had all been blown *way* out of proportion. Yeah, Nick might have put a little scare into him for thinking about getting a little action from a girl who was too drunk to make good decisions, but did he beat Scott up? Come on.

Sam kind of liked being notorious; people's eyes would follow her as she walked down the hallway and every time she walked into the room conversations stopped. It would have been different if she were staying in Baxter of course, if she had to attend school with these people next year and she developed some kind of reputation; that would have been terrible. But she wasn't, so what the hell? She decided to go with it and enjoy the drama and misinformation, to enjoy being the center of attention for once, for as long as it lasted.

The only one she felt sorry for was Scott Temple. It sounded like he got the short end of the stick with all these rumors. Becky told her not to worry about it, that if Scott Temple got knocked down a peg or two, it was far from a bad thing. But Sam did feel bad about it. The whole thing was fun for her, in part because she got to leave it all behind, but also because no one thought she did anything wrong. When people started actually talking to Sam, they told her terrible things, like that she was naked when Nick busted in, that Scott was about to rape her or something. Sam was horrified when she heard that, she told anyone who'd listen that, no, it wasn't true at all. Everything was exaggerated by the rumor mill. But try as she might, Sam couldn't seem to make the rumor go away.

She felt so guilty she decided to talk to Scott herself, to at least tell him that she was appalled by how far the rumors had grown and explain that she did what she could to set the record straight.

But the thing was, she never seemed to be able to talk to him. They shared only one course that semester. She wasn't ever able to make eye contact with him, and he was the first one out the door when the bell rang. The one time she saw him in the hall and it was relatively empty, he saw her coming and took off in the other directionas fast as he could without actually running. It made her sad; she figured he was upset with her for what people said or didn't want to be seen with her for fear that more rumors would spring up from it or something like that. It was a shame, but at least she tried.

Things went better with Nick.

Her pledge to not talk about what happened until he did, to give him his space, didn't last very long. He came back to take her driving on Tuesday, and was acting pretty okay, but she still felt the distance between them; it was subtle, but he was definitely nervous and it was really driving her nuts. So she caved, she pulled over, kind of abruptly actually, into a Wawa parking lot, turned to him, and just apologized.

She babbled about not remembering anything from Friday between talking to some weirdo Goth kids outside and waking up on his couch the next morning. She told all the details Becky had filled her in on, but beyond that it was all a blank. She would be devastated, she said, if she said or did anything to upset or alienate him that night, and she was so, so sorry that he was involved at all. She was sure that he had better things to do with his Friday night than to crash some stupid high school party and babysit (and clean up after, how could she ever thank him enough for cleaning up her vomit?) a drunken teenager who didn't know when enough was enough.

Then she told him about her epiphany in his truck on the way home Saturday morning, about how being an adult meant not making excuses for herself but accepting responsibility for her mistakes. How she was determined to give him the space he needed to process his anger or disappointment or whatever it was he felt about her, but it was just too hard. She felt the crushing weight of the weird tension between them, and she couldn't take it and she knew that meant she was regressing but she had to get it off her chest how sorry she was. She said she was so grateful for everything Nick did for her over the last month, and it tore her up to think, even for a minute, that she somehow ruined it.

When she finished, Nick looked, well, he looked a little stunned actually. There were a lot of times when she went on tangents and he was off in his own little world and not really paying attention, or other times when he looked at her when she was done with amused eyes that seemed to say *you just talked for longer than I've ever heard anyone talk about* anything, *about something completely trivial/silly, something I don't think I've wasted more than two minutes total in my life thinking about.* She got that look all the time from just about everyone. She was very familiar with that look. That wasn't the look he was giving her now.

Sam couldn't remember ever seeing the look Nick had on his face, and it was only there for a second before it snapped back to one of his normal faces.

"I'm not angry with you at all," he said. "You're a good kid."

He said she was way better than he was at her age, and she made a really big mistake running out on her mom; she totally shouldn't have done that, but as for getting loaded and needing a place to crash? That happened to everyone once and a while. He said he was glad that he was able to help out, that he'd hate if something happened that hurt her that he could have prevented. How bad that would make him feel.

She tried to thank him, to tell him how grateful she was, but he wouldn't hear of it. Kept cutting her off whenever she tried–*don't thank me, really. It was nothing*–until she finally let the matter drop.

Involuntarily, Sam thought about her conversation with Val in the kitchen Saturday morning, and all the things she said about Nick being a fuck-up and unreliable and all that. She would never tell Nick all the things his aunt said, or how they confused her. It just went to show how sometimes the closer you were to a person, the less clearly you could see them. Val had her own ideas about who Nick was and that was based on some past experiences that cemented in her mind. Nothing Nick said or did would be able to shake her of that view. It made Sam sad because she could see how much Val loved Nick, how much she cared about him, but her perspective was poisoned by years of disappointment. It would be so much better if she could see the person Sam saw when she looked at Nick, someone caring and decent, who would help a girl he barely knew at the drop of a hat and then refuse to even be thanked for it.

It just went to show, she guessed, that sometimes you could understand the least, the people you loved the most.

Nick asked her, while they were still sitting in that Wawa parking lot, how many hours she had left before she was eligible for her driver's license. Sam said she wasn't sure, but about twenty she thought. He said fuck it, why didn't they just finish the hours before she left next week? He told her to calculate the actual number of hours she needed, divide it by the amount of days she had left and, if she wanted to or had the time, they could try and get her license test in too. That way, she'd be set to drive around on her own the moment she stepped foot in Chicago.

His offering that, mixed with the relief she felt that he wasn't angry at all with her, made Sam so happy that she was afraid she was going to cry again right there.

It was kind of eerie how smoothly everything was going.

It was like that blow-up with her mom, getting wasted at that party, and her night on Nick's couch all combined to close out this chapter in her life in Baxter. She was still sad about leaving, of course she was, but it wasn't the same as it was before. She made peace with Chicago somehow, made peace with the idea that it was happening and, while she still wasn't exactly looking forward to going, she was as ready as she was ever going to be. It felt almost like whatever her life in Baxter was, it wasn't fighting her anymore. After the drama of the weekend, she wanted to make the last two weeks as calm and drama-free as possible.

And what helped more than anything, was the simple fact that the bond she felt with her mother hadn't faded.

When Sam took ballet all those years ago, the instructor droned on about rhythm and timing, how important it was to be in synch with the other dancers. That, she said, was what was most beautiful about dancing, the sight of all these people working together to create something larger than any one individual. She said a group of mediocre dancers working together could create something far more beautiful and special than any individual virtuoso. And she emphasized how even the best dancing looked bad if it was out of synch with everyone else, that even that virtuoso needed to understand that she was a part of a larger whole, or the performance would dissolve.

Sam didn't take much away from her dancing years, but the idea of synchronicity made sense to her. It was easy to think about relationships in those terms: people she moved well with and people she didn't. For years, she was resigned to the fact that she and her mother were out of synch, while taking comfort in her good and easy-going relationship with her dad. That was just the way things were.

But now, it was as if she and her mother suddenly fell in synch with one another, and things that were once laborious and awkward were graceful. Sam always figured if she ever stayed out all night and came home hungover, her mother would be apoplectic, that Sam would be dead before she hit the ground. But it was totally the opposite—her mother wasn't interested in punishing or scolding her or even talking about it, which was also weird because she was normally such a talker, always wanting to go over what Sam did wrong, why it was wrong, and how she wasn't going to do it again. *And what have we learned?* This time Sam got none of that. Not a word. Frankly, Sam couldn't believe her luck.

Maybe her mom did something similar as a kid and remembered how bad she felt, or maybe Nick talked her down. Or maybe, just maybe, she saw how difficult everything was for Sam and she was just going to let this one go. No matter the reason, Sam was grateful. She caught a break and she wasn't going to blow it by being petty or obnoxious. If the last few days in her house were going to suck, she wasn't going to let a bad attitude make it worse. Her mother must have felt the same way because she seemed almost maniacally determined to make her kids happy. She didn't nag them to pick up after themselves or to do chores. Every dinner was an old favorite, either something she made or a meal at their favorite restaurant. She seemed to make cookies or pie or some other delicious dessert every day. And she even took them shopping for *Goodbye Baxter/Hello Chicago* presents. Sam got three new books and a skirt, and Oscar got a pile of new toys.

On Thursday, the day before her last day of classes and a little over week before they left for good, Sam's mother even apologized to Sam about not letting her stay a little longer with Becky. She said it was really important to her that they have those first weeks together to acclimate to Chicago as a family, but she should have been more understanding of Sam's desire to stay.

Then, she pulled an envelope out of her pocket and handed it to Sam. Inside was an airplane ticket from Chicago to Baxter dated three weeks from that day. Her mother said she already checked it out with Sam's dad and Becky's parents. After Sam gave them two weeks in Chicago, she could come back for a whole week and stay with Becky, and then, maybe they could bring Becky out in August.

Sam screamed with joy and threw her arms around her mother, squeezed her tighter than she ever squeezed her before.

The last day of classes was weird. Weird because, while it wasn't the last day of school—that would be the following Thursday when she completed her last final—it was for all intents and purposes the end of her time as a student at Baxter. The school system that she'd attended her entire life and that she, up until very recently, believed would be the only one she would ever attend. She looked at all the classrooms and hallways and stairwells and corners, at the gym and fields, and the auditorium and lunch room and wished she could, just for a second, remember every experience she ever had there, good or bad.

She knew it was cool to not like school and high school in particular, but the truth was, Sam always kind of liked it. She liked learning, liked having access to books and computers and teachers and all of that. And she liked the people, not all of them sure, but even the ones she didn't like, she liked seeing them. She liked watching them grow into different people that she might still not like, but appreciated somehow all the same. They were lousy people, but they were *her* lousy people. And the ones she did like, and there were more of them than ones she didn't like, she was bummed about leaving behind.

On the last day of classes, Sam sat with Becky on the hill above the parking lot and watched as the buses filled up and one by one the cars in the student parking lot started and pulled out of their spots. They waited for an hour and a half, just watching and waiting and talking about the people they recognized, memories they had of them, and making predictions about what would happen to them in the future. When the last car pulled out, and only Becky's remained, the two of them stood up, brushed themselves off, walked down to Becky's car, and went home.

The Saturday before she left, Sam spent the night at Becky's, just like she did when they were young. Sam rode her bike over, like the old days, just in time for lunch. Then they ordered a large mushroom and pepperoni pizza and a Caesar salad from Baxter Pizza, which they ate while watching *The Wedding Singer*, *Pirates of the Caribbean,* and *Napoleon Dynamite,* the three movies they watched the most when sleeping over at each other's houses growing up. When the movies were finally over, they re-dyed Sam's hair red, with her mother's permission of course, and stayed up until one o'clock planning an overnight trip to the shore that they could take during Sam's upcoming visit. When they couldn't keep their eyes open a minute longer, they got into Becky's bed and went to sleep. Just like the old days.

And the last week was kind of a blur.

Her mother had been packing up the house ever since her dad announced the move, but it happened in subtle ways. One day Sam noticed the picture albums weren't in their usual spot; another time she opened a kitchen cabinet and found it empty. The junk in the basement was mostly in boxes anyway, but when Sam went down one afternoon to throw some clothes in the laundry, it seemed to her that the boxes were a little better organized than previously.

But that last week, things really kicked into overdrive. They were leaving on Friday, or at least Sam and Oscar were. They were flying out to be with their dad and her mother was driving out in her car with the moving trucks the day after they left. Sam's finals were scheduled every morning until then and she drove with Nick in the afternoons after each exam. Every afternoon she entered the house to find it drastically different from how she left it that morning.

On Monday, she came home to find the entry room, her parents' room and her dad's office empty, stripped of all non-essential items, the items in the rooms boxed up, and the furniture bare. On Tuesday, the dining room and kitchen were all packed; it would be paper plates and take out from then on. Wednesday cleared the den and the bathrooms; and on Thursday her mother finally did Oscar's room (which her mother said wasn't easy, and Oscar wasn't happy) and the living room (except the TV).

Sam was only really responsible for packing up her room. And she dragged her feet on it for as long as possible. But by that Wednesday she figured it was time. She grabbed a pile of boxes and finally started going through her stuff.

It was a slow process, taking all that day and into the next. Virtually every item Sam pulled from the back of her closet or found in a drawer had to be considered, remembered, and contextualized before it could be moved into its box. Posters were carefully rolled up and placed in cardboard tubes. Photos were unstuck from her walls, and carefully put in albums. All those photos were on her computer, and could be easily re-printed, but she wanted the physical copies she always had. They were her friends. Old books she grew up with had to be paged through, stuffed animals had to be held in their old room one more time, then paired up with an appropriate moving-buddy before the lid was closed on them. Jewelry, what little she owned, was tried on again, and old clothes that she hadn't worn in years, were held against her cheek and their musty old scent breathed in. And her shoes, her beautiful shoes. Well, she knew she'd kept all their boxes for a reason.

In her suitcase, she packed items for the plane ride to Chicago. She packed two pairs of jeans, three shirts, some underwear, her toothbrush, her MP3 player, a few books and, wadded up in a tight ball, hidden in the pocket of her jeans, the lingerie Becky made her buy all those months ago. She just couldn't risk putting it in a box that might break and some sweaty mover coming across it somehow, or worse still, her mother. She felt closer with her mother, but there were limits.

When the last box of her room was packed, and all that was left were the sheets on her bed, Sam took a seat on one of the sturdier boxes, looked around and let her mind wander. When she walked out of Baxter High earlier that day, after her last final, it was with the thought that she might never walk back inside again, and certainly never again as a student. And now, here she was, in the skeleton of what was once her room, that would also never be hers again.

She went, a few days earlier, with Becky and a few other friends, to watch the seniors graduate. They sat in the bleachers of the football field behind the school and watched them get their diplomas; they hooted and cheered for the seniors they knew and liked, and, under their breath, booed the ones they didn't. It was a tradition, one that they always figured would culminate in their own graduation. But of course, for Sam, that was one more thing that wasn't going to happen. That made this last ceremony all the more important to her.

It was a weird tradition really, as graduation ceremonies were pretty much all the same and all very boring. But there was something that Sam loved about watching the mass of caps and gowns separate to allow each member of the crowd his or her individual moment of triumph, as they got to hear their name announced and got to walk across the stage, accompanied by the applause of their friends and loved ones. It was cheesy, and silly, and utterly, utterly charming.

Usually the speeches that people gave were forgettable too. A local celebrity, relatively famous college professor, or super-successful graduate would go up and say the same thing every year using slightly different words. They always talked about moving on and growing up and how proud everyone was of the graduates; someone usually talked about caterpillars and butterflies, and Dr.

Seuss and Winnie the Pooh seemed to work their way into at least one speech a year.

But for some reason, actually for pretty obvious ones, the commencement speech this year made an impression on Sam. She'd never heard of the woman speaking, she had something to do with the college, but Sam didn't catch what, and it really didn't matter. Most of it was pretty standard stuff about growing up, but at a certain point it took a turn and drew her in.

"It's common," the woman at the podium said, "for people to say that they've graduated from whatever school they attended, as if graduating was an active thing the person did. *I have graduated.* That's something you hear a lot. It's not technically correct though. A person doesn't actively graduate. You," she said, gesturing to the crowd of seniors in caps and gowns, "none of you has the power to graduate from here. What happens is, your school, having decided that you have met its criteria, *decides* to graduate *you.*"

She took a second, flipped a note card, and started again. "It's a subtle distinction, but I think an important one. To say that someone actively graduated implies an agency, a control, on the part of the graduate that is, I think, misleading. To *be* graduated means that you, the graduate, don't actually get to say when you're ready to move on to that next level, that's not a choice you get to make. Instead, it's up to us, the authorities, to decide when you are ready. And when we've decided, that's when we *allow* you to go. You, the prospective graduate, can work and strive as hard as you can, but if we, the institution, don't think you're ready, we are not going to let you leave. And that's so important to understand because so much of adult life is about giving up control to other obligations: community, work, family. When you're a child, it's common to believe that adults *control* everything, that they always get their way."

She paused there, as a wave of laughter went through the crowd of parents. "Of course those of us, who *are* adults, know how far from the truth that is. We're always doing things we don't want for our families and friends and jobs; we're *always* waiting for things, waiting for our kids or spouses to get ready to go somewhere we don't even want to go; waiting for a diet to show results; or for the weekend so we can finally get a minute to rest and catch up on all the stuff that didn't get done because we were too busy waiting. We're waiting for paychecks, for a promotion at work, for recognition of some kind that may never actually come. Adults don't get to decide when they're ready any more than kids do. It's something that gets decided for you. And it's not always when you want it either."

That was when the woman started to really catch Sam's attention.

"Sometimes, a lot of the times actually, graduating can be a painful, difficult process. It isn't always caps and gowns and celebration. Sometimes it involves making it through an experience that you never thought you could, that you never *wanted* to learn if you could, go through. It could be surviving some kind of loss, a death in the family maybe, a sick child, or an injury, sustained perhaps overseas in combat. Something that caused you to change the way you thought about yourself and your capabilities in order to overcome. And you find that you can. That's a form of graduation too, and really a more vital one. And it's the kind we don't come together to celebrate; rather, it's the kind we celebrate just by surviving."

A wave of nodding heads followed that last statement; there was scattered respectful applause.

"You are all here because you've passed tests, literal tests with paper and pencils and questions and answers, and have proven mathematically that you are ready to be graduated by your school and move to the next stage of life. And that's great. But there have been other tests, more abstract ones, ones that don't have definitive right and wrong answers and no way of really telling if you've passed or failed, or if the test is even over. And as you're celebrating your graduation tonight with your loved ones, I'm just asking you to keep in mind, that the real tests in life, the ones that matter the most, are going to be more like the latter than the former. Remember that, and respect it, and you'll truly have learned something, and you'll be worthy of being graduated. That, and don't ever say *but yet.* It's *and yet* or *but* or just *yet*; *but yet* is redundant and makes you sound foolish. Thank you."

Sam sat on that box in her room and she thought about the speech and the last month of her life and how much sense it made.

She felt different. She felt older. Like the last months, facing the challenge of leaving Baxter, her relationship with her mother, learning to drive with Nick, had all culminated with her running out the door and staying out all night two Fridays ago. Maybe, maybe she *had* changed somehow from all that, gotten a little wiser or something. Maybe it was one of those experiences the woman at the graduation ceremony had been talking about. One she hadn't wanted to go through but was forced to, and grew up a little in the process. Maybe it happened just for that.

On Friday, Nick came by to take Sam to her driver's test. On the drive, he reminded her to stay calm, that it was the test administrator's job to be harsh. If he was super nice and supportive and all that, kids would walk out of their tests with big heads, not pay attention to their driving and get into accidents right away. He told her to just be cool, and do whatever the instructor told her to and she would be fine.

And she was.

The test was over in a flash. The instructor made her do the basics: three point turns, reversing, parallel parking. Then, they drove around Baxter for about fifteen minutes and she was done. She passed. She expected… she didn't really know what she expected, but certainly more than *that.* Some sort of obstacle course maybe, or having to go onto the highway, anything really. Nope. There was another written test, and then she took the car for a spin around the block a few times, and that was it. All those hours practicing in the car, all that time, and when the test finally came, she didn't even get to drive above forty.

The instructor was even nice. She wasn't Miss Sunshine or anything, but she wasn't particularly judgmental. She even smiled a few times and said Sam did a good job when they were finished.

All and all the whole thing was kind of a letdown. Okay, a letdown with a positive outcome, but a letdown all the same.

The disappointment about the test wrestled with the exhilaration that came from actually passing as the two of them drove back to Sam's house. But those two emotions were both dwarfed by the knowledge that the closer they got to home, the closer she was to never seeing Nick again. There was so much she wanted to say, so much she felt like she *needed* to say to make him understand how grateful she was to him; how much of an impact he made on her life in such a short amount of time. She wanted to thank him for introducing him to his family, for letting her get to meet Val and Robbie, Christ, for letting her sleep on his couch after rescuing her from the party.

She wanted to say that she knew he thought he was a loser because he hadn't made it as a baseball player, that his life had no meaning after that. She wanted to tell him she knew all that and he was wrong. He was good and decent; she didn't know anyone else who would have done all he'd done for her.

She wanted to tell him she loved him.

But she didn't. There was so much she wanted to say, and so little time, and all the words she could think to say felt so inadequate and, in the end, she didn't say anything. When they got to her house, she turned off the engine, walked with him to his truck and, right before he got in, she hugged him. She hugged him and said, "Thank you." And that was it.

He looked at her a little funny when she said it. He smiled, but it was a kind of a sad smile. She almost asked him what it meant, but he got into his truck and then he was gone.

Later that afternoon, Sam drove her dad's car by herself for the first and last time. She followed her mom to the house of some guy her dad knew from his job who was buying the car from them. Sam pulled up behind her mom and got out of the car. She waited outside as her mom went in the house to pick up the check and drop off the keys. Less than three hours after her triumph at the DMV and Sam found herself in the passenger side of a car again.

She guessed change didn't get you very far.

Later that night, after Sam stood in her house for the last time, after she went into each and every room, touched the walls one last time, after her father arrived from Chicago in time to eat dinner with the family, pick her and Oscar up, and head straight back to the airport, when Sam was sitting with the two of them at the departure gate, her father turned to her.

He said, "So this is it, huh? How does it feel to finally be on your way?"

"Different," she said. "It feels different than I thought it would. Like, I'm still sad about leaving? I'm definitely still sad, but I'm not as sad as I thought I'd be. I guess I feel like maybe I'm finally okay with it or something. I guess I'm ready."

"I'm really glad to hear that, Sam. Really. We all know that, in some ways, this is hardest on you and to hear that you're even a little more okay with it, well, it's a huge relief to me and your mom."

"Well," Sam said smiling, "I mean it wasn't like I had a choice, right?"

"That's one way of looking at it. Another is to say you always have control over how you choose to react to anything. You can hang on to anger and pain for as long as you want, or you can try and adapt. Try to see how you can take what's in front of you and move forward. It sounds to me like you're making the right choice."

"Trying anyway."

"It sounds to me like you're succeeding," he said. "I know you and your mom were really butting heads a lot while I've been gone. But your mom tells me that's changed over the last few weeks. She tells me you've been making a real effort with her. That sounds like someone who's making good choices to me."

Sam shrugged. "I just started looking at stuff from her perspective more," she said. "Tried to see things through her eyes."

"Well whatever it is you're doing, it's good. I'm really glad you guys are getting along."

She laughed. "You know, it's funny. I was thinking the other day—it's too bad I'm flying out with you guys instead of driving with her. That's crazy, isn't it? To think there would ever be a time when I'd *miss* not being able to take a two day car ride with mom, alone."

"That is funny," her dad said. Then, after a minute, he said, "Why don't you do it?"

"What?"

"Yeah, why not? Just go home, spend one more night in the house and leave with your mother in the morning?"

"Uh, because I have a ticket to fly and I'm already checked in and everything?"

"So what?"

"What do you mean *so what?*"

"I mean, so what? I can tell the airline you had to change your plans, it happens all the time."

"But the ticket. Won't you lose your money?"

"Who cares? I don't care about the cost of a lousy ticket. I'd much rather lose that money if it means you and your mom can have a great trip together that you'll never forget."

Sam chewed on her lip, started to really consider the idea. "I guess I could," she said. "I could even help with some of the driving maybe."

"There you go," her dad said, "now you're getting it. And think of how much it would mean to your mom if you did this. It'd be better than a million Christmas and birthday presents."

Sam laughed. "Maybe not that big, Daddy, but it would be nice." Why not? Things were going so well between them.

"Okay," she said. "I'll do it. I'll call her to come get me." She went to pull her phone out of her bag.

"No," he dad said suddenly, as he reached into his back pocket and pulled out his wallet. "I've got a better idea, take a cab. Really surprise her."

"You think? I've never taken a cab before."

"Easiest thing in the world," he said. "Just go to the baggage claim, there's tons of them. Get in, give the driver your address and he'll do the rest." He counted out three twenties and handed them to her. "This will cover it," he said, "and use whatever change there is to buy some lunch or something on your drive tomorrow."

Sam took the money and hugged her dad. "See you Sunday, Daddy," she said.

"See you Sunday."

"Bye Oscar, see you Sunday." She waved to her little brother.

"Bye Sam." He waved.

Sam left the gate, pulling her suitcase behind her, made her way to the baggage claim, and got in the first cab she saw. It was as easy as her dad said.

The trip back to her house took about forty minutes. Sam stared out the window and imagined the look on her mom's face when she walked in the door, how surprised and happy she would be. She tried to imagine all the things her mom might say, and what Sam would say back. She could play music on their trip to Chicago, and talk, and find some place to spend the night. She thought about how it would feel the first time her mom pulled over to let her drive, how amazing it would feel to readjust the seat and mirrors and pull back into traffic with her mom sitting beside her, not as a parent or a teacher or anything like that, but as an equal.

The cab pulled into the driveway of her house. Her mom's car wasn't there; Sam looked and saw it parked in front of the house instead of in the driveway and remembered her saying something about leaving the driveway empty for the movers. The whole street was filled with cars actually. Their neighbors were throwing a party; nicely dressed adults stood all around their lawn. Sam paid the driver, making sure the tip was generous. Then she pulled her suitcase out of the trunk, walked up the driveway, slid her key into the front door, and went inside.

The entry room was dark, and filled with boxes ready to be carried out as soon as the movers arrived in the morning. There was light however, spilling out from under the door to the living room, and the sound of music, a group Sam recognized but couldn't pin down. Sam made her way toward the door. She cursed when she bumped into one of the boxes. She was so used to the room the way it had always been, all these boxes were throwing her off.

Sam called out, "Mom?" and pushed the door to the living room open.

# DISINTIGRATION

They decided it would be best if they didn't see each other again.

Liz called him later that Saturday night, after he dropped Sam off and took Dana out shopping. The two of them talked it over and that was the conclusion they came to. That was fine with Nick. It was more than fine; it was what he hoped she would say. The whole thing was just too weird for him, too serious or sad or too something, anyway. He needed to get space, let his head clear a little. Then maybe he could get back on track again. Somewhere he lost sight of who he was and what he was doing with the whole Heller family, and that in turn managed to fuck up how he saw everything else too. They'd gotten into his head and he didn't like it.

He intended to stay away from the whole family, Liz *and* Sam. Driving Sam home after was excruciatingly awkward and left him feeling miserable. That wasn't entirely true, the bad feeling actually started right after the conversation with Liz where she told him about her dad and her husband and he thought *what have I gotten myself into here?* That was when it started. But it got worse when he went to pick Sam up at his place. That was the thing about it, he left Liz's and was on his way home, and was feeling better, and then he saw Sam and the bad feeling returned, worse than ever. It stayed with him, through the drive home and taking Dana out. So when Liz called late that night and said it would be better to keep their distance he thought *thank God* and he was off the hook.

He figured he'd tell Sam he got a really big job and he was sorry but he wouldn't be able to take her driving anymore and that'd be it. She'd be bummed about it, but it would be for the best. But for some reason, when she called the next day to see if he'd take her driving that Tuesday, for some, reason he agreed.

He felt bad and weird the whole day leading up to it and even worse when they were driving. He geared up to call the whole thing off, when all of a sudden Sam pulled into a Wawa and started apologizing. She had no memory of the near rape and apparently no one told her the entire truth. Not just that, but Becky told her some sanitized SFW version of what went on in the room that night. Which he was cool with, the less Sam knew about that night the better, but what got to him was this idea she had that she somehow alienated or upset him and that he was mad at her.

He told her there was nothing to apologize about, that he just had a lot on his mind. He was on the verge of giving her his story about the big important job that was going to take up his time but instead he found himself offering to spend *more* time driving with her. As much as it would take for her to qualify for her driving test.

It was the damndest thing.

Normally he could cut people out of his life with no problem, he just stopped coming by or calling or whatever, and sooner or later they got the message and that would be that. As uncomfortable and weird as he felt when he was with Sam, as much as it reminded him of things he didn't want to think about, her apology suddenly mixed everything up even more and the thought of *not* finishing teaching her to drive, the thought of disappointing her, made him feel worse. So he pushed through.

It wasn't guilt, well it wasn't *all* guilt. He was all too familiar with guilt. Guilt was a manageable emotion that he was an expert at identifying, attacking, and eliminating. It was one of the skills he mastered back when he thought he was going to go pro. In high school there were always hangers-on—friends, girls, whatever, people eager to hang out with him. When he started to take off, started experiencing new things and started out-growing some of those friends, some of them grew angry at him, laying guilt trips on him about how *he owed them* this or that because of the past they shared. Nick realized a lot of his so called friends had never been anything of the sort. They were just parasites looking to latch onto someone they thought would hit it big and then they could cash their ticket in.

That was when he figured out that you can't afford to become too invested in other people's feelings or how they perceived your actions. There's just how you felt about yourself, and how others felt about themselves. Beyond that, things got too complicated and too unclear to put any kind of stock into.

He didn't feel bad about what happened between him and Liz either; they were both adults, they knew what they were doing and they'd made a decision. Feeling bad about it wasn't going to change anything or somehow make it not have happened. The only thing to do was put it behind him and move on. Getting hung up on the past was another aspect that his days in baseball helped to annihilate. If, when you played, you had a bad day at the plate, made some errors in the field, and you spent too much time thinking about it,it got in your head and you sucked the next game too. All anybody has any control over are the things that are going to happen; once they've happened, put them behind you and move on.

No, this was something deeper, and more alarming. His clear, uncomplicated life was now confusing and messy and… weird. He didn't like it. Somehow, in the last few months, he became entangled in all these other people's lives and he didn't know how to proceed. He couldn't think about Dana or Liz or Sam or anyone without becoming anxious and uncomfortable. All he knew for sure was that he felt the overwhelming need to get Sam her license. He didn't know why he felt it, he didn't even care at all really until he was sitting in that parking lot. And, as the week went by, that goal was the only thing he could think about without feeling miserable.

So he focused on that.

If things started to get fuzzy for him during the day, if that bad feeling crept into his brain, he just pushed it out by focusing on the hours left in the car and where they were going to go next.

They spent two, sometimes three hours a day in the car over the next week and a half. They ran Nick's errands, picked up food for Sam and her family, toured the places Nick hung out when he was young, the neighborhood Sam's grandparents lived in before they moved to Florida. The Sunday before she left they even went all the way up to Weston, past the dentist office where his mom was a receptionist. He didn't tell her that of course; she just thought they were getting some highway time in, but that's where they went.

When the day finally came for Sam to take the driver's test, he was almost as nervous as she was. The test was the same Friday she was leaving, so, if she messed up and failed, she wouldn't be able to retake the test in Baxter; it would have to wait until she was in Chicago. He couldn't let that happen. They'd come too far, did too much work, to fall apart at the end. They went over the finer points of driving on the way to the DMV. He told her to keep cool, not to worry about any attitude the instructor gave her, to just do what she went there to do. She knew how to drive, and she was ready for this.

The whole thing took less than an hour, but it felt like an eternity. He waited inside with her until she was called to take her written test, then she disappeared into another room and Nick went outside to pace and smoke and wait.

He watched as Sam and her instructor got into the car and drove away. He was a little up the block, and she didn't see him. He'd considered calling out to her as she walked across the parking lot to the car and giving her a few more words of advice and encouragement, but he restrained himself. Even with all the weirdness and the nerves, that was a little too much like a soccer-mom. Besides, he didn't want to throw her off. Once the game started and you were at the plate, it was just you and the pitcher. The manager wasn't allowed to run out and tell you what to do next, whether to swing or not and when. And you wouldn't want him to if he could.

Sometimes, you just had to do things by yourself.

Sam drove back onto the lot about twenty minutes, or five hours later, depending on whose measure of time was being recorded. Nick tried to gauge how she'd done by the glimpse of her face as she returned to the driving center. But it was impenetrable. Sam was usually so animated, he could usually tell her mood within five seconds. But the face he saw walking from the car to the main building was blank. There wasn't a big smile or a frown dripping with disappointment. Instead she looked, passive. Calm. Like nothing had happened at all.

When she came out and told him she passed, he just about screamed with relief. The accomplishment he felt was almost overwhelming. He couldn't remember feeling that good about anything in years.

It meant that he could still function in the chaos that swirled in his head; that he could find a way out of the mess that his life had become. Sam getting her license was the last step in removing himself from the Hellers and all that came with them. He was done. All he had to do was drop her off at home, get in his truck and drive away and that would be it. No more Liz, no more Sam, no more bad, confused feelings.

And once he was clear of them, he could get clear of Dana too, he just knew it. He was too deep in all of it, he could see that now, too attached, too involved in various dramas. But now, the Hellers were leaving and all he needed to do was cut ties with Dana and get a fresh start.

It had been too long since he'd had one of those.

He said goodbye to Sam in front of her house. She hugged him and thanked him and that was it. He got in his truck and drove away and left them all behind forever.

Driving away, he had to admit that, like everything with that girl and her family, he was unprepared for how mixed his emotions were. As much as he wanted to get away, as much as he *needed* to, when that moment came it was hard. He really *liked* her. He liked driving around with her, talking to her, listening to her babble about her life. He liked the enthusiasm she seemed to have for life; it was charming and he was going to miss it.

But sitting at home that evening, drinking a beer and watching *SportsCenter*, a wave of satisfaction washed over him and he felt peaceful. It was done, he did his job, and now they were gone. He looked at the clock on the cable box; it read six-fifteen. When had Sam said her flight was taking off? Was it six or seven? Was she in the air right now? Sitting on the plane on the tarmac, or still in the terminal waiting to board? It didn't matter, she wasn't at home anymore. She was out the door and on her way to Chicago and he didn't have to worry or think about them ever again.

He was finally free.

He was feeling so, so good about it, and that's why it didn't make any sense that he found himself back at the Hellers' house an hour later.

Here's what happened. His phone rang and he saw that it was Liz and his first thought was that something was wrong. An accident or something, the plane or driving to the airport, there was a problem and she needed his help. That was what shot through his mind in the second he saw the ID flash on his phone, so he picked up.

She sounded wary. Warm, but wary. Nothing was wrong, Steve just left with the kids and the house was empty and she was all alone and thinking and she felt bad about how they left things between the two of them and she just wanted to call and say there were no hard feelings and she was really glad that she got to know him.

He was glad she called, and he said so. He admitted that things were...complicated for him over the last couple of weeks, but that he didn't regret anything either. He told her about how irrationally proud he was of Sam that morning when she passed her driver's test, what a great kid she was, how much he liked the whole family.

They talked for a few more minutes about Sam and Oscar before Liz said they were being silly and why didn't he just come over and they could talk face to face. She said it wasn't like they were a couple of teenagers who couldn't control themselves or anything; he could come by, they could talk, smoke, have a nice evening and then say goodbye, face to face, like proper adults.

He said why not.

Liz was parked in the spot in front of the house, and there was some kind of party going on across the street. Nick drove almost down the block before he found somewhere to park. He locked the truck, and trotted down the street, back to the Hellers.

"I remember when we moved into this place," Liz said, refilling Nick's glass of wine. "It was the first place we ever owned, and I just learned I was pregnant with Sam and I was a couple of years shy of thirty and I felt so grown up. Like I made it through adolescence and early adulthood, whatever that was, and now I was going to be an adult."

"I'm still waiting to feel that way," Nick said.

"Me too," said Liz. "I think I thought there was going to be some corner I turned or switch I flipped and I would just *be* an adult. But it never happened. Instead, I was just the same old me, but I was *doing* grown up things. I was the same silly girl inside, but I was cleaning my house instead of an apartment; I was driving around suburban streets instead of city ones. There were times I felt like an adult, sometimes when I was with Sam or Oscar, driving them somewhere, or disciplining them, or something like that. But even then there was a part of me that was always aware that I was doing these things that I was just unprepared for, that I had no business actually doing. That's what I think adulthood really is—it's just little kids playing dress-up."

"I hear you." Nick said. "My aunt is the most grown up person I know, like the most responsible, bill paying, dinner preparing, *don't horse around inside you'll break something*, adult type person in my life. And even she spends all her free time watching John Hughes movies and listening to *The Cure*."

"Oh my God, I used to love *The Cure*," Liz said.

"That's funny, you don't seem the type."

Liz shot him a mock indignant look. "What's that supposed to mean?"

"It means," he said, "I don't know, it means I never pegged you for being into that whole beautiful sadness thing that they sold. The self-obsessed tragic poet type; I guess I always figured you were more of the jock type or something."

Liz lit a cigarette. "I did that too," she said, "but that was more high school. I still ran track in college, though; it's actually how I met Steve. He was a junior when I was a freshman and he was a real gym rat, you know? He played on the college baseball team, or maybe he'd just stopped to focus on grades? I don't remember, but he was always in the gym either way. So I'd be out on the track running and Steve was in the gym, which was right next to the track and had all these windows that looked out over it, and he said the first day he saw me running he thought to himself, *I gotta meet that girl*, and he jumped off the machine he was using and went outside to talk to me."

Nick nodded along; he'd heard the story before actually, from Sam. Twice.

"I wasn't really into guys like him at that time," she said, "I dated athletes throughout high school and I wanted something else, a fresh start, you know? I'd been going with more, I don't know, artsy, intellectual types since getting to college, but he was so smart and so charming even then. *Man,* he had a way with words; he always said people told him he should be a lawyer. He talked me into dinner and we've been together since."

She stared off into space for a minute, lost wherever her thoughts had taken her. Then, she blinked back into the present.

"What was I talking about anyway? Why was I telling you all that again?"

"*The Cure*," he said.

"Right," she snapped. "*The Cure*. So I just said I thought I was over jocks, right? Well, earlier that year I was seeing this guy Max, Max the painter. Max was a real intense guy and really into acid and Kurt Vonnegut and he loved *The Cure*. He always played their really weird druggy stuff, like *The Top* and *Pornography*. But I was more into *Head in the Door* and *Kiss Me Kiss Me Kiss Me* and that sort of, more pop stuff. Max said those albums were *The Cure*'s sell out stuff. He said *Head* had some good stuff, but *Kiss Me Kiss Me Kiss Me* was an abortion, he really said that. An abortion. It was just released and *Just Like Heaven* was all over the radio and every time he heard it, he just got so mad."

She laughed.

"Max and I didn't last that long. He was a little *too* intense. But, he got me into *The Cure*, and that was the soundtrack to my life for a while, so I guess I've always been grateful to him for that. I remember when *Disintegration* came out, and I opened it and it had that little note, what did it say?"

Nick shook his head.

"It was something about how loud to play it," she said. "Hold on." She got up and went over to a box and opened it up. "Pour yourself another glass of wine while I dig this out. Get me some more too."

Nick got up and walked to the table where the bottle was sitting, picked it up, and looked at it. There was a Kangaroo on the label. It was good. He wasn't much of a wine guy, but he liked this stuff, this Kangaroo wine. He filled his glass and then hers.

"Here we go!" Liz pulled a CD out of the box, one he'd seen many times at home on Val's shelves. Liz opened the case, took out the book and read from it. "*This music has been mixed to be played loud, so turn it up*. And see, look, it's all printed in capital letters, like it's not a suggestion, it's a command. See?"

She handed the book to Nick so he could verify that it was indeed all in capitals.

"I bought that CD the day it came out. I was just finishing up, I think it was my junior year, and I opened the packaging and read that little note and it was like *Oh my God.* It was the coolest thing I'd ever read."

"Sounds pretty cool," Nick said.

Liz laughed, took a sip from her glass, "You think I'm just the lamest right now, don't you?"

"No," said Nick, "not at all. I've just heard a lot about *The Cure* and *The Smiths* and *My Bloody Valentine* and all those bands over the years."

"From your aunt?"

"From my aunt, from girls I've dated. Lately from Sam."

She looked surprised, "Sam likes *The Cure*?"

"I don't remember *The Cure* specifically, but maybe; all those bands kind of sound the same to me. She just plays it when we're driving."

"How about that."

"Oh yeah, she loves all that stuff. Val's been making her mixes, I guess."

"I had no idea," said Liz.

"Well, look at it this way, it's something you guys can bond over and listen to together now."

She laughed. "I guess we can." She looked at him. "I'm going to miss talking to you," she said.

"I'm going to miss talking to you too." It was true.

"You always say the right thing; I wish there was some way I could thank you."

"Don't worry about it," he said.

Liz smiled mischievously; she picked her CD up and put it into a small portable CD player that sat on the mantle. She pressed the track advance button a few times, then, a guitar started playing and Robert Smith was whispering. Liz turned around to face him, her smile wider and wickeder than ever. Smith started singing about the spider man coming and Liz's eyes were hooded; she ran her hands through her hair. She advanced toward him in time with the music.

"What are you doing?"

"Saying goodbye."

She slid up close to him so their hips touched, wrapped her arms around his waist, and smiled at him.

"I thought we made an agreement about this."

She looked at him dreamily. "The bad thing's already done, one more time can't hurt."

She stood up on her tip toes and kissed him, he tasted the wine on her lips and tongue.

They fell onto the couch, Liz on top, Nick beneath her. Liz straddled him; she smiled, reached down, crossed her arms and pulled her blouse up over her head and tossed it across the room. Nick did the same with his t-shirt; he sat up and pulled her against him and kissed her again. He felt up her back towards her bra and, with ease, unclasped it with one hand.

Still kissing him, Liz pulled away just far enough to pull the straps down off her shoulders and the bra off her chest. She tossed it after her blouse.

She got his belt off and was unbuckling his jeans when they heard it, a sort of muffled bumping noise in the next room, followed by a quiet curse.

They both froze.

Nick looked at Liz.

Liz looked at Nick.

"Mom?" It came from behind the living room door.

Then, from the other side of the couch, came the sound of the door opening.

# PART THREE

The average speed of a major league fastball is ninety miles an hour when it leaves the pitcher's hand.

The distance between the mound and home plate is sixty feet six inches.

That means that, factoring random variables like the length of the pitcher's arm at the point of release, the average fastball travels from the pitcher's hand to the catcher's glove in about point four seconds. That's less than half a second for the hitter to find the ball, identify the type of pitch, the speed, where it's going to cross the plate, and swing before it's already gone. They say that the difference between a line drive and a foul ball is about a one-one hundredth of a second differential in reaction time. One-one hundredth of a second between standing on first and popping out. One-one hundredth of a second between winning and losing, between living and dying.

Some people believe that once the batter hits the ball he has no control over where the ball goes. They say all the batter can do is make contact, and whether it goes to left or right field, is on the ground or in the air, whether it finds the hole, splits the gap, drops in or goes off the wall, and is just another routine out, is left entirely to luck.

People who believe those types of things don't tend to be the ones playing the game.

Hitting a baseball is the hardest thing in professional sports.

Fact.

"Mom, are you in here?"

From the other side of the couch, there was the sound of the door opening.

Sam was in the room.

Liz looked down at Nick, then across the room to where her blouse and bra were lying on the box.

She looked terrified.

There was no time.

No time to move or talk or breathe.

"Mom?"

She couldn't see them. They were on the couch, she was behind it.

If she took two steps into the room she'd see them.

Sam's face emerged behind the couch.

She stared at them uncomprehendingly for a second.

Then, the color drained from her face. Her eyes went wide with surprise; she covered her mouth with her hands, turned, and ran from the room; the screen door slammed a second later.

She was gone.

Liz shot up from the couch and across the room where she grabbed her shirt.

"Oh my God," she was saying as she pulled it over her head, "*oh my God, oh my God, oh my God, oh my God, oh my God.*"

Nick sat up, said, "What…" and trailed off. He wanted to say, *what should I do?* But it seemed so inadequate. There were no words that could express what he wanted to say, what he needed to do. There was a part of him screaming that he could somehow still stop it from happening. That he could, somehow, go back in time thirty seconds, a minute, and change it all, if he could just figure out *how*.

Liz turned and looked with bugging eyes. She looked like she'd forgotten he was there.

"What?" Her voice cracked, she was on the verge of really panicking.

"What do I, what am I…?" Still no words.

"I don't know, *I don't know*! Just stay here, I'm going to go… if she comes back… I don't know." She ran out of the room and out the front door after Sam.

Nick waited.

He found his shirt, put it on. He sat down on the couch, got up, sat back down again. Got up again, walked around the room, sat back down again.

Nothing felt right.

Nothing felt natural.

When he was sitting, he could only think: *why am I just sitting here? I look like a fucking asshole just sitting here, I should be doing something.*

So he stood, but then he thought: *where am I supposed to go? What am I supposed to do? I'm supposed to wait; that's what she said.*

He was a caged animal.

He looked around the room; everything was the same as it was a few minutes ago. The bottle of wine sat on the coffee table; the glasses were on the floor. The bottle was open and the glasses still had a little wine in them.

Should he close the bottle? Empty the glasses?

Should he look for the cap?

Was that what he should be doing?

What if Sam came back and found him calmly capping a bottle of wine or rinsing two glasses out in the sink? What would that look like?

Would it look like he was covering something up? Would it look like he didn't care about what happened and he was just casually cleaning up after himself?

Then again, what if she came back and the bottle and glasses were still there? Would it be a kick in the face about what she just witnessed?

Oh God.

Sam.

He couldn't stop thinking about her face. Couldn't stop thinking about the look on her face when she saw them. He would never, ever, forget that look. It was horror and shame and confusion and disappointment and just, sadness—deep, deep sadness. It was all there in one face all at once.

And it was his fault.

The worst look he'd ever seen in his life, and he'd put it on her face.

Him.

Jesus.

Nick rubbed his chest, his neck, his chin, the back of his head.

He felt itchy, twitchy, all over. His skin was burning.

He stood up.

Sat back down.

His hands felt heavy and awkward.

There was a prickling pain in his right knee.

He was coming out of his skin.

What was he going to do?

What would he do if Sam came back before Liz? What would he say to her? What *could* he say to her? How could he undo or lessen the damage he created? Wouldn't seeing him there just make things worse?

Maybe he should just go.

Maybe that was the smart thing. To just slip out and go, leave a message on Liz's phone or something, just explaining why he left.

Unless.

Unless they were right outside on the lawn or somewhere on the way to his truck.

If they were out there and saw him running away like the pussy he was, that might be just as bad as him staying at the house.

He was so turned around and confused that he didn't know which way was up.

God, he was an asshole.

The music.

The music, the CD, was still playing.

Nick raced across the room and ripped the boom box cord out of the wall. He took out the CD and looked at it. How long ago did he tell Liz that she could bond with Sam over this album? Ten minutes? Fifteen?

What a fucking asshole.

He wanted to destroy it. To break it into a million little pieces, grind it into dust. He wanted to smash its case, rip the cover in half, destroy its existence.

The front door opened, he put the CD down and spun around in time to see Liz walk back into the room, alone.

Her face was red and splotchy, her hair in shambles. Her bare feet were scuffed and a little bloody, as was one of her hands. She looked wrecked.

"She's gone," Liz mumbled. "I caught up with her, down the block. I tried, tried to talk, to talk to her, to get her to calm down. But I didn't know what to say."

Liz closed her eyes and took a deep, shaky breath.

"She was crying and screaming and calling me names and I didn't know what to say. There was nothing I could say."

She opened her eyes and looked at Nick, imploringly, as if he had any power to change what was happening.

“I tried to calm her down. I reached out, to soothe her. I tried to hug her and she shoved me.” She held up her scraped and bloodied hand. “I fell,” she whispered, “she ran again. Disappeared. I didn’t know if I should keep, keep following her or let her go or come back and get in the car and look or…”

She pressed her palms into her forehead, gritted her teeth, the veins and tendons in her neck bulged.

She screamed.

And Nick just stood there and watched.

Lost.

Nick sat on the edge of his bed and unscrewed the cap from the bottle of whiskey he’d picked up on his way home. He took a long drink straight from the bottle. What buzz he had from the wine earlier was long gone, and he definitely needed help to find any kind of peace tonight.

Liz told him to go. He offered to stay with her, make sure she was all right, but she said no. He said he’d drive around, see if *he* could find Sam. But Liz squashed that too. He asked her what she was going to do; she said there was nothing to do. Sam’s phone was off, she called Becky to see if Sam was there, she wasn’t; she tried everyone she could think of, no one had seen her. Liz would just have to wait until someone saw her or she called or showed up.

He asked her what she planned to do about the movers in the morning. She had no idea. Steve expected her to arrive on Sunday, the movers were paid, and she had no idea what was going to happen. She started crying again.

Was she sure there was nothing he could do to help? He’d do anything; he had to do something. She shook her head. He just needed to go. She told him it would be better if, whenever Sam resurfaced, he wasn’t there. It’d be easier that way.

She was right, as much as he hated to admit it. If he wasn’t the last person on Earth Sam wanted to see, he was a close second.

He felt a driving urge to *do something*, to stay involved, help clean up the mess that he made. But there was nothing he could do.

He hated feeling so useless. Worse than useless, he was destructive; he was the problem. And now that the damage was done, he'd been shoved aside. Like a child who messed up and was sent up to his room while the adults figured out what to do next. He took another swig from the bottle.

*You motherfucker, you stupid selfish motherfucker, why did you have to go back over there? How the fuck could you have been so fucking stupid?*

If he just listened to the voice in his head, to his instincts, none of this would be happening right now. If Liz hadn't called, if he said thanks but no thanks, if he hadn't drank that last glass of wine, if she hadn't put on that goddamn CD.

The look on Sam's face wouldn't go away. That fucking look. He saw it every time he closed his eyes.

*FUCK*!

He was so, so stupid. He had made it, he was free! Sam earned her license; she was gone, he was clear of that whole family. And he went and fucked it all up because he was too fucking stupid to follow his own fucking rule.

And now, she was out there, somewhere, hurting like crazy, and there was nothing he could do about it. Anything he did would just make things worse. That was all he ever did.

It didn't matter the reason, *intent* didn't mean shit. All that happened was things got worse.

Always.

He took another drink.

Here was this girl, this sweet, trusting, happy little girl. All she asked was that he teach her how to drive. All he needed to do was be her friend; to sit next to her while she drove and listen to her talk.

She didn't even really need him to listen; she just wanted him there while she talked. Had anybody, anywhere, ever, asked for less of a friend than that?

All he had to do was not go back into that house.

Why had he thought it was a good idea to go back there? How could he have thought it was anything but a bad idea?

How did it all get so fucked up?

He sat on the edge of the bed and drank until he couldn't sit up anymore. Then he dropped the bottle on the floor and closed his eyes.

"Nick... *Nick*!"

Nick opened his eyes. Slowly, ever so slowly, Dana came into focus.

"Quite a night you had last night, huh?"

He squinted at her. "What?"

"We were supposed to have brunch today? You were gonna pick me up? I called like a hundred times before I came over. And I find you, in bed, totally dressed, shoes and everything, no covers, and this"—she held up the empty whiskey bottle—"on its side by the bed."

Nick rubbed his face, he felt like he swallowed a cat. "What time is it?"

"Eleven thirty."

"And we're having brunch?"

"We *were*," she said.

It started to come back to him. Yes. Saturday. He told Dana he'd see her on Saturday, they were going to go get brunch before she went to work in the afternoon. That all sounded familiar. He sat up.

"What happened here last night? Did you just decide to have a little party by yourself or something?"

Last night?

Last night.

"Oh yeah," he said. "I was just… I had a hard day. Needed to relax. I must have overdone it."

She looked at him, concerned. "Is everything all right?"

"Everything's fine," he said. "It's all fine. I just need a minute to get my head together. I should clean up, take a shower."

"I have to be at work by two," she said.

"That's fine, two's fine. I'll be in and out. Just, stay here, gimme ten minutes."

He got to his feet and headed for the bathroom where he started the shower.

He used the time in the bathroom to fix his head, figure out what to do next. He had three voice mails, all from Dana, no missed calls or texts from Liz or Sam or anybody else. He considered calling Liz, find out how she was doing, if she'd heard from Sam, but he decided against it. If no one reached out to him, it was because they didn't want him involved. Whatever was going on, he wasn't a part of it anymore.

That left Dana, and he was of two minds on what to do with her. On the one hand, he wanted to call the day off, tell her he wasn't feeling good, send her home. His life was dramatic enough without adding her into the mix. He could offer to take her out after she was done with work, or tomorrow, or something. She'd be disappointed but she'd understand.

On the other hand, maybe she wouldn't. It was tough to predict what was or wasn't going to piss Dana off at any given moment, and breaking a date with her just because he was hungover might not fly. Plus, who knew if she'd buy it? She could get pissy and start asking questions he didn't want to answer. He didn't have the energy for another fight, or the strength to face another disappointed girl.

He turned up the heat in the shower, put his face square in the stream and tried to blast the image of Sam's face out of his head.

Fuck it.

If Dana wanted to go to brunch, and that's what he told her he'd do, then that's what would happen. He was done changing plans and going back on his promises, to himself or to anyone else. That was over.

He thought about Dana, about all the shit they'd been through, and how she was still there. She never ran from him or gave up on him. Maybe he was too hard on her. She could be annoying sure, but who wasn't from time to time? She wasn't that bad, if he really thought about it. Most of their fights stemmed more from his doings than hers. Had to do with him breaking promises or getting angry with her for stuff that was, when he thought back about, probably fairly petty. If he was honest, then he had to say that he never really gave her a chance.

Today was a perfect example: how many girls would patiently wait for their boyfriend (yeah, he said it) to shower off a hangover before taking her out to brunch without complaining?

She hadn't yelled at him or guilt tripped him or anything; she was even worried about him when he said he had a rough night.

That was the girl he was always complaining about?

Dana might get too emotional at times, or have annoying friends, but she was good and loyal. Her expectations of him might be too high, but at least she thought he was capable of more.

What had she said the other day at lunch?

*I have faith in you.*

Why was he spending so much time pushing away someone who had faith in him?

He always reached for something else, something just beyond his grasp, instead of appreciating what was staring him in the face. It was the competitor in him, the part that always wanted to compete, to excel, to *win*. Maybe it was time to stop competing, maybe it was time to settle down and start living.

Dana wasn't in his room when he walked back in, freshly showered. Instead, she was sitting in the kitchen with Val and Robbie.

"I hope you don't mind," she said in explanation. "Your room kind of smelled."

"I was just telling Dana about pancake Saturday," Val said.

"Pancake Saturday, right," Nick said. "You ready to go?"

Val looked at Nick as she stirred the batter. "Maybe she wants to eat here with us?"

Dana's eyes flicked nervously over to Nick; the opportunity for her to spend time with his family was one of their biggest sources of conflict. "Oh, no," she said, "I couldn't intrude on your family time."

"It's no bother, Dana; I wouldn't have invited you if it was. What do you say, Nick?" Val smiled. "Take a load off."

Yesterday, this wouldn't be a question. Yesterday, he would have gotten Dana the hell out of there the second he saw her. Yesterday, he would have been more concerned with Val's clear attempt to piss him off by inviting Dana to stay.

But it wasn't yesterday anymore.

"Why not," Nick said taking a seat.

"Really?" Dana looked shocked.

"Sure, if you're okay with eating Val's shitty pancakes, so am I."

"Language, you ass!" Val said, and gestured toward Robbie.

Dana's face twitched, like she was fighting a smile, "Okay," she said, her voice still unsure but happy. "Then I'd love to stay."

They were almost finished when they heard it.

Nick fed the last bit of his pancake to Gertie, and Val and Dana talked about some celebrity he'd never heard of and didn't care about. Gert was licking syrup off Nick's hand and Nick thought this wasn't so bad at all; he could live with something like this. Tom came in from his office and told everyone to be quiet for a second.

Then there was a sort of thump sound.

"There, did you hear that?"

"Yeah," said Nick.

"What is it?" said Dana.

They heard it again.

"I think it's coming from outside," Val said.

Thump. Thump. It was getting faster.

"I'm going to go check it out," Tom said, and disappeared out the kitchen door. A moment later they heard him again, alarmed. "HEY!" he shouted. "WHAT THE HELL ARE YOU DOING?"

Nick jumped to his feet and ran toward the sound of Tom's voice. Gertie followed, barking all the way.

Tom was outside, in the driveway, his arms wrapped around a wriggling figure holding an aluminum bat. The hood of Nick's truck was covered with dents; his windshield and one headlight were broken. Gertie ran to the struggle and barked up at the intruder.

"What the fuck?" Nick growled.

Tom turned around, and Nick got a look at the figure with the bat.

It was Sam, her face red with rage and tears. Her hands were wrapped in gauze; Nick saw brown stains of dried blood on her knuckles. And her head, her head was shaved right down to the scalp. All that was left was a thin layer of brown fuzz and a few thicker spots where the clippers missed. Gertie ran around her feet, barking up at her.

Sam glared at Nick with a fury he'd never seen before.

"Drop the bat," Tom said. "*Drop the fucking bat.*"

"Sam?" Val appeared from the doorway, Robbie in her arms, Dana right behind her. "What's going on? What happened to your hair? *Were you just hitting Nick's truck with a baseball bat*?"

Gertie was going nuts.

"You know this girl?" Tom asked.

"Yeah," Nick said, "I do. *Gertie! Enough! Come here!*" Gertie, satisfied with a job well done, stopped barking and trotted over to Nick, tail wagging. "Sam, drop the bat."

"*Fuck you,*" snarled Sam.

"Sam…"

"*Fuck. You.*"

Val handed Robbie to Dana, marched across the lawn to where Tom held Sam, and pried the bat out of her hands.

"What the hell is going on?" she demanded.

"Ask him." Unable to use her hands or arms, Sam pointed her chin at Nick.

"I'm not asking him right now. If he did something, we'll deal with that later. Right now I'm asking you, *what the hell is going on?*"

"You want to know what's going on?" Sam laughed. "Nothing's going on, nothing that matters anyway. Nothing matters anymore. Not after what he did."

Val closed her eyes, sighed. "What'd he do?"

All around him, there were people, people who came out of their houses to witness the disturbance.

Sam laughed again. Her eyes were crazy with rage. "What'd he do? *What'd he do? WHAT'D HE DO?* I'll tell you what he did—he fucked my mom, that's what he did. The whole time he was taking me around, teaching me to drive, being my friend, he was fucking my fucking mom. That's what he did."

There.

Done.

Val turned, and faced Nick. "What's she talking about?"

Nick didn't say anything.

"Why would she be saying…?"

He looked straight at her; there wasn't anything he could say.

Her jaw dropped. "Oh Jesus, Nick," she said. "Really?"

The back of his head was on fire, he couldn't move.

Val said, "How could you?"

Tom looked at Nick with a mixture of shock and confusion. Sam broke free of his grasp and took off. She hobble-ran down the street and disappeared around a corner. Nick wanted to go after her, try to calm her down, apologize, do something to fix things. But he knew there was nothing he could do to make anything better anymore. There was no way to make it look like anything other than what it was.

Val glared at him with tears in her eyes. "What is *wrong* with you?" She stormed past him and into the house, scooping Robbie up off the ground on her way inside.

"Christ, man," Tom said, and walked into the house after his wife.

Nick took a seat on the front lawn, rested his arms across his knees. More sitting and waiting while the grown-ups figured out what was to be done about his mess. Gertie walked over and pushed him with her head and licked him until he relented and pet her.

It was only then he realized that Dana was gone. Dana, who had been standing in the doorway holding Robbie. Dana, who unquestionably heard everything Sam said and made an exit all her own that he hadn't even noticed. Dana, who had cared about him and trusted him and who he finally appreciated. Dana, who would never, *never*, forgive him.

Gone. Just like that.

He put his head in his hands.

He sat there in the grass and watched the lazy Saturday traffic pass by on the road for a good half hour until Tom came back outside and took a seat on the grass beside him.

"She's, uh, she's really pissed at you, man." He stared straight ahead, his eyes on the road.

"Yeah, I kind of figured."

"No, I mean *really*."

"Yeah."

"Well, the thing is, she doesn't want you in the house anymore."

Nick looked at him. "What?"

"I mean, look, I fought for you, but…"

"But?"

"But what am I gonna do?"

"I don't know, stand up for me?"

"What did I just say I've been doing in there? There was nothing I could say, she's just, she's had enough man."

"Enough? What does that even mean? Enough what?"

"Just, enough, enough of the bullshit. Enough of *your* bullshit."

"What bullshit? What are you *talking* about?"

"Nick, stop it, you know what I'm talking about."

"No, I really don't."

"You're really going to make me say it?"

"I guess I am, because I have no idea what you're talking about. Look, I fucked up; I can see that, *anyone* can see that. What I *don't* see, is how it's got anything to do with her."

"Do you think she doesn't see what's going on with you? Do you think she doesn't care just because you don't? You're killing her, you're absolutely killing her. You're a fucking train wreck man; no one understands what you're doing anymore. You're angry all the time. You work when you want, don't when you don't. You don't show any interest in actually, you know, turning it into a *career*. You run around with these girls. Girls who aren't old enough to pay for their own drinks; you fuck around with them, then take off when things even smell serious. You're just wasting your life. And you're doing it in her house. Do you have any idea how much it hurts her to see you acting like this? She only let you live with us in the first place because she thought we'd be a good influence on you, that we could be some kind of example of adulthood or something, and you pull this? You're fucking some married lady and playing weird head games with her daughter? Seriously?"

"It wasn't like that," Nick said.

"So, we got it wrong and you didn't sleep with that girl's mom?"

"No, I mean, yeah, but it wasn't, I mean," he gave up. "I don't know."

"What were you thinking?"

"I don't know."

"You don't know? What are you, twelve? If you don't know what you were thinking, how's anybody else supposed to understand?"

He said the only thing he could. "I don't know."

They both laughed when he said it. It was sad, but it broke some of the tension.

"God," Nick said, "you really didn't hold back, did you? How long have you been waiting to say all that?"

"I didn't like having to say any of it. But you kept pushing."

"Figure I wasn't feeling bad enough. Jesus."

"It would have been worse coming from her, believe me."

"Tom..."

Tom held up his hands. "It's just how she feels man, that's it. Bottom line, you may be my oldest friend, but she's my *wife,* okay? I *have* to live with her. If she wants you out, you're out, sorry. And I gotta tell you, I don't think I disagree with her."

"Well," he was struggling for something, anything, to say, "if she wants to kick me out, why can't she come out and do it herself?"

"She doesn't want to talk to you."

"But, maybe if we talked for a minute-"

Tom cut him off. "Dude," he said, "it's over, all right? It's just, it's over."

Nick ripped a chunk of grass out of the ground, "*Fuck!*"

Tom put his arm around Nick's shoulders, "Look, it's not, you're not homeless, okay? You can stay here until you find somewhere more permanent."

Nick laughed darkly. "Yeah, whatever."

"Maybe," he said, "maybe in the end this is gonna work out for the best. Maybe this is just what you need to finally get your shit together."

He laughed again, "Maybe it is."

He didn't blame Val, not really. He didn't have any fucking idea where he was going to go, but that didn't change the fact that everything his aunt thought about him was right. He was a fucking train wreck.

He finally understood.

Finally saw the scope of how bad he fucked everything up.

There was no one else to blame for this one either. No misunderstanding, no mistaken impression, or inflated expectation he could turn around and use to shield himself against guilt and accusation. There was just him, what he did, and the people he hurt.

*You deserve whatever happens to you, you piece of shit.*

A woman was talking on the TV bolted to the upper corner of the waiting room, but there was no sound. Instead, a modern rock radio station pumped music through the speakers. The woman on the TV screen was excited about something, she was holding a blender in her hands; occasionally the camera cut to a studio audience. A telephone number scrolled across the bottom of the screen. The music playing was loud and aggressive. It was one of those post grunge, post metal, post quality bands, what Val called *butt rock*. He listened to the angry driving song and watched the peppy, excited woman on the TV talking to the enthusiastic audience and waited for the guy to finish replacing the windshield on his truck.

"Wow," the mechanic said when he drove up Sunday morning, "who'd you piss off?"

Nick had no desire to get into that, or anything really, with some grease monkey. "No idea," he said. "I just woke up yesterday and found it like this."

The mechanic ran his clean hand over one of the dents in the driver's side door; he whistled softly. "Fifty bucks says it was some woman mad at you. Women always go after your ride. You piss off a guy and he'll wanna fight you, you know? Prove he's a man by standing face to face with you. A woman doesn't think like that. She just wants to fuck your day up, right? Let you know she'd mad."

"I guess so."

"What's that saying? Hell has no fury. I knew a guy, he did his girl wrong; she set his car on *fire*. No shit. She broke a window, sprayed the interior with lighter fluid and tossed in a match. Whoosh, bye-bye Jetta." He laughed. "My boy was leasing that car too. He had all *sorts* of explaining to do after that."

"Anyway," Nick said, "I just really want the windshield taken care of today. I can fix the headlights myself."

"All right, all right, I can do that," the mechanic said. "What about all the body work? You want to try and knock out some of these dents? Order replacements?"

"I'll worry about that later. Right now I just want it to be legal to drive."

The mechanic wiped his hands on a rag. "Cool man, cool," he said. "Waiting room's inside, take a seat. If you want, have some coffee or something, there might still be some donuts. I can knock this out real quick for you, be an hour or so."

"All right," Nick said. "Thanks."

There were big black bars across the top and bottom of the TV screen. Whoever turned it on hadn't bothered to synch it correctly with the cable box so it was broadcasting in the wrong aspect ratio and the image was stretched wider than it should be. What was the point of turning the TV on if you (A) couldn't hear what anyone was saying; (B) the image was of some shitty infomercial and not sports or something else you didn't need sound for; and (C) the image wasn't even displayed correctly anyway?

He could fix the dents eventually, the truck wouldn't pass inspection with that much damage to the body; but even thinking about it made him feel bad. Like he was trying to whitewash over what happened or something. There was a part of him that felt like he should leave the dents right where they were forever, like scars or a limp. They could be a constant reminder of what a shit he was. Sam and Dana and Val and Liz would have to live with the damage he did for the rest of their lives. Why should he, or his truck, be any different? The windshield and headlights were one thing, he needed them to function; but cosmetic fixes? He wasn't sure.

There was so much he didn't know about anymore.

He had to find a place to live, like, right away. Tom might have *said* he could stay with them until he found another place. He might have said that, he might have gotten Val to agree to it,but he could have said he was the king of Siam too, and that didn't necessarily make it so. The night before was excruciating. Val didn't say anything to him all night, not a word. If she saw him, one of the few times he ventured out of his room, she looked away or left the room.

He knew she was mad at him and that it would take time for her to get over it. But still, it was intense and very clear that, as far as she was concerned, the faster Nick was out of there the happier she would be.

The problem was that he hadn't lived on his own, pretty much ever. He lived at home of course; then he had roommates when he was with the team and after, and then Val and Tom. He was never totally by himself before; never worried about paying bills or rent or buying food or anything like that. He contributed to the house, but it was a thing where Val told him how much to pay, and he handed her cash when he had it. Did he even have a check book? He didn't even know where to begin. It was the middle of June, did he have to wait until the start of July before he could sign a lease somewhere? Did he have good credit for that? How did you find something like that out? There was always spam in his email about finding out his credit score; then again there was always spam about making his cock bigger too. Whatever his credit was, it was good enough to buy the truck, but Val had co-signed on that one. She probably wouldn't want to help out with this, even if it did get him out faster. The thing to do he supposed, was to find somewhere else to crash while he figured out a more permanent solution.

Speaking of permanent.

There was no way Dana would ever forgive him. That was completely out of the question, right? Or was that him pussying out of something he needed to face up to? Was this one of those times he was supposed to stick it out? Would it be like Val—if he gave her time, she could forgive him? It seemed like a long shot, but was he supposed to try anyway? Even if it only gave her a chance to spit in his face, was that something he should do? Like some sort of cathartic moment for her or something?

Christ, what a mess.

The woman on the TV seemed happy; she apparently had all the answers. But whatever it was she knew, Nick wasn't going to hear it.

She came back Tuesday during the day, knocked on the door a few minutes after Val and Robbie left. She probably waited somewhere on the street until their car drove away.

He wasn't home all that often if he could help it. He spent the last couple of days mostly driving around and thinking, trying to figure out what to do next. When he wasn't driving, he was in his room, the only place in the house where he felt even remotely comfortable. Val still wasn't thawing; she said less than a dozen words to him since Saturday, and the ones she did say were short. The house didn't feel like his home anymore, he felt like he had to ask permission just to sit in the living room. And forget about food; that was out of the question. He ate every meal out, drove, and sat in his room.

He drove past Dana's house a couple of times, trying to work up the courage to knock on her door. Try and see if, maybe, somehow, there was something salvageable to be found in the wreckage of their relationship. But he chickened out every time. He parked down the street, watching her house, trying to man up and just walk up to her door. It was the easiest thing in the world; he'd done it dozens of times before. But he couldn't make himself do it. He couldn't even make his hand open the door to his truck. Once, when he was almost ready to do it, he saw the curtain in their living room window flutter, like maybe someone looked out of it or something. He started the engine and drove away.

Everything was awful—up was down, black was white. Nick always relied on his instinct to figure out what to do. It was easy: whatever felt right, he did. But *nothing* felt right anymore, so there was nowhere to aim. Every direction felt equally wrong. He was nervous and jumpy all the time, and the things that always brought him pleasure in the past seemed weird and intimidating. When he played ball, he went into slumps every once in a while like anyone else; times when his swing was fucked up or his timing was off or he just wasn't seeing the ball. He just had to believe things would get better again, that he'd be back in the rhythm of things eventually.

Sometimes though, guys just lost it. They hit the wall and that was it. Their whole lives they were the best at something. Then, just before they broke into the big time, just when it was all about to pay off, all those hours at the batting cage, all those nights and weekends working with a pitching coach, all that work and all that dedication and single minded obsession with excellence, would just, poof, disappear. And they were left with nothing. Close, but no cigar.

Nick and the other guys on the team sympathized when that happened. And it happened pretty often. They'd take the guy out for drinks after he was cut, if he wanted, give him a proper send off. Not all of them wanted to go out. Some guys got cut and just vanished; no one ever saw or heard from them again. That made sense too. After some poor bastard's dream got its throat slit, the last thing he wanted to do was hang out with a bunch of dudes who were still in the game.

It was just as well when the guy didn't want to go out anyway. As much as they all said they wanted to give him a sendoff, as much as they *acted* that way, the truth was, no one wants to be around a guy who just got cut. It wasn't any kind of personal thing against the guy, whoever he was; it was because they were afraid of getting whatever inflicted him that made him suck all of a sudden. Every time a guy washed out, every other guy on the team had the same thought, *what if I'm next*? As much as they might say otherwise, every professional athlete in the world has that thought. Because, eventually, it will be their turn. Eventually, every athlete knows that his body will fail him, and his time will be up. Whenever that time is, if it's ten years or ten minutes after the thought occurs to him, that's the mystery, that's what keeps a guy up at night.

A guy in a slump will do anything to try and change his luck. He'll spend more time in the cage, he'll spend less. He'll change his swing, his stance, his bat weight. He'll cut his hair, grow a beard, wear women's underwear, anything to get his mind off the fact that he suddenly can't manage to get good wood on that fucking ball.

On Tuesday, he thought he might spend some time packing up his room. Maybe the act of getting his shit together and throwing it all into boxes would be the break he needed to get some direction back. That's when he heard knocking at the front door.

She wore jean shorts, a black t-shirt with a pair of blue plastic sunglasses hanging at her collar, the frames shaped like stars, and her sneakers were red and white checkered. They looked like tablecloths. Her head was still shaved of course; but sometime in the last three days someone went over it again and smoothed out the rough spots. The patchy, mental patient look was replaced by a sort of 'alt-rock grrrl' thing. She looked kind of like the lead singer of *The Cranberries*. Or the girl in that movie about the record store. It was another one of those movies he hated but that Val used to watch all the time. It wasn't important really, but his impulse to call and ask her the name of that movie, and the fact that he couldn't do it anymore, made him sad.

In the absence of any hair, her green eyes took over her face. They loomed, bore into him. It made him very, very uncomfortable.

He stood there, completely at a loss for words.

"Hey Nick," she said after almost thirty seconds of the two of them just standing there, her in the doorway, him in the house.

"Hey Sam," he said, trying to sound casual. "What's up?"

"Nothing," she said, "what's up with you?"

"Nothing, I guess," he said. "Did you want to, come inside or anything?"

"No thanks," she said. "I'm pretty good out here."

"Okay."

They stood there for another minute, neither of them speaking. Nick had no idea what he was supposed to do. His weird nervous feeling was as bad as ever.

"You can come out here if you want," she finally said. "I was going to have a smoke."

"Is that what you want? For me to come out there?"

Suddenly she was angry. "I just asked you to, didn't I?"

"I just didn't want to-"

"Forget it," she said, and turned around. "Just forget it."

"Wait! Don't... just gimme a second, okay? You kind of took me by surprise."

He opened the porch door, stepped outside. He pulled his pack of cigarettes out of his pocket, and shook a smoke out. He offered the pack to Sam. She shook her head and pulled her own pack out of her bag.

There was another long silence while they stood there smoking. Nick had never been so uncomfortable in his life. He was dying to ask her why she came back, but he had to wait for her lead.

Sam waved towards his truck. "When'd you fix it up?"

"Sunday."

"I sort of did a number on it, huh?"

"Sort of."

"You can't say you didn't deserve it."

"No, I can't."

"You *deserved* worse."

"Probably."

"No, not *probably, definitely*."

The edge in her voice kept startling him. "Okay then, definitely."

She took a long drag. "Did you fix the windshield yourself?"

"Took it to the shop."

"Is that expensive?"

He shrugged. "It wasn't anything I couldn't handle."

"That's a relief," she spat.

He winced, what could he say that wouldn't make her angry? Why wouldn't she just cut the bullshit and tell him why she was there? Did she want or need to talk about what happened? How could she not? Maybe it was his job to start, but he had no idea how. "Listen, I don't know, I mean, I'm not sure, but, the other-"

She put her hand up to stop him. "Don't, okay? Just, don't. That's not why I'm here. If we go the rest of our lives without talking about that, it'll be too soon."

Then what the fuck? "Okay."

"So how much is it?"

"How much is what?"

She gestured at the truck again. "The windshield. How much?"

"With labor, a little north of three hundred."

"And you couldn't just do it yourself?"

"I'd need to know about, like, glass and stuff, angles. It's complicated." This was ridiculous. "Look, I know you didn't come here to talk about how much truck repairs cost. And if you're not here to talk about the other day…"

She took a final drag on her smoke, dropped it on the asphalt, ground it out with her foot. "I need to ask you something."

"Okay."

"It's important."

"Whatever you need."

"I need a ride."

"I can do that, where to?"

"Chicago."

“What?”

“You heard me.”

“You want me to… drive you to Chicago?”

“Did I stutter or something?”

“But what about…” He couldn’t bring himself to say her name in Sam’s presence.

“Gone,” Sam said. “Left Saturday with the movers; we worked it out.”

“Wait, so you’re just here? Like, by yourself?”

“I told her,” Sam said, “to go. I told her to go, and I’d find my own way out when I was ready. I told her if she didn’t leave with the movers like she was going to, I’d tell everyone what she did. I’d tell Dad, I’d tell Oscar and her parents and sisters and all of dad’s family and everyone I could think of. I told her I’d write a big email that night, and cc everyone I knew.”

Nick was impressed, and more than a little freaked. “Wow.”

Sam made a sad puppy face. “Oh dear, was that not very nice? Was I too hard on poor old Mom? Fuck her.” She threw him a contemptuous smile. “Oh wait.”

He rubbed his temples. “Jesus, Sam.”

“*Jesus Sam*,” she said, like a kid mimicking someone.

This didn’t make any sense; she was practically boiling with rage. Why would she want to drive half way across the country with someone she seemed to barely be able to stand the sight of? All she had to do was call Mom or Dad and they could buy her a plane ticket and she could be in Chicago by the end of the day. Instead she was going to spend two days driving with someone who made her furious every time he opened his mouth? There was some weird sadistic thing going on here that he couldn’t quite get a handle on.

“Sam, do you know how long it takes to drive to Chicago from here?”

“Obviously, I do. Look, can you do it or what?”

"I mean, yeah, if you want, I guess. You know, I just, I don't understand, why you want me to do this."

"Why?" Her eyes flashed. "*Why*? Because *FUCK YOU* that's why! Because you destroyed my family and ruined my life and are the worst, most disgusting, horrible *fucking* person I've ever met in my *fucking* life and the least you can do is give me a *fucking ride* when I *fucking* ask you for one!"

It was crazy and pointless. Worse than pointless, it was guaranteed to be a miserable, punishing experience. One that, if he had even half a brain, he would just walk away from. Every time he got close to this family, bad things happened.

"What the fuck," he said, "it's not like I had anything else going on."

***

"Do you ever think about dying?"

"What?" Nick quickly glanced over at her then snapped his eyes back on the road.

Sam unhooked her blue star sunglasses from the collar of her shirt, put them on; she flipped down the passenger visor, checked herself out in the mirror. Behind her, Gertie lay sleeping in the back seat. "Dying, do you ever think about it?"

"No," said Nick, then, "Why? Do you?"

"Sometimes," she said. "I used to think about it a lot, like when I was a little younger. I guess I went through a phase. I would picture my funeral, who would come, what people would say, what boys would be sad because they missed their chance with me. That kind of stuff."

"Okay..."

"What? That's normal, lots of people think about death. I saw a movie once on TV, it was called *My Life* something, *My Life Without Me*. It was about this girl who found out she was dying and how she didn't tell anyone and instead went out and lived her life to the fullest, did all the things she never got to do before."

"So, like *Bucket List*?"

"Kind of but not as cheesy; she doesn't go skydiving or anything like that. And not like, old guys. This was sadder because it was a girl, or like a young woman, you know what I mean, someone who never got a chance in life. Someone who should have gotten to live a whole full life and wasn't going to and how she handled it. It was really good."

"It just sounds like *Bucket List* to me."

"Well it was different, okay? It was better."

"Fair enough," said Nick.

"She like, tries to get everybody ready for what life will be like when she's not around. That's why it's called *My Life Without Me*, because all these people who rely on her or whatever are going to have to manage when she's gone and she's setting them up to be okay without her, without them even knowing she won't be there anymore."

"But she doesn't tell them she's dying?"

"Nope."

"I don't know," Nick said after a moment. "I think I'd be pretty pissed if someone I cared about was dying and they didn't tell me."

"Yeah," Sam said, "like you care about anyone."

Nick's jaw tightened; he gripped the steering wheel and he stared straight ahead.

Sam pushed her glasses up on her nose, smiled.

After a while, she rolled her window down and let the June air rush across her face.

The wind on her head was weird.

Her whole life she had hair to keep her head warm; it kept the low temperatures and cool breezes off her scalp. Now, with only a thin layer of stubble on her scalp, she found she was ultra-sensitive to even the slightest stimulus. It was the same with her neck. She got these nagging itchy sensations or chills that started at the base of her skull and quickly spread down her neck and across her shoulders. Her head felt lighter, felt faster, without the extra weight of hair sitting on top of it. But it also felt a little more vulnerable, a little more exposed. She kept touching her head, feeling the sharp little points of her hair scrape against the palm of her hand.

She kept thinking people were staring at her, and she felt naked all the time.

It was definitely different.

Sam crossed her arms on the open passenger side window, rested her chin on her arms, watched the scenery rush by and felt the wind on her head.

The fact was, she didn't know why she wanted Nick to drive her to Chicago. She didn't understand it any better than he did.

When she ran out of her house the other night, it was with the conviction that she never wanted to see him again, never wanted to see either of them again. She wanted so badly to just get away from how she felt that she'd have gladly forgone any vengeance or recompense for just a moment of peace, just one moment when the inside of her head wasn't screaming.

She spent that night in the clearing in the woods. She didn't want to see *anybody*. Her head was still too messed up; she couldn't get a straight thought in it. Her phone buzzed in her pocket, her mother calling. She hit talk, screamed, "Leave me alone!" into the mouthpiece, then smashed the phone against the trunk of a nearby tree and threw it as far as she could. There was so much energy inside her that she thought she would explode. There was a branch on the ground next to the tree—a big thick ridged one with little twigs growing off of it. She picked the branch up and bashed in against the trunk until it came apart in her hands. When the branch splintered, she battered the trunk with her fists. She punched it like a boxer working a heavy bag until her knuckles were raw and bloody. When she couldn't stand that anymore, she started swinging wildly, hitting it with the sides of her fists and palms. Then she kicked the tree over and over until her foot was sore and pounding.

When her whole body ached and she could barely stand, she gripped the tree, reared back and closed her eyes. Maybe if she head butted it, maybe if she smashed her face right into the bark, she'd knock out the thoughts in her head. She closed her eyes and grit her teeth and she gathered what was left of her focus to prepare for the shock of impact.

But she couldn't do it.

After everything she saw, after everything that happened, she still didn't have the willpower to force herself to slam her head into a giant oak tree.

The wind blowing into the truck smelled like rain. At least it hadn't rained that night or turned really cold or something. Sam hadn't spent a night outside since she was a little girl and went camping with her brownie troop. Man, she hated it.

"What's your favorite season?"

"I don't know," said Nick. "Summer, I guess."

"Mine's fall, then spring, then summer and winter are tied. I love the seasons where things change, where it's windy and raining and you get to dig out all the clothes you haven't worn in months."

Sam took a cigarette out of her bag and lit it.

"Do you like summer best because of baseball?"

"I don't think so. I never thought about if I had a favorite season until you asked me a second ago; summer was just what popped into my head."

"But it wasn't because it was when you got to play baseball?"

Nick shook his head. "No. I mean, when I was a kid, baseball was a spring sport. Like, for high school sports. And I practiced year round."

"What, like, playing for other teams or something?"

"No. Like batting cages and practicing with coaches and stuff."

"Oh." She was quiet for a second, rolled what he said over in her head. "Like what kind of coaches?"

"All kinds: hitting coaches, throwing coaches, fielding coaches, running coaches."

"Like school coaches?"

"Personal. Private."

"Doesn't that cost a lot of money?"

Nick nodded.

"So, did you have money?"

"Not really."

"How did you pay them?"

"Different ways. My grandparents had a little money, and they took out another mortgage. I worked. Some of them worked on sliding scales, cut us breaks."

"Oh." She didn't know what to say to that. All that time and money, a mortgage.

"You need coaches to know how to run?"

"Sure. Look, you've seen guys run the bases, hit doubles and triples and steal and stuff like that?"

"Uh-huh."

"Well, you learn how to do all that. Like if you're stealing a bag, you pretty much have to go from a complete stop to a run and then stop again on a dime in a couple of seconds. It's not something you can just *do*. You have to learn how. Or if you're trying to score from first, you have to run as hard as you can, but you have to touch second and third too, and you need to learn how to hit the bag at just the right angle without having to slow down and think about it either. You just have to know."

"I guess I never really thought about that."

"Most people don't. A lot of athletes don't. If you watch a game and know what to look for, you see bad base running all the time. Guys who aren't disciplined and don't know how to play the game the right way. They just want to get big hits, make big plays and get on a highlight reel. That's not how games are won. It's the details that decide who wins and who loses."

"So, like, how do people run bases wrong?"

"Okay, well, for one thing, when a guy gets caught stealing, when they show the replay, look at his feet. Watch how many steps he takes when he runs, how long his strides are. If you're running, it's better to take fewer, longer strides. A lot of times, if a guy's running bad, he's taking a lot of short, quick, steps, instead of long strides. That's something you want to avoid. Another thing is when to slide and when not to. Slides are dramatic and cool-looking, but they actually slow you down. If you're trying to get to the bag and you're trying to beat a close throw, it's sometimes better to just stay on your feet and beat it out. But guys almost always slide."

"So, why slide at all if it just slows you down?"

"It makes you a smaller target for the tag."

"Sure."

"And think about sliding," said Nick, "think about how dangerous that is. You're throwing your body on the ground towards a bag and another guy's feet. And, oh yeah, the feet are moving and are spiked. And you're trying to get your hand in there. That's all base running too. Do you know how easy it would be to get hurt sliding into a bag head-first? Of course, you can hurt yourself if you don't slide too. If you're coming into a bag and you slow down too fast, you can pull a muscle or strain something like that." Nick snapped his fingers. "It's precision stuff and the body is super sensitive. I had a doctor tell me once that you can break a rib in your sleep. He had a patient who woke up with pain in his side and they took x-rays and he just slept on his side a little wrong and he cracked a rib. It wasn't a serious thing, but still."

Nick trailed off, lost in his own thoughts. Sam tossed her cigarette butt out the window, went back to watching the scenery.

She'd woken up in the woods clearing with a crick in her neck, bugs on her arm and a wicked urge to pee. She'd shaken the bugs off and sat up; she tried to massage her neck but found that her hands were swollen such that she could barely move them, let alone massage any soreness. It was hot; the sun was low in the sky, but it felt like it was beating down on her face anyway. She'd had no idea what time it was, her only clock was on her phone, and that was gone.

Her stomach growled. Sam reached into her pocket and pulled out a five dollar bill, all that was left of the money her dad gave her for the cab ride the night before. That wasn't going to cut it. She stood up, brushed herself off and slowly walked out of the woods.

It was probably a two mile walk to Becky's house; under normal circumstances Sam could walk it in twenty minutes. But her foot was still tender from kicking that stupid tree, and she ended up hobbling most of the way. It took almost an hour.

By the time she made it, her foot throbbed so bad she was visibly limping and wincing with every step. She didn't even know if Becky was home; she couldn't call ahead and check, and the two of them hadn't discussed her plans, seeing as how Sam wasn't even supposed to be in the state anymore.

As it turned out, she wasn't home. But her mom was. And when she saw Sam's state, her bloody hands, her dirty clothes and messy hair, she rushed her right in. Sam took a handful of ibuprofen for the pain in her hands and foot and went to the bathroom to clean up while Becky's mom called Becky, who was out getting groceries with her dad for breakfast. Sam took a long, hot shower. She washed her hair three times, rubbed her skin raw with the loofa, let the steam build up in the room and open her pores; she did everything she possibly could to try and wash the horrible feeling out of her body.

But it wouldn't go away.

She wiped the steam off the bathroom mirror and took a good long look at herself.

How could she not have seen what was going on with Nick and her mom? Did she really think he came over all those times to help her? Did she really think that he actually liked her? That he cared about her? Had she really thought, way back in the recesses of her mind, that she might some way, somehow have some kind of shot with him herself?

She was so stupid.

In the trash can by the sink sat the box of hair dye they used less than a week ago. They were so happy doing it, it was so much fun. Becky told her how good she looked with red hair, how it popped, made her look sexy.

Fucking idiotic.

Sam pulled open the drawer next to the sink, grabbed the scissors from inside and went to work on her hair. She chopped it down as far as she could. Then, when the scissors were no good anymore, she plugged in the clippers in the drawer below and finished the job.

The girl Sam saw in the mirror looked kind of like the one who walked in half an hour earlier; she had the same face, same eyes, nose, mouth, but at least that stupid fucking red hair was gone.

She didn't feel any better; if anything, she felt worse. It was almost like her trying to feel better, even for a second, somehow offended the pain she felt. It was like the pain saw that she was feeling almost okay and said *no, no, this is so much deeper than a simple shower and haircut, you don't get away that easily. Do you think I'm fucking around or something here?* And the pain came back, stronger than ever. It coursed through her veins and cracked her bones and pushed out at her skin until she could almost see it.

Whatever was going on, whatever it was she felt, she was going to have to deal with it. Was going to have to understand it and maybe live with it, because it wasn't going away.

It was like some horrible soap opera or something.

That was exactly what it was. Her life was being overrun by silly, stupid, soap opera bullshit. Bullshit that, if someone told her was happening to them, she'd barely be able to stop herself from running out of the room and calling Becky.

It would have been the weirdest, funniest thing that she'd ever heard.

It would have been a joke.

Her life was a joke.

Sam laughed. She opened her mouth and laughed out loud at the ridiculousness of everything. The Sam in the mirror laughed too, and Sam watched her laugh. She tried to connect the girl in the reflection to herself, but it wasn't happening. She couldn't make the leap. The person Sam was had been replaced by a new angry, crazy, wild-eyed girl who was laughing and crying and shaking apart.

She had to do something, she needed time to figure out what was going on in her head or she was going to explode.

Carefully, Sam opened the bathroom door and tip-toed down the carpeted hallway to Becky's room where she grabbed the phone that sat on her dresser. She took the phone back to the bathroom and called her mother.

Her mother picked up right away, barely before the first ring. Her voice over the phone sounded defeated and far away and scared.

Good.

Sam told her to leave. She told her to drive away with the movers to Chicago and to never come back to Baxter ever again. Sam would return to the house in two hours to get her bag with her stuff and she better find the bag on the porch and her mother gone. She'd stay with Becky and she'd find her own way to Chicago when she was goddamn good and ready. She said if her mother tried to talk to her, or to Becky or anyone she knew, she'd tell everyone what she saw the night before. She said she'd write the email to everyone she could think of, and describe in detail everything that happened.

She said if her mother ever, *ever*, spoke to *him* again, she would leave, and her mother would never hear from or see her again. Did she understand?

Her mother said yes. Her voice was barely a whisper.

Sam said she couldn't hear her, she told her mother to *speak the fuck up*.

Her mother cleared her throat, said she understood in as clear a voice as she could manage.

Sam said she'd see her when she fucking saw her. Her mother started to say something, but Sam hung up the phone.

*That* made her feel better.

"Sam?" Becky's voice came through the other side of the door. "What are you doing here?"

Sam leaned up against the door. "Hi Becks," she said. "Change of plans."

"Mom said you were all dirty and your hands were bloody?"

"Yeah, I guess I had kind of a hard night. I might have tried to beat up a tree."

"You tried to what? Sam, what are you talking about, *what's going on*?"

"Oh, Becks," Sam could feel her throat closing up, the tears welling up in her eyes, "everything's so fucked up."

"Well, just open the door and talk to me, okay? Whatever's going on we can figure it out, but open the door. Because you're kind of starting to scare me."

"All right," Sam said, "just gimme a minute." She washed her face one more time in the sink, wet a towel and brushed off as much of the lose hair as she could. She put on the clean clothes that she'd taken earlier from Becky's room.

"Becks?" she called. "I'm coming out now."

"Okay," said Becky.

Sam opened the door.

“You haven’t said if you like my hair.” Sam peered at Nick over the top of her sunglasses. They were at a gas station. Sam sipped from her blueberry Slushee and Nick filled the truck.

“Uh, well, I wasn’t sure I was supposed to say anything,”

“Supposed to? What do you mean supposed to?”

“I just didn’t want to…”

“What, you didn’t want to tell me? You thought I hadn’t noticed my head was shaved?”

“I don’t know anything, okay? That’s why I didn’t want to say anything.”

She waited a beat, took another sip of her Slushee. “So, you don’t like it then?”

“That’s not what I said.”

“What else am I supposed to think? You said you didn’t want to piss me off? And why would it piss me off at all?” She smiled. “You think I care that much about what you think of my hair?”

“No, I know you don’t… you wouldn’t… I didn’t want to piss you off, that’s all,” he said, “if this was, like, a thing or something.”

“A thing?”

“Yeah, like an acting out thing.”

She laughed. “Oh, okay, like a childish acting out thing.”

Nick sighed.

“Is this what girls do when they walk in on their mom with some guy? Is this how it goes? Did you catch a Dr. Phil one afternoon or something?”

Nick closed his eyes, banged his head against the column of the pump station.

Sam laughed again, harder. “Would you relax? I’m just fucking with you.” She punched his arm but pulled her hand back with a wince. “It’s a long way to Chicago, you’ll never make it if you don’t relax a little.”

Nick rubbed his neck and shoulder. “Okay,” he said, “whatever.”

All right, maybe she shouldn’t have gone after his truck with the bat like that.

And yeah it was stupid and dangerous, and no it didn’t solve anything. But, in her defense, it felt fucking amazing when she was doing it.

It was just, after she explained everything to Becky, after she just laid it out, it seemed so unfair that Nick should get to walk away without any consequences.

She wanted to scream at him, to punch him and rip at him and burst his eardrums and break his knees and his hands so that he could never walk or hear or do anything ever again without being reminded of what he did to her. How he betrayed her heart and her trust and how she’d never see the world the same way again and she’d have to carry the memory of what he did forever. She wanted to scar him so deeply that he was never happy again, the way she was never going to be happy again.

But she couldn’t do that.

A little later, when she went back to her house to get her bag, her dad’s baseball bat was just sitting in the garage, forgotten in the flurry of last minute packing.

She picked up the bat, and she thought about her dad coming home happy after an afternoon with his buddies at the batting cages, and how her dad recognized Nick because of his baseball career. She thought again about how Nick was sitting in his house living his life and would never understand just how much he hurt her.

She couldn’t stop thinking about that actually.

And then she just saw red.

The next thing she knew Nick's friend's arms were wrapped around her, the bat was on the ground and Nick's truck was all fucked up.

She figured that was it. She was never going to get any kind of long term cathartic resolution with the piece of shit, so she had to settle for getting what satisfaction she could from a single act of violence.

It was something at least.

"I remember these." Sam picked a pair of cheap blue star-shaped sunglasses from Becky's dresser. "Didn't I get them for you at the beach a million years ago? I can't believe you still have them." She put the glasses on, checked herself out in the mirror. It was Sunday night. She spent most of her time sitting on Becky's couch watching TV and goofing off. She excused herself periodically to cry in the bathroom, but that was happening a little less frequently.

"Yeah," Becky said. "I was in my acting phase. You said they reminded you of me because I was going to be a star someday."

"I can't believe you kept them."

"I found them in the back of my closet in this old box filled with notes and movie stubs and bracelets and all this other stuff I didn't know what to do with but couldn't throw out."

"I have a box like that too," said Sam. "It's sitting in a bigger box in a room in Chicago."

"Yeah..." Becky said, "about that—look Sam, you know you can stay here as long as you need to. I mean, my folks are totally cool with it, and I'd love it if you stayed the whole summer. But, you're going to have to talk to your family eventually, right? And you're gonna have to go to Chicago and all that."

Sam took off the sunglasses and sunk into a chair, her head down. "I know," she said. "I know. I've tried calling my dad, like, ten times. But every time I pick up the phone I think about what I'm going to say, how I'm going to get through the conversation, and I start to lose it and chicken out."

"I'm not saying I know what you should do. Just that, you're going to have to do something, that's all."

Sam looked at the glasses in her hand, "I just wish I could go back, you know? Just make it so I went on the plane with Dad and Oscar or make myself forget what happened or something. I just want to figure out how to get past it."

"Then maybe you have to go through it. Maybe you just need to go to Chicago and get everything over with."

"Maybe," Sam said. "Maybe."

"Or not," Becky said and laughed. "What do I know?"

Sam sighed, "No, you're right. I just hate it, is all." She got to her feet, held up the sunglasses. "Where do these go?"

"Anywhere," Becky said. "I don't care, I just had them out to show to you. Hey, why don't you keep them?"

"I can't do that Becks, I got them for you. They were a present."

"Yeah, but I'll just put them back in a box and forget about them. Keep them; I didn't get you a goodbye present. Think of them as a memento of me."

"But, that's why I got them for *you*. Can you use something that's already a memento as a memento of something else? Is that allowed?"

"Allowed by who? Just take them."

"I don't know," Sam said. "What if it messes with karma?"

"The karma of the glasses?"

"The karma of the glasses or my karma for taking something that was given to you as a gift. What if they bring me bad luck or something? I don't think I could take any more bad luck."

Becky laughed. "Take the glasses Sam, please. And promise me no matter what happens, you'll never change." Becky took the glasses, opened them up and slid them onto Sam's face. "You'll always be a star to me, kid."

Sam felt herself choke up again. One of these days, she was going to be able to get through ten minutes without crying. "Thanks Becks," she said, "you're the best."

"Not really," Becky said. "I just know a good thing when I see it."

Two days later she was out walking, not really paying attention to where she was going and before she knew it she found herself on his street. She could see Val putting Robbie in the back of a car, getting in herself and driving away. She saw Nick's truck, its dented body and repaired windshield and, without knowing why she was going or what she would say when she got there, she walked up to his front door and knocked.

She didn't have a plan, or scheme, nothing beyond smoking a cigarette with him on the lawn. When she told him she needed to ask him something she had no idea what it was going to be, but when he said whatever you need, it just popped into her head. It popped into her head and she knew she was going to ask, and she knew he was going to do it.

They weren't done yet.

They drove through all sorts of towns, starting with her upscale quiet community with its giant houses and nice cars, which gave way to more modest but also somehow livelier suburbs. She saw a lot of flags hanging from porches: American, revolutionary, the *don't tread on me* one with the snake, and various sports teams; inflated balloons sat in some lawns for no reason Sam could see. The summer brought a lot of people out into their yards; they sat on lawn furniture, watered flowers; kids ran around everywhere. It was all very nice, very much like a beer commercial or one of those paintings her grandparents had in their dining room. Baxter was great, and she loved it dearly, but sometimes it felt like the whole town was a library or something. Some of the places they drove through just looked so *alive* to her.

Then again, some of the places seemed just the opposite. The deeper into the state they got, the more beautiful the land became, and the bleaker the towns. There were a lot of empty store fronts, and consignment stores and old beat-up cars with angry—and frankly a little scary—bumper stickers on the roads. Years ago, before she died, Sam's great-grandmom warned Sam about *ghettos*, and how if she ever found herself in a car going through a *ghetto* she should make sure her windows were all rolled up and her door was locked, because someone might run up to the door, open it, and pull her right out. And there'd be nothing she could do about it. It scared her, and her mother explained that great-grandmom was sweet and we loved her, but she also came from a different time and had ideas about types of people that were misinformed and wrong. It wasn't really her fault, and she didn't mean any harm, but there it was.

It wasn't her finest moment, but driving through some of those towns, Sam fought the urge to lock her door.

It wasn't that Sam had never seen a run-down area before, or a simple suburb, but there was something about watching the progression that made it all so linear. Sam never drove cross country before; the family took a plane if the trip was going to be more than a couple hundred miles. There was no continuity between one place and another. Sitting in a car she could watch the land ebb and flow—hilly to flat, clean to dirty.

Sam drove with her parents a few times to New York to see shows. They went to see the Empire State building when she was younger after her dad showed her *King Kong*. But those trips were all on the highway. Jump on 95, drive until you get there, jump off. Nick was using highways too; but it wasn't like 95; they were driving through a lot of places, driving close enough for Sam to look at what was around her. They were getting off the main roads to get gas or food, hitting lights, listening to the radio. Sam felt like she was really getting a sense of a place she'd never known existed. The place in between places.

Ohio, though, was awful.

The minute they crossed the border it felt like the sky turned grey and the land flattened out and all she saw were billboards for fireworks, guns, and Jesus.

The last time she took a car trip was the previous Christmas when her mother thought it would be fun if the family went to see the lighting of the Christmas tree at Rockefeller Center. Sam's mother assumed the tree would be lit on a Saturday night, that would make it easiest for people who might want to come from out of town with their families to see it. But it wasn't; apparently the tree was always lit on either the Tuesday or Wednesday after Thanksgiving; apparently it was a tradition. And while getting there and back in a night was doable, it wouldn't be much fun, and if they waited until Sam's school day was done, it would almost certainly mean hitting traffic on the way too. But once her mother got an idea in her head, she could move mountains to make it happen. She decided that not only would Sam miss school that day so they could have a nice day in the city, she also said it would be fun to get a hotel room nearby and make a whole thing out of it.

Sam's mother didn't usually let school slide on some kind of whim. Like when it came to sick days, the rule in her house was, unless there was vomit, *actual* vomit, you were going to school. So the sudden change in attitude was a surprise, certainly welcome, but a surprise all the same. She justified the trip by saying that in a few years Sam would be too old to care about something like watching a giant Christmas tree light up, and she wanted to show it to her before that happened.

Her mother had never understood her.

Sam didn't think she'd ever get too old to care about something like that. Christmas was her favorite holiday, always had been, always would be. She loved going around and seeing all the decorations people put on their lawns and the lights on the lamp posts in town; she loved the specials on TV and the music in the stores and the Santa at the mall and the fake snow in shop windows and all of it. She loved spectacle and artifice, loved the idea that people regularly went out of their way to try and construct a totally false reality to enjoy. It was like, for a month of the year, people did their best to *make* the world a little cozier, a little warmer and a little more magical. It didn't matter that it was fake, if anything, it was better *because* it was fake. That just made things shinier and prettier and brighter. It wasn't like it was possible to have peace on earth and good will towards men for real anyway.

The idea that Sam would ever not want to go see a giant Christmas tree was preposterous. The idea that she would ever not be interested in almost any garish tacky spectacle was ridiculous. She still loved visiting *Disney World* with Oscar when they went down to Florida, for heaven's sake. She probably enjoyed it more than he did. But two days off from school to see a giant Christmas tree was two days off from school to see a giant Christmas tree. So Sam kept her mouth shut and let her mother go right on thinking the clock was ticking on those sorts of things.

So they went and it was glorious.

That night Sam stood in a huge crowd with all the other out-of-towners, sipped hot chocolate and ignored the glares from actual New Yorkers trying to get on with their day. The tree was dark, but Rockefeller Center was bathed in blue light, and spotlights projected snowflake patterns across its walls. But suddenly, a single light flickered on and off on the tree, then another, and another. The blue lights went down and the crowd started to cheer as the lights continued to sparkle all across the still dark tree, faster and faster, brighter and brighter, like a thousand cameras flashing until it exploded to life in a dazzling display of light and color and sound as the crowd gasped and cheered and applauded, and Sam was right there with them.

Sitting in the backseat of her Dad's car on the way home the next day, Sam watched the city become smaller and smaller in her window. Oscar sat next to her, strapped into his car seat, fast asleep, and her parents in the front were deep in a conversation that she couldn't hear because her headphones were on. Maybe it was because she was still a little buzzed from the excitement of the night before or maybe it was because it always gave her a thrill to be out of school on a weekday, but sitting there, surrounded by her family and coming home from that wonderful, surprising trip, in that moment things seemed perfect to her. They seemed perfect and Sam thought: *I'm going to remember this moment and feel good about this moment for the rest of my life.*

Driving through Ohio was pretty much the opposite of that.

Behind her, in the little seat in the back, Gertie panted happily. Occasionally, she stuck her muzzle over Sam's head and out the cracked window, so that she could sniff whatever it was that caught her attention.

Sam gently patted her seat; Gertie leaned forward and rested her head where Sam indicated and sighed as Sam scratched behind her ears. "How old is Gertie anyway?"

"About seven," Nick said. "At least, I got her seven years ago, and she was a puppy."

"We're not allowed to have dogs," Sam said. "Mom's allergic." Then in a high pitched baby voice she turned her attention back to Gertie. "Oh, who's good?" she asked her.

After a moment Nick said, "Have you thought about what's going to happen when you get to Chicago?"

Sam kept her attention on Gert, "Not really," she said in the same voice. "I just figured I'll see when I get there, won't I? Yes I will, *yes I will.*" Gertie's tail thumped heavily on the back of the cab.

"It just might be better if you had some kind of plan."

"What do you care?" Sam said to Gert. "Just drop me off and you'll never see me again."

"I just care, okay?"

"Oh stop pretending," Sam said, and rubbed her nose against Gert's, still using her puppy voice. "Stop pretending you give a shit what happens to me or my family."

He sighed, "Look," he said, "you're furious with me, I get it, that's fine. And your mom too, okay, fair. But there are other people, there's your brother, your father-"

Sam's head snapped up. "Don't you fucking talk about my dad," she said.

"I was only-"

"No, you don't get to talk about him. You never talk about him. You never even *think* about him. Do you understand?"

"I just wanted to-"

"*Do you understand?*"

"Yeah."

"Good. Then just drive. Drive and keep your fucking mouth shut."

Once, when she was bored in class, Sam tried to imagine what it would be like to think without words. What it would be like to organize her thoughts and recognize things without using words to classify and distinguish them, like an animal might. If Gertie saw a tree that smelled good, or a squirrel she wanted to bark at or another dog she wanted to meet, she didn't think the words *tree, squirrel,* or *dog,* did she? But somehow, she was able to recognize the thing and put it in a context where she knew how to behave toward it. Sniff tree and hopefully pee on it, bark at, chase, and if possible, bite squirrel, meet other dog, judge danger of said dog, treat accordingly. These were all complex ideas, involving recognition, judgment, and action, and Gerite figured it out all the time without using language. Sam knew she was *smarter* than Gertie, knew she was more sophisticated; she couldn't understand how Gertie pulled it off.

But of course, she hadn't always thought in words, had she? That was the bitch of it. There was a time when she was more like Gertie, when she didn't know any words, and then, little by little, she'd learned individual words and eventually sentences and finally a whole language. Or a good portion of it anyway. The point was, she was once like Gert, and now she wasn't, and further, she couldn't access any memories from that time to see what it was like.

Maybe, Sam decided, it was *because* she'd learned language that she couldn't remember what it was like to not know it. Maybe whatever it was that made her able to think in words made it so she *had* to. Like a survival mechanism. Maybe language was a type of organism that wanted to survive and so it made itself indispensable by, among other things, eliminating any memory its host might have had of surviving without it.

Because the fact was, when she thought about it, there were far more animals in the world that didn't have language than did have it. And they got along just fine using a system that she couldn't hold in her head for more than a second at a time.

And maybe all that was bullshit anyway; just because Gertie couldn't *say* squirrel or tree didn't mean she couldn't *think* the word. She knew a girl once named Sarah, and she had a dog named Daisy. Daisy was a snuffley, sad-faced hound dog and Sam loved burying her face in the folds of Daisy's skin. It was so warm and soft and comforting, she used to wish she could fall asleep and use Daisy as a pillow. Anyway. Sarah's mom was a vet, and Sam asked her once if Daisy knew that Daisy was her name the way Sam knew Sam was her name.

Sarah's mom said no, it wasn't the same. She said that Daisy knew that the sound *Daisy* applied to her, that it was her sound, but she wasn't smart enough to know that it was her *name*. It was just her *sound*. Sam lived with that explanation for years, but then one day she was thinking about it and the whole thing kind of fell apart.

What did that mean, Daisy was just her sound? How was that different from recognizing a name? It wasn't like *Samantha* had any actual meaning or power, it was just a sound too, one that her parents designated to signify and label their daughter years ago. It might have some special specific meaning to *them*, but that was only because they had some experience that related to the series of sounds that was her name. It was just a focal point for organizing thoughts or memories or whatever around an actual person who was real. But the name itself was meaningless; all that mattered was what it represented. How was that different than Daisy the hound dog recognizing her name as a sound that was familiar to her?

It was only because people were stupid and self-centered that they thought the words themselves had any special meaning.

Maybe because it made them feel special and good that they thought in words to begin with.

But words meant shit.

Gertie didn't need them, and she was, by far, the happiest creature in the truck. She didn't care where they were going or why; she just wanted to go for a ride. She ran up to the truck at about a thousand miles an hour back at the house when she saw that Nick was leaving. He'd tried to get her to go back inside, but she'd looked so happy and so excited; her tongue was out, her eyes were bright and she'd kept taking little half steps in the direction of the truck while looking up at Nick for the okay. Eventually Nick had just looked at Sam and shrugged, w*hy not*; Sam had opened the door and Gert leapt inside.

Now there were three of them.

What did Gertie care what Nick did, what he put Sam through? All she knew was that Nick loved her and took care of her, and she loved him for that. And Sam conceded that Nick did love his dog. For all his faults, and they were legion, there was something about the purity of his connection to his dog that Sam still liked.

Why weren't personal relationships like the relationships people had with animals? You can't lie to a dog, bullshit it, string it along; you either treat it right or you don't. It's simple and direct, cause and effect, right and wrong. She never asked for anything more and he didn't expect anything from her. No reading anything, no misunderstandings, no miscommunications, and no hurt feelings, just two creatures co-existing.

That would make things so much easier.

He was still an asshole though.

They had to stop at three motels before they found a vacancy. "What, is Ohio like the convention capital of the Midwest or something?" Nick asked. "I thought people went to Atlanta, or Miami, or places like that. Why is everyone all of a sudden in a rush to get to Toledo?"

It was one of those places that just had a row of rooms, each one with a big window next to the door and a view out onto the highway. Nick and Sam's rooms were next to each other, and there was a door inside that led from one room to the other. Sam pulled at it absently as she was making her way around the room and was surprised when it opened without any resistance. Weren't they supposed to lock somehow? She examined the lock on her knob; there was a little lock on it, and it seemed to be in working order, but when she closed the door to test it, the thing opened right up again.

They had pizza delivered for dinner. Sam didn't know you could get pizza delivered to a motel room, but you could and they did, and it wasn't too bad. The delivery place only carried Pepsi products, and that was kind of annoying, but Sam got root beer and the fries were good and *Law and Order* was on TNT, so things could have been worse.

But she was still in a shitty motel room in Ohio.

And she was still there with Nick.

The *Law and Order* marathon ended at ten; after that they aired an episode of *The Closer*, which her mother watched and Sam never liked. Sam tossed the remote to Nick and went back to her own room to get ready for bed.

It was a little bit of a pain in the ass these days. Her hands still throbbed whenever she held something, like a cigarette or a toothbrush, for too long. And showering was almost impossible. She had to unwrap the bandages from her hands, which was weird and painful because her hands still hurt a lot and some of the gauze from the wrapping always stuck to her scabs. Then she had wash off all the gauze that was stuck to the scabs, clean the scabs with peroxide, and rinse them out with water. All that she did in the sink before she could even step into the shower.

When she was *in* the shower, she had to be careful not to open the scabs again, either by rinsing them or brushing her hands too hard against the washcloth or even her own skin. Her whole showering life, she'd lathered the soap by holding it and running her hands over it again and again in the shower stream. It wasn't anything she even thought about, it was automatic. She'd done that when she showered at Becky's the other day after spending the night in the woods, and the pain that shot through her from the simple contact of her skin and soap on those fresh cuts was so sharp that she almost cried out. Now she had to *remember* to take it easy and watch her hands when they were unwrapped and exposed, which wasn't easy, because she used her hands constantly. Not to mention worrying about putting too much weight on her bad ankle or losing her footing on her good foot and falling.

It was all so protracted and ridiculous. When she was out of the shower, she had to carefully, *oh so carefully*, pat dry her hands and re-wrap them before she even got dressed so that her knuckles didn't accidentally brush some rough fabric and disturb the scabs. It was so fucking annoying. And the whole time she was cursing herself for being so stupid as to almost break her hands punching a fucking oak tree. Or maybe it wasn't an oak, but it was big, whatever it was. It accomplished nothing and now the simplest things were so much more difficult.

And all the while, her ankle was *throbbing*. She kept her weight on her left foot as best she could, but days of that caused her left ankle to ache with all the extra use. Every step was a little harder than the last.

And then, after all that, when she was going through her bag after her shower and she came across the lingerie she'd hidden in the pocket of a pair of jeans, the unfairness of everything just overwhelmed her and she said fuck it.

Fuck it.

No more fear.

No more hiding.

No more *thinking* and *considering*, and *wondering* and *dreaming*.

Thinking was nothing.

Words were nothing.

All that mattered was the moment now.

She pulled on the underwear, put on the thin top she always slept in, the tight one with the lace fringe that stopped half way down her belly. She limped out of the bathroom, across her carpet to the door that connected her room with Nick's room. She turned the doorknob before she could convince herself not to, opened the door, and stepped across the threshold.

Sam had never witnessed a genuine real life double take before—like a real, unscripted double take. But that was exactly what Nick did when he saw her. He glanced over at her when she walked into his room and went back to *SportsCenter*. Less than a second later, when it registered with him, his eyes snapped back to her, wide with surprise. He shot up from his chair.

"How did, how was, why wasn't that door locked?"

She shrugged innocently, "I dunno, it just wasn't."

"What is this?" There was a real edge in his voice.

She liked that.

Sam put on her innocent voice. "What's what?"

He took a step toward the door. "Don't fuck around here, why are you dressed like that?"

"This is just what I wear to bed."

"Ok, well, go back to your room and go to bed then."

"I will," she said, "when I'm ready." She advanced toward Nick's bed, the color drained from his face. This was fun.

"Go to your room."

Sam laughed. "What are you, my dad now?"

His eyes narrowed. "Go," he said.

She glared right back at him. "No."

"*Sam*," he said, and stopped; he took a breath, and wiped his hand across his chin. "Look, fun's over, okay? Yeah, you shocked me, congratulations. If you want to hang out in here, that's okay. But you need to change into something else, like *right now*."

"And I said no."

His voice wavered, like he was about to lose control. It made her stomach warm. "I know you're mad at me, okay? And I know you're going through a bad time and it's my fault. But if someone sees you dressed that way, I could get into really serious trouble. Like, jail trouble. Really. So I need you to go and get changed."

"Or what?"

"Or I'm leaving."

"No you're not."

"Yeah, I really will."

The warm spot in her stomach just kept growing. "No," she said, "you won't. Wanna know why?"

"No."

She smiled at him. "Because if you walk out of here, I'll just follow you out, and I'll make a big scene and everyone will come out of their rooms and they'll see me and you and they'll go on their own from there."

He looked at her. "You wouldn't."

"Sure, I would." She wouldn't. Probably she wouldn't.

He was taking tiny steps backward. "Sam, you have to stop this."

She limped toward him, slowly, her ankle aching, but she didn't care. "Stop what? *I'm not doing anything.*"

"Sam…"

"C'mon," she said, "what's the harm? It could be our little secret." She reached out and brushed his cheek with her fingers. "You're telling me you've never been the least bit curious?"

He grabbed her hand. "*Stop it.* I'm serious now. You can't do this."

Pain exploded through her knuckles where he grabbed her and down through her wrist and arm. The game stopped being fun. She ripped her hand out of his. "I can't? *I can't*? What do you mean I can't? Why can't I? You do whatever you want."

"I don't-"

"Fuck you, yes you do." Her eyes stung. "Yes you do. You do whatever you want, Mom does whatever she wants. People do whatever they want. Why can't I? What, am I not good enough for you or something?"

"It's not like that-"

"Then what is it like? Huh?" She felt a tear drop down the side of her face. "It seems to me, you'll fuck just about anyone! Doesn't matter if they're married and too old, or too young. How old was that girl holding Robbie at your house the other day, huh? That was the girl wasn't it? That girl you were dating that you were always talking to Mom about?! Fucking how old was she, Nick? Eighteen? Nineteen? She looked about my age to me!"

"You leave her out of this," Nick said, his voice darkening.

"Fuck you, leave her out of this. You were the one who brought her into it! You were the one who ran around on her! Cheating on her! You were the one who cried on my mom's shoulder how *she didn't understand you,* and how *she didn't appreciate you*!"

"You don't know what you're talking about, so fucking just drop it, okay?"

Now the tears streamed down her face. "Of course I don't know what I'm talking about," she yelled. "No one will let me play in their little reindeer games, will they? You bust down doors to make sure I don't know what I'm talking about!"

"You were *unconscious!*" Nick was yelling back now, his face red with anger. "That little fucker was about to rape you!"

Sam laughed. "Sure, he was. And I should believe you why? Because you're so trustworthy? Tell me, tell me why I should believe that Scott Temple, a boy I've known my whole life, and would have willingly done *anything* with, just *decides* to rape me. Why would he do that?"

"I don't know, Sam. I don't know why he would do that! I don't know why he did what he did; I don't know why I do what I do, or why your mom does what she does. I don't know why your dad fucked some little bitch at his office either! Because if he hadn't, maybe none of this would be fucking happening now would it?! *But people just do things Sam! That's the way it is, and the sooner you stop feeling sorry for yourself and accept it, the better off we'll all be!*"

Wait, what?

"What did you just say?"

All the color drained from Nick's face; he closed his eyes and said softly, "Fuck."

Did he just say that?

"Nick, what did you just say about my dad?"

"Nothing, I didn't say anything."

No. He did.

"Why would you say that?"

"I don't know, I was angry."

It was a lie. It had to be. But the look in Nick's eyes, the fear. It was true. It was the truth. She was sure of it. Her head spun until suddenly everything came into a new, sharper focus.

Sam fell to her knees. With her head in her hands, she tried not to scream.

Nick knelt down beside her, he put his arms around her, but she pushed away. He didn't back off, he put his arms around her again. She buried her head in his neck and sobbed.

"What is happening?" She groaned. "What is happening, what is happening, what is happening, what is happening?"

"It's okay," he said. "Everything's going to be okay."

Sam coughed out a bitter laugh. “How can you possibly say that?”

“Because…”

“Because why?”

“I don’t know,” he said, “because it has to be.”

They sat there on the floor, Nick with his arms around Sam, stroking her head. And Sam collapsed against him, hugging him tight, her head on his chest.

After a long while, after Sam started to relax, Nick spoke quietly. “When I was really young, like in second and third grade, my mom used to lock me out of the house.”

Sam sniffled. “Really? Why?”

“Really. Sometimes she would just get really tired or angry or whatever, and if there wasn’t anyone around to watch me, she’d tell me to go outside and lock the door and leave me out there until someone else came and let me in. And I’d be out there, and I’d get so scared and so lonely. Sometimes I would just sit between the screen door and the front door and just wait.”

“How long would you wait there?”

“Hours,” Nick said.

“Did you ever tell her you didn’t like it when she did it?”

“All the time,” he said.

“What did she say?”

“She said it wasn’t her job to entertain me, and little boys needed to spend time outside.”

“What a bitch,” said Sam.

“Totally,” said Nick.

“Was that supposed to put things in perspective or something?”

“I don’t know,” he said. “Maybe, or maybe not. I just, I don’t like to see you unhappy. And I was thinking about what it’d be like to go through all you've had to go through with your parents. But I really have no idea what it's like to feel the way you do because my parents, well, my parents weren't like that. I don't know, maybe it was stupid. I don't really talk about that stuff a lot. I try not to even *think* about it. But I just wanted to-"

"It's okay," Sam said. "It's okay. I know what you're trying to say."

"Really?"

Sam nodded.

"Could you explain it to me then? Because I really have no idea."

Sam laughed. "I don't think I could actually. But I appreciate it. And it helped."

"It did?"

She sniffled again. "A little. For a second anyway."

"I guess that's good."

Sam took her head off his chest and looked at him. "You're really an asshole, you know that?"

"Yeah," he said, smiling sadly. "I know."

"But you're sweet sometimes, too. I think that's actually more of the problem."

"I'll try and work on that," he said.

"Don't try too hard," she said. Then she put her head back on his chest and closed her eyes.

They sat like that a long time.

Things went much easier the next day.

They woke up late, got some bagels and orange juice from the Dunkin Donuts down the street and were on the road just after check out. Nick figured if traffic wasn't too bad they could be in Chicago in the late afternoon.

They talked while Nick drove. It was like the old days when he was teaching her to drive, but better too. Sam talked about books she planned to read and where she might apply to school, and Nick talked more about his days playing ball, told funny stories like the time he played pool in a buddy's basement and the buddy's older brother had been standing on a table that collapsed underneath him on the floor above them, and how he fell through the dining room floor but stopped his fall with his arms so that his legs were dangling above the pool table and how Nick and his buddy tried to push the guy back up by poking him in the ass with their pool cues.

Sam laughed so hard at that story that Dr. Pepper came out of her nose.

She still felt sad of course, still flashed on Nick with her mother, or what she learned about her dad. She knew there was a long, difficult summer ahead of her, and the rest of the year after that. But there were moments when she forgot it too. Very brief, sure, but every once in a while as they drove, she'd be talking to Nick, or listening to one of his stories and it occurred to her, *I wasn't feeling bad there for a second.* And thinking that brought the bad feeling back, but at least she knew it was gone for a moment. And maybe if it could be gone for a moment, it could be gone for longer.

It was a start.

"I know I shouldn't be talking to you about this," Nick said. "And I know it really isn't any of my business, but you should try and go easy on your folks."

"I know," said Sam.

"No, really, I mean it. They might be fuck-ups, okay? And they might be selfish and stupid and all that other stuff you think they are, but they also love you. And they're doing their best."

"I said I know," teased Sam.

"Yeah, you said it. But you don't know. You don't. Because you haven't been there yet. People do stupid shit all the time for no good reason. And they hurt each other and they're ignorant and cruel and all that stuff. But they're just people. That's just part of what people do. And I don't think you can really understand that until *you* get out there and start making stupid decisions for no good reason. Then it starts to get a little clearer. People aren't *bad,* not really, or at least most people aren't; they're just stupid. *We're* just stupid."

"So, is that the moral of this whole thing then? People are stupid, but that's just how they are?"

"No," he said, laughing. "What have I been saying this whole time? There *is* no moral, no lesson, there's just what is. So you just, have to go with it."

"I'm sorry, but that sounds like a moral."

"Okay, I've never told anybody this before, but I seem to be telling you things that I don't tell people, so what the hell." He paused, then said, "When I got in that fight with that guy and dislocated my shoulder and I knew, like really knew, I was out of baseball, that I'd never get to the bigs, there was a part of me that was relieved."

"You were relieved? Like happy?"

"I was relieved. Relieved because it was over, that I didn't have to think about it anymore. But also, because I never had to really find my limit. I never had to give my all and just come up short."

"Okay," Sam said, "that makes sense."

"Does it? It makes sense that I would spend tens of thousands of dollars that I didn't have and countless hours practicing, training, working, just to throw it all away at the last second just because I was tired? That makes sense?"

"It does to me."

Nick shook his head, but he was smiling. "I'm going to miss you," he said.

***

Things started to look familiar pretty soon after that.

She saw the skyline first. Then she recognized some of the smaller buildings from her trip a month ago, started to see signs on the highway counting down the miles to Hyde Park and the University of Chicago. Nick took the second Hyde Park exit, and started winding through the streets of Chicago's south side.

"Do they even know you're coming?"

Sam shook her head.

"What are you going to do if they aren't home?"

"I have a key."

"Did you want me to… wait with you or anything?"

"I don't think that would be a very good idea, do you?"

"Well, no, obviously. But I would have done it if you wanted me to."

"Thanks."

"What do you think they're gonna say about your hair?"

"I dunno, probably not much. Hair grows back."

"I guess. Hey, you want to stop off somewhere first, get a tattoo?"

She punched him in the arm, then shook her hand; it *hurt*. "Stop being a troublemaker," she said. "You've almost pulled this off. Don't mess it up now."

They drove past the Barnes and Noble that she'd gone to with her dad. They were pretty close now, just a few more minutes.

"What are you going to do?" Sam asked. "Just turn right around and go back to Baxter?"

"I've been thinking about that," Nick said, "and I don't think so. I think me and Gert are gonna head out west for a while. Go to Oregon, or Northern California maybe. I have some friends from forever ago that ended up out there. Humboldt County, I think. Figure I'll see what it's like, maybe try and get a job or something; maybe my luck will change, you know?"

"Maybe it will," Sam said.

"Maybe it will."

It was just after four when they turned onto Sam's new street, pretty much when Nick said they'd be there. She told him to stop the truck a couple blocks down from her own, no reason to tempt fate any more than they already had. She made sure she had all her stuff. When she was satisfied, she unfastened her seatbelt and smiled nervously at Nick.

"I'm not worried about today," she said. "I'm really not. I'll go in there and whatever happens, happens. I'm fine with that. It's after that I'm worried about. What happens after I see them and there's a big scene and it's all emotional and we talk and cry and whatever, and I go to sleep and when I wake up in the morning, I'm still here and this is my life now? What do I do then?"

"You do what everybody else does when that happens," Nick said, "you get up."

"That's it?"

"That's it. If I knew something better or smarter, I'd tell you."

"Thanks," she said, and opened the door.

"Sam?"

"Yeah?" She already had one leg out of the truck.

"I just, I wanted to say, I'm sorry."

She smiled, "I know. But it's nice to hear it."

"Does that mean you forgive me?"

"Not a chance. Not yet anyway. It just means that I know you're sorry."

"Okay," said Nick. "I can live with that, I guess."

"Take care, Nick."

"Take care, Sam."

Sam leaned back and pet Gertie one last time, then swung her other leg around and dropped out of the truck onto the sidewalk. She pulled her bag out after her and closed the door.

Nick gave her a little wave. He started the truck, put it in gear, and drove off. She watched the dented truck as it headed down the street away from her; its right turn signal was already blinking. It paused at the corner to let a car go by; then it turned and was gone.

Sam stood there a moment, watching the empty spot in the road where Nick's truck had just been.

She took the pull-handle of her bag and walked up to her new house.

Made in the USA
Middletown, DE
13 September 2017

2-P